Praise for *The Actor and the Housewife*

"This effervescent story reads like a romantic comedy screenplay . . . Sweetly satisfying, it's the perfect diversion on a sunny day."
—Darcy Jacobs, *Family Circle*

"*The Actor and the Housewife* is completely unbelievable and totally credible . . . The dialogue is witty, the romantic suspense genuine, and the finale? It ends the way it should."
—Sherryl Connelly, *New York Daily News*

"And while cynicism makes it difficult for readers to believe that such a platonic relationship could actually occur in the real world, author Shannon Hale does a fine job of making a case for this dream come true . . . The novel is light, fun reading material for the beach or airplane and will cause more than a few readers to wonder what would happen if they happened to run into their favorite celebrity."
—Jae-Ha Kim, *Chicago Sun-Times*

"Like *Austenland*, *Housewife* is entertaining and is far above many books in its genre . . . [Hale] is a talented writer who creates compelling characters."
—*Deseret News*

"Hale's prose is friendly and funny."
—*Kirkus Reviews*

"Hale keeps the prose crackling with humor and has a sure hand in creating nuanced, believable characters."
—*Publishers Weekly*

"Hale offers a pure wish-fulfillment fantasy, one that readers, especially housewives, will thoroughly enjoy."
—*Booklist*

Praise for Shannon Hale's *Austenland*

"Funny, moving and a real surprise."
—*USA Today*

"Gloriously satisfying."
—*Glamour*

"Adorable! This is the best tribute to obsessed Austen freaks (like me) that I've ever read."
—Stephenie Meyer, author of the Twilight series

"An utterly enjoyable tribute."
—*Miami Herald*

"An homage to Austen and Fielding . . . *Austenland* offers hope that after years of fruitless searching for a companion, just when you're ready to give up on love, it will find you all on its own."

—*Houston Chronicle*

"Allow me to direct you to the best Austen tribute since Karen Joy Fowler's *The Jane Austen Book Club*: Shannon Hale's clever and imaginative *Austenland* . . . Hale's charming first book for adults (she is also an award-winning young adult writer) is chick lit with soul. Though there's a laugh on nearly every page—Hale, like Austen, is adept at subtly skewering the ridiculous—there's also the more serious story of a woman learning the difference between fantasy and reality, and discovering that real life can be better than your dreams." **—*BookPage***

"Cheeky irreverence . . . For all her breezily amused tone . . . Hale treats Jane and her fellow park 'clients' with affection, and she shows that the Janes of today are as likely as the Darcys to shy from commitment."

—*Los Angeles Times*

The Actor and the Housewife

A NOVEL

ooooooooooo

Shannon Hale

B L O O M S B U R Y

New York   Berlin   London

*For the Bryner and Bronson clans—sixty grandparents,
parents, siblings, aunts, uncles, and cousins—who lent their names to
the characters in this book in a completely random fashion and under no
circumstance resemble their fictional namesakes. Except for that one.
You know who I mean. No, not you, silly, the other one. Riiight . . .*

Published by Bloomsbury USA, New York

All papers used by Bloomsbury USA are natural, recyclable products
made from wood grown in well-managed forests. The manufacturing processes
conform to the environmental regulations of the country of origin.

LIBRARY OF CONGRESS CATALOGING-IN-PUBLICATION DATA
Hale, Shannon.
The actor and the housewife : a novel / Shannon Hale.—1st U.S. ed.
p. cm.
ISBN-13: 978-1-59691-288-5 (hardcover)
ISBN-10: 1-59691-288-X (hardcover)
1. Chick lit. I. Title.
PS3608.A54584A65 2009
813'.6—dc22
2008049699

First published by Bloomsbury USA in 2009
This paperback edition published in 2010

Paperback ISBN: 978-1-60819-255-7

1 3 5 7 9 10 8 6 4 2

Designed by Sara E. Stemen
Typeset by Westchester Book Group
Printed in the United States of America by Worldcolor Fairfield

Contents

○○○○○○○○○

ACT I

ooooooooo

First Kisses

Then I did the simplest thing in the world. I leaned down . . .
and kissed him. And the world cracked open.
Agnes de Mille

In which our story begins

Becky was seven months pregnant when she met Felix Callahan. She was on her first trip to California that didn't include Disneyland, and by a twist of luck, selling a screenplay.

"So, you haven't found an agent?" Annette the producer asked, thrumming through the dozen bracelets on her wrist. She was wearing a striped scarf, hoop earrings, a white blouse, and a shin-length full skirt. The outfit was a little disconcerting in a sleek Los Angeles high-rise, a good three weeks before Halloween, and on the body of a fifty-year-old woman.

"Nope, no agent," Becky said. "Frankly, I wouldn't know how to get one."

"Uh-huh, that's fine. We'll just deal woman to woman." Annette smiled, and Becky was reminded of the myth that gypsies carried off babies into the night . . . or was it a myth? She had a crawly suspicion Annette would claim the life of Becky's firstborn if given the chance. Barring loss of offspring, Becky wasn't too concerned about the details of the contract. After all, what were the odds that a stay-at-home mom from Utah would sell a screenplay in the first place? Why look luck in the mouth?

"Here's our boilerplate contract. Just sign the last page, and we'll get this ball rolling!"

Becky hefted the pile of paper. "Okay, it'll take me a minute to read through."

"Mm-hmm," said Annette. *Clink-clink-clink* went her bracelets. "Take your time." *Clink-clink-clink.* "I'll just wait."

Becky tried to sift through the legalese, keeping an eye out for such phrases as "the life of your firstborn," but it was a beast of a contract. All the while she was mindful of the diabolical pings of the bracelets, and the gypsy woman staring, staring . . .

Becky was about to just sign and get it over with when Annette's door opened and in walked Felix Callahan.

According to the celebrity magazine *Exclusive!*:

FELIX CALLAHAN
Exclusive! heartthrob #14

HEIGHT:
>   6'0"

BUILD:
>   British sexy

AGE:
>   37

BORN:
>   Devonshire, England

RESIDES:
>   London and Los Angeles

MARITAL STATUS:
>   Happily married (sadly for the rest of us!) to French model
>   Celeste Bodine

MEMORABLE ROLES:
>   Calvin the sexy pet shop owner in *Rattled Cages* and
>   Edward the alcoholic pilot in the twisted comedy
>   adventure *The Stabbist*

BEST FEATURES:
>   Those dark, bedroom eyes and that kissable dimple on his
>   chin

READERS' RATING:
>   Superfine!

"Annette," Felix said, "Matthias isn't in, and I need—"

"Whoa," Becky said, because the baby kicked her hard in the bladder.

Felix startled, backing up and nearly falling over a chair.

"Sorry, I was *whoa*-ing because right when you came in, the baby kicked, not because you're Felix Callahan. Oh, you know what it reminded me of? When Elisabeth's baby kicks just as Mary greets her? Isn't that funny? As if I had some spiritual sign when I saw you."

Annette smiled, her eyebrows raised. Felix glared handsomely. Becky stamped down a desire to squirm.

"No, it's not terribly funny," Felix said, "particularly as I have no idea what you're talking about."

"Elisabeth, wife of Zacharias, cousin to Mary, mother of Jesus? No? Nothing?"

Felix looked at her with a careful lack of amusement.

"Oh, maybe you don't have the Bible in England. See, there's this guy named Jesus and his mother is named Mary, and well, it's a really interesting read if you don't mind parables."

Okay, Becky was not on her best form here. See, she was trying to be funny to relieve the tension, but the nerves and Felix Callahan and the clicking of gypsy jewelry and all made a mess of her head.

"So, do you already know Felix?" Annette asked, confused.

"Yes," Becky said, because she felt she did know him. She'd watched *Rattled Cages* an embarrassing number of times. "I mean—"

"No, we've never met," Felix said.

Becky couldn't stop a laugh. She faced Los Angeles like an anthropologist in the field—observing and taking notes in order to amuse her husband later. Between the producer in gypsy attire and this conversation, Mike was going to be thrilled. "That's true. I just meant that I knew who you . . . *whoa!* You must be important! Baby just kicked again hard."

"Ah," Felix said. "By 'baby' I assume it's one in your womb, meaning you're pregnant. That is something of a relief, as I thought that you were just fat."

Becky readjusted her smile to something that felt more caustic. "Don't be so hasty. I might be fat too." (Sans baby, she hovered between a size 10 and 12, if you were wondering.) "Now that I hear your accent, I realize that you actually are British. What a relief. I had assumed that you were some actor performing a caricature of a British jerk."

Becky did her very best not to wince after saying "jerk." Besides being rude, it was just so pedestrian.

Annette stared between them, then rose to her feet, bracelets quarreling. "Felix, happy to help you, but Becky here is about to sell me her screenplay and—"

"You know a lot of British people, do you?" Felix kept his eyes on Becky, his gaze boring through her skull. "You're an expert?"

"Oh, I know enough," she said, enjoying herself much more than she knew she should. " '*Ello, love!*" she said in a really horrible English accent. Then she explained to Annette, "That's how all British talk. *'Ello, love! Spare me a coppa?* Copper—that's what they call their money."

"Interesting," Felix said. "So if they call money 'copper,' what do they call a policeman?"

"Bobby."

"Then what do they call Bobby?"

"Frank."

At that point, Felix Callahan pressed the back of his hand to his mouth. At first Becky suspected he was trying to push a laugh back in, but when he spoke, there was no humor in his voice. "You are by far the most fatuous woman I've met today."

"Hey, enough with the fat commentary already!"

He started to scoff, saying, "I didn't—" then noticed her amused expression. "You're teasing me."

"All part of being fatuous! Annette, my flight isn't until tomorrow, so I'm going to take the contract back to the hotel to read and bring it by in the morning. Thank you! I mean, cheers, love!"

She gathered her purse, glasses, and contract in an awkward bundle and saw herself out the door.

The offices of Bub and Hubbub Productions sat a couple dozen stories above Los Angeles, the windows squaring off with other high-rises against the grayish tint of polluted air. She'd been expecting something fancy, it being the movie biz and all, but the offices evoked a high school teachers' break room. She supposed movie folk saved all the razzle-dazzle for the screen.

Becky had to use the ladies' room, so she waddled across the hall to a law firm. It looked pretty posh, and Becky wagered its bathrooms would be nicer.

She was doing her very best not to panic.

Felix Callahan. *Felix Callahan!* She'd just met him, and insulted him, and walked away! She waved to the law firm's young, blonde receptionist, entered the ladies' room, and paused in front of the mirror to see if the humiliation of having a horrible encounter with her favorite actor mixed with pregnancy hormones could make her cry. She squeezed her eyes, held her breath, and . . . nope. Well, given her temperament, it hadn't been likely, but it would have made the story even better. She might have been able to squeeze out a little moisture if she hadn't been so distracted by the bathroom itself. Endless chrome, olive-colored walls, tile at eight dollars a square foot—and not a single place to set her purse.

Stupid, narrow-minded male architects, Becky thought.

It took her some time to relieve her squashed bladder, wash her hands (holding her purse between her knees), and toddle back down the corridor. By then, Felix Callahan was at the elevator, his finger pressing the Down button.

She squeaked to a stop and had started to back away when he turned and saw her. Caught. Oh-so-casually she pushed that backward step forward, suddenly excruciatingly aware of her outfit—canvaslike maternity shirt/tent in a luscious shade of rotting plum, and khaki-ish pants left over from her first pregnancy nine years ago. Mmm, baby.

Felix pretended she wasn't there. The baby kicked again. Becky stifled a laugh.

The doors opened, he let her enter first, and the doors closed, sealing them inside the plummeting box. It was going to be a long ride if she didn't speak.

"I'm sorry for calling you a jerk," she said, keeping her eyes on the ticking floor numbers. "I didn't mean it."

He spoke blandly, also not looking at her. "I thought it showed you had some bottle."

She suspected "bottle" had a different meaning to the Brits, but she didn't ask. "What kind of a mother would I be to tell my kids they shouldn't call people names then go ahead and label a perfect stranger as a jerk?"

"You'd be a hypocritical mother."

"Exactly."

"Though surely not a perfect stranger. Didn't you claim to know me?"

She ignored that. "It would've been one thing if the insult had been clever, but I very happily retract the word 'jerk.' In any case, my reaction to attack was uncalled for, and I apologize."

Now he looked at her. "You're serious?"

"Of course I'm serious."

"Where are you from?"

"Utah."

"You're from Utah, and you're selling a screenplay to Annette. Where's your agent?"

"Nowhere. Annette seemed pleased that I didn't have one."

Felix shook his head. "Most producers will only deal with agents. There's no doubt Annette plans to wipe the floor with your face."

She shrugged. "I assumed so. It doesn't matter, so long as she doesn't take one of my children in the deal. Which, as you know, gypsies are wont to do."

"Right. The baby-napping is a habit that would be too horrible to ignore, if they weren't so inhumanly skilled at fixing pots."

"Yes, you have to give them that. And they can fiddle the moon down onto your tongue."

His lips played with the idea of a smile.

The elevator opened and he put his arm against the door while she exited. She mumbled thanks and hurried on, hoping to outpace him—or out-waddle him at least. Mike was going to enjoy this anecdote, and she really should keep chatting to get as much story fodder as possible, but there was only so much insane heart pounding she could take before going into labor.

She went to the curb and looked left. And looked right. And put a hand on her hip (or where her hip had been before she'd morphed into Prego Beast). She could hear footsteps behind her. It was him; she knew it was him. She wasn't going to turn around. She looked left again. Right. Left.

"What are you doing?" he asked from behind her.

"Waiting for a cab."

"Did you call one?"

"No, but I took one here from the hotel and I thought—"

"Utah," he muttered.

She stiffened, and her mind began to grope for a suitable insult. Something about his smell perhaps? Those digs were always popular among her children's friends. No, no, no, Becky! She was not going to stoop to that. She'd make her kids proud.

A short black limousine pulled up, and the driver hopped out to open the door. Felix stood beside it for a few moments before sighing dramatically.

"I am headed to the Parkside on Ocean. Where are you staying?"

She blinked. "The Parkside."

"Really? What a coincidence."

"I'm not making that up, if that's what you think. Annette made my reservation and—"

"You know if you give her half a chance, she *will* come for your firstborn in the night, her bracelets tinkling, her voice cackling, her toe bells sounding alarm . . ."

"Toe bells?"

"Er, don't gypsies wear toe bells? Didn't I hear that somewhere?"

"As in 'rings on her fingers and bells on her toes,' that nursery rhyme?"

"She will have music and babies wherever she goes. Look, it doesn't make sense for me to leave you pregnant and clueless on the pavement when I am headed for your very hotel."

"I can manage to find a phone and call for a cab. I graduated from college and everything."

"You don't say? Can you take a degree in childbearing in this country?"

"That was my minor. My major was social grace with an emphasis on tolerating the obnoxious—ack! I did it again! I keep telling myself, 'Be nice, don't insult him.' Then you say something and out it comes."

He stepped back from the door. "Hop in, my gravid lady. I have no doubt you could rustle up a horse-drawn carriage if you wished, but this ride is on me. It would seem the proper way to absolve myself of the fat comment—my wife would not approve. She is passionate about eating-disorder awareness."

Felix swished his hand, inviting her in. She didn't move, but she *was* looking at him, which was risky. For one thing, he was abnormally good-looking. It was just wrong, looks like that. They could confuse a person. And for another thing, looking at him made it very hard to pretend he was someone else, which is precisely what she would need to do in order to turn him down. If he had been *anyone* else, no matter how impressive his résumé or photogenic his face, she would have said, "Thank you, but I'm married and I don't get into cars with strange men." She had drawn strict moral lines around herself and never crossed them, didn't so much as prod them with her big toe.

But this was Felix Callahan. The man who had been her unattainable crush, her occasional just-before-sleep daydream for the past twelve years. She'd spent so much time with his movies (one in particular), he didn't seem like a stranger. And they wouldn't be alone, she reasoned, what with the driver there to chaperone. Besides, it was just too surreal. It couldn't actually be happening. And if it was, could she in good conscience pass it up?

So, okay, she said yes. It was an incredibly un-Becky-like thing to do, but can you blame her? She had a weakness, and there he was.

But the real question that haunted her as they rode in silence to the hotel was, why had he insisted? She suspected kindness wasn't a primary motivator in any of his actions. She assessed the watery reflection her face made in the darkened window, though she didn't need to see it to know she wasn't a looker.

Here's what *Exclusive!* magazine would have said about her.

BECKY JACK

HEIGHT:
> A bracing 5'5"

BUILD:
> Cuddly

AGE:
> 34

BORN:
> Ogden, Utah

RESIDES:
> In a genuine 1972 bi-level brick home (kitchen remodeled in 1986!) in posh and exclusive Layton, Utah

MARITAL STATUS:
> Excruciatingly happily married

MEMORABLE ROLES:
> Incubator, prize dairy cow (when nursing), and She-Who-Motivates-with-Popsicles

BEST FEATURES:
> The enchantingly brown shade of her hair, sturdy glasses, and her, uh . . . her shapely kneecaps

READERS' RATING (OF HER LASAGNA):
> Superfine!

She wasn't hideous. There had been that unfortunate hairdo that she'd sported far too long—the bad corkscrew perm with lots of bangs curled and heavily sprayed like some *Star Trek* alien ridged forehead. But a couple of years back, her friend Melissa had dragged her to a salon for a bad-hair intervention.

Bless you, Melissa. Bless you.

Still, there was no way Felix was giving her a lift because he was attracted to her—unless he had a fetish for hugely pregnant women. But she wasn't getting creep-o vibes. In fact, even in the silence, she didn't feel the least bit uncomfortable.

Hey, that was another strange thing—they should be trying to make stilted small talk and squirming at gaps in the conversation, not riding at ease. She watched him as he stared out his window, trying to see in him the character of Calvin from *Rattled Cages*. But the man beside her wasn't Calvin. She was riding with a stranger.

However, there was something intensely familiar—more than just what she knew of him from the screen. There was something about the way they'd been conversing, especially in the elevator.

"I know it's a stupid question," she said, "but is there any way we knew each other when we were younger?"

"I seriously doubt it."

"You seem . . . familiar."

"Yes," he said tiredly.

"No, not from your movies, you doofus. Something else."

"Well . . . you do resemble my great-aunt Hydrangea."

"Stunning, vivacious, and witty, was she?"

"Hydrangea? She was, er, she was . . . Hullo, what do you know? Booze!" He opened a hatch and pulled out a minibottle and two glasses—holding one up to her with a questioning look.

"No thanks." She pointed at her belly as if it were a badge for the Women's Temperance Society.

"Right. I don't know how you survive for nine months."

"I don't drink alcohol even when I'm not in the family way. Never have."

"Never?"

"Nope."

"Never drank once in all your life? That's impossible."

"It's partly a religious decision. I'm a Mormon. From Utah, you know."

He stared, mouth slightly agape. "How many wives does your husband have?"

"Oh please. Mormons aren't polygamists."

"Yes they are," the driver piped up. He wore one of those cliché chauffeur hats low over his eyes. "Everyone knows. The men have loads of wives, make them all wear bonnets."

Becky sighed and gave her speech. "Some Mormons were polygamists in the nineteenth century, but they gave up the practice in 1890. There are small religious groups around the Utah area who practice polygamy, but they have nothing to do with the LDS Church."

"That's not what I saw on TV. Mormons, they said. Polygamists. Loads of 'em."

"I *am* a Mormon, from Utah, lived there my entire thirty-four years, and I've never met a polygamist."

The driver straightened the Mets plush baseball that dangled from the rearview mirror. "You must not get out much."

"Yes, that must be it."

"It's tragic really," Felix said. "She's agoraphobic and hadn't been out of the house in, what was it, fifteen years?"

"Sixteen," Becky said.

"Right, sixteen. Last time was when Charles and Diana wed."

"You're thinking of the last time I leaned out the window. The last time I actually left the house was for a sale at Sears."

"Of course, the day you bought those trousers. Sixteen years later, here she is! And in the same trousers, but still . . . We're so proud of our little Becky!" Felix patted her head. "You dug deep, but you found the courage to step out of that door."

"I did like you told me, Felix. I just shut my eyes and chanted, 'The polygamists are not going to eat me, they're not going to eat me,' and I wasn't afraid anymore."

"She is a rare example of true bravery. Don't you agree?"

"Uh, yeah," said the driver. "Congratulations."

"Thanks." Becky smiled politely. "Go Mets."

The driver snorted.

Becky sneaked a glance at Felix before returning her gaze to the window. That whole exchange had felt as unaccountably familiar as Felix's presence. She had an ah-ha moment as she thought, Augie Beuter! That's who Felix reminded her of—well, actually, the two men looked and acted about as much alike as Margaret Thatcher and Cher. But the way she and Felix had followed each other's lead, the way their conversation flowed together, tuned for an audience, that's how she and Augie used to be. He'd been her assistant editor on the high school paper and partner in debate club. Their five-year best friendship ended when they both married other people. Augie Beuter—she hadn't seen him since her wedding, and she still missed him.

When the car stopped at the hotel, there was some fumbling with wallets. Felix assured her that Bub and Hubbub had paid for the limo, but then he added his own tip in cash. Becky protested that she should pay the tip, and they were still arguing about it after the car had driven away.

"Just take five bucks," Becky said. At times Augie had been irritating too. "I swear I'm more stubborn than you."

"I've already paid. It's your duty to be gracious."

"Argh!" She stuffed the money back in her wallet and grumbled as they walked. "Why'd you have to say 'be gracious'? Hitting below the belt. I don't like being a freeloader. I'm not a mooch. I'm—"

"Mooch?"

"—capable of paying my own way, and with you of all people, Felix Callahan. You'll think I just wanted to ride with you because you're famous and rich, and that's not it at all."

He held open the door to the hotel. "Then why did you want to ride with me?"

She ducked under his arm, then stopped, trying to find a reasonable answer to his question.

"Did I say I 'wanted to'?"

"Yes, you did."

"Really?"

"Well, your verbiage did imply it."

"Huh. I don't know. I don't know why."

She became conscious that she was close enough to smell his cologne (a light sandalwood), so she hurried inside.

And there they were. At the hotel. This would be good-bye. She was in one way anxious to get away from him and the awkward drumming of her heart, and in another way a little sorry. She really did miss Augie.

"Well, thanks. For the ride. And good luck." She held out her hand.

He gave her hand a light squeeze. "All right then. *Au revoir.*"

She did a half wave, half salute and walked away.

And . . . yes, once again, he was behind her, his shoes tapping the marble floor. She rolled her eyes. He *would* be going the same direction. She tried to walk faster so at least they weren't side by side, though that was tricky given that she was carrying an extra thirty pounds and pregnancy hormones had made her hip joints as loose as wet sand.

The restaurant, she thought. He's going to the restaurant too, darn him!

She hadn't eaten anything since the granola bars and orange she'd packed for the plane trip that afternoon, and she hadn't seen a single restaurant around the hotel or she'd have taken the quickest path to a ninety-nine-cent hamburger. It was the hotel restaurant or starve, and starve was not an option.

"You're going for dinner?" she asked over her shoulder.

"A drink," he said, still one step behind.

"Well, I would be polite, veer left and leave you to it, but I'm ravenous and so is the fetus. I have an urgent mission to hunt down some steak and potatoes and dark green veggies and some kind of frosty dairy product to follow. But mostly I want red meat. And ice cream. But not at the same time. Though maybe . . . would that be yummy? Anyway, just so you know I'm not following you."

"Technically I'm following you."

"Yeah, I didn't want to mention that. You should do horror movies—you're kind of creepy."

"I get that a lot. *People* magazine's Creepiest Man of the Year, Lifetime's Top Ten Hunks Who Give Us the Willies, that sort of thing."

"Where do you keep all the trophies?"

"In an abandoned shed in the forest."

"Infested with bats and rusty farm equipment?"

"Naturally."

He opened the restaurant door for her. It was at least the fifth door he'd held for her so far. And the last, she was sure. She thanked him, said good-bye again, and made for the maître'd, a very thin young man with shiny black hair.

"Nonsmoking, please," she said.

The maître'd picked up two menus and said, "Table for two, right this way."

"Uh, no," she said, and glanced over her shoulder where Felix was waiting his turn for a table, "not for two. We're not together. I'm just me."

The maître'd gestured grandly to the bar. "We seat single patrons at the bar, madam."

The bar. The air around the dangling lights was thick with cigarette smoke, as if the area were in the process of creating its own atmosphere. It was 1996—if this had taken place just two years later, smoking would have been banned in California bars and there would be no issue. Even from a distance, the odor was making Becky woozy. Strong smells and pregnancy were about as pleasant a combination as rotten seafood and roller coasters. Then her gaze fell to the bar stools—faux art deco contraptions with tiny round seats and three stainless steel legs that looked fit for holding, say, a potted geranium, but certainly not a pregnant woman.

"Do you have a nonsmoking bar perchance? And one with sturdy stools?"

Behind her, Felix groaned.

"I'm sorry, madam," the maître'd said.

"In that case, don't I count as two people and deserve my own table?" she said, patting her belly.

Felix groaned louder. The fact that he didn't go to the bar himself made Becky think he wanted to drink in some privacy—she was certain the maître'd could find *People*'s Creepiest Man Alive a table for one. Pregnant women should be pampered over celebrities, shouldn't they? The thought made Becky outrageously angry, the emotion quickly transforming inside her hormone-ridden body into heartbroken misery.

"I am sorry," the maître'd said, though when his gaze passed over her belly he seemed mildly disgusted, as if he believed Becky thoughtless for getting pregnant in the first place and so doomed to pay the consequences. "We expect a significant dinner rush, and hotel policy dictates single patrons sit at the bar. Are you a hotel guest? Perhaps you could order dinner in your room?"

Becky's bottom lip quivered. She was getting dizzy with low blood sugar, and she was feeling pouty too, not to mention broke. "Room service is so expensive. Are there other restaurants nearby where I could walk? I don't—"

Felix grabbed the two menus out of the young man's hand, took Becky's elbow, and said, "Table for two, nonsmoking."

"Oh. Very good. Follow me please."

As he began to walk them to the table, the maître'd glanced at Felix for the first time, did a double take, and excited recognition warred with professional reserve. In the end, he gave Felix a sheepish, adoring smile over his shoulder, the kind of smile that would have been at home on the face of a six-year-old girl.

"Thank you," Becky whispered to Felix, removing her arm from his, though they immediately had to descend some stairs and on her first wobble, Felix took her arm again. "I wouldn't have survived that stool. It would've been 'Humpty Dumpty had a great fall.'"

"With rings on your fingers and bells on your toes even," he said.

"Curious that meeting you is more nursery rhyme than fairy tale. If I see a farmer's wife with a butcher's knife, I'm running and not looking back."

"And I'll have no nonsense from my dish and spoon."

The maître'd placed them in a padded booth (A padded booth! Becky thought happily, for the sake of her pelvis), hidden around a corner and private from any other table, in a prime location facing the dance floor. The maître'd glanced back lovingly at Felix before leaving them in awkward silence.

Because it *had* become awkward suddenly. They ordered (Becky a three-course meal, Felix a whiskey sour), and with no menus to stare at, they turned their gazes on the empty dance floor and the enthusiastic DJ in his red-and-gold caftan and cap. Becky tried to restart the conversation, asking why he was staying at a hotel, and he explained that he'd be there for a few weeks while his house was renovated and his wife was in Europe. He made some polite inquiries about her stay, her flight, her home. She said she was from Layton, Utah, only she pronounced it as Utahns do, replacing the "t" with a glottal stop—*Lay'en.*

"You're from where?"

"*Lay'en.* It's near Salt Lake City."

"Spell that for me."

"Um, that would be S-A-L-T—"

"No, the other one. The city you're from."

"Oh. L-A-Y-T-O-N."

"Ah—Lay-*ton.*"

"That's what I said."

"No you didn't. You said, 'Lay'en.'"

"So I did. But just go ahead and pronounce 'aluminum' for me, Mr. British Man. How are you going to defend that piece of insanity? Why don't you spell it and count syllables and see if your al-um-in-ium makes any sense whatsoever?"

He bowed his head. "Touché. So . . . if you're from Utah . . ."

"How did I end up in Los Angeles selling a screenplay?" she gushed, relieved to have a topic of conversation. "A fluke. On road trips as kids, my family used to play a game where we invented original but plausible movie plots. A few years ago I checked out a book on screenplays from the library and wrote out a couple of my ideas. So I was on a TV movie set one day—my friend Melissa is a second assistant director and she's always roping me and the kids into being extras. Anyway, I was hanging out at craft services with my two older kids—"

"Just how many children do you have?"

"It'll be four with this one. So—"

"And you're interested in breaking into professional acting?" His look became a little cagey.

"Yes, that's right. And I was hoping," she leaned forward, resting her chin coyly on her hands, "I was so hoping that you could help me get cast. I've heard tales from the other girls about a certain couch . . ."

His eyes widened in alarm.

"Oh come on, do I look like the actress type to you? I just do the extra stuff as a favor for a friend and to have a little adventure with the kids. As I was saying, I was at the craft services snack table, the best spot on set, and one of the producers for the show and I got to talking about why we like yellow M&Ms better than the other colors, and somehow that led to how there's been a real dearth of good romantic comedies lately—"

Felix groaned. "Romantic comedies . . ."

"I repeat, *a dearth of good romantic comedies*, the kind of which you starred in years ago before you got too old—"

"I grew bored of the hackneyed—"

"Uh huh. So I tell this producer my idea for a romantic comedy called *Arm Candy*, about an up-and-coming supermodel who gets into a fake relationship with a young actor for publicity purposes. By being photographed together and developing a public relationship, they hope to help each other's careers soar, but they both start actually falling in love with each other while believing that the other still feels platonic, and it escalates until a scene when they've been roped into getting married and the actress calls it off at the last minute because she can't bear to marry someone who isn't in love with her, because she is actually in love with him, and he's heartbroken, thinking she called it off because she really doesn't love him, but when he finds out how she feels . . . well, you get the picture. Anyway, the producer liked the sound of it and gave me her card. I mailed her the screenplay and she must have passed it on to Annette, because a few months later, Annette called me to fly out to L.A. and negotiate a deal. Okay, now you may interrupt."

He was staring at her. "Be honest, no embellishments. That's really how it happened?"

"Yellow M&Ms and everything."

"But that never happens."

"I was pretty surprised myself."

"No, it *never* happens. No one actually reads a spec script written by an extra for a made-for-telly movie and then *actually* passes it on to a producer like Annette, who then flies said Nobody to Los Angeles and *actually* buys it. I would call you a liar, complete with pants afire, as they say, if I hadn't seen you in her office myself. How could . . . That's preposterous. Just how did you do it?"

"I'm one of God's chosen people, and he looks out for me."

Felix didn't blink.

"It's too easy! You'd believe me if I said I sacrificed a goat to get the good will of the north wind."

"Don't you?"

"No. Goats are cute. Anyway, it was just a colossal fluke, like I told you. I fully expect the screenplay to languish on someone's desk for eternity, never becoming a movie, and to never sell another screenplay in my life. Which is why I wasn't so worried about the contract."

His eyes flicked to the stack of paper, sitting on the table under her purse. "Annette is going to own you."

Becky shrugged. "Yeah, but what can you do? Can't cross a gypsy without getting cursed." She leaned forward and tried to whisper judiciously. "Her outfit . . . I've been keeping an eye out for other women in poofy blouses and hoop earrings, or men in caps and vests carrying fiddles. I mean, for all I know, everyone's going gypsy this year and Utah is egregiously behind the times."

He shook his head slowly.

"So, does Annette always dress like a caricature of the Roma people?"

"Last time I saw her, she was wearing a sort of . . ." Felix mimed something like a bib over his chest. "Something silver, with buckles . . ."

"Like a . . . space suit?"

Felix's gaze returned to the contract. "My curiosity is piqued. Let me just . . ."

He reached across the table and slid the contract from under Becky's purse, upsetting the purse in the process. ChapStick, wallet, keys, and receipts spilled onto the bench.

"Hey," Becky said, trying to catch the detritus before it hit the floor.

"Apologies." Felix didn't look up from the papers.

She managed to stuff everything back in her purse except a travel-sized lotion, which had fallen under the table. Her belly wouldn't allow her to bend over enough to reach it, but she managed to kick it out from under the table. She had to sit on the very edge of the bench with her legs apart in order to scoop it up by hand. Her face was flushed and she glared at Felix, who hadn't budged. He was on the third page of the contract now, a pen in hand.

Her (surprisingly delicious) food came and kept her pretty well occupied, and Felix finished making margin notes by the time dessert arrived.

He heaved a big breath. "She's a clever girl, I'll give her that. No one like Annette. So. It's not reasonable to expect profit participation on your first deal, but from a producer like Bub and Hubbub, you should get a guaranteed payout for the script option and then a percentage of the budget if the project gets a green light. Also there needs to be a time limit—if the movie isn't in production in eighteen months, say, then they need to renew the option or else return the rights to you. And this clause here basically states that anything you write for the rest of your life belongs to them. That has to go."

"I don't want to be pushy, scare them away or anything."

"This is entirely reasonable." He paused, drumming his fingers on the script, looking at her with a considering squint. "I'll take it over to Annette myself tomorrow morning. Is she going to argue with me?"

"She'd be crazy to try. You might call her fat."

"To Annette? I wouldn't dare without wearing protective eye gear."

"Thanks for offering. That's very sweet of you . . . I think. I'm not sure why you're being sort of sweet all of a sudden—"

"Neither am I," he said, glaring at the script.

"But you don't need to take it over. I can—"

"I'm going there again tomorrow anyhow. Look, don't argue with me, all right? Just be gracious and say 'thank you.'"

"Again with the 'gracious'!"

"It appears to be the only thing that works with you. Just—I'm not used to running little errands for people and I'm feeling fairly irritated about it."

"Then why are you offering now?"

"I don't know! Drop it, please?"

"Okay. Fine. I'll never bring it up again."

"Good."

Their gorgeous redheaded server chose that moment to come by and ask if they needed anything else.

"A muzzle," Felix grumbled, just as Becky said, "A fly swatter."

"Um, sorry?" the server asked, her expression adorably quizzical.

Becky sighed. "There was this enormous fly over here a minute ago—"

"It was trying to lick her ice cream," Felix said.

"I thought we should swat it, but he is so humane."

Felix held up a finger. "'Just muzzle it,' said I. 'Just muzzle the wee creature so it cannot consume your confection.'"

"He always goes Scottish when he's trying to protect his pesty pals. He's very tender-hearted actually. Don't believe those tabloids about punching reporters and sucking the marrow from the bones of the elderly. Mostly rumors."

"But for that one time . . ."

"There was no evidence, so it doesn't count," she said through clenched teeth.

"Ooo, right. At any rate, the winged creature seems to have flown away."

"So we're good." Becky smiled pleasantly at the redhead. "Thanks for checking."

The redhead tried her best to smile cheerfully but mostly she looked confused, and she stumbled on a stair as she walked away.

Becky took a deep spoonful of ice cream to keep her mouth occupied, because she wanted to grin right at him, a big old embarrassingly pleased grin.

He's not Augie, she reminded herself—he's Felix Callahan. And you're wearing a purple canvas tent for a shirt.

But she did glance at him and saw that Felix was smiling in his slow, sweet way, a smile full of fondness and ideas, and she felt it hit her in the gut. He was most definitely Felix Callahan.

"Would you like to dance?" he asked.

"What, are you serious? I can barely plod."

He looked at the dance floor, where a tourist couple who seemed pretty well toasted were spinning and swaying to the DJ's music. "In this crowd, plodding would be an improvement."

"Wait a minute . . . You just want to dance with me because you think it would be funny."

He raised one eyebrow. "Wouldn't it?"

She tossed down her cloth napkin like a gauntlet. "I'll have you know that I'm a fairly decent dancer."

He held out his elbow, she took it, and they walked out as "A Kiss to Build a Dream On" began. He held her left hand and put his other hand on her theoretical waist, deftly leading her into a gentle two-step. After a time, he would switch up the steps, lead her backward, swing her out, and she was proud that she could keep up, belly and all.

"When I was a teen and going to church dances," she said, "the adult advisers told us to keep a Bible's distance between our bodies during the slow songs. This pregnant belly does the same thing."

"It is rather rudely bumping into me."

"Can't be helped. Oof, he just kicked again. This kid knows right where to boot me. You'd think this swaying would rock him to sleep."

He spun her out and brought her back so that they danced side by side.

"You're right," he said. "You can dance."

"Aren't you at all worried that some smart-aleck paparazzi might take our picture for a tabloid? Imagine the headline: 'Who Is Felix Callahan's Secret Pregnant Girlfriend? And Does His Wife Know?'"

He stopped dancing. "Excellent point. Shall we sit?"

"Not yet. I love this song."

He scanned the room looking for cameras, dancing her toward their table.

"You are paranoid," she said.

"With reason."

"Seriously, who'd believe that the man married to French model Celeste Bodine would frolic with pregnant me?"

"Who'd believe that the man in a relationship with Elizabeth Hurley would pay for professional attention?"

"Oh, all right. The song's almost over anyway."

They returned to the table and Felix tried to claim her bill. She refused and gathered her purse and things, keeping possession of the contract as they walked to the elevators.

"Listen, I don't want to bother you anymore," she said. "I can just write Annette a note with the ideas you suggested and—"

"And next thing you know she'll be standing in your labor and delivery room with a catcher's mitt. No, strangely, I insist." He frowned. "I never insist. What's come over me?"

"I have magical powers of persuasion."

"God's chosen people and all. By the way, you know that there actually isn't a god, right?"

"You don't say? You mean I've been fooling myself all these years?"

"I'm afraid so."

"Golly, thanks for setting me straight."

"Think nothing of it."

At the elevator door, he held out his arm, gesturing for ladies first. He really was a sweet boy when he didn't open his mouth.

He asked her floor, pushed the button, and they rose up in silence, watching the numbers.

"You're thinking something absurd, aren't you?" he asked.

"Just that you're a sweet boy when you don't open your mouth."

"Boy? I think I have a few years on you."

"I'm thirty-four, but I already feel like everybody's mother."

His eyes were still on the numbers—ten, eleven, twelve . . .

"Would you like to come up to my room for a bit?" he asked.

She stared. Up to his room. To Felix Callahan's room. Whoever this guy had been during dinner, this person who felt like an old friend, he was still Felix Callahan. And she was in her third trimester and wearing maternity pants she'd purchased in 1987. "Come up to your room? You've got to be kidding me."

"I didn't mean for . . . I only meant that . . . just to keep—never mind. I don't know why I wanted to prolong the evening."

That was nice, actually. He wanted to prolong the evening! He wanted to keep chatting . . . or something. But though she had gotten into his car, though she had shared dinner and a dance, they'd never been alone. Now the lines became more clear. Becky Jack wouldn't go into a man's hotel room alone, no matter if he was a dear friend, the prophet Moses, or Felix Callahan.

When the elevator doors opened, she shook his hand. "Thanks for the contract advice. And the company. And the dance."

"You're welcome. Good-bye, Becky Jack."

He smiled politely as the doors shut. She had no doubt that she'd never see him again.

In which Becky tells all and Edgar Poe falls asleep

Mike picked up Becky at the airport, coming inside to help her with her bag.

"It's just a carry-on," she scolded him when he met her at the gate. "It's not going to send me into preterm labor." But of course she was thrilled and let him buy her an expensive airport frozen yogurt, holding his hand as if they were on a date. Really, any moment together without the three kids was a date, and lately those were as rare as warmed beef.

So she didn't tell him about Felix right away. The thought of it was on her tongue, around her shoulders, rubbing against her neck. But her husband—the former varsity high school tight end, big as life—was holding her hand and wearing a smile fit to dazzle. His presence was even more delicious than the nonfat strawberry-cheesecake twist. It would seem like such a slap to bring up the happenstance meeting of her number-one heartthrob right away. Later, then.

She did describe Annette's attire with relish, as well as her bus ride to the airport that morning and her in-depth conversation with the driver on the subject of "Which are cuter—animal babies or human babies?" Mike laughed at all the right places and kept bending down to kiss her cheek.

"You're in a good mood," she said.

"I missed you."

"You missed me taking care of the kids and the house."

"That too." He kissed her again.

She was going to have to remember to go away more often.

It took half an hour to drive home. They headed east, the Wasatch Mountains growing larger, rust red smudges of autumn gathered on their lower slopes, the craggy peaks of the highest already white with snow. She glimpsed the building cluster of downtown Salt Lake City before they veered north, leaving behind sight of the palatial peaks for the older, rounded hills of Davis County. The road lifted, and to the west she could see the mysterious purple outline of Antelope Island and a glint of the Great Salt Lake. Becky sighed, meaning that even though she'd only been gone one night, the landscape already felt new and it was nice coming home. Mike smiled, meaning that he understood and was glad to have her back. Early in their marriage, Mike and Becky had driven from

Boston to Utah, and Becky had learned she could spend hours in silence with her husband and never get bored.

When they came in the garage door, Becky could hear nine-year-old Fiona's voice from the family room. She put a hand on Mike's arm to stop him, wanting to listen in.

"I'm a princess who can turn into a dragon, and you're my maid."

"I wanna be a princess too," said Polly, who at age six had just learned to pronounce her *r*'s, though they were soft.

"No, Polly."

"Fiona will give in," Becky whispered. She had a theory that no one could deny Polly anything—she was unaccountably sweet in every way.

Mike shook his head. "She's getting stubborn."

"Please, Fiona!"

"Okay, but you can't turn into a dragon. Hyrum is the evil ogre. Here he comes—run! Run!"

Two voices squealed as footsteps pounded down the hall, resembling the stomps of ogres more than princesses. Behind them four-year-old Hyrum growled in his high-toned little-boy voice, more princess than ogre.

Fiona shouted, "And now behold my transformation into the dragon Princess Firemouth!"

"And I'm Princess Hot Mouth!"

"No, I told you already, you can be a princess but you can't turn into a dragon."

"Rwaaarrrr!" said Hyrum.

"But—"

"No, Polly. I said no three times. You need to listen to me when I'm talking to you."

Becky nodded at Mike. Apparently Fiona was mother when Becky wasn't around.

"You can't be a dragon 'cause I'm already a dragon."

"Pwease—please, Fiona?"

Fiona sighed. "You can turn into something else—like a hamster."

"A fire-breathing hamster?" Polly sounded intrigued.

"Sure, okay."

"Rwaaarrrr!" said Hyrum. "You are dead. Rwaaarrr!"

"I like home," Becky whispered to Mike.

"Home likes you," he said. "Also, the cat knocked an open ketchup bottle over on the rug."

"And what was an open ketchup bottle doing on the rug?"

"Um . . . let me go put your bag in our room."

"Uh-huh."

Polly came around the corner, abandoning the game to fall into

Becky's arms. She was petite and darling, freckles high on her face and hair blonde, like her father's. Fiona and Hyrum both took after their mother's side: brown hair, angry cowlicks in front and back, sturdy and unremarkable features. With those two, Becky did most of the hugging. She drove thirteen-year-old niece and babysitter Kayla to her home and then whipped up an improvised dinner (apparently in the thirty-two hours Becky had been gone, her family had nearly expired from starvation).

Right around the cleaning up of the dishes, it occurred to her that waiting too long to tell your husband about a heartthrob encounter can make it seem even more important than it was. It took the usual hour and a half to coerce her children into clean teeth, PJs, and beds, but it felt like at least an hour and three quarters.

Alone in their bedroom, Becky began to unpack and said casually, "You'll never guess who I met in L.A."

"Carol Burnett." Mike was sitting on their bed, reading the hunting magazine *Big Buck*—lead article: "Five Deer Scents You Can't Live Without!"

"Carol Burnett? What made you guess her?"

He shrugged. "She seems like a fun person to meet. Now you're going to tell me who it really was, and I won't know the name and I'll have killed your story. But try me anyway."

She tossed the purple tent/shirt into the hamper. She did feel a touch disheartened because, in fact, Carol Burnett would have been awesome. Still, the actual person was no one to sneeze at, so she straightened up proudly when she was able to report, "Felix Callahan."

"Who?"

And, she slouched. "Come on, Mike! He's an actor and completely famous. He was in that weird drama you liked, the one with the baseball and the live bats."

"*Furry*. Which one was he?"

"The British one. The good-looking one."

Mike stared blankly.

She sighed and mumbled, "The one who eats the gopher."

"Oh, okay. He's in that what-cha-call-it movie you and Jessie watch every year when Mark and I are on the elk hunt."

"Yeah . . ." She was embarrassed he knew that.

"So you met him, huh?"

"Get this: I didn't just meet him. We had dinner together. Steak. At least, I had the steak. It was good. And some ice cream. Ooh, do we have any ice cream left in the freezer or did you guys eat it all while I was gone?"

Mike had lowered the magazine. "Wait, wait . . . you had dinner? As in, on a date?"

"What? Oh, no, not a *date*. A . . . a . . . I don't know, just dinner."

"Just dinner."

"Yeah, in the hotel. We were in the same hotel. And then we did dance, but just because it was funny."

He stared at her. "You had dinner, just the two of you? And you danced? It's been a while since I was on the *scene*, but as far as I know, that would be considered a date."

"Can you blame me for not . . . I mean, sheesh, look at me." She stuck out her belly. "I'm nearly my own continent. And he's a famous actor. It was hardly a recipe for seduction."

Mike smiled into the corner of his mouth. "You charmed him, didn't you?"

She clicked her tongue. "You are the only person in the world who would assume I could charm some actor, and in my third trimester, no less. It's very sweet of you, but, no."

"You did. You charmed him. You know you can be very charming when you set your mind to it."

She threw a pillow at his head. He snatched it out of midair like a ninja catching a thrown knife. He could be quite agile. When he set his mind to it.

"I'll bet he's never met anyone like you. He's probably twitterpated and doesn't know what to make of it."

Becky snorted. "Not likely."

"That's my wife, so pregnant she's about to pop and still getting men to buy her steak dinners."

"Oh please, as if I'm some femme fatale. Besides, I paid for my own dinner."

"But he offered, didn't he?"

She didn't answer. He smiled at her, and the sweetness of this man and his smile made her feel all warm and gooey, as if her heart were hot brownies. Until the smile turned sneaky.

"No," she said, trying to flee, "no, no, no!"

But he weighed well over two hundred pounds, most of that muscle, and she was slowed down with child. She never had a chance. She shrieked as he grabbed her and tickled her sides, going on about her powers as a temptress. The temptress part at least proved to be true. Becky started to kiss him just to distract him from tickling her, which worked almost immediately, as his fingers left her ribs and found the small of her back and her neck, and then he was kissing her neck, which so wasn't fair, and down into the hollow of her throat. The brush of his lips there nearly made her sigh, but she held it in, determined not to let him know how easily he could make her knees weak. All the same, it was fun to discover that she was in the mood after all. She melted into his hold and seduced him into bed with the lights still on.

The next day Becky told him the story properly, playing up the extended awkwardness and coincidental meetings. Mike thought it was a riot and absolutely not for one moment took it seriously. And neither did Becky. Now that she was home again and back in her routine, that brief foray into the jungles of Hollywood seemed like a *Twilight Zone* episode she'd watched late at night and only half-remembered. She certainly never expected to speak to Felix Callahan again.

About a month after Becky's return, she received four copies of the contract from Bub and Hubbub to sign, Felix's improvements applied. Unsure if she was supposed to send them all back or keep one for herself, Becky phoned Annette and left a message with her assistant.

She was unloading the dishwasher when the yipping started up.

"Nubbin," she said under her breath.

The dachshund next door shimmied free from its fence at least once a week and terrorized the neighborhood with its jackhammer bark and twelve-inch vibrating body of doom.

"Mom, you should come see this!" Fiona called from outside, just as the phone rang.

"Just a minute, hon . . . Hello?"

"Becky! This is Annette. Tangerine said you called earlier."

"Tangerine?"

"My assistant."

"Tangerine. Right. Thanks for calling back." Becky really, really wanted to know what Annette was wearing. Was she still a gypsy? Or perhaps a disco mama with hot pants and platform sandals? Becky tried not to picture her in jeans and T-shirt—that would have been a letdown. "I had a quick—"

"I had to call you right back, because as luck would have it, Felix Callahan is coming to speak with me any moment and I know you two have become fast friends!"

"Fast friends? Well, we—"

"Here he is now!"

A scuffle, a muted handset, then she could hear a whispered conversation.

"Who is it?"

"Becky Jack. I thought you'd like to say hello."

"You did not need to—"

"She's on right now."

There was a pause and the click of speaker phone.

"Hello, Becky."

Her heart thudded. "Oh, hi. Hello. Felix."

"Thank you for the gift. That was . . . thoughtful."

"You're welcome." Becky had mailed Felix a note of thanks for the help with the contract, care of Bub and Hubbub. She'd included a large Ziploc bag full of chocolate chip cookies, because who doesn't like cookies? "I guess I lost a wager, though. I bet Mike, my husband, that Annette would eat the cookies herself."

"There were cookies?"

"Hey," Annette squealed over the speaker phone. "You big teaser!"

"Yeah . . ." Becky had no idea what to say next.

"What's that noise?" asked Felix.

"The yipping? The neighborhood hot dog. He does seem to be trying to pop an eyeball." Becky stretched the twenty-foot cord so she could stand out on the porch.

Fiona, Polly, and Hyrum were on the front lawn, sitting cross-legged as if watching a show.

"Oh, the dog's trying to get our cat, who is wisely just out of reach. See, our driveway and the Kellys' driveway touch, but ours slopes down more, so by the garage it's about eighteen inches lower than the Kellys'. Our cat, Edgar Poe, is sitting on the upper driveway."

"The cat's name is Edgar Poe?" Felix asked. "What about the Allan?"

"She's not that pretentious."

"Yes, I see. Go on."

"The barking is Nubbin, hopping frantically on the lower driveway. On his hind legs he's just about one inch too short to reach the cat."

"A fearsome creature," said Felix.

"Exactly. But the cat—hang on. Nubbin's changed tactics. He's zooming down the driveway . . . hauled a quick U-turn . . ."

"I can hear the little toenails clicking."

"Speeding up the Kellys' driveway. Almost there. And . . . ah! Genius! Who said dogs are smarter than cats?"

"What? What's happening?" Felix sounded truly desperate to know.

"Nubbin was one length away from his black quarry when Edgar Poe dropped to the lower driveway. Nubbin followed down. So the cat promptly hopped back up, leaving Nubbin back in position one."

"That is to say, hopping on hind legs and yipping at a cat just out of reach?"

"Exactly."

"Has the cat used this tactic previously?"

"Hey, Fiona," Becky called, "did Edgar trick Nubbin like that before?"

"Oh yeah, like ten times," Fiona said. "We have the coolest cat ever."

"I love him so much," said Polly.

"What's the cat doing now?" Felix asked.

"Batting her tail just above Nubbin's nose."

"Cheeky minx."

"That's our Edgar."

"Nubbin sounds like a puppy bomb ticking towards explosion."

"Hang on . . . Nubbin's taking the bait again. Streaking down the driveway. Around that turn the only thing keeping him upright is the grip of his claws on concrete. Yipping all the way."

"A beast of stealth and style."

"He's almost got her. He's so close! He's—nope, missed by a hair. Down goes the cat, down follows Nubbin, up goes the cat, and we start over. Nubbin's on hind legs, yapping up a spleen. And Edgar Poe . . . oh, she is so coy. She's curling up and appears to be . . . yes, folks, she's taking a snooze."

"Let me understand—the dog is barking at a hundred decibels approximately four inches from her face, and the cat is faking slumber?"

"Eyes closed, head down. And she's rolling . . . she's rolled onto her back, paws limp in the air."

"Exquisite."

Then Annette piped up. "Wow, that's a crack-up, huh? What a silly cat, huh?"

Becky felt that familiar tight sensation rushing from her belly, up into her throat. She tried to clamp down on it, but that only increased its power. She squeaked, and out it came. But here was the curiosity: Felix laughed with her, as if they were old pals on the same side of a joke. It gave her a strange, fluttery feeling in her middle—a kind of happiness, and a kind of alarm. She quickly dismissed it as the delightful rarity of laughing with a famous person.

As soon as the conversation ended, Becky ran inside and found Mike, who'd been peering into the oven at Becky's chicken enchiladas.

"That was him again—hey, shut that door; you'll let all the heat out. That was Felix Callahan. I was talking to Annette about the contract and he was in the office, and we spoke. Isn't that weird? That I would speak to him again in my life? I think it's so weird."

"That is weird," Mike said, though his attention was mostly taken up by the enchiladas. They did smother everything with their tauntingly delicious aroma.

She rolled the strangeness over in her thoughts from time to time, wondering if it all meant something. There was a queer beating in her heart when she thought of that man, and she felt something like pregnancy food cravings when she considered she'd never speak with him again. Which she fully expected. So when he showed up a few weeks later, it was strange and wonderful but disturbing too. And also quite interesting. Enough adjectives. You'll see.

*In which Becky tries on the Professional Screenwriter
mantle and does okay until an unexpected incident*

"You *are* a professional screenwriter," Becky's friend Melissa said on the phone. "You sold a screenplay. For money. To a major Hollywood production company no less."

"Sure, but . . . it was a fluke and I don't know anything about . . . oh okay, fine. I'll do it."

And so Becky presented at the third-annual Greater Salt Lake Filmmaking Conference. It was a favor to Melissa, who was helping to organize the conference, and Becky planned on appearing as the poseur and not enjoying it at all.

Melissa was waiting for her at the downtown library. Her skirt was self-shredded, her boots combat, and her ash-blonde hair streaked purple. Becky felt a stitch of jealousy—Melissa looked cool with torn clothing and wild hair, while Becky would have resembled a Care Bear beaten and left for dead. Melissa's mother had abandoned her at age ten, her father resembled a block of slowly melting cheese more than a human being, and her brother was a passive-aggressive predator. It was fifteen years late, but Becky couldn't begrudge her friend a good old-fashioned teenage rebellion.

"There you are," Melissa said in tones meant to be urgent and angry but sounding more like an excited Elmo. She had one of those babyish voices with a high pitch and a narrow tone. Becky adored it, especially when her language turned blue. Of course Becky couldn't approve of vulgarity in general, but when Melissa got to swearing, Becky just wanted to pinch her cheeks. Sometimes she wondered if Melissa's voice was actually the driving source of her rebellion. What if you had a soul forged in fire but a voice cut from felt and feathers?

"Hurry up. There are people waiting for you," Melissa said, taking her arm.

"Really?"

And sure enough, when Melissa dropped Becky at her assigned conference room, eight people sat patiently on folding chairs. Eight people interested in writing screenplays and eager for some hints and encouragement and hope. Eight people who thought Becky was a superstar for having done it. So she sat in the chair in front, patted her pregnant belly, and let herself feel awfully pleased as she told her story.

First she had to admit that she didn't deserve to be successful. "I sold the very first script that I wrote—I gather that's not the way it works. I've been making up stories all my life, but I'd never written them down."

She talked about format, writing both for and against formula, and her own unlikely contact with the producer, warning them that becoming extras on a movie set wasn't likely to pan out twice.

"But be prepared when any opportunity strikes," she advised.

Then she described the trip to Los Angeles. She drizzled on the details, emphasizing the quirky bits, playing for laughs. A few more people straggled in, filling out the audience, and Becky was feeling jubilantly popular. She got to the part in Annette's office, how pregnant she felt ("It's one thing to be an expectant mother in Utah, but being pregnant in Los Angeles felt like a lazy and irresponsible thing to do"), the constant clicking of Annette's bracelets, and . . . she faltered, hesitating to mention Felix Callahan. Why? That would be the climax to the story. It was something to brag about, wasn't it? Why did she want to keep it to herself, as if it were some precious secret? That was just plain silly. It wasn't a secret or precious. The encounter was good for nothing but retelling. So she brushed aside her doubt.

"I was about to sign that tome of a contract just to stop the clickety-click of gypsy jewelry when someone walked in that I never expected, never hoped to meet, looking as if he'd just peeled off the front cover of *People* magazine. You cannot guess. You won't even believe me when I tell you." She paused. "Felix Callahan."

A woman in the front row gasped, both hands on her chest as if preparing to give herself CPR. She was in her midforties and wore a large purple hat that might have been in style if seventies retro was in. Was it already? Becky made a mental note to ask Melissa later.

"You. Are. Joking." The woman in the hat spoke in overcome staccato.

"He waltzed right in, as if my airfare, hotel, and celebrity sighting were all a package deal."

Becky stopped. It turned out she could laugh about it with Mike but flinched at flapping the story around in public. (Okay, maybe it was a tiny bit precious.) So she quickly wrapped up and asked for questions.

"Do you use adverbs to describe how your dialogue should be spoken?"

"Will you give my screenplay to your producer?"

"How do you format a screenplay?"

"Did you get that blouse at Motherhood Maternity?"

"What things should be in a contract?"

"Can you help me sell my screenplay?"

"Do you think there's a market for another robots-take-over-the-future movie? Mine kicks butt."

She thought it was a good sign that there were so many questions, that maybe she'd been interesting enough, and she answered them spryly, until the last one tipped her over.

"So, what was Felix Callahan like?"

The question came from a man in the last row, one of those who had straggled in halfway through. He'd spoken in an American accent, which confused her at first. But no, it *was* him, hidden to all but her at the back of the room, in dark sunglasses and baseball cap, his long legs stretched out before him in a manner of casual relaxation.

Becky felt her face flush. And her neck. It was one thing to blush daintily on the cheeks, something that could be blamed on a warm room, but when the neck got in on the deal, she might as well just announce to the world, "I'm extremely embarrassed and would like to curl up and hide. Now go about your business."

She shook her head. Then she smiled. Then she answered in a jaunty tone.

"Felix Callahan was . . . what's the word?"

"Gorgeous?" the hatted woman offered, to tittering sounds of laughter.

"He was okay," Becky said. "I mean, he was dressed all movie star-ish, so you were aware you were talking to someone beyond the norm. But still, he wasn't *so* handsome. I mean, you see these men on the big screen and you expect them to take your breath away."

"You're lying," said the woman under the hat. "Tell me you're lying, because you're ruining my favorite daydream."

"Oh, all right, he was a little more than so-so. He was okay. He was fine. And besides being a brutish kind of British, he did end up being kind of nice. More or less."

"More," said the woman with hat. "Definitely more."

Felix was smiling. "But don't you think he's terrifically gosh-darn talented?"

He was such a faker with shades and hat, pretending a preference for circumspection; but underneath all that, she could tell he was just a big ham. Her heart was pounding and her neck was probably bright purple by now, but her voice stayed cool.

"He's good enough. I mean, he's no Laurence Olivier."

"You think he's more of an Anthony Hopkins?"

"Not so dignified."

"Kenneth Branagh? Robert De Niro?"

"No, he lacks that intensity."

"Sean Penn?"

"Doesn't have the range."

"Chevy Chase?"

"Getting closer."

The audience members were looking back and forth between them as if trying to figure out whether the guy in the back row was being difficult or whether this was a preplanned part of her presentation.

"Then how do you account for his superhunk reputation?"

"I can't," she said frankly, returning his gaze. "I'm utterly mystified. Okay, look, no one's going to say that Felix Callahan isn't *photogenic*, and it's true that he's brilliant both at comedy and that moody and disenchanted thing, and every woman who's seen *Rattled Cages* put him at the top of her secret list of crushes. He's got that accent going for him, and even though he's a jerk, he can be a nice boy."

Felix smiled, like an imp who's cornered his victim. "So what you're saying is . . ."

She glared, suddenly annoyed, and gestured in his direction. "I'm saying . . . ladies and gentlemen, may I present Mr. Felix Callahan."

There was the hard sound of eleven people taking a sharp intake of breath and the clutter of chairs as everyone turned to stare.

Felix stood, reluctantly, walked to the front of the room, took her hand and kissed it.

"Nice to see you again," he said quietly.

"Sure thing," she said, because the moment felt both too bizarre and too important to say anything profound.

He turned to the small audience, who hadn't moved. "Don't believe a word this woman says. For one thing, I've never met her in my life."

He left.

And the clamor began.

"Was that really—"

"Did he just—"

"I can't believe I said—"

"Did you see how—"

"He was right in the room and I said he was—"

"This is unbelievable!"

Becky listened as if half awake and looked down at her feet to see if they were touching the floor. They appeared to be.

She expected to find him waiting outside the room. When he wasn't, she walked slowly to her car, in case he'd hidden himself somewhere out of sight of autograph seekers and intended to find her alone. She got into the car without incident. She started it slowly, inched out of the parking lot, then when no Felix appeared, sped home.

She cruised on the freeway, scarcely aware of the landmarks rolling by: Bountiful temple, amusement park, flour mills . . . Her thoughts tumbled. Felix Callahan. Felix Callahan! Could this really be happening? The whole Los Angeles thing had been just a surreal, sliding moment that sparked and was gone. Having dinner with Felix had been like seeing a UFO flash through the night sky—so real one moment, but the next explained away as the combined effect of a lightning storm and dry eyes. Even speaking to him on the phone had seemed like a daydream gone strange.

But now, she'd seen him on her home turf. That was passing surreal. That was getting downright dangerous.

Felix Callahan. From *Rattled Cages*. She'd seen it, oh, let's say, a dozen times, because she'd never counted (and if she had, it would be closer to twenty-one). Enough, anyhow, to know most of the dialogue. Enough to be able to replay that final scene in her head . . .

Calvin watches Katie with those dark, soulful eyes. He is painfully shy, but Katie needs him to speak. She can't risk everything on a hope.

CALVIN: Katie, I . . .
KATIE: Yes?
CALVIN: I'm . . . we're out of birdseed. I need to reorder.
KATIE: Oh. I guess you're busy. It was nice knowing you,
        Calvin. I'll stop by again, if I'm ever back in the city.
CALVIN: That'd be . . . that'd be great.

He watches her go, his face pained. We know he'll lie awake for days just picturing her face. We know he'll never love again.
   He stares down, angry at himself, at his own failure, and picks up the change she left on the counter. Beneath it, he sees again the mark she scratched into the wood—the reason his boss flipped out at this troublesome customer, the reason Calvin first stepped in to protect her, the way their friendship started, how he had the courage to buy the shop from his boss, strike out on his own, change his life. He'd never noticed before what she'd scratched there—it's a heart . . . and we know he's reminded of those conversations they had about what a heart is. Just a vital organ? Or the house of the soul? The most precious thing one owns and yet is eager to give away?
   He runs out into the rain.

CALVIN: Katie! Katie, wait!

She stops, her heart pounding, wondering if he's going to say it. Her love life has been an endless succession of men who appreciated

*her looks but never saw her heart, and like Katie, we believe that
Calvin is the first and perhaps only man who could love her right.
But she needs Calvin to speak this time. Please, Calvin, speak . . .*

CALVIN: I . . . I . . .
KATIE: You're getting wet!

*She pulls him under the umbrella, their faces inches apart. His
dark hair is dripping, water running down his face. The rainstorm
thickens, so it almost seems there's no world outside that space. They're
both breathing a little faster.*

CALVIN: Katie, I . . .
KATIE: Yes? What, Calvin?
CALVIN: For your birthday, I was thinking of getting you a
hamster. Unless there's something of mine you might
like.

*And he looks at her, in her eyes, and smiles just a little. It's
enough. Man, even the barest wisp of a smile from that man is
breathtaking. He doesn't say "I love you," but by cleverly echoing
what she'd said earlier about hamsters and the giving away of one's
heart, we know that's what he means. (I love you, you're perfect,
you're everything, you toast my marshmallows, baby.)
Katie's mouth twitches as if she'd like to laugh, but he's so close
it's all she can do to just keep breathing.
His hand touches her face, tentative, and he looks at her as if
she were the world. Her eyes close. He comes a little closer, as if
melting into her. Then his lips—those wonderful, wonderful
lips—are on hers. One long slow kiss. Then another. Another. The
umbrella droops. Her arms go around his neck, she drops the umbrella entirely, and they kiss long and deeply in the pouring rain.*

Yes, she'd seen it a dozen times (or twenty-one). And yes, each time
that final kiss made her heart sputter, and she'd returned to Mike feeling particularly amorous and often downright frisky. Mike once declared it his favorite movie of all time. And he'd never seen it.

Becky was standing in her driveway. She wasn't sure how long she'd
been there, reliving the last scene in *Rattled Cages* and waiting for Felix
to show up. He didn't. She peered behind the leafless shrubs then walked
around the mammoth sycamore in their front yard, eyeing Hyrum's
treehouse for any occupants. Nobody. But Felix had been at the library,
right? There, in the back row. In Salt Lake City. That hadn't been an

incredibly vivid daydream, a sign that a stiff white jacket would be in her future? No. If there was one thing in this world Becky was sure of, it was her own sanity.

"That was one of the weirdest things," she said to the rosebush. "Ever. Weirdest things ever."

The rosebush needed pruning. It didn't respond.

Putting out of her mind the "Why on earth did he come see me?" question because it was impossible to answer, she asked instead the "how" question. How had he known where she'd be? She went inside the quiet house and opened the white pages to "Jack." In the Layton area, there were only three, and the first one listed was her brother-in-law Clark.

His wife, Angela, answered the phone—Angela of the Perpetual Happiness, Angela of the Ubiquitous Exclamation Marks.

"Becky! Hi! How did your little thing go?"

"It was great, thanks. Hey, listen, did anyone . . . one of my friends call your house asking where I was recently?"

"Yes! Your nice friend from England called! Hendrix, was it? Just this morning! He thought this was your number! Well, I gave him yours and Mike's number, but I told him, I happen to know she's not home now, because her kids are here while she's doing a little thing! 'Did you know that she's a professional screenwriter,' I said, 'and she's presenting today at a conference for professionals?' Well! Wasn't he happy for you! I can tell you! He said I was helpful beyond words! Wasn't that nice?"

"Yes, that was nice. And helpful. Thank you." And part of Becky thought, thank goodness Angela didn't give all her private info to some creepy stalker. Then again, did Felix fit that bill? It seemed he had flipped through an airport phone book to find her, taken a cab or something to sit in on her "little thing," and then left again. Definitely questionable behavior.

"Okay, I'll see you later. Say hi to Clark."

Angela cleared her throat. "So, um, Becky, are you home now?"

"Yes, I'm all done."

"So . . ."

Becky waited. So . . . ? She was feeling antsy standing in the kitchen, tethered to the wall by the phone cord, and really wanted to go sort laundry and sort her thoughts with it.

Angela's voice turned shy. "So, will you be coming to pick up your kids sometime soon?"

Her kids! Mike had gone with Fiona to a father-daughter church party, so Becky had dropped off Hyrum and Polly at their aunt's house, and she was supposed to go straight there, not wander home to talk to unresponsive shrubbery and flip through an expired white pages! What was the matter with her? Usually she was the first minivan waiting outside the school, the first mom to sign up for the bake sale, the responsible one, for Pete's sake! And now here she was completely forgetting her kids and thinking in gratuitous exclamation points!

"Yes! Yes. Thank you. I'm on my way right now, so I'll see you later, you know, like, in five minutes. And I'll just wait in the car—you can send them out so we don't take up any more of your time. So say hi to Clark for me, you know, since I might not get a chance to talk to you from the car. But thanks so much for watching the kids for me, and I'll see you later . . . in five."

There was a pause. Then Angela's voice piped up, as enthusiastic as ever.

"Okay, see you later in five!"

Oh great, Becky thought as she jogged back to her car. Now Angela would be using that phrase, convinced it was a real idiom. And it would be all Becky's fault. As if the poor lady didn't have enough communication problems as it was, what with the excessive exclaiming.

Becky drove the familiar route to Angela's, past the brick bungalows, down Gentile Street, turning by the field with horses that Hyrum loved. What would Layton look like to Felix? A dull little backwater, she guessed. Just then, it did seem run-down to her, squatty and rough compared with Los Angeles, with its glossy skyscrapers and expensive pollution. Her backbone straightened. How dare he make her sweet town look dumpy? Who did he think he was?

Polly and Hyrum raced for her car as soon as she pulled up, none too sorry to leave their cousins. Apparently there had been a prolonged incident where seven-year-old Jayden had chased Polly with a "snot rag." Polly was exhausted from her desperate flight, and Hyrum was glum because no one would play Dinosaurs Rule the Earth with him (probably, as Becky suspected, because Hyrum wanted to be the dinosaur and make everyone else Doomed Cavemen). Both kids were silent on the ride home, giving Becky a chance to keep thinking. But the meditative time wasn't especially productive, churning out such thoughts as, *That was weird. Is he gone for good? Weird, definitely weird. But fun too?*

When Becky pulled into the garage, Felix still wasn't there.

"Mom, Mom, Mom," Polly said, panic quivering her voice, "I think one of my teeth is loose."

"Okay, honey."

"It's loose, Mommy, it really is. It's loose!"

"It's okay, honey, it's okay. If it's barely loose, it won't fall out before Monday and we can run to the dentist after school."

Because Polly, you see, was petrified of loose teeth and so had to have each of her baby teeth professionally removed by a dentist. This was all thanks to her sister's son Luther, who convinced Polly that if you accidentally swallow a tooth, it will eat through your stomach and come out your belly button. The little rat.

So Becky was pretty well occupied the rest of the afternoon keeping Polly calm and distracted, the Felix question barely twitching there in the back of her skull until she and Mike were alone in their bedroom that night.

"Maybe he's insane?" she asked.

"That'd be my vote. Did you get that crazy vibe?"

"No," she said, disappointed, because it would have been such an easy explanation.

Becky had recounted all the details from that afternoon—except how Felix could make her heart skippity-skip. In Becky's opinion, you don't *ooh* over a fine young actor on the screen in front of your husband. That's not okay, any more than it's okay to hear him say, "Check out that babe" at the community pool. Maybe Mike did notice other women, maybe he did have secret crushes on Sharon Stone and Teri Hatcher, but exclaiming about their perfections in front of your wife is like saying, "Why can't you look more like her?" So Becky kept her mouth shut. Besides, she was embarrassed about the whole thing.

Not that it mattered. This time, she was certain, she'd never see Felix again. He'd shown up to see her, sure, but then she'd outed him. He must have been upset, since he hadn't even stayed to say hello. So that was it, the end of the Felix sightings. Thank goodness, really. Who needs that kind of heart-smacking hassle?

Right?

In which Becky receives an unexpected phone call

"Hello?" Becky clamped the receiver between her ear and shoulder. Her left arm held a nursing baby, her right hand turned off the oven timer and stirred the green beans, her left leg was occupied with Hyrum, clutching her and screaming that he was starving, and her right leg itched. Probably a spider bite.

"Hello?" she said again, not hearing a response over the noise.

"Uh . . . Becky Jack? This is Felix Callahan."

"Who?"

"Felix Callahan? We met in Los Angles four months ago. I accompanied you and your fetus to dinner."

She stopped, baby still nursing, four-year-old still screaming. The sound of his voice made her limbs freeze and her heart pump—that is, Felix Callahan's voice had that effect. She was used to her toddler's screams. Nothing a predinner cracker couldn't cure.

"Felix Callahan," she said flatly, once Hyrum had run off with his cracker, crisis cured.

"Yes. I am. That is my name."

"You're calling me. On the phone. At home. Felix Callahan. *Ahem*, well, hi, how are ya?"

"Fine, thanks. I am—"

"Just a second." She muffled the receiver against her shoulder and shouted, "Fiona, just because I'm on the phone doesn't mean I can't see you sneaking those olives! Finish setting the table, young lady, or there will be no dessert." She tucked the phone back under her shoulder. "Sorry, you were saying?"

"I was . . . er, how are you?"

"Uh, fine. I'm fine. The whole family's fine. Thanks for, you know, stopping by my presentation in November. That was—sweet? Or something? Actually, it was odd."

"Yes, I suppose it was."

"But kinda funny too?" she offered hopefully.

"It was impulsive. I had a layover in Salt Lake City on my way to Los Angeles."

She wasn't going to let him get away with that. "A layover that just happened to coincide with the exact time I was presenting?"

"Yes."

"Really?"

"I was surprised myself. I just . . . I realized you were the only person I knew in Utah and . . . it was impulsive."

"Okay."

"Hmm. So." He paused. "My wife, Celeste, and I are coming out your way on the twelfth for a skiing holiday, spending a week in Park City. We thought we might"—he cleared his throat—"we might meet up with you. And your husband. For dinner."

Becky didn't say anything for some time.

"I think you're still there," he said. "I think you're shocked."

"Sort of. Sort of still here. Sort of shocked."

"Dinner is always a shocking proposition."

"That's the truth. Lunch, supper, after-school snack—all respectable and appropriate sessions of nutritional intake—"

"Whilst dinner is practically Neanderthal."

"I couldn't agree more." Becky took a deep breath, reminding herself that she was not talking to Augie Beuter. "Well, okay, well . . . we'd be happy to have you over for dinner, as shocking as that is. You could meet the kids and see the new baby. Sam is four weeks old, and he got Mike's looks, thank goodness, narrowly escaping my family's tendency to resemble hairy little trolls at birth. I guess I'm just a bit subjective, but I think he's worth looking at."

"Oh. I see. That might do, except we'd most likely stand round staring at it, and I'd know that I was expected to admire it and I wouldn't know what to say, which would be awkward for everyone."

"Especially if you kept referring to him as 'it.' Well, then—*Polly, you can either clear your crayons off the table or help your sister set it! I'm not going to ask you again.* Sorry, um . . . dinner . . . well, Mike and I are going to the Valentine's Ball the Saturday after the fourteenth . . . whatever date that is. It's our yearly tradition, and the first time I'm getting out of this house since the baby. You and your wife might like to come. The Salt Lake Chamber Music Association puts it on—dinner, ballroom dancing, rather nice, though you're bound to roll your eyes."

"I most certainly will not! It will be a delightful experiment in anthropology."

"Okay. Then it's a date—uh, I meant, it's an anthropological experiment."

"Right then. Saturday it is."

"Okay, we'll see you then."

"Very well."

"Good-bye."

"Yes, good-bye."

There was a silence. After a time she said, "You're still there, aren't you?"

Pause. "So are you."

"I guess I am." She hemmed. "Did you want directions or anything?"

"It's in Salt Lake City, isn't it? I imagine if we wander round, we should run into it before long."

"I really am hanging up now."

"That's probably for the best." His voice went low, quiet, and made her stomach drop. "I'll see you soon."

"Soon." She hung up and looked at Mike, who'd been frozen in the kitchen, staring at her since she'd spoken the words "Felix Callahan."

"That was him?"

She nodded. "He and his French model wife are coming to the Valentine's Ball. So they can hang out with us."

"So they can hang out with us."

"Yep."

"Okay," he said.

And they laughed.

They kept talking and laughing about it until four-year-old Hyrum gave the prayer on the food. Then it was time to focus on the eating of shepherd's pie and the official Family Talking Around the Dinner Table. Mike was solemn as he listened to Fiona recounting her third-grade spelling bee, and Becky guessed he'd become as thoughtful as she had.

Felix Callahan. And Celeste Bodine. Coming to Utah to hang with the Jacks. There was that funny tickle in Becky's stomach again, and she didn't think it was the shepherd's pie. At least, she hoped it wasn't. She prodded the meat for signs of undercooking.

The question of Felix Callahan ran under everything she did that night—cleaning up, dressing kids, reading to kids, kissing good-night. It was ten o'clock before she and Mike had their sacred time, just the two of them alone in the bedroom—well, almost just the two of them, and no, not for that yet. She hadn't been cleared by her doctor postpartum. No, just to see each other, hear each other, maybe smell each other a little.

With Sam curled up in her arms, Becky leaned into Mike and inhaled the scent of his neck. It was like drinking water, how it filled her. Sure, Mike had first wooed her with his attention, his strength, his stability and future-father-ness, but let's be honest—a hearty slice of what had attracted Becky to Mike were his highly compatible pheromones.

Sam began to cry with a little dry cackle, squirming, his face rooting around Becky's chest.

"He's not very subtle, is he?" Becky said.

"The kid knows what he wants."

Becky climbed onto the bed, settling into the stacked pillows. When Sam latched on and began to nurse, his twelve-pound body relaxed into blissful contentment, and hers followed in kind, calm radiating out from her middle. She sighed. Kids asleep, baby happy. Life was good. And now her undercurrent thoughts jumped back up.

"But you know what's weird, honey? That it's not weird." She didn't name the "it" and Mike didn't need clarification. He was sitting on the floor, smearing brown polish on his good work shoes. He was a marketing analyst at a biotech firm, and he liked having polished shoes.

"How is it not weird?"

She pulled one knee up to rest her elbow. Four weeks old and the little fellow was getting heavy. "Somehow. It's just not."

"I don't know about that. He's starting to sound stalkerish."

"Mike, come on. Felix Callahan is not going to stalk some frumpy mommy from Layton, Utah. That's not how these things work."

"I don't know if we should go."

The idea was impossible to her. Not see what would happen next? That would be like turning off a movie ten minutes before the ending! "But aren't you curious?"

He shrugged.

"I think you have a good thirty pounds on Felix anyway, so if it comes to that, my money's on the hubbie."

"Fifty pounds," Mike mumbled. He went back to polishing his shoes. "This spring I'm thinking of pulling up that honeysuckle vine and planting a silver birch instead. I think the kids would rather have some shade in that part of the yard. What do you think?"

She agreed, and they talked about the yard and the kids, dance lessons and piano lessons and chess club events, who was going to parents' night at Hyrum's preschool on Friday and who would stay home with the baby, until they read scriptures together, prayed together, and went to bed.

The first time Mike snored, Becky opened her eyes and stared at the ceiling.

Why isn't it weird? she asked herself.

It was nearly two A.M. before she fell asleep.

*The Valentine's Ball, in which someone gets punched
in the face but no one is seriously injured*

Becky and Mike were going to be late. Her parents drove up from Centerville, where they had moved in retirement to be closer to a community theater. (Last season, Alice Hyde had portrayed Mama Rose and Casper Hyde had played Don Quixote.) After the obligatory greetings, Becky went through the how-to-care-for-the-newborn list, with such important items as "never microwave the bottle of breast milk—heat it by placing it in a cup of hot water" and "watch Polly with the baby—she thinks 'kissing' and 'mauling' are the same thing," while her mother kept insisting, "I know, Becky, I know. I raised six of my own." And Becky said, "Yeah, back in the day when they thought smoking was medicinal and breast milk inferior to formula."

"And dinosaurs walked the earth," her father added.

Alice laughed her wonderfully loud cackle.

"You're the only ones in the world I trust to take care of my teeny guy," Becky said, hugging them both.

"I know, I know." Alice stroked her hair. "I give you my grandmother's oath that Sam will still be alive when you get back. Forget about it all for a few hours and go be carefree."

Carefree, Becky thought ironically. Her mother didn't know who might or might not be waiting at the ball.

Just as Becky and Mike were leaving, Becky decided she had to hold Sam one last time, and he spit up on her dress—not just a dribble, but a couple of pints of cheesy regurgitated milk. It was the only nice dress that she could fit into postpartum, so she was forced to change into her maternity Sunday dress. She had put in contacts for the evening, because glasses felt informal, but they were pokey and irritating, so she pinched them out and shoved back on her sturdy wire frames. Then there was an accident on the freeway and the twenty-minute drive from Layton to downtown Salt Lake took thirty-five minutes. Parking was chaotic, Becky's corsage got caught on the seat belt, but finally, at quarter to eight, they speed-walked into the rotunda of the state capitol building, red-faced, breathless, and only mildly surprised at the sight that awaited them—Felix Callahan in a black tuxedo and Celeste Bodine in a sparkly scarlet low-cut gown, both looking like they'd just waltzed off the red carpet.

They were standing in one corner of the gray stone chamber, whispering to each other. The rest of the ball-goers danced or bustled or moseyed through the buffet line, all the while keeping an eye on the Hollywood couple.

Felix spotted Becky and said something to Celeste, who looked up and smiled. The Frenchwoman had chestnut hair, twisted up with a little spray escaping from the top. Her face was long and lean; her nose was long too and would have looked ridiculous on anyone else's face, but on her it was exotically beautiful. Her slender neck was bare of jewelry, as if to say, do I need any adornment beside this fabulous bust? (The answer was no.) But she wore gems the size of nickels in her ears, glinting in that we're-real-diamonds-and-we-know-it way, that you-couldn't-afford-us-if-you-sold-your-house way.

Becky fingered one of her own earrings—genuine pink enamel, $11.95 at Fred Meyer.

"There they are," Becky said, waving.

"You don't say? I never could've picked them out of the crowd."

"I can't believe they actually came. What on earth are they thinking? Come on."

"Okay," Mike said, which meant he'd rather go back home and watch the news, if that was all right.

"Hello, hello!" Becky called. "Look at you two. My, don't you blend in like cougars in a petting zoo."

Felix adjusted his bow tie. "Yes, we thought we'd dress down tonight."

Becky believed Celeste was showing remarkable restraint by not so much as glancing at Becky's pink cotton maternity dress.

"Hi, I'm Becky." She extended her hand to Celeste.

"How do you do? Celeste Bodine," she said, her accent as rich and yummy as rum sauce.

Celeste took Becky's hand but then leaned in for a cheek kiss. Becky had never encountered a Continental greeting before, and in her panic, she planted her lips on Celeste's cheek, leaving two lines of lipstick.

"Oh, whoops." Becky tried to smear the mark away with her thumb, momma-style. "I nicked you there with my Seashell Pink grocery store lipstick. I did that wrong, didn't I? Sorry, I'm not used to the whole cheek-kissing thing."

"Let me show you." Celeste took Becky's hand. "Now lean in, touch your left cheek to mine, and gently kiss the air. That's right. Now we switch, touch right cheeks and repeat. Ah, you are a natural, Rebecca!"

And despite the fact that Celeste was way beyond Barbie doll,

Becky already liked her. She tried to imagine what she herself would look like in that red sparkly getup. It was enough to make her flinch.

"Hey there!" A woman with a razor-perfect bob came upon them like a bulldozer, dragging her husband behind. "You're Felix Callahan! Wow, you're taller than I expected, and paler too. Maybe it's all the makeup you wear on-screen? That helps? Anyway, I need an autograph for my daughter or she'll never believe me!"

Felix gave her a half glance. "To be fair, I don't believe you myself. Tell me you're a singing telegram in the Stepford model someone hired as a joke, and I'll breathe a sigh of relief."

"Huh?" she said. "I . . . I really need an autograph for my daughter."

"Unfortunately, I don't keep a surplus of damns on hand, so I don't have one to give right now." He turned his back.

The couple blinked a lot as they walked away, as if trying to decode the insult.

"Somebody's grumpy," Becky muttered.

"Oh no," Celeste said, looking through her clutch purse as if to ignore the scene. "This is Felix with his fans. Ever diplomatic."

They browsed the buffet, taking plates back to their table to eat while watching the Brigham Young University ballroom dancers. Mike barely tolerated this part. He liked dancing with Becky okay; watching others prance around was just a bit too close to sissy.

The two other couples at their table flicked their gazes at the Hollywood pair and whispered in each other's ears. The glances morphed into stares, and Becky steeled herself for another obscure and biting comment.

"Excuse me, aren't you famous?" the balding man asked, raising his voice to be heard above the music.

Celeste looked away, and Felix opened his mouth to speak when Becky interrupted with a laugh.

"You win, Rufus!" she said to Felix, offering him a fake name. "I thought you were kidding when you said people mistook you for that British actor. I owe you five bucks."

Felix hesitated the barest moment before smiling a very un-Felix-like smile, tight-lipped and toothy, and saying in an American accent, "Happens all the time. Thought we'd play it up tonight." He straightened his bow tie and made a clicking noise with his tongue while winking.

"I told you, honey," his date said. "He doesn't look like him at all."

"I've heard stories about that actor." Becky leaned forward conspiratorially. "His looks are all fake, loads of plastic surgery, you know, and they say he doesn't eat food like a normal person, just drinks glass after glass of whiskey. He's actually ninety-five, but the alcohol preserves him, like pumping a corpse full of formaldehyde."

Celeste laughed into her napkin. Felix shut his eyes and shook his head. Mike pressed his knee against Becky's under the table, his way of sharing a joke on the sly.

As soon as the floor opened to dancing, Becky and Mike hit it, pulling out their favorite—the fox-trot. He slid her along, the firm pressure of his hand on her back directing her steps. It gave Becky a thrill. At home she was the CEO, in charge and responsible for everything. It was lovely to feel so light, to turn over her motions to Mike, to feel a part of his strength. He didn't love to dance, but he did it for her sake, and that made him completely lovable.

"You have to admit that this is bizarre," Mike said.

"I admit it. But isn't it funny bizarre?"

Felix and Celeste whirled by. They looked like an ad for expensive things—luxury cars, gold watches, purses that cost more than a minivan.

After a couple of songs, Felix tapped Mike on the shoulder. "May I escort your wife for a number? My own has kindly offered to keep you occupied. On the dance floor, I presume."

Celeste smiled mischievously. "Or wherever he likes."

"She's not so dangerous as all that," Felix said. "You should be safe so long as you don't do anything foolish, such as give her diamonds or feed her human blood."

Mike looked to Becky for help. Becky shrugged, no more certain of the situation than he was, though probably more curious.

"If you want to, hon . . ." Mike said.

Celeste took Mike's arm. "That's right, I will take care of your husband. You go have fun." Celeste seemed eager for Felix and Becky to dance, for some reason, and showed not the least sign of jealousy—and really, why should she? Becky was so aware of her stiff pink maternity dress that she might as well have been wearing the skin of a grizzly. Besides, it would be unfair to deny Mike a chance to dance with a supermodel.

Becky let Felix lead her to the dance floor.

After Mike, dancing with Felix felt strained. First, she kept remembering who he was, and that made her suspect that she was in a movie, which then turned on her underutilized self-conscious glands, because she didn't belong in a movie. What on earth would she be doing in a movie?

Besides, she was used to Mike, and Felix's hands confused her. Dancing with him while pregnant had been one thing—the weight of her belly and the twisted, bloated, stiffened peculiarity of every limb made her feel a stranger in her own body. It hadn't been *her* body then—her mind had been transplanted into a 180-pound incubator.

Now that she was back to being Becky, dancing with Felix wasn't just a joke.

But by the second song, they stopped knocking knees and pulling away from each other and began to move as one. He held her in three places—hand on her lower back, hand holding her hand, and then sometimes, his leg against hers. Mike didn't do that.

She laughed, because how does a grown woman and mother of four interpret such a thing as dancing with Felix Callahan? And she laughed because she glimpsed Mike and Celeste, and Mike's arms and back were stiff, his expression uncomfortable bordering on painful, and he seemed to be looking everywhere in the room but at Celeste's highly visible cleavage.

The cleavage reminded Becky of that place in the bathroom where the baseboard was pulling away from the wall. She needed to glue that back on and recaulk. Around some of the windows too. Maybe she and Mike could make that their project next Saturday. And maybe replace the hinges on that one cabinet. And this was a good time of year to go shopping for winter clothing, buy the kids' next-year sizes from the discount racks—

What are you doing, Becky? Focus! You're dancing with Felix Callahan. You need to be enjoying this on behalf of every woman in America.

She snapped back. He was still there, holding her. Back, hand, thigh. Back, hand, thigh. Felix Callahan. Felix Callahan?

It had seemed safe to have a crush on Felix Callahan from the sanitized distance of the screen, but having him this close was . . . well, a little confusing. She'd fallen in love with characters all her life—Gilbert Blythe, Mr. Rochester, Harry Hamlin as Perseus. Then she'd met Mike. Real men had thinned into the scenery; fictional men were briefly entertaining but faded out of her consciousness as soon as she closed the book or emerged from the movie theater.

So her only dalliances were inside those story moments. There was that pesky romance gene that needed a little twanging from time to time, and crushing on a fictional character or unattainable movie star was completely kosher. Everyone knew those rules. Of course, those rules assumed that said Unattainable Crush would never actually step into your very real life. So, how to deal with the disorientation when the man you've blushed about from a movie seat is suddenly quite real and leading you in . . . what dance were they doing now?

It was the waltz (one-two-three, one-two-three . . .). The music had a rubbery, echoey tone in that large, round room, the wails from the stringed instruments bouncing off stone. That particular waltz wasn't as circusy as some, nor as stately—it was a tender tune. The melody rolled under her, made her feel as if she were dancing on water. It curled around her, wrapped her up, and spun her out, till it seemed the music itself was moving her body. The waltz . . . there was something about the waltz she used to know . . .

The Waltz (according to Desdemona Yap, instructor of "You Can Ballroom Dance!"): "The Waltz took Europe by surprise, the first dance where the man holds the woman to his body. To dance it properly, you must feel the romance of that music. Mike, hold her tighter there. Becky, relax your upper body. Surrender yourself to the movement. It is intimate, it is erotic, it is—"

"Ack!"

Yes, Becky said "ack" right then on the dance floor of the Valentine's Ball. She was in no way a fan of the word "erotic," and she had just thought it while dancing with Felix Callahan. (Felix Callahan!) She let go of him as if of hot metal and took a step back.

"Maybe we shouldn't dance anymore," she said.

"All right." He gestured with his chin toward the far part of the rotunda. "I glimpsed some interesting statues that way, and I wouldn't mind removing myself from all the—how would you say?—rubberneckers." He offered his crooked arm. "Walk with me?"

Even though she was still thrumming with that *e*-word, she didn't want to interrupt the evening. It never entered her thoughts that walking with Felix might be dangerous in a moral sense. For one thing, she was clad in that hideous pink maternity dress she'd purchased in 1987. It wore like armor. Besides, she trusted herself absolutely, as much as she trusted Mike with those most perfect breasts west of the Mississippi. He wouldn't be biting into any off-limits apples, and neither would she.

On top of that, she was sleep deprived (Baby Sam was a cutie, but he still had day and night confused), she hadn't put on makeup or gone farther than the grocery store in six weeks, and before she cracked and went completely insane, she wanted to see where this crazy night was going. Because it was going somewhere, and on Felix's arm. So she took it. And they walked toward the edge of the room.

She caught Mike's eye and waved so he would see where she was going. He nodded, still dancing.

Moving into the quiet corner was as much of a relief as walking into shade on a blazing day. She'd never in her trimmed-and-tidy life been so accosted by stares—except that one time when she'd left the church restroom with the back of her skirt tucked into her pantyhose.

"Thanks again for your help with the contract," she said as they passed a marbleized Philo T. Farnsworth, inventor of television. "Nothing's happening with the film, of course, but Annette gave me five thousand dollars for the option. After taxes and all, it'll be enough to cover the baby delivery bills, and just in time."

"Oh, I see, you're still expecting. For some reason, I thought you said you'd already had your baby."

Becky stopped so fast, her low heels squeaked, and she glared at Felix until he actually stepped back and adjusted his tie.

"Were you raised in a barn? Don't you know that you never, *ever* assume a woman is pregnant? Not even if she's nine months and in labor—Not ever, never, never!"

He winced. "I . . . er . . ."

"I just had the baby six weeks ago, and it was my fourth pregnancy and it takes time for a body to readjust, and I haven't had more than two hours of sleep in a row since December, and I'm normally a very nice person but I would like to hit you."

"Then you probably should. On the jaw."

"Are you serious?"

"Quite." He stuck out his jaw. "I'm ready. Bombs away."

She readied her fist.

"No, no," he said, "get your thumb out of your fist, and you need to pull back more. That's it. Get a good range and extend your arm all the way."

She pulled back, pictured hitting her target like Mike had taught her to do before driving a golf ball, then swung. She struck him dead in the jaw. He wheeled around, clutching his face.

"Ow! Oh!"

"Really?" she said, rubbing her knuckles. "Did I really hurt you? You're just faking it to make me feel good."

"No, not faking." He was still hunched over. "That was a proper punch."

She clapped her hands. "Wow! I've never hurt someone before, especially not someone who deserved it so much. Can we do it again?"

"I'm certain I'll do something else to deserve it before long. In the meantime, mind if we step outside and let the night air cool down the swelling?"

He offered his arm again and she took it. His left elbow was becoming familiar. Mike and Celeste were still dancing, Mike's back to her. Becky waved, indicating that they should join them outside, and Celeste nodded, holding up one finger.

No one else was out in the chilly February air. Felix gave her his tuxedo jacket. The sleeves reached her palms, and she thought of how Mike's coats engulfed her fingertips.

She reached to touch Felix's red cheek, then stopped herself. "Is it sore? Does it hurt to the touch?"

"It does, actually."

She giggled. "That was so great!"

"I'm so happy to have obliged."

"You did offer."

"I did. And I deserved it."

The cold hadn't touched Becky yet. She folded her arms and leaned against the stone balustrade, looking over the sporadic lights of Salt Lake City, up to the black outline of the mountains against a sparkly, starry sky. Beside her Felix was quiet too. She figured he was bored and was waiting for Mike and Celeste before restarting the conversation. That was fine. At the moment, she couldn't drum up enough energy to make herself be entertaining. She sensed his eyes on her, probably gazing at the Fred Meyer surgical-steel-post earring with genuine pink enamel flowers in her right ear. That little beauty should charm him more than anything she could say.

She felt deeply content to be out of the house and in a world full of air and a moon and Felix Callahan too, even if he was contemplating the abomination that was her cheap earring. The air between them was becoming warm, like the pockets of tepid water her toes found when swimming in a cool lake. And she felt—she actually felt a little tug on her chest. On her heart. As if her heart were tied to his by a string. No doubt a hallucination caused by new-mommy dementia, she thought.

It *was* strange, though, wasn't it? That she was standing in silence with Felix Callahan, and neither of them seemed the least bit uncomfortable? That he'd come at all, that he'd wanted to dance with her. If she were a different kind of woman, she'd suspect Felix was falling in love with her. Which of course was impossible. But she was in the right setting—attending a ball, dressed in a gown (or at least, something of that genus), leaning against a marble balustrade with a handsome, famous, wealthy man. It was a shame that such a moment was wasted on Becky Jack, married mother of four. She tried to imagine what it would be like if she were someone else, some single, childless beauty, staring up at a sly moon. It was a scrap of a moon really, a fingernail clipping, hardly worth contemplating. If this were a true romantic moment in a screenplay, Becky would beef the moon up, round it out, make it silver and startling in its beauty. She relaxed into a sigh and got carried away rewriting the moment.

Rachel [that's the name Becky assigns the single, childless beauty]
sighs under the lusciously full moon. She turns to Felix, and sees that

*he's not looking at her earring in disgust, but at her face . . . with
longing.*

RACHEL: It's good that we're together. I can't believe I just said
that. Why did I just say that?

*She wants to take it back, yet feels in her bones that it is one of
the truest statements that she's ever spoken.*

FELIX: Yes, I think so too.

Felix speaks with a little smolder in his voice.

RACHEL: Oh.
FELIX: I've changed since our first meeting. *You* have changed
me, Rachel. I can't stop thinking about you. The
thought of you fills my very senses.
RACHEL: But that's ridiculous. We're so different. I mean, I'm
just me, and you're . . . you're *you.* You can't possibly—

*He takes her hand and kisses the backs of her fingers, once.
Chills travel down her arm and through her whole body. She has
nothing left to say.*
*The moment slows. The moment feels like silver. The night isn't
cold, the lights of the city rise up and surround her like stars crowning
her head. She feels her knees go soft, her middle woozy. Man, she
really is tired. [Strike that—she's not tired at all. She's young and
vivacious and twenty-nine.]*
*He cups his hand around her jaw, running a thumb over her
cheek.*

FELIX: Rachel, I don't know what I'm feeling . . . but I . . . I
think you feel it too, don't you?

*She nods, afraid to move, afraid to think. She stares into those
eyes now, feeling like a heroine in a romantic movie. She labels
it—Romantic. It helps her brain process what is going on. Felix
Callahan touching her face, feeling something for her. Does she feel it
too? He starts to lean forward, inviting her body to do the same. She
should turn away, she should run away, this must be some kind of
joke on her. But instead she's staring back at him, unresisting. Did
she lean too?*

Kiss him, instinct urges. *Kiss him and see if it's like being
struck by lightning, if your world changes from mundane to movie,
if everything you thought was true is a lie and you fall wildly
in love.*

*And as he leans and she almost leans, the synapses in her brain
begin to fire like a lightning storm. A kiss. Now. Here. Is this her
moment? Has she been living in a movie without knowing it, her
story leading up to this? The rush of warmth through her limbs, the
frantic kick of her heart, the deliciously cold jolt in her belly—maybe
this is the best thing in the world. And forget pragmatics and
sanity—live for such a moment as this. Live.*

*She is definitely leaning now. Her body sighs—her joints
soften, her breath relaxes out of her lungs, her eyes even start to
close—and his lips are so near . . .*

"You're cold?"

"What?" Becky jerked around much faster than Felix's question
could possibly warrant. No more daydreaming. Sheesh, thank goodness
mind reading only existed in comic books, because if anyone had overheard her thoughts just then, she'd have to bury herself alive.

"I was wondering if you're cold. You shivered."

"No, I'm fine." Goose bumps lined her arms, thankfully hidden by
his jacket.

"Mind if I put my arm round you?" he asked.

"What?"

Felix smiled. "You love that word."

"What? I mean . . ." Definitely no more daydreaming. Just imagining that had made her feel all swoony and discombobulated. And had
he just asked to put an arm around her? She took a very tiny step away.

Where were Celeste and Mike? Standing beside Felix (post-
daydream) was becoming chancy. He was her number one, after all, and
here they were, alone. Well, alone besides her pink maternity dress, the
bulk of which should count as its own separate entity. But still.

She turned to face Felix, meaning to say something smart, churn
up the sudden solemnity, find something to laugh at again. But his look
made her forget what she'd been about to say—he was intense, no humor about him now. She'd never noticed his eyes before, not even on
the screen (she'd been too wrapped up in the whole package to analyze
the parts). But seeing them now made her feel as if she'd known them for
years. Wise eyes, sad eyes.

"It's good that we're together." She snapped her mouth closed. Had
she just spoken that line aloud? Shut up, Becky, shut up!

Felix breathed out. "It's a relief to hear you say that."

Her mouth was gaping, and completely without her permission.

"Because the thought of you has been driving me crazy," he said.

She barely stopped herself from saying, "What?"

"I need to ask you a favor." He turned to her fully. His eyes took her in. They were bedroom eyes, I-vant-to-suck-your-blood eyes. She shivered.

His voice was all soft and yummy, and the sound of it went inside her, down into her knees. "Becky, may I kiss you?"

Did he just say that? Not possible. She'd imagined it audibly. Maybe she was the one who'd been hit in the head.

But then his hands were on her shoulders. His look was full of purpose, his eyes saying that she was the only thing worth looking at in the whole world. She was so disconcerted she didn't extricate herself from his hands and back away, as she surely would have had she been normal, sane Becky. That was when his lips parted just a little, and he started to *lean*.

Becky made a face. "Whoa, wait, hold on a sec. What are you talking about?"

"A kiss," said Felix, raising one hand to the back of her neck. "One kiss."

"But . . ." She laughed in disbelief. "But why?"

There was something in his look now, his quiet features, the way he glanced at her and then down again as if too shy to stare straight-on—it was more Calvin the sexy pet shop owner than the Felix who didn't have a surplus of damns.

He's acting, she thought.

"I need to see if what I'm feeling means what I think it means," he said.

"You do not."

"I do actually."

"Balderdash. You just got thumped in the head. Wow, I didn't know I could hit so hard. I might've really done some damage."

His hands dropped from her. "Why won't you let me kiss you? This isn't something I envisaged we would argue about."

"You *envisaged* kissing me?"

"Well . . . yes, but I was eloquent and you were rational."

"And in your fabulous daydream, what happened next?"

"Actually it ended there, which is why I wanted to kiss you, to see what would happen next. But I'm rapidly reconsidering that desire."

"Well, thank goodness for that, since, according to your envisaging I'm so enthralled by your sexual powers I have no self-control."

"It's not as if I was happy about having to kiss you."

"What is this, some bet? Some bad-boy prank?"

"It is not a prank," Felix said, his voice strong, his eyes angry. He slammed his fist down on the very hard marble. "I thought I was falling in love with you!"

She stared at him, and he stared at his fist, and the staring went on long enough for Becky to realize that she was finally getting cold.

"That's crazy," she whispered.

He wagged his head in a kind of befuddled, helpless agreement. Should she pat his shoulder consolingly? Check his pupils? Scream for security? Then it started. She tried to hold it back, but the harder she tried to hold it back, the more insistent it was, until she choked on it. Then out it came—a hard, loud laugh.

"Sorry . . . I don't mean to . . . sorry." She cleared her throat. "I'd rather you didn't kiss me, if that's all right."

Felix leaned back and sighed, his smile cheery. "Do you know, I don't think I'd actually fancy kissing you after all. That's good to know."

"Isn't it? Man, when we got to the eye staring, I was sure I was living in Bizarro World."

He looked over her dress, his chest shaking with a chuckle. "That really is an unsightly rig."

"At last I get some honesty out of the man!"

"I was being honest before."

"What, when you wanted to kiss me?" she said with a teasing smile. "When you thought you were falling in love with me?"

He shrugged. And that motion stilled her to her core, made her stand fast and look at him now, read him as she would a child she suspected of lying. But she detected no telltale signs of dishonesty. He was serious. He'd really thought—

"You really thought—"

"I don't know what the hell is going on," he said, raising his arms in a helpless gesture. "If you were the least bit attractive—"

"Hey!"

"If I felt the smallest itch of desire for your body—"

"Take it easy now!"

"Then I could dismiss all this"—he gestured madly at his chest and head—"as mere sexual desire. That I can manage. I had a wild past before Celeste, and there are still the occasional cracks of temptation, but they are not difficult for me to overcome."

"Wow, you are a modern-day hero."

He ignored her. "I have never loved another woman as I love Celeste, and now you're confusing things. This wasn't simple desire, so naturally I assumed I was falling in love with you—"

"Naturally, because there could be no other explan—"

". . . and I wagered that a kiss of passion could help sort it all out. But now that seems unnecessary, and I'm still left in the muddle. I find no logic to my interest in you. First off, you're Mormon. What does it mean to be Mormon anyway?"

"That's a nickname for people who belong to my church. It's a Christian religion."

"So, you read the Bible, pray, have lots of kids, go to church on Sunday and all that."

"In a nutshell."

He shook his head. "Sounds god-awful."

"And you're a cynical atheist, can't stand children, and combine the words 'god' and 'awful.' Even if we weren't both married, we'd make a horrific couple."

"Well, what a relief to get that out of the way!"

"Absolutely."

There was a shiver of silence in which Becky wondered what would happen now. Would he walk away? And she'd never see him again? Well, at least she'd have a good story to tell Mike.

But Felix leaned against the balustrade, looked at the moon, and said, almost shyly, "But I'm feeling rather protective of you, as if I don't want to let you go."

She stared at the moon too, that pathetic little shred of it, her recent laugh still curling her lips. "I wish you wouldn't."

"What does this mean?"

"Have you considered that maybe—this is a wild idea but hear me out—maybe you might like me in say, oh, a *friendly* way? I absolutely without question refuse to be the least bit romantic with you. And yet"—she turned to face him—"and yet I feel kind of giddy, like I just made a new best friend at camp, and he's supercool."

"I am mortified to admit this, but I know what you mean. This has never happened to me before, and I find it all not a little unsettling and quite nearly shocking."

"Making new friends with cool people always makes me kind of twittery-excited. But you . . ." She laughed. "Gosh darn it, this is so bizarre. I can't believe I'm having this conversation with Felix Callahan. We're somewhere in La-La Land."

"This is precisely what I'm talking about—you say things like 'La-La Land' and 'gosh darn it.' I should be eager to scrape you off my shoe."

"I know, sweetie, I know. But maybe we're just *keen* on each other, as you limeys would say."

"'Ello love, 'oos your uncle and all that."

"Exactly. But we fell into the keenness pretty quickly. I mean, if we'd grown up together, come into a friendship slowly, it'd be one thing. In a way, it almost feels like falling—" No, she wasn't going to say it. "There should be a new term—*falling in friendship* or something like that. I wish there was a word for it! The English language is seriously flawed. It reminds me of Gonzo's song from *The Muppet Movie*. Do you know it? No? Seriously, you have no culture."

So she sang it for him, starting with the part that bemoans the lack of a term for old friends who are meeting for the first time. She paused, intending to stop, but the edge of the melody was hanging there in the cold like the decimated moon, aching to wax round. So she took a breath and kept singing through the verse. Her voice was small and raspy because she knew better than to sing out, and it ended up sounding less like a melodious bird and more like a tree branch scraping against a house.

Still, the words, the tune, seemed perfect for a night under the stars—full of wonder and mystery and yearning. And then the song went and tugged at her emotions unexpectedly, and had she known she'd start to tear up, she never would've squawked a note. So she opened her eyes wide to dry them and bit a lip until pain trumped sentimentality.

Felix sighed and she thought he might say something tender, share the heartfelt moment.

He said, "You really shouldn't sing in public."

Her laugh was so unexpected, she snorted.

"I mean it," he said, putting a comforting arm around her. "Never again."

"The day that you qualify as 'public' will be a very sad day."

"Also, you shouldn't snort."

Prompted by a surge of gratitude, she hugged him. She had sung Gonzo's song and cried, he had told her not to sing ever again (or snort), and that made her want to hug him till his bones creaked. What was happening? Everything from her sore right knuckles to her elephantine maternity dress made impossible sense.

"Felix." She let go, suddenly shy to speak. But that tense, tickly sensation running from her throat to her belly was giving her some kind of superhuman nerve. And besides, he wasn't really Felix Callahan anymore, not in that ethereal, big-screen sense. So. She cleared her throat. "Felix, will you be my friend?"

He did laugh at her, though he didn't seem to mean it. "Yes, we'll get matching lockets holding strands of each other's hair."

"I wish the English language gave us a better option. 'Pals,' 'chums,' 'buddies' . . . but a word that implies the sudden and unusual nature— like 'metabuddies.'"

"'Metabuddies.' Wow. This *is* getting serious."

"So?"

"So. Yes. Let's be friends. That would solve some of this confused muss. Do we spit in our palms and shake?"

"I think this calls for a pinky pledge." She hooked her pinky around his. "I, Becky Jack, agree to be Felix Callahan's pal, even though he's way overrated as an actor and screen hunk and can be such a brat."

Felix cleared his throat. "I, world-famous and fabulously wealthy Felix Paul Callahan, agree to be mates with Becky, even though she wears grandmother shoes and insists on popping out children with reckless abandon and shows no remorse for her vicious right hook."

"That was very nice. I almost shed a tear."

"Apparently all it takes to make you weep is a singing puppet."

"Hey, don't sell me short. I also cry at talking socks and animated washcloths."

"You cry in terror."

"Well, yeah, that's true."

He leaned back and exhaled. "Celeste will be so relieved. So am I."

"Yeah, where are Celeste and Mike?"

"Oh, they're not coming out. Celeste's mission was to retain him so I could speak with you alone."

"Seriously? Did she know you were . . ."

He nodded.

"No way," she said in the same tone Fiona used.

"Truly. My lady is game. We . . . you see, after our sordid pasts, when we married, we agreed that if we were ever tempted to cheat, we would have the decency to inform each other first. It was her idea to occupy your husband, giving me a crack to test my falling-in-love theory."

Becky slowly shook her head. "You are the oddest people I've ever met."

"Well, I had to give it a go, didn't I? The thought of you has been driving me insane."

"I think this boils down to a lack of imagination. You like me, but because I'm a woman, you assume it must be either a physical attraction or infatuation. But it's something else."

"And what about you? You thought you might be in love with me as well."

"I did not."

"You did. You said yourself you had been feeling confused and giddy."

"I didn't—in *no way* did I think I was in love with you, and the uncharacteristic giddiness was just because . . ." she finished in a whisper, "I thought I was in a movie."

"You thought you were in a movie?"

She raised her hands to the sky. "You're Calvin the sexy pet shop owner and I owed it to women everywhere to at least see it through, because that's how these stories go and . . . It was very confusing."

"And now?"

"And now I'm cured and sane again."

They smiled at each other, almost shyly, until she laughed.

"What?" he asked. "What is funny? Tell me."

"You. You thought you were in love with me. And I thought I was in a movie. And there's no way we're actually going to be 'mates.'"

"We might," he said indignantly.

"No possible way. In a few years you'll be outside under a moon scrap and it'll remind you, and you'll say, 'There was this odd woman I almost kissed once—haven't thought of her in years . . .'"

"I'm going to call you tomorrow."

She shrugged. "We'll see."

"Hey, I don't take pinky pledges lightly. Ask anyone."

"And if you don't call, it's okay, Felix. Tonight, I'm the luckiest gal in the world to have you as my friend."

"Yes, you are."

"Let's go find our spouses."

"Right, our spouses. Isn't that an odd word? 'Spouse'?"

"I've always thought so. Sounds like an animal. Or a disease."

"Or a diseased animal."

Felix offered his arm, she took it, and they turned their back on the gaunt moon.

She felt perfect, as if her belly was full of hot chocolate, all the kids were in bed, the house was clean, and there was nothing to do but put her feet up on Mike's lap and enjoy the night. She was going to get a new Augie—that wonderful friendship that had made her laugh through high school and college had been as lost to her as a childhood doll. She'd met Mike, Augie had gotten engaged, and the friendship had unceremoniously died. You cannot support a spouse and a best friend of the opposite gender. It just cannot be done! Or so she'd thought. But she was thirteen years older now, full of world wisdom and top-notch maturity, and her chest swelled with hope that it was possible after all. They could do it. And she'd taken a pinky pledge to that effect.

When they entered the ballroom, Becky became conscious of the grin on her face. A couple she knew from her Layton neighborhood two-stepped by, their looks full of gossipy indignation when their eyes flicked to Felix's jacket around her shoulders. It made Becky laugh. If they only knew!

"Are you always this giggly?" Felix asked. "I don't know if I can approve."

"I certainly hope I am. I mean, I certainly hope you're not making me more giggly than normal—that would be plain gross. But really, if you have the option to laugh, why ever hold it back?"

A warm burning sensation flashed in her breasts, and she pressed them with backs of her wrists to stop the milk before it flowed.

"Ugh, I'm letting down. We'll have to make this fast so I can go pump in the bathroom. I'm used to nursing every couple of hours."

The horror in Felix's eyes was so intense it seemed painful. "Pretend you didn't just say that."

"Say what? I didn't say anything."

He shook his head in disgust.

Back at their table, Celeste was talking, her hands flashing in the air, her eyes wide, as if she were recalling an impressive fireworks display. Mike was listening with polite though somewhat feigned interest, but when he saw Becky approaching, his eyes brightened.

"Hey, there you are. You okay?"

"Oh yeah, fine. It's just that Felix thought he was falling in love with me."

Felix slapped a hand over his face, which gave Becky a good snicker.

"He . . . what?" Mike looked around, trying to figure out if there was a joke he didn't get.

"It's okay, really," Becky said, rubbing his back.

Celeste stood slowly. In that slinky dress, she flowed like a waterfall falling up. "She rejected you, *ma puce*?"

"No, she did not reject me—I realized that I was mistaken."

Becky nodded happily. "We confirmed that there was no love falling anywhere around us and so we had the wacky idea that we could play at being friends." Becky turned to Celeste. "I gather Felix has never had a female friend? He liked being around me and he saw only two options: either it was a romantic or physical attraction."

"It's just as I thought. I was never worried, Rebecca. But I wanted him to see this through so he would know for himself."

The two women gave each other knowing glances.

"Now be clear," Felix said, and if he'd had feathers, they would have been ruffling. "I *didn't* find you physically attractive, and that was a bit of my confusion."

"Hey!" Mike's hands were fisting and unfisting, caught between outrage and relief.

"Sorry," Felix said. "Sorry, sorry. Unintended insult."

Mike glanced at Becky, as if to make sure she wasn't offended. She was smiling, so Mike shrugged. "That's okay. It's not like I think that way about your wife either."

Celeste looked at Mike in unabashed amazement.

"Sorry, I meant . . ." Mike rubbed his eyes and turned away. "I can't believe I'm having this conversation."

Becky looked from aghast Celeste to befuddled Felix to mystified Mike and clapped her hands with glee. After so many winter weeks housebound and half-crazy, this was turning out to be the best outing ever.

"You realized that you are not impassioned?" Celeste asked her husband.

"Not in the slightest."

Celeste muttered something in French and slinked over. Felix put his hands on his wife's hips and let his eyes admire her in a bedroom way. They kissed. Becky coughed. It was a bit much for public.

"He's in love with you?" Mike whispered.

"No, no, no. He was confused. He wanted to be friends, I think, and since I'm apparently a female alien, he had no idea how to interpret that data. So I set him straight. We agreed that there's no romantic feelings floating about, that we're both absolutely in love with our spouses— 'spouse' is really a weird word isn't it?—and decided to be friends. We took a pinky pledge."

"You took a pinky pledge."

"I know it's weird, hon, but he feels like someone who should be in our lives. In a different way from our family. It's all new. But it'll be good." She put her arms around his neck. "So, can I keep my new friend? Please? You luscious, luscious man?"

Mike eyed the couple as they whispered Frenchy things in each other's ears. "If that's what you want . . ."

"Thank you." She planted a kiss square on his mouth. "Okay, I really need to go pump now."

In which we listen in on phone calls,
track down Slurpees, and are privy to a flashback

"He's not going to call," Becky said.

"He is." Mike nodded fervently, keeping his eyes on the road as he drove the minivan home. "He took a pinky pledge."

"He thought he was in love with me. Now that he knows he's not, the reality of a Utah housewife as a friend will sink in."

"You sound pretty confident there. Willing to put your money where your mouth is?"

"The usual?"

"You're on."

Becky lost the bet quickly. Felix called the next morning from Park City before hitting the slopes.

"I told you I would phone."

"And thus you prove you are a man of your word. Now quit wasting your time and go skiing."

"Excellent suggestion. Good-bye."

"Bye."

Mike was reading to Hyrum while keeping one eye on a golf match when Becky leaned into the TV room to announce, "He called."

Mike peeked over the couch. "He did? Felix? What did he say?"

"'I told you I would call.' 'Yeah, you did. Shouldn't you be skiing?' 'Right, cheerio.' 'K-bye.'"

"Huh."

"It was obligatory. He won't call again."

"Double or nothing?"

"Of course."

Even though their friendship was surely doomed, she'd really liked Felix. That fact bothered her, and that night she listened to Mike snore and pondered her giddiness at each Felix encounter. By one in the morning, she'd determined her fond feelings weren't caused by the novelty of his celebrity or a warped infatuation. What a relief! The idea that she could be so easily affected by a movie star had nettled her, and she had covered her ears and shouted "LALALA!" (metaphorically) at the barest hint that she might be harboring some secret and untoward attraction.

No, she just liked him. Felix, the guy who talked with her as Augie had, the guy who'd been fascinated by Edgar Poe versus Nubbin, even the guy who told a complete stranger, "I don't keep a surplus of damns on hand." Who talked like that? Felix. And though she could not approve of such behavior, she was still a teeny bit amused.

He didn't call on Monday.

"Pay up," she said.

"He'll call," Mike said. "He took a pinky pledge."

Mike made a good point, but how long could even a sacred vow sealed by the tiniest and most loyal of digits forestall the inevitable?

They decided to give it a month. Tuesday morning the phone rang.

"Hello," said an increasingly familiar British voice.

"Oh, hello," Becky said, and thought both "darn" and "hooray!" at the same time. She hated to lose a bet.

"Yes, hello," said Felix.

Becky cleared her throat. "Did you go skiing?"

"Yes, you know, we did."

"Have a good time?"

"Mm hmm."

"Good. Sounds . . . fun."

"So, what do we do now, swap stories about our exes? Watch a reality show on the telly and narrate to each other in scandalized voices? 'Can you believe she said that? I can't believe she just said that.'"

"You don't have many friends, do you?"

"I have thousands of fans, dozens of itinerant co-workers, a handful of acolytes, three stalkers, and a wife."

"You have no idea how this friend business works, do you?" she asked.

"Ha!" Felix said.

"Ooh, that was a nice 'ha.' Full of derisive laughter and effectively evading any answer."

"Thank you. I've been practicing."

"Yeah. So, um, you have no idea how this works, do you?"

"I know there's talking involved, don't I? And phone calling. I'm not such an amateur as all that."

"Felix, are you really sure you want to be friends?"

"What do you mean, am I sure? I took a pinky pledge."

"Yeah, okay, you're right." It was true. He had, in fact, taken a pinky pledge. "It's just that . . . I bet Mike this would deflate and go nowhere, so—"

"How much did you wager?"

"No money. We bet Slurpees."

"What?"

"Slurpees? You know, those slushy icy concoctions, the perfect mix of cold and sweet that descends directly from heaven above? The winning Slurpee has to be grape flavored, which often requires driving to multiple 7-Elevens on the hunt, and we went double or nothing, so I'd have to get him two, which is really awkward to carry, because I'll have one for myself as well, and I'll be balancing three frozen beverages and a baby. So I was hoping, if you're going to renege on the pinky pledge sometime in the future, could we jump ahead now so I can win the bet?"

"Sorry, love."

That afternoon Becky had to go to eight 7-Elevens. Her afternoon was shot. But that grape slush was oh-so-scrumptious.

What with the Slurpee search, she hadn't had time to make dinner, so she fed the kids cold cereal and she and Mike dined on their shockingly purple slush, sitting in the basement while watching *The Little Mermaid* on VHS.

"What do you make of all this?" Becky whispered through three children—Fiona and Polly crammed between her and Mike, Hyrum on Mike's lap.

"I think that octopus is up to no good," Mike said, his eyes on the television. The corner of his mouth twitched. She knew he couldn't help it—he was always so pleased with himself when he made a joke. Then he shrugged. "I don't know, really. I don't know."

Becky nodded. "He doesn't have any other friends besides Celeste, not really. I think this will be good for him. I think he needs us."

"Yeah," was all Mike said. The crab was singing now. It was his favorite part.

Wednesday morning she called the Park City number.

"Hi, it's Becky."

"Hi," Felix said, with a hint of an exclamation point.

The degree of his enthusiasm made her feel all warm and squashy.

"You know, this friends thing means we get to hang out together if we're in the same state."

"Right. Right! I didn't think about that. You mean, as in, a date?"

"Noooo. As in hanging out, as in friendly lunches or dinner. Why don't you and Celeste come over tonight?"

"We're flying home this afternoon."

Becky had not realized how light and happy her heart had been until she felt it plummet into her midsection. He was leaving. Of course he was leaving. He didn't live there. Wow, this really was intense, this new friendship or whatevership. That sticky, achy missing feeling was already burrowing into her chest.

"Oh," she said, and she must have sounded pathetic, because Felix said, "You're not going to cry now, are you?"

"Just hide the puppets. When do you go?"

"We leave for the airport in two hours."

"What, are you taking a limo?"

"A hired car of some sort."

"No, no, no. You don't take a limo in Utah, and you *never* pay someone to drive you to the airport, not whenever there are friends or family around. I'll take you, of course."

And that's how Becky found herself packing up four-year-old Hyrum and baby Sam into their car seats and driving an hour to Park City. Long car rides with two small children should only be undertaken with trembling caution; yet off she went when Felix and Celeste could have afforded a fleet of stretch Hummers. Becky merged onto I-80 West, threading the snowy canyon, reaching back to reinsert Sam's pacifier for the thirty-second time, and answering Hyrum's whining with, "Just a few more minutes. Let's sing 'Wheels on the Bus' again!"

She pulled up to the four-star lodge where Felix, Celeste, and their mountain of luggage were waiting, and her heart bounced back up.

She hopped out and ran to Celeste, trying out the cheek-kissing thing and succeeding moderately well. At least Celeste said, "Well done, *ma belle*." Becky turned to Felix and wasn't sure what to do. She usually hugged friends, but he was a *guy*. This was going to take time to figure out. So she just sort of waved and said, "Hi."

Felix looked over her ten-year-old lemon yellow parka and unlaced snow boots. "What are you wearing?"

Becky rolled her eyes, and Celeste said something French and scoldy.

Becky helped toss the luggage in the back and offered the front seat to Celeste.

"No, no. I want to see the baby."

Becky relocated Hyrum's car seat to the back bench so Celeste could sit next to Sam and coo and stroke his palms.

"All I need is to smell a baby from time to time, and I am satisfied."

Becky was pretty sure she heard maternal longing in Celeste's voice, but Felix didn't so much as glance at Sam.

Felix rode shotgun, and while Celeste cooed and stroked, Becky and Felix laughed.

Later when Becky was trying to recount the conversation for Mike, she couldn't remember what had been so funny.

"I think he said something about traffic lights, and he just sounded so British, then I said something about the British but I got it wrong. And we just kept laughing the whole way. You remember Augie Beuter, right? That's how it was with Augie too. I ended up parking at the airport and taking the boys in the stroller, going through security and everything with them, so Felix and I could keep talking. We sat by the gate, and I nursed Sam—under a blanket, but it still freaked Felix out, which was also funny, and . . . this is a really lame story, isn't it?"

Mike scratched his chin. "You've told better."

"Well, anyway, I've paid up in Slurpees and I agree that he was serious about the pinky pledge."

They were in the kitchen, the kids asleep upstairs. Mike sat at the counter going over some papers while Becky rolled dough. It was a weekly tradition for Becky to make three pies—one for the family and the others for giving away to persons yet unknown. By the next night two names would invariably pop into her head, neighbors or family members or even relative strangers who, for whatever reason, might especially need the sweet comfort that came with a home-baked pie.

"It was good to see Felix again, after the ball and all," she said. "He really is Felix to me now, not Felix Callahan, not the actor or any of his characters. I'm relieved. At the ball, I was still disoriented and caught myself daydreaming about a romantic moment with him and . . . not me, but someone sort of like me."

She peeked up from the dough. Mike was looking at her as if she'd just confessed to murdering her parents and storing their bodies in the Deepfreeze.

"I know, that sounds really bad," Becky said, laying dough in the tin and pressing ridges with her thumb. "I don't know why I do that—I don't mean it. But I couldn't daydream about him like that now, even if I wanted to. It's one thing to have cheesy thoughts about a far-off movie star, but now . . . well, I just don't think about him like that. Still, for the sake of full disclosure, getting his calls does make me a little giddy, like I'm twelve and I have a crush on him."

Becky had always gotten a little crushy with new friends of any gender. She'd meet a like mind and her heart would skip about and she'd want to brag to the whole world about this marvelous person. It was a common-enough occurrence to be unremarkable, though from his expression, it seemed Mike could not empathize. Everything about Mike's face opened wide—eyes, lips, jaw. His nostrils may have even flared.

"Honey, I don't mean . . . you need to take that the right way."

"What right way is there to take that?"

"Not lovey crush, like, friendship crush, like . . . ugh, there's no word for it! Maybe it's a woman thing. I don't think it's unusual for women to feel affectionate about lots of people—not in a romantic way, just in an I-love-this-person way, I'm-excited-to-have-this-wonderful-person-in-my-life way."

Mike's horrified expression was frozen on his face.

"No, no, it's not like that. I just wanted to tell you, since Felix is a guy and it might seem like a different thing and I wanted to be honest about everything. Never mind, never mind, pretend I never used the word 'crush' and go about your business."

"Becky . . ." His tone was concerned.

"Honey." She reached across the counter and took his hand. "Is this too hard for you? For me to have a friend who is a man?"

"When you start saying you have a crush—"

"Wrong word. There's probably a word for it in French or Sanskrit or something. I am so violently in love with you. He's just another Melissa. That's all."

"But he's . . . an actor, one of those, whatdoyoucall'em, heart-throbs."

"Not to me."

"But . . ." Mike scowled. "I've always thought it was weird, the way you and your friends sometimes talk about seeing a movie with this actor or that, as if you're in high school and the actors are guys who might ask you to prom."

Becky's smile was aghast. "Really? Are we that bad?"

"You know what I mean."

"You know we're not fantasizing about them in a vulgar way."

"Yeah, I figured. But I still think it's weird."

She shrugged. "Maybe it is. I don't know—it seems so normal. But Felix's friendship isn't about that. He's not a character from his movies. He's just some guy, a friend. An Augie."

"Yeah?"

"Yeah. Absolutely."

"Okay," he said. She was pouring the filling, and he watched like a dog under the dinner table. "Can I lick the bowl?"

"And the spoon, baby."

Becky watched him scoop up sweet appley goop. He wasn't settled, but he wasn't upset. She would have to take care. But maybe this was a good thing. They had gotten into such a routine the past few years; there had been no bumps in their marriage, no doubts, no serious conflicts. She didn't want to get lazy. A little imaginary threat would give her a chance to fight for her man, prove her devotion.

And she would fight. She had chosen Mike thirteen years ago and never regretted a day.

She and Mike had both been part of a large group of friends at Weber State University in the 1980s. They held monthlong foosball tournaments, played music in backyards and held impromptu dances, went on day hikes and picnicked on mountaintops.

In the group, there were funny guys whose casual anecdotes were like stand-up routines. There were smart guys who could explain string theory and built backyard rockets. There were ambitious guys who would one day start their own successful businesses, taking their wives on vacations to islands strung with hammocks and glistening with virgin piña coladas.

Maybe that was why Becky didn't notice Mike at first—he wasn't making the whole room laugh or wowing them with brilliant insights and obscure knowledge. But then again, all the other guys seemed to be trying so hard, flexing their muscles and wit anytime a girl was in the room. Mike just *was*—vulnerable and strong and goofy and nice.

Ultimately it had taken an "ah-ha!" moment. They'd been at a potluck in someone's backyard, a pool party where no one had brought a swimsuit, the chlorinated body of water more of a large, awkward centerpiece. Mike and Becky were at the food table, standing side by side, reaching for the same spoon in the potato salad, and their hands touched.

"Sorry, I got greedy there." He handed her the spoon and stepped back. It was the first time he'd ever spoken to her.

What a nice voice he has, she thought, noticing how deep and rumbly, how she felt the sound in her ears and in her belly. While scooping the potato salad, she dredged up what she knew of this guy: spying Mike on campus with his freakishly smart sister Virginia, talking and laughing not like siblings but close friends; a movie night crammed into someone's basement, when the host played a few moments of a pornographic movie and laughed at everyone's surprise, and Mike quietly got up and left the room; Mike arriving late for a pizza-making party but still taking the time to crouch down and chat with the host's five-year-old brother.

Mike. Michael Jack. She looked at him then, noticed him, the pleasing oval of his face, his straight blond hair falling down his forehead, how much larger he was than her, large enough that she'd feel tiny inside his arms. She liked how she felt standing next to him, and with a thrill that shocked her scalp and ran like lightning down her spine, she thought, I could be happy beside him for the rest of my life.

"Hey, Mike," she said, meaning, Wow, I just noticed you and this could be happily-ever-after, pal.

"Hey, Becky," he said with a smile, and she realized how often he was near her, quiet but leaning forward, listening, relishing.

"Want to go eat with me over there?" She nodded toward a cluster of trees hiding a bench, apart from the noise.

So they sat alone and ate and talked. Let's be honest—it was a Potential Husband interview. Even at age twenty-one, Becky was auditioning guys for the post.

Soon they left the bench to ramble the yard, then went out into the neighborhood, wandering streets until they came upon an empty park. The air temperature was the same as Becky's skin, making her feel embraced, just another part of the summer night.

Hope and expectation were bubbling inside her, and she felt thrills bigger than roller coaster drops. She wanted to kiss him. That was all she needed. Her friend Melissa was in love with any guy she was kissing at the moment, then complaining to Becky the next day that she'd been confused. But with that most perfect of touches, Becky's mind and body just knew, and her heart followed.

She'd kissed five guys. Post-kiss, three of them disappeared from her life without a backward glance. Two had electric kisses, stay-and-hold-me kisses, and those boys she'd dated for a good amount of time before one or the other decided to end things. The kisses hadn't lied, she reasoned—they'd both very nearly secured the post of Mr. Becky.

With Mike that night, it started with a held hand. He took hers as they climbed onto the jungle gym, and then he just kept holding on. Perfect, perfect sensation. A held hand was a hug to her whole body. The conversation drifted away, and she stepped in closer. She rested her head on his shoulder and breathed in. His smell was more delicious than hot chocolate. Genetic Compatibility had spoken. They had the potential of having beautiful babies.

His brown eyes were warm with the sight of her. He seemed so big and yummy, manly and wonderful. But when his lips first met hers, they were tentative, intruder lips, uncertain lips. She kissed him back, inviting him to fall in love with her. And as he fell deeper and deeper into the kiss, Becky's heart exploded. Her arms wrapped around his neck and pulled him as close as she could. The kiss left no doubt. She would never be without Mike again.

Smell and kiss aside, three things sealed the deal for Becky:

1. Two weeks later, Mike called to tell her about a new job he'd been offered. She said, "Sounds great. Did you take it?" He said, "I told them I wanted to check with you first." So it was with Mike—he began to think of her as his partner from the top of that jungle gym and never stopped.

2. Everywhere they went, Mike opened doors for her. Melissa had scoffed at this detail, but truth be known, it made Becky melt.

3. Mike and Becky could curl up on a couch and talk for hours. It never got old.

She'd thought she was in love before, but now those faded relationships seemed quaint and childish. Being in love with Mike lifted her off the ground, swathed her in fuzzy blankets, kept her warm and cozy everywhere she went. Awake or asleep, her heart thrilled, her lips smiled.

The whole world was gilded, water was nectar, cloth was silk on her skin, every child was an angel and every stranger her best friend. Yay! Yay for love and the perfect man and the absolute complete gorgeousness of everything, everything!

Beyond the rich emotions pouring through her, she felt herself change at the core. Mike merged into her every thought and action and hope and plan, her existence transforming from Becky-ness to Becky-with-Mike-ness. Five months after their first kiss, they were married. And the explosion of Mike in her life only expanded with each baby. They were a *family*. That word alone felt stronger in Becky's mind than "army" or "fortress" or "Justice League."

That's why it never crossed Becky's mind that Felix's friendship could threaten her marriage. That little kick she got after talking with Felix was a star prick compared with Mike's sunlight.

So when Felix returned to Los Angeles, she didn't hesitate to call the number he'd given her just to check on his trip. He called a few days later when he was bored during a break in some production meeting. Soon she was phoning him whenever she thought of something that would amuse him, and they'd have brief, bright conversations. She didn't need to talk long—five minutes, and she'd get that jolt, that goofy happiness that made the day a little better. It took a few weeks before "Hi Felix, it's Becky" turned into "Hey, it's me," and eventually . . .

"Hello?"

"Did you see it?"

"Yes." Felix groaned. "I was hoping you hadn't."

"Did you really tell *Vanity Fair* that you're more Cary Grant than Sean Connery?"

Another groan.

"And say, and I quote, 'I think women love me because of my world-weariness, my droll outtake on this absurd life. They feel that emptiness in themselves and recognize it in me. Mutual understanding is sexy.'"

"For the love of—please, not another word!"

"I'm going to put that on a T-shirt—Mutual Understanding Is Sexy."

"Interviewers coerce you into these statements," he said, his voice a little desperate. "They ask you leading questions and push you into saying something idiotic, and then print your stuttered reply as if it represented your core philosophy."

"Yeah, I understand what you're saying." She paused. "Wait . . . I *understand*. That means I'm sexy!"

"Stop! I'm begging you!"

"Do you know what's funny? I mean, besides that interview. I thought everything you said was adorable."

"Adorable. That's just what I was going for."

"No, really. Every word you said. Even when you were being arrogant and narrow, I just wanted to pinch those three-days-unshaven cheeks. I must be completely smitten with you—I mean . . ." That had sounded wrong. "Platonically. Smitten platonically."

His voice was low and sweet when he answered, "I know what you meant."

She exhaled. "Good."

Felix knew. And Mike understood too, or so she thought. This would work. Becky was going to keep her new Augie.

In which Becky employs a positive reinforcement lollipop

Becky was friends with Felix Callahan, and she hadn't told anyone but Mike. Nine-year-old Fiona, the eldest Jack child, had never seen a movie with Felix Callahan and if shown his photo would only think, "Yep, that's an old guy." Polly was . . . Polly, and happily enshrined in her day-dream world of pink-drenched princesses and sparkly faced sprites. Hyrum was at the age when the coolest kid on the block was the one who could walk up the slide *in his socks*, and Sam had yet to discover his own feet. So, she didn't bother telling the kids.

She thought of phoning her parents, sister, brothers, sisters-in-law, neighbors, the local news—not to brag to them, mind you, but it was *such* a story and she was bursting to spill the beans. In the end, the first to hear was the last person Becky wanted to tell: her oldest friend, Melissa.

Melissa was in the movie business, a freelance second assistant di-rector in Salt Lake City. Being in the off-off Hollywood movie biz, she not only knew who Felix was; she would care *very* much about Becky's news. Melissa had already heard about Felix Callahan showing up to the screenwriting presentation—her face had turned almost as purple as her hair. If Becky didn't come clean about the whole story, the day Me-lissa found out from another source would mark the end of their friend-ship. It almost did anyhow.

"What the hell do you mean Felix Callahan is your friend?" Me-lissa demanded over the phone.

Becky couldn't help smiling—not at Melissa's question, but at the way it sounded. That sweet baby voice, that squeak of anger in the upper registers. Endearing.

"He is, sort of. Well, not really, he's—"

"Oh, you really had me for a second! You goofball."

"What I mean is, Felix and I . . . you know how sometimes you meet someone and *bam!* Just like that there's some connection and it feels as if you've been friends for years? Is there a word for that? Like 'metabuddy,' but something real?"

A pause. "Becky, are you studying conversational Yiddish? Because I have no idea what you're talking about."

"Felix Callahan and me. We're sort of friends now."

"Elucidate the 'sort of' part."

"We took a pinky pledge."

"You took a pinky pledge."

"Yeah, it was funny but kind of sweet too."

"What are you saying? Do you guys, like, hang out or something?"

"Well, he's in England right now, but we talk."

"You talk."

"Yeah, every so often. About once a week."

"Who calls whom?"

"We take turns. He called last night."

"Are you serious?"

"Yeah."

"But . . . but you're the last person . . . I mean, I can imagine Shauna or Ava going off to California and coming back with some famous best friend, but you? I know you liked him in that movie, but you're just not the type." She took a breath. "Are you still serious?"

"Still serious."

There were rustling and stomping sounds, then Melissa's voice strained as though it hurt her throat to talk. "Do you know that at this very moment I have a picture of Felix Callahan taped to my headboard? Between Johnny Depp and Bono?"

"I know."

"I think I hate you."

"He's married and so am I, obviously. Mike's met him. There's nothing remotely romantic about this. We just clicked, somehow."

"Okay, I know I hate you."

At that point, Melissa availed herself of more colorful diction—especially of the color blue. Per usual, Becky tried to shush her back to the straight and narrow but without much fervor. She couldn't help herself—she found Melissa's squeaky voice speaking those words just as cute (and wrong, but still cute) as a waterskiing squirrel.

The same sort of conversation went on for a month, straining the friendship to the point of ripping.

"It hurts her," Becky told Mike.

Mike didn't have much patience with the sob story. "If I'm putting up with it, then so should she. What right does she have to get mad at you for making other friends?"

Becky glowed when he got riled up on her behalf. The big sweetie. But it was easier for her to feel tolerant of Melissa's occasional tantrums, knowing her history. They had met at a community theater where Becky's parents dragged the whole family several months out of the year. Alice and Casper Hyde swore it was so the family could spend quality time together making art, but Becky had often suspected her parents just wanted to perform in plays without having to pay babysitters. Becky often won speaking parts because she was fearless and had personality, though she didn't get any particular high from it.

On the other hand, Melissa's home felt like a half-dug grave. She dove headfirst into theater with a duffle bag full of needs. Her unusual voice relegated her to bit parts, but she dreamed of a playbill with her name at the top and a script so thickly highlighted with her own lines it glowed. It wasn't fair that Becky didn't care and yet still got her photograph in the program.

Unfulfilled and too often rejected, Melissa abandoned live theater for film production. Now, here was Becky making friends with a film star—that should be Melissa's territory. Again, it wasn't fair. Becky agreed, but she wasn't going to give up her famous friend to placate Melissa's jealousy.

Still the tension got exhausting, so Becky tried to work out the resentment from another angle, engaging Melissa in the "why" discussions.

"I don't understand why he wants to be my friend."

"Pheromones," said Melissa.

"No. No! No way. No chance Felix is attracted to me. Not all men are shallow about physical appearance, but I would bet my dishwasher Felix is. He doesn't even think of me as a woman—more as some kind of large, humanoid insect."

"What do you guys talk about anyway?" Melissa was sitting on Becky's counter, sorting through a bowl of popcorn for the half-popped kernels.

"Nothing." Becky smeared peanut butter on toast for Hyrum. "That's the thing. It's not like we're unloading deep secrets and purging our souls onto each other. We just . . . laugh, I guess."

"So there you go—you make him laugh."

"But he could hang out with the likes of Chris Farley and Lily Tomlin if he wanted."

"Maybe there's some novelty about a guy like him having a random Utah housewife for a friend."

"Sure, he's the reverse of me in L.A. In Utah he's the anthropologist, taking notes home to Celeste Bodine to make her laugh. 'Four children she has,' he'll say, 'and no help! She actually cleans her own house and makes her own dinner!'"

"'And she dresses like a circus tent,'" Melissa said in strained, lower tones, as if imitating Felix's tenor.

It was true. Becky was in a red and white striped shirt, a choice made even more regrettable by the fact that it was three sizes too large, as her body was still pulled and stretched in so many directions as to make her pre-pregnancy wardrobe look like doll clothes.

"Send in the clowns." Becky smoothed her hair around her face. "But at least I have a rockin' hairdo, thanks to my best friend."

Melissa leaned forward and gave Becky an uncharacteristic hug. A heavily hair-sprayed lock of Melissa's purple-streaked hair stabbed Becky in the eye, but other than the pain, it was a tender moment.

"Melissa's okay with it now, I think," Becky told Felix on the phone a few days later. "But if Celeste doesn't work out, she says she'd like to buy you a plate of cheese fries and discuss your future together. Or just skip to the making out."

"Excellent."

"Yeah, I think it'd be best to avoid Melissa next time you're in town."

"Oh, will I be in town?"

"Friends should visit each other. Haven't you seen *Beaches*?"

"It's my all-time favorite film."

"Really?"

There was such absolute silence Becky imagined Felix didn't breathe, blink, or swallow.

"That's what I thought," Becky said. "Anyway, if we don't get to see each other, it won't make sense for me to take care of you someday when you die slowly of a terrible illness. Besides, it's logical for you to come here. Salt Lake is between London and L.A., and my family of six won't be making a trip to England anytime soon. Even if we had the cash, imagine entertaining an infant and a four-year-old on a transatlantic flight."

"I lack the imagination, Zeus be praised." He paused. "I'd pay for your airfares, you know."

"Please. That is never going to happen, Mr. I'm-So-Wealthy. Don't run up your platinum card on me—go save some endangered species."

"It wouldn't be a—"

"Never."

"It's not as though—"

"Not gonna happen."

"It would be—"

"In your dreams."

After one phone call that broached the subject of religion, Becky sent Felix a copy of *The Book of Mormon: Another Testament of Jesus Christ*. Before it had even reached him, Becky received a package from Felix—*The Invention of Religion: How the Powerful Few Made Fools Out of the Ignorant Many*.

She tried to read it for Felix's sake, and to prove mightily to him and everyone else that she *was* open-minded, thank you very much! So what that she belonged to the same church as her parents had before her—it wasn't blind following or laziness; she'd made a choice! Every night she tackled a chapter, even going so far as to make notes in the margins. But she found the book so boring and irrelevant to her life that she soon relegated it to some lower shelf. She gathered that her gift to him had embraced a similar fate. They didn't bother about spiritually enlightening the other again, except for the occasional jabs.

"Hello, this is your liver speaking," Becky said when he answered the phone. "Lay off the booze, bozo, or I'm shutting down and cutting you off from all that sweet, sweet bile."

"I'll climb aboard the hideously dull temperance wagon when you confess that god is a scam and we're merely the offspring of evolved apes."

"You are hysterical! Anyone ever tell you that you could be in show business? I mean it, baby. You've got potential."

When weeks sloughed off since the last phone call, Becky thought about Felix in a distant, dreamlike way. Were they really friends? It couldn't be. She changed Sam's poopy diaper and thought, what on earth does such a man have to do with my mothering, housekeeping day-after-day life? She glimpsed his face on a magazine cover and thought, what on earth do I have to do with his glitzy fast-lane highbrow life?

So she determined not to bother him anymore, and really believed, in the exquisite way she had of innocently playing the martyr, that he would never call again.

Then a few days later . . . "Hallo, you loon. What passes as news?"

His voice was cozy against her ear, his conversation like play, and she ran loose with it, happy as a toddler in a room full of balls.

"Yo ho ho!" she said, holding the phone on her ear while unloading groceries.

"Repeat that?"

"It's National Talk like a Pirate Day. Didn't you know?"

"Somehow I missed the memo."

"You mean, 'Somehow I missed the memo, arrr!'"

"Precisely. Arr. So, Mrs. Jack . . . er, is that still your name? Or, I tremble to ask, have you adopted a pirate identity?"

"Arr, matey, of course I have! It's . . ." She pulled an eggplant from the grocery bag. ". . . Captain Eggplantier." She needed to stop speaking the first words that popped into her mind.

"Captain Eggplantier." He sounded very doubtful.

"That's right. A family name. It's Belgian."

"You don't say. I didn't realize there was a *Belgian* language."

"Most definitely."

"And what is this language called?"

"Waffle."

"Ah-ha."

"And this brings me to today's burning question, Mr. Callahan. Why on earth are you calling me? Why haven't you run for your life?"

"No one crosses Captain Eggplantier and lives! Arrr!"

"Ooh, that was good!" She was sincerely impressed. It had been a superb pirate accent.

Felix sighed as if getting serious. "Lord knows I have tried to run, Mrs. . . . . er, *Captain* Jack. I've gone to every doctor in England, but you have no antidote."

"Don't say 'Lord' unless you mean it."

"Oh, but I do mean it. Good Lord, but I mean it."

"Please flick yourself in the forehead for me."

"Ouch."

"Good boy. Now each time you take the Lord's name in vain, flick yourself again."

"Why would calling on the Lord's name ever be in vain if he were really there to listen?"

"Also you should flick yourself each time you're obnoxious."

"Now you've gone too far. I'd be too bruised to show my face on camera."

"You're right. Besides, all the books say we should focus on positive reinforcement. Call me each time you had the opportunity to be obnoxious but stopped yourself, and I'll put a sticker on your sticker chart. When you fill it up, you get a lollipop!"

"Mmm, lollipop. You've got my number, darling, indeed you do."

It took Felix a year to fill up the chart. Becky sent him a package—a single Dum Dum wrapped in a yard of cellophane with a note that said, "We're so proud of you!" signed by all six of the Jacks (Becky signing on behalf of eighteen-month-old Sam—she had his permission).

Mike sighed as he signed. "I don't even want to know what it means. I have a feeling I couldn't comprehend it."

It had been a year and a half since the Valentine's Ball. Felix was busy—in France with Celeste, at home in London, working in Los Angeles, shooting on location in New York or Australia or Toronto. Becky suggested driving the family out to California, but twelve hours with a one-year-old (and five-, eight-, and eleven-year-olds) intimidated Becky so much she consumed half a bag of Oreos just at the thought.

"If we're going to take a trip," Mike said, "why don't we go visit my brother in Vernal? We haven't gone to Dinosaurland since Fiona was five, and that's a heck of a lot closer and less expensive than L.A."

"But Felix isn't in Vernal."

"The kids don't care about seeing Felix."

He had a point. So Becky let the idea slide away.

Now let's not give the impression that Becky's life revolved around Felix's calls and visits. They were brilliant little distractions; they were the occasional breezy lifts to Becky's wings (pretend nonchalance as she might, Becky loved *Beaches*). If we were going to examine Becky's life in earnest, we'd tell the story of how Hyrum broke his arm, and the mini-crisis that created in Becky's marriage when in a moment of frustration Mike blamed her for negligence. We'd tell about that weekend trip Becky and Mike took to St. George, how their car broke down and the motorist who stopped to "help" stole Becky's suitcase. What about Polly's first piano recital, when she was so terrified, she refused to play unless she was sitting on her dad's lap? And Hyrum's angry refusal to try to read? The disastrous bake sale when Becky had been distracted by Sam's rash of diarrhea and forgot to add sugar to the apple pie. Fiona's birthday party, when Becky nearly threw her bratty little "friend" Cassie out on her rear end. Sam's first step, first animal noise, word, sentence, leap, joke . . . everything!

Time ticks on and too much happens to tell it all. So let's focus.

"I miss you," Becky said.

Felix paused. "You really do?"

"I know it makes no sense."

"That's it. How can I put a mother of four through so much torture? By the way, you're not pregnant again, are you?"

"Nope. We're going to hold steady at four."

"Thank the fertility goddess. I feared you might be preparing to form your own colony off in the Rocky Mountains."

"Well, of course we still plan to do *that*. Won't you reconsider and join us? I make a lovely fruit punch."

Felix would have the chance to sample some punch (or a green and chunky substance claiming to be such) very soon.

In which Becky doesn't lock her front door and someone walks in

Becky was in the front room lying on her back and flying Sam above her, aiming to get some sort of arms workout while still playing with the toddler. It was Hyrum's second week in afternoon kindergarten. Mike was at work. Fiona in fourth grade. Polly in second. Leaving Becky and Sam home. Alone.

The first week of school had been awesome. In the mornings, she and the two boys ran errands and took trips to the park. In the afternoons, Sam napped as soon as Hyrum left for school, giving Becky time to clean corners of the house previously untouched by human hands and sort drawers cleverly masquerading as temporary holding bins, but actually harboring expired coupons and receipts dated 1989.

When Sam woke from his nap, they read and drew and chased, and she showered on the kind of attention she hadn't been able to give a child since Fiona was an only. It was great. It really was.

It was just that when she spoke to Sam, the house had a weird echo to it, her voice bouncing off the empty walls. And Sam didn't have much to say in response. The sunlight seemed to shuffle in unwillingly through the windows, and the floors groaned more than usual, the house apparently aware of its unforgiving bulk.

Sam giggled as she lowered him to her face and pushed him back up again. Her pectorals burned.

"You're my cute guy, yes you are!"

"Haaaa! Mama-mama. Bababa zooo zoo!"

She glanced at the door to the basement, where the television awaited, offering its own kind of comfort. No, she would not resort to daytime television and that greasy, stomach-sick hangover. But the truth was, Becky thrived on some well-managed chaos. Noise was good. And hullabaloo even better. Heck, cacophony wasn't out of line. Give her pandemonium and she'd wrestle it into four bathed and pajama'ed children, a clear kitchen counter, and three casseroles—one for dinner, one for freezing, and one for a sick neighbor. She was not the type to invent drama for drama's sake. Happiness was good, and she'd take it in hearty slices, thank you. But blissful quiet calm also meant . . . nothing for her to do.

"Yes, you're a cutie. Yes, you're clever!"

"Mmmfff," said Sam. He could only take so much adoring, and puttered away, enchanted by an empty cracker box. Becky stayed prostrate, watching him flick the tabs, breathe into the box, then growl at it menacingly. She was so proud.

Becky sighed at the ceiling. She had precisely twenty-seven items on her to-do list, but the silent house was enervating. Maybe if she called someone, she'd perk up and get productive. She'd already bothered Mike at work that morning, keeping him on the phone for twenty minutes to talk over her grocery list. Melissa was on location in southern Utah. Her neighbor-friend Jessie had started working half days while her own kids were in school. Fridays were her sister Diana's errand day. Maybe she'd phone her mom; or Laurie, her favorite sister-in-law; or her cousin Tina . . . There was a knock at the front door.

Ooh, she thought, company! And called, "Come in!"

She wasn't expecting a repairman, she rarely got packages, and her family and neighbors all knew she kept the door unlocked and would walk in without the knock. So, who? The suspense was positively exciting! It never occurred to Becky that it might be some unsavory character who meant harm. That sort of thing didn't occur in her cleaned and folded life. Besides, if robbery was afoot, then good luck—the most expensive item in the house was her standing mixer.

The door squeaked as it opened. Becky craned her head to see around the corner. Felix peeked back.

"No way," she said in a slightly garbled voice, forgetting until that moment that she was sucking on a pacifier.

An explanation: From infancy Sam was a very giving sort of fellow, and having two pacifiers, liked to share. Whenever he had one in his mouth, he was determined his mother should have the same luxury, and was continually trying to shove the spare "paci" between her lips. She'd long ago given up resisting, habitually holding the paci with her teeth while she spoke or unconsciously sucking away. So it was that as Felix peered around the door, he happened to catch her lying on the floor and nursing a bright blue teddy bear pacifier.

She blew it out of her mouth, sending it arcing into the air, and careful not glance at it plop on the carpet, she said again (this time the words less muffled), "No way."

He shut the door and in seconds was on his back beside her, staring at the ceiling. He looked boyish and seventeen, and yet still debonair. His mere scent (no cologne today, but even his laundry soap smelled swanky) wafted ideas of faraway places and lavish things, a home full of shelves with precious objects that gleamed in the chandelier light.

"Hi," he said.

"Hey there."

"Were you . . . I could have sworn . . . did you spit a dummy out of your mouth?"

"How could I? You were all the way over there by the door."

He blinked at her. "I'm not following."

She blinked back. "Neither am I. Dummy?"

"Oh," he said slowly, "you were making a joke, implying that I am a dummy. Yes, exquisitely clever."

"And you were being British, and since I don't speak British, I can pretend I don't know what you're talking about and never admit to what you think you saw." She squinted as she examined his face. "You look pale. Have you been checked for anemia?"

Sam crawled over his mother to land smack on Felix's stomach.

"Oof. He's bigger than I expected."

"Hundred and tenth percentile," she said proudly. "So, you were in the neighborhood?"

"I just don't get to Utah enough."

"Don't beat yourself up. I mean, who does?"

"Sometimes you need the mountain air and a few million Mormons to perk up your spirits."

"As I've always said."

"Precisely." He turned his face to her. She adjusted onto her side to see him better. His voice became a little uncertain. "Can I stay a few days?"

She smiled. "Please do."

"You cut a fringe," he said, indicating her bangs. "You shouldn't have a fringe, not with your face. You really need to consult me before doing anything semipermanent to yourself—hairstyles, plastic surgery, tattoos, shoes . . ."

"What percent gay are you, do you think?"

He considered. "I max out at fifteen."

"I'm going to go with thirty."

"You've never seen me bench-press Marlon Brando."

She patted his hand. "You are a shining specimen of raw masculinity. But while you're here, I'm going to set you up a blood test. Really, you look awful."

"I feel awful, frankly, my red blood cell count aside. Early reviews for *A Boy Called Skeeter* aren't promising. Celeste is in Milan for a couple of months, and I'm filming next week, so there isn't enough time to join her. The house was so empty."

"I'm afraid you've exchanged one cavernous wasteland for another, but just wait until the kids get home from school—blessed bedlam. And in the meantime . . ." She grinned. "I have the makings for zucchini bread."

"Zucchini bread? Shall we top it off with turnip muffins and asparagus cake?"

Becky sat up. "You've never had zucchini bread? Criminal. Get Sam and come to the family room. You can entertain him while I bake."

"Er . . ."

She started toward the family room without looking back. "It's about time you learned to like children."

"Er . . ."

"You're such a wuss. Come on."

He followed, holding Sam away from his body so the boy dangled from his hands like something dirty. She rolled her eyes, set him up with some books on the couch, and plopped Sam on his lap. As she forced zucchini through her food processor in the kitchen, she could hear Felix's stiff, forced voice.

"'Once upon a time there were'—why are you squirming? Don't you like this book? *Ahem*, 'there were three pigs: a big pig named Pig, a bigger pig named Pigger, and the biggest of the three named Piggest' . . . you're squirming again. Becky! This book is boring him!"

"It's not the book's fault," she muttered.

"Pardon?"

"An actor, paid ridiculously huge sums to speak lines on camera, and he can't even read a child a picture book."

"He isn't my ideal demographic."

"Try using some *inflection*. At this age, a kid doesn't understand all the words. But if *you* don't sound interested in the story, he won't be."

"If he doesn't understand, then what is the point?"

"I'm not even going to answer that," she sang back.

By the time she'd dumped the canned pineapple into her standing mixer (that's right, the most valuable item in the house, so thank goodness Felix hadn't been a robber), Felix was employing nasal voices for the pigs, and Sam was enthralled.

With the first couple of loaves baking, Becky joined them, sitting on the floor. Sam hopped onto her lap, and Felix wiped his brow.

"It's not that I don't like children; I just don't comprehend them. What's their purpose? Why can't they just say what they want? Why are they always touching things and knocking things over and whining?"

She dumped a basket of socks on the floor and began to sort and match. "Here's the thing: Given your profession, you should have that skill of observing people and getting inside them and understanding them, blah blah blah. Why can't you just do that with children? I mean, you were a child once."

"I hatched from an egg at age twenty-three."

"I almost believe you." She squinted at him. "What *were* you like younger?"

"Same but smaller, with slightly less facial hair."

"Stop. You don't have any siblings?"

"No, it was just me and Mum. When I was five, the father figure left us for Spain and had the good grace to die a few years after that."

"I bet your mother loved you half to death."

"Yes, that would describe it."

The conversation had turned a little chilly, and Becky backed away from the pit of unsaid things. This was not the fodder of their friendship, and Becky was feeling waterlogged with the awkwardness drowning the room. She cleared her throat.

"Even more reason for you to catch a sniff of normal family life and learn to fall in love with the wee ones. Here, let me get out of your way . . ."

"No, don't leave us alone!"

"Just have fun with him. He's a happy kid, it won't take much. And if you're capable of multitasking, go ahead and sort the socks while you're at it."

She showered for the first time that day, blew her hair dry superquick, and put on jeans and an almost clean shirt. (She was back into prepregnancy clothes by now—huzzah!) The jeans were freshly washed, and made her feel prettyish—they came out of the dryer a little tighter and held everything in, sort of pants and girdle in one. Her butt alone felt ten years younger.

It wasn't until she was rubbing lotion over her face before running back into the kitchen that the whole man-in-my-house complication occurred to her. From the moment he'd walked in, it had felt as normal as having Melissa drop by or her brother Ryan come over to play.

But he's not my brother, she reminded herself. And he's a man. And I'm married, and alone with him in my house.

Usually she was so strict about those things. As soon as she and Mike married, she'd become conscious of a layer between her and other men. She no longer reached over to touch their knees when making a point, as she would with her women friends. Her brothers she could still hug, tousle their heads in passing, rub their backs to say hello. Cousins and uncles were different too—any relative. So in one way, she reasoned, it wasn't so unusual to have a man in her life she treated differently from the rest. If only Felix were family, then their relationship wouldn't be strange.

Because it didn't feel strange. It should, said the logical part of her brain. But it doesn't, said her heart part, where that soft little tug encouraged her to keep him close. Boundaries were getting fuzzy. She'd have to talk this over with Mike.

She rushed back to check the loaves just as the timer was ringing. Then she heard it—little-boy laughter.

She peeked around the corner and spied Felix on the floor with Sam, singing the lyrics to "Short People." He shook the little boy's legs as he sang about the bitty feet and tickled his hands for the line about grimy fingers. Becky glanced at the unmatched socks—nope, apparently Felix wasn't a multitasker.

"'Gain, 'gain," Sam said, enjoying the humiliation tremendously.

So Felix sang it again, shaking body parts and tickling along with the song. Becky leaned against the doorway, soaking it in. The sound of her little boy's laugh made her heart feel so light it might float away, and seeing that Felix caused the joy about burst her through. She remembered Celeste's face as she gazed at baby Sam, and had a wild hope that she might send Felix back to his wife converted to having children.

Felix noticed her and let go of Sam's toes, looking highly embarrassed to have been caught playing with the child.

"You have a singing voice," she said. "I didn't know that. Do you do musicals?"

"Not since university."

"You should sing in a movie. You'd knock them dead."

Felix shivered. "Musical movies are nasty business."

"I know—a film version of *Anything Goes*. You'd be hysterical as the uptight Englishman who falls for the nightclub singer."

Sam, bored with the talking and the lack of tickling, began to hike up Felix's back.

Felix shrugged his shoulders in an awkward attempt to interact with him. "I'm an actor, not a producer."

"But you have producer friends. I haven't seen you do a real comedy in years, and you're so good at it. Plus you'd sing! Talk about a talent showcase."

"Your son just sneezed on my neck."

"I'm taking that as a committed yes."

There was a honk and Becky ran outside to fetch Hyrum from her friend Jessie's car. Jessie had violently curly hair in a pale brown 'fro. She was tall and toned and looked great without makeup, her eyelashes long and dark and lips pink naturally. It really wasn't fair.

"Felix Callahan is inside my house," Becky said through tight, conspiratorial lips as she unstrapped Hyrum from a back seat.

Jessie grinned. "Really? Can I—" She glanced back at four impatient five-year-olds waiting to be carpooled home. "Never mind. Are you going to bring him to the potluck tonight?"

"Possibly."

Jessie raised her eyebrows. "Wow, you are daring. I won't complain, though, since I'll get to sneak a peak."

Becky herded Hyrum through the front yard and into the house at a record speed of three minutes even, and reintroduced her five-year-old to her friend.

"Look how long my tongue is," Hyrum said, sticking it out with a *bleh* noise twelve inches from Felix's face.

Felix recoiled. "Ooh. Long. Yes."

It really was impressively long, Becky thought as she tidied up the family room before Mike got home. She herself often bragged, "You should see my Hyrum's tongue. He could catch a fish with it." She was sorting toys into their boxes, only half aware of the continuing conversation on the couch.

"Look how long my tongue is. *Bleh* . . ."

"Yeah, that's a proper tongue."

"Look how long my tongue is. *Bleh* . . ."

"You mentioned that before."

"Look how long my tongue is. *Bleh* . . ."

"Er . . ."

"Look how long my tongue is—*bleh*. Look how long my tongue is—*bleh*. Look how long my tongue is—*bleh* . . ."

"Becky?"

She popped up to attention. "What? Oh. Yes, Hyrum, we all see how long your tongue is. It's impressively long. It's catastrophically long. It's amazing! Go play in your room please."

Hyrum needed no further incentive to be alone and trotted off. Felix cleared his throat.

"So, that's the chip off the old block, eh? He's . . . er . . . what am I supposed to say now?"

"You're supposed to exclaim about how smart and good-looking and clever my son is and say you wish he were your very own."

"Right. Yes. Your son . . . has a very long tongue."

"Why, thank you, Mr. Callahan! You are all compliments today."

"Hmph."

"I really am glad you're here, grumpypuss." She leaned over and nearly kissed Felix on the cheek, as she might have done to one of her children, but stopped herself short, ruffling his hair instead. It was stiff with gel. "Ouch! Your hair just stabbed me."

"Uh, hi there," Mike said from the doorway.

"You're home early!" Becky went to him, this time delivering a cheek kiss that she didn't have to pull short. Mike's presence filled up the house, relaxed Becky's bones, and made her realize she'd been more anxious about having Felix there alone than she'd guessed. But the next day was Saturday and Mike would be home, so the problem was temporarily solved. "Felix is going to stay the weekend. Isn't it great?"

"Yeah." From Mike's reserved expression, "great" wasn't the word he would have chosen. But he shook Felix's hand and smiled. "Welcome."

"Dada, Dada, Dada," Sam was chanting as he toddled over.

"Actually, I thought I'd get a hotel," Felix said.

"No, stay here. That's great, that's fine," Mike said, holding Sam upside down by one ankle and swaying him back and forth to evoke the maximum amount of squeals.

"The girls will camp out in the basement," Becky said. "They'll love it, and I know you'll be in heaven in Fiona's twin bed with *Little Mermaid* comforter and matching shams."

"*Little Mermaid* comforter?"

"*And* matching shams. We don't cut corners here, mister."

Felix offered an impossibly fake grin. "I can scarcely wait for night to fall."

Becky left the men in the family room to get to know each other while she finished up the zucchini bread and changed the sheets on Fiona's bed. When she peeked from the kitchen, Mike was on the sofa playing with Sam. Felix was on the love seat flipping through a magazine.

Becky rolled her eyes and hand-washed the mixing bowl. For years she'd yearned for a dishwasher. She'd never had one, not in her parents' home, not in college or her first apartment with Mike. Then for Mother's Day 1991, a brand-new Maytag dishwasher in almond (to match the fridge) with a fat red bow! She wiped down the front of it at least once a week just to make sure it still shined.

But half the time, she found herself hand-washing the dishes anyway. The warm water, the suds and strokes—it was meditative, like pruning rosebushes or folding laundry. She entered a Zen state, taking chaos and filth into her hands and turning it into order and cleanliness.

So she washed and thought. Felix was in the other room. She felt a little patter of excitement like she did whenever Mike first set up the Christmas tree. Yeah, Mike clearly wasn't in on the whole patter-of-excitement part. But it was good for him, she thought, as she ran the spatula under the faucet, sending suds bubbling down the drain. It was good for a man to be reminded that his wife was interesting to other people. Last night she'd worn her deliciously satin pajamas to bed and he hadn't so much as touched her knee.

Felix was here. And the sweet, warm scent of zucchini bread filled the house with contentment.

The girls came home. Fiona at age eleven was unimpressed with the actor and soon absconded to the basement with *Classy and Fabulous*, a photograph-heavy biography of Coco Chanel. Becky had been mystified by that choice, but her rule was her kids could pick out their own library books. Polly, enchanted by Felix's accent, scooted closer and closer to him on the couch until their sides touched. Felix tried making faces at her, but she just stared. He cleared his throat.

"Polly's second-grade class has been learning folk songs," Becky said. "Felix, would you sing 'Danny Boy' with her?"

Polly's voice was dry and soft, and always made Becky think of buttercups because her mother had once remarked, "If buttercups could sing, they'd sound like Polly." Felix sang softly as well, and his robust man's voice on harmony and her little-girl sweetness on melody was breathtaking.

They finished, and Polly snuggled in closer, hugging his arm. He looked at Becky and mouthed, "I am in love."

"I knew you would be," she said.

Polly was Becky's secret weapon. Add the duet to Sam's laughter, and Becky was feeling quite triumphant. She turned to share her happiness with Mike, but he'd already decamped to the office to make work calls. He didn't pop up again until the whole family was readying for the potluck dinner at the church building.

"Sorry we're not having a family dinner for you tonight," Becky said. "But Mike's in the bishopric in our ward and—"

"Slow down, you're speaking Mormonese."

"He's . . . there's no professional clergy in our church. All the members take on different volunteer jobs and we switch around from time to time. He's in the bishopric, which is three people who oversee the entire ward. A ward's like a parish, you know, a certain neighborhood that all meets together as a congregation—"

"You're quite bad at this."

"I know! There's just so much lingo! When we have an hour, I'll give you Mormonism 101."

"Your excuse to try to convert me to your secret, cultish practices."

"You wish. Anyhoo, because Mike's in the bishopric, he needs to be there. I'd let him go alone and the rest of us could stay home, but I signed up to bring zucchini bread. And besides, I know how much work the Activities Committee goes to for these nights. I teach Sunday school now, but I used to be on the committee and I'd really like to support them."

"Of course. I'll tag along tonight, get an insider's view of your life. It will be a delight."

He was wrong.

In which two worlds collide, taxis are not readily available, and no one learns a helpful moral

Mike had to go to the potluck early, so Becky was left to get the four children ready and shepherd them into the car. It took twenty minutes.

"Mom, can I bring my Game Boy?"

"No, Hyrum. Fiona, put on your shoes please."

"I can't find my pink ones."

"Just wear your brown ones, sweetie."

"Eee, eee!"

"We're eating in a minute, Sam. Polly, I asked you to take off that tutu. Shoes, Fiona."

"I can't find my pink ones."

"Just wear your brown ones. Hyrum, if you're ready, wait for us in the car."

"Can I bring my Game Boy?"

"No, just go please. Sam, careful, don't—!"

"Uh-ooooooh."

"Aw, Sam, what a mess. Fiona, can you toss me that rag?"

"I'm looking for my pink shoes."

"Wear the brown ones, Fiona."

"Eeee!"

"We're going to eat at church, Sammy. Careful, don't walk in the—great. Sam, take off those socks."

"NOOOO!"

"We need new socks, these ones are sopping with milk. New socks, Sammy."

"NO! EEEEE!"

"Here's a banana. Hyrum, I thought I told you to get in the car."

"I'm just finishing this one game."

"No, get moving. Lovely twirling, Polly. Now just twirl your way out of that tutu. Fiona—"

"I'm looking for my pink—"

"Fiona Jack, for the love of all that is holy, WEAR YOUR BROWN SHOES!"

"Found 'em!"

Four kids shoed, seated, and strapped in, Becky sat in the driver's seat and exhaled.

"Alrighty," she said with a bright smile. "Off we go!"

Felix was gaping. "How do you stay sane? Not that you are sane in the strictest sense, but you are functional, and I cannot fathom how."

"What, that? You get used to it. I mean, what if I had four children who stood quietly in a row waiting to be told what to do? *Cree-py*. Well, some days I think I'd trade a few toes for that miracle, but long term, no thanks. Give me kids with a little verve any day."

"You are a goddess."

Becky wished Mike had heard that. Some days he came home and gave her that look—you know, that "I've been out earning money while you have nine free hours, and I come home and the house is a mess and I have to wonder what have you been doing with your time" look. Some days it made her want to throw her body over the sticky linoleum and weep with shame; some days it made her want to slug him in the jaw.

As she turned to back up, Becky noticed that the minivan smelled strongly of french fries. She couldn't remember the last time she'd taken the kids through a drive-through and gotten fries to qualm their troubled little souls. How could the smell still linger? Were there fries hiding under car seats, stowing away under benches, squished beneath floor mats? And when was she going to have time to check?

There were lots of things Felix's presence made her notice—how tiny the houses were in her neighborhood, how unkempt many of the lawns. At the entrance to their development was a low brick wall with scripty metal letters spelling out SOMERSET ESTATES. When she and Mike had been house shopping, she'd thought the name of the development completely lovely, evoking at once a dreamy English countryside and something ancient and regal. Now, she squirmed.

A block later, he cleared his throat. "Somerset Estates?"

"Yeah, I was hoping you hadn't noticed."

The ward potluck was held in the church's "cultural hall," which was an indoor basketball court with a stage at one end and wide doors connecting to the kitchen. She found Mike, but he was chained to a conversation with the elderly and apparently angry Brother Brunson, so he just greeted her with a nod and returned his attention to the ranter.

Her heart gushed to see him. There was no one better in the room to take care of whatever the problem was than her Mike.

White and pink plastic sheets covered round folding tables, with centerpieces of elaborate tole-painted wooden daisies on beds of intricate paper grass—the kind of homemade art that would make Martha Stewart shed tears of envy. It was clearly Christine's doing. Last spring they'd had an Under the Sea–themed party, and Christine had created a twenty-foot-long humpback whale out of construction paper and hung it from the ceiling.

"Hi Becky!" Christine rushed up, her hands full of paper petals that left a clumsy trail behind her. "What do you think of the center-pieces?"

Becky almost said, "What, they don't spin in circles and sing 'It's a Small World'?" But sarcasm-as-compliment would be lost on sweet Christine, so she said, "They are so gorgeous I still can't catch my breath."

Christine was staring at Felix's face, then down to his left hand, which didn't bear a wedding ring. He never wore his ring when in production. Christine was single, forty-three, and of the steamroller personality when looking for a mate. That was the word she would use—*mate*.

"Uh, Christine, this is Felix, a friend of the family, who's staying with us for a few days."

"He's staying with you?" Christine was standing on her toes. "For a few days? You come to dinner at my house tomorrow. Tomorrow night. I insist. I'll have a feast prepared. I'll see you at six."

"Er," Felix said.

Becky had a sudden instinct to throw herself in front of her friend, as if he were an allergy-prone boy facing a hive of angry bees. "Christine, we're busy tomorrow night, actually, and—"

"Sunday then. See you at six!" She scuttled away before any protest could reach her ears.

Felix whispered, "Which was she, Arsenic or Old Lace?"

Fiona, the only Jack child who hadn't wandered off to play on the stage, was snickering. When had her little girl grown up enough to understand adult social situations?

"Fiona, don't you want to run along and play?"

"Not really."

"Run along now," Becky said with emphasis. Fiona rolled her eyes and stalked off. "Felix, I'm sorry. I should've called you Rufus or something."

"Just tell me, what is that?" He pointed to a huge punch bowl filled with orangish-green liquid, blobs of unknown origin floating on the soapy surface.

"That's . . . that's . . . it's a drink. Probably Sprite and orange juice with lime sherbet."

Felix's eyes widened. "By the ghost of Hamlet's father . . ."

"It does look pretty revolting, now that you mention it. Why don't we find a table?"

Felix was still holding the bag with the six loaves of zucchini bread and he dropped them off on the buffet tables. A woman with salt-and-pepper hair in a heavily sprayed helmet-do turned to take them. It was Kirsten Nutter. Stop, Felix, Becky wanted to warn. Halt! Desist! Danger ahead! But Felix was already in physical contact with that darling, lovely, meddling woman.

"Let me help . . ." Kirsten paused. She stared, her mouth open. "You're famous, aren't you? I know you."

"Er, I'm a friend of the Jack family. I'm just—"

"You're Felix Callahan! I didn't know you were LDS. That's so fantastic that you're LDS!"

"I'm not . . . I'm just . . . I don't know what you're talking about. I'm a friend of—"

Kirsten grabbed a young, blonde woman by the arm. "Look, look, did you know that Felix Callahan was LDS? I'd heard that Steve Martin was, but I didn't know—"

"You are?" The blonde squinted and adjusted the infant in her arms. "But your last movie was rated R."

"I . . . I'm a friend of—" Felix started.

"Well, don't bother him, Kirsten," the blonde said. "I'm sure he doesn't want to be fussed over. I hope you feel at home, Brother Callahan. Have some punch." She handed him a cup of the punchlike concoction with an extra lump of melting green sherbet.

"Were they accusing me of drug use?" Felix whispered as Becky hurried him away.

"'LDS' stands for 'Latter-day Saint.' They think you're Mormon."

"Ah. That's just . . ."

"Tabloid-worthy?"

"I doubt even the tabloid readers would believe that." He was staring at the lumpy punch in his hand with undisguised horror.

"And yet in Layton, Utah, it's no doubt already considered fact. I wouldn't be surprised if the news has reached as far as Ogden. We are a hopeful lot."

She spotted the shivering 'fro of her friend Jessie across the cultural hall and rushed Felix that way. Becky was extremely fond of her fellow ward members, and it just wasn't fair that he'd met some of the quirkiest among them right off. Jessie would balance things out.

"Jessie! I want you to meet my friend Felix."

Jessie stood up to shake Felix's hand. "It's great to meet you. And you couldn't have picked a better friend than Becky."

"Likewise, I'm sure."

"Jessie studied dance at Juilliard and was a member of the Martha Graham Dance Company before she gave it up to have children," Becky bragged.

Felix glanced at the five-year-old girl engrossed in a coloring book at the table then turned back to Jessie. "You gave up professional dance to have children?"

"Yeah, I did."

"And moved to Layton, Utah."

"Well, yeah, my husband's job brought us here."

"So . . . congratulations?"

"Um . . . thanks?"

Becky considered smacking Felix, but she could see he didn't mean to be offensive—he was sincerely confused. She cleared her throat.

"Jessie's youngest is in school, so she decided to go back to work and just started with Ririe-Woodbury, this really amazing local dance company. She'll be choreographing a piece for their upcoming show."

"Ah," Felix said.

"Yeah . . ." Jessie said unsurely. "It's . . . it's nice. I feel very blessed. I mean, it's hard to have it all, but I'm doing my best."

"That's all anyone can do, I suppose." Felix spoke like an automaton programmed to sound almost interested.

"That's the truth. So . . . what do you think about Utah?"

"The mountains are lovely. My wife and I skied in Park City last year."

"Oh yeah, Park City's beautiful. So . . . I think Becky mentioned you have an apartment in New York. What neighborhood?"

"Upper West Side, near the park."

"Nice. My first place was in the West Forties—not so nice, but it was New York. I still miss it."

"It is a unique city."

"Yes, that's true."

Both Jessie and Felix were looking at Becky now, expecting her to save them. Her mind blanked, and she smiled with so much teeth she felt like an alligator.

"Becky, tell me you brought your famous zucchini bread," Jessie said.

"I did indeed!"

"I'd better grab some before it's all gone. Nice to meet you, Felix!" And Jessie scurried off.

After that, Becky picked out a far-flung table in the corner, placed Felix with his back to the room, and decided to keep him to herself. She even filled up a plate of food for him at the buffet table, along with Sam's and Hyrum's plates. Because her hands were full, Mike made up a plate for her, then Fiona got a plate for her dad. Polly was the only one who served herself and so ate only white dinner rolls.

During the dinner hour, there were stares. And whispers. And people slowing down as they passed the Jacks' table and gaping at Felix as if at a traffic accident. A few bold ones approached.

Mari Moss, age seventeen: "So, hi, so my friends bet me I wouldn't dare to come talk to you but I totally am, and I'm even going to ask you to autograph a napkin. I know, I am so bold."

Melanie Bradford, PTA president and mother of two sets of twins: "I just wanted to tell you how much I enjoy your films, but I wondered, do you have any control over the editing and such? I just hate to see so much violence and profanity."

Lorrie Kimball, CPA and mother of three boys, ages one, two, and three: "I just want you to know that while everyone else is either standing back and staring or fawning and drooling, I'm going to treat you like a completely normal person. I'm not fazed at all."

Occasionally, Mike laughed into his napkin. He seemed to be the only person at their table who was having a terrific time.

"Thanks for not pulling out Diplomatic Felix," Becky whispered. "You're showing admirable restraint. They really are very nice people. The more sane ones are being polite and giving you space while the others . . . Well, they're just . . . they're . . . we're not used to . . . if Tom Selleck showed up here, I'd probably make a complete idiot out of myself."

"And why didn't meeting me cause the same effect?"

"Come on, sweetie. You're great and all, but you're no Tom Selleck."

"What does he do? He smiles with dimples and grows a mustache."

Becky patted his arm consolingly. "Someday you'll be able to grow a mustache too. Just give it time."

They partook of ham and rolls, green bean casserole, green salad and fruit salad and pasta salad and Jell-O salad, and in the silence Becky became more and more aware of the conversations around them.

"Hey, Bonnie, did you say you want one baby hamster or two?"

"Oh, we'll take two, if they're both little boys or little girls. I don't want to open their cage one morning and find a nest of them."

"Wish I'd thought of that a few weeks ago."

"Are you still with Weight Watchers?"

"Nah, I went off it again. I mean, all the counting. Me with math! I mean, I can't add two and two, you know what I mean? Two and two! I'm serious, you know what I mean? I can't add to save my life."

"Yeah . . ."

"Yeah, can't add to save my life. Not even two and two, you know what I mean? Ha!"

"Yeah, it's good to be healthy."

"Yeah, that's important. And I've been reading about eating fruit every day, but not the peels, because that's where the pesticide toxins live. That's important."

"Yeah."

Becky's face was set on permanent wince. She kept her eyes on her plate and poked at her Jell-O salad, letting its fabulous green body (neither solid nor liquid!) wiggle gleefully. The harder she tried to tune out the conversation, the more she absorbed every word, eavesdropping with an ear for how it must sound to Felix. What did his friends talk about? Not hamsters and Weight Watchers, she was pretty sure. Not that there was anything wrong with that. These were perfectly wonderful people, and who said that the rich and fashionable are superior to anyone else? Who said their conversation is any more important than that of a middle-class housewife?

"I mean, it's not like I have time to work out. I chase around a toddler and two schoolkids all day—now that's a workout!"

"Well, you look . . . I like those pants. Where did you get those pants?"

"T.J. Maxx. Four bucks. Can you believe it? Four bucks. How can you say no to four-dollar pants?"

"Wow, that's . . . what fabric is that?"

"Polyester or something. They're a size too small, but really, can you say no to four-dollar pants? I mean, really! I mean, come on!"

Becky smiled at Felix through her wince. "Having fun? You just wait—this magnificent feast and riveting repartee is only half of tonight's gala. Next up is a world-class talent show."

"Maybe I'll call a cab and leave you all to it," Felix said.

Becky's smile felt sad. "This isn't New York. It'd take at least half an hour to get here. By then the program will be over."

He nodded and leaned back as if readying himself for the worst. The bishop stood to get everyone's attention so the program could begin, and in the sudden hush, someone could be heard to whisper too loudly, "Who's Felix Galahad?"

The program consisted of several casual musical numbers: two members of the high school marching band played a squeaky clarinet duet; a sixty-five-year-old soprano sang an Italian aria (sans Felix's presence, this one would have impressed Becky to death); the ward's token over-forty bachelor played the theme from *The Godfather* on the accordion. Then the four- and five-year-olds sang "I Am a Child of God." Hyrum was there with his classmates, singing boldly, completely un-self-aware, their chins raised, their tiny voices scratching out a melody, their arms and legs unable to hold still for a moment, fidgeting as they sang.

Becky couldn't see Hyrum after the first verse because the waterworks started. Becky hadn't cried for sadness since she'd been thirteen years old and her older brothers had discovered her singing to the mirror. Ah, the hours of entertainment her brothers derived! As part of her recovery, she forced herself to stay dry-eyed for a good ten years, not even weeping at the movies. Then she had children, and suddenly there were a thousand sparkling moments of beauty that seized her by her throat and shook the tears right out.

After the song was over, she realized Felix was staring at her.

"Why were you crying?" His voice was soft with curiosity.

She didn't know how to explain how she felt about Hyrum, let alone the song. He'd been her baby, cradled in her arms and nestled into her chest. Now he was five, so big and clever, in kindergarten, wrestling with his new identity as an individual who makes his own decisions and has friends and suffers the teasing and insecurities and danger that every five-year-old must face. She wanted to snuggle him and keep him safe and warm. But it also thrilled her to see him enter the world, so brave and excited, ready to conquer it all. And to hear his little voice singing that song—the pure childhood sweetness of it, the simple faith of it, laying out all that she felt in her soul for God and family. Describing that sensation seemed like trying to describe the taste of salt.

"Beauty makes me cry sometimes," she said finally.

"Beauty? But . . . they were . . . never mind."

What had he been about to say? That they were just children, that they were all off-tune and forgetting words, that their performance was nothing worth admiring?

They looked at each other, Becky and Felix, and she guessed that he too was feeling a gap press between them. Perhaps she looked as strange and foreign to him as he did to her, and she wondered what could possibly hold them together.

When Hyrum dashed back to their table, he went straight for his daddy. Mike grabbed him and swooped him into the air like a fighter plane then back into his arms for a quick hug.

"Great job, chief," Mike said. "I could hear every word you sang. Your lungs are so strong they must be made out of titanium."

"Yeah, Dad! Titanium!"

Becky glowed at her boy then turned to Felix, gloomy confusion on his face. Why all the praise for such a mediocre performance? he seemed to question. Why care so much for the squeals of a child?

On the ride home, everyone was quiet, even Sam. As if he sensed tension, he looked around with wide eyes, sucking ardently on his pacifier. At least he was strapped into his car seat and couldn't force one into Becky's mouth.

The next morning, the family ate one of the leftover loaves of zucchini bread for breakfast. Felix had oatmeal. By noon, he was on his way to the airport, returning early to Los Angeles. He'd insisted on calling a cab rather than bother Becky for a ride.

"Well, good-bye, thanks for coming," Becky said at the door.

"Perhaps you could let Christine know I won't be able to make our dinner date?"

"Sure, right. I'll do that."

"Good. Thank you. Good-bye."

He stood in the doorway, holding his suitcase, then nodded in farewell and left.

It was not the first time she thought she would never see him again, but this time she had no doubt she was right. She didn't let herself feel any which way about that. Shutting the door, she went back to the kitchen to clean up after breakfast.

"What do you want to do today?" Mike asked.

Becky smiled. "Everything."

In which long-distance charges apply

The calendar clung to September, but Becky was still in mourning for the wide open weeks of summer, a full and noisy house, outings to the zoo and pools and canyons. Becky didn't see autumn as a glorious and exciting time of change, wind peeling away layers, alternately breathing chill on your neck and cuddling you in bright bursts of warmth. No. She saw autumn as Not Summer.

So she kept the Saturdays in autumn so packed with amusement and frivolity that no one (especially Becky) could slow down to realize what they weren't.

One week after Felix's sudden departure, the Jacks did something for everyone: a picnic up the canyon for Fiona, who loved the early autumn colors (though Becky refused to acknowledge them, the traitors); back to civilization to fetch ice cream sundaes for Hyrum; a jaunt farther west to look for buffalo on Antelope Island for Polly; and some free running on the white beaches for Sam, sending kamikaze kites into the frantic, gusty sky. Mike was magic with kites, keeping those be-tailed jewels aloft in hurricane or vacuum. He put Hyrum on his shoulders and chased down the wind, the string trying in vain to tear loose from his iron hand.

It had been a sweater day, sunshiny with the sky a summer blue, the grasses a shy shade of green. It had been nonstop good times, and when they drove home, all the kids (except stubborn Hyrum) fell asleep in the car.

Becky dressed sleeping bodies into jammies and tucked them in, leaving Mike to coax Hyrum down, and had just collapsed on the couch when the phone rang.

You'll never guess who it was. Becky certainly didn't.

"Hello, Rebecca."

"Celeste?"

"This is not too late? I didn't wake you?"

"No, you're fine. It's about eight. Where are you?"

"Milan."

"Isn't it the middle of the night there?"

"Is it? I never sleep. Felix is here with me."

"He is?"

"Yes, he flew out. He must leave tomorrow. He can be impetuous, but only when he is running away from something. I think he was running away from you."

Becky sighed. "Yeah, he cut his visit short and fled like a rabbit from a fox."

"What happened, Rebecca?"

"I think he glimpsed for the first time who I am, you know, here in my home with my people around me, and it disgusted him."

"Not disgust. Fear. He is a frightened little boy. He was afraid of who he was in that place, I would suppose, just as he is still afraid of who he was in Devonshire. What does it say about a man that he never returns to the town of his childhood? You see what I mean."

This was good stuff, and Becky didn't so much as breathe, afraid to set Celeste off track. But Felix's voice crackled in the background.

"Who are you talking to?"

"Rebecca, of course."

"What? What are you—" He began to rant in French, and Celeste ranted back. Oh, why hadn't Becky studied French in high school? It almost killed her to know that intensely interesting things were being tossed around and she couldn't understand a word. But she soaked up every inflection—Felix was annoyed, embarrassed, and Celeste was soothing but stubborn. Then she sighed.

"I am apologetic. I have spoken quickly because I'm French and I love this man. This silly, silly man." Celeste laughed. "They are so much trouble, aren't they, Rebecca?"

"That's the truth."

"I was curious what happened, but now he is standing here, wide awake with the jet lag, and looking at me in such a way—"

Sounds of someone handling the phone receiver, a pause, then Felix's voice. "Hello, Becky."

"Hi," Becky said with a laugh. "You, uh, you've concerned your wife a bit."

"She's fine. She's used to me. Aren't you, Celeste?"

A faint voice shouted back, "The stories I could share, Rebecca!"

"Yes, let's just put a stop to that, shall we? Celeste, shoo. Shoo, my love. Yes, I worship your very shadow, your body is the Elysian Fields, I will fall upon a sword at your command—now please shoo before you say anything else." There were shuffling sounds, Celeste calling something back, perhaps a farewell, then a door clicked shut.

Felix groaned. "She means well."

"She's fantastic!" Becky said, though mourning the stories Celeste could but didn't tell. "So, it was that bad? That you couldn't just leave Layton behind but had to flee the entire continent?"

"Mm," Felix said noncommittally. His voice went raw. "I am sorry I left like that."

"It's okay. You don't belong here. You were a wild toad caught in a mason jar."

"With a stick and a leaf."

"Hold on . . . am I the stick in this metaphor? Because I have lost some weight . . ."

"I didn't know what I was doing. There was something uncomfortable about it."

"I can't imagine what."

"Certainly not *The Little Mermaid* comforter. That felt oh-so-right."

There was a curl in his voice that implied a smile. So she smiled back across two continents and an ocean. Maybe he heard the smile, because his voice relaxed, and she was talking to Felix again.

They fell into their old rhythm of conversation, though at first it was more habit than sincere, a stale awkwardness filling in the spaces between words. Becky tried to keep the conversation light, harmless, deftly skirting the topic of her aggressively happy neighbors, or Hyrum singing "I Am a Child of God," or how Becky could possibly be at home both at the church potluck *and* as Felix's chum. Their conversation wandered from *The Little Mermaid* to dinosaurs, comic book superhero movies to the reasons Canadians weren't as neutral as they seemed. Then before the energy could start to dwindle, before there was a pause where they'd have to listen to the silence and consider what hadn't worked, they said good-bye.

Becky stayed on the couch for a few moments, just feeling glad. So glad. She'd never given that word much thought before, never paused to experience it as a valid emotion, a stable kind of happiness, a glow that warmed but didn't overwhelm. It used to seem like a throwaway emotion that just sat in her chest, smiling awkwardly. But now it was perfect.

She went in the bedroom where Mike was dumping himself onto the bed with a groan.

"Long day," he said. "Good day."

"Tired?" she asked.

"Yeah. But good tired. How do you feel?"

"Glad."

"Mmm," he said, rolling over. She thought he might be near sleep, so she didn't explain. Sometimes he took a twenty-minute nap in the evening to sustain him, then he was good again till midnight. But Becky wasn't tired anymore. She dimmed the bedroom lights and went down to the kitchen, cleaning out the fridge while humming "Raindrops Keep

Fallin' on My Head." Glad was not a boring emotion after all. Glad was awfully nice.

Becky wasn't surprised when Felix phoned on Sunday, and they talked for five minutes about nothing. She *was* surprised, however, when he called Monday as well. She picked up the telephone to clean refried beans off the receiver, accidentally answering it before it had rung. She was using her fingernail to loosen dried brown smears out of the mouth speaker when she heard a British voice say, "Hello? Hello, is someone there?"

She dropped the phone then brought it hurriedly to her ear, smearing refried beans on her cheek.

"Hi! Um, Felix? Is that you?"

"It was."

"Sorry, I was cleaning the phone. There was a refried beans incident and—"

"Those qualify as 'incidents'?"

"They do when your marvelous toddler manages to get bean gunk into every crevice of a crevice-prone phone."

"That's all I needed. Good-bye."

The line went silent, and she stood, stunned, gloppy phone in hand.

He called again on Tuesday, and they spoke a little longer. Soon almost every day included a quick conversation with Felix. His calls were like polishing off a Snickers bar at four in the afternoon to hold her over till dinner.

Felix rarely offered info about the movie business and his exotic exploits; their talks maintained a fluffy, frivolous tone. But curious about what stories Celeste could have told, Becky got Felix to reveal slivers of his past. Eventually she was able to piece together a snapshot.

It would seem that as soon as Felix was old enough to think about girls as anything other than pests, his good looks won him admirers. The older girls pulled him into corners at school, grabbed him in the corridors, sent him witty love notes. Felix studied the movies of Sean Connery and Cary Grant and picked up some charmer skills, playing up his youth and innocence, feigning sheepishness to lure them in. At age fifteen, a girl about to leave for Oxford took it upon herself to teach him the ways of the world. He didn't go into great detail about this event (not that Becky would have allowed it), but she gathered it was at once shocking and life altering. A new world opened up—easy, uncommitted love. Theater, and eventually film, became a means of widening the playground.

"Before Celeste, I thought committing to one woman was complete rubbish," he said.

Then in 1992 he attended a charity banquet, and the model Celeste

Bodine shared his table. He was fascinated—the words she spoke, the movement of her body. She was gorgeous in every way. She spurned him that night. The infatuation grew hotter and he pursued. Surely once the chase ended, he would grow tired of her. He didn't.

"Let me see if I can explain without sounding like a nancy boy," Felix said. "Being with her, I felt myself change, as if down to the atoms I was rearranging, becoming a person who only needed one woman. I lost the desire to conquer lovely young women or go out at night and get pissed as a newt. Even bad reviews, which used to unsettle me for days, barely touched me anymore. I felt myself become, first, the man who loved Celeste, and second, everything else. I never in my younger years imagined this would happen, but I knew I had found my soul mate." He cleared his throat. "So much for not sounding like a nancy."

Becky in turn couldn't help gushing about Mike now and then. She seldom mentioned the children, because it seemed to make Felix uncomfortable, and covered the handset when she spoke inevitable asides such as "We don't eat gravel, Sam. We are not chickens." If Polly was home from school with a stomachache when Felix called (as she was about once a week), she would speak with him or sing a duet across fiber-optic lines.

One time Becky started to tell Felix a mothering story, thinking it was funny, but it morphed into something else altogether.

"This morning Hyrum came to me with a booger hanging out of his nose, hollering 'Mom, help! Help, Mom, help!' He refuses to wipe his own nose. He's so independent in so many ways, but with his nose, he's still a baby."

"That is revolting."

"I know! I mean, I know it should be. But what was funny was how I felt a rush of warmth at the privilege that I was the one this boy would go to for help. I know that sounds ludicrous, but I felt so happy I kissed him all over his face. After I wiped his nose."

"Yes, I was going to ask that."

"I'm continually shocked by how much I feel for these kids. I don't know if I can even explain it, let alone comprehend it. You know Michelangelo's *La Pietà*?"

"Of course I do. I own it."

"What do you mean you own it?"

"Well, I've seen it. And I purchased the ticket to see it with my very own money. So in a sense—"

"*Anyhoo*, the first time I saw it—"

"You were in Italy? I can't imagine you in Italy."

"No, not in Italy. I've never even been out of the country, unless Arizona counts."

"Never? Are you mad? That's—"

"Shush, I'm telling you a story! I was young, maybe ten or fourteen, and I saw a photograph of *La Pietà* in a textbook. I remember being stunned by its beauty. But after I had children, I saw a photo of it again, and this time I actually sat down and cried. As a mother, the meaning of Mary holding her son's body changed for me so completely, I wondered how I'd seen any significance in it before."

There was a pause.

"That got kinda serious, didn't it?"

"So . . ." Felix said. "Seen Nubbin lately?"

Sometimes she happened to be talking to Felix when Mike got home from work.

"Gotta go, my man's here," she'd say and hang up.

"Felix?" Mike would ask.

"Yep." And she'd repeat some bite of conversation to help Mike feel included.

"Felix went bowling last night because Celeste had never been. Time after time he knocked down every pin except the one right in the middle, and he thinks that's the bowling equivalent of getting the bird."

Or, "Felix spent twelve hours in a milk sauna because *Entertainment Weekly* used the word 'weathered' to describe his face. Celeste said he smelled like goat for a week."

Mike was being awfully good natured about his wife's male friend, and she tried to be careful not to push it. Most of the time, anyway. One fateful Thursday in the spring, two-year-old Sam pried open a childproof cabinet and knocked a jar of pear preserves onto the linoleum. Fortunately Becky arrived in time to pull him from the disaster area before he'd taken a step, but in the process a glass shard stuck between her toes. There was something entirely vulgar about glass and jam mixed with blood. She locked Sam in his room to keep him safe while she bandaged herself then scraped up preserves and glass.

And things went downhill from there. The furnace stopped working, the car wouldn't start, Fiona and Polly missed piano lessons, two separate neighbors had emergencies and asked Becky to watch their kids, so she had eleven children running around her house—one of them had a penchant for yanking on blinds, and another climbed on the kitchen table, disrupting her careful piles of tax papers. At five thirty P.M. she ushered all non-Jack children home, peeled a frozen lasagna out of the freezer, and answered the phone. Felix. She felt her body soften from shoulders to knees.

Then Mike walked in.

Now, Mike never noticed if the toilet bowls developed hard-water stains or the counters were sticky, but clutter made his neck cramp.

Before even greeting the kids, his gaze fell on the floor littered with blocks and various and sundry plastic ponies, then jumped to the table smeared with receipts, bills, and bank statements, and the kitchen counter teeming with food-encrusted dishes. He looked at Becky, the phone in her hand, and his features tightened in barely restrained condemnation as he said, "This place is a disaster."

She bristled.

Normally Becky would have hung up the phone and said to Mike, "Honey, can you help me reach something in the closet?"—their code for "Please come into the bedroom so I don't have to yell at you in front of the children." Did he think she couldn't see the mess? He had to rub it in with that self-righteous little gleam? And after the day she'd had? While he was leaning back in his cozy office chair making calls and answering e-mail, did he imagine she had her feet up too, sipping cold drinks and watching *Oprah*? Well. She was revving up to throw some blame back at her quick-to-judge-an-untidy-house-and-blame-the-wife husband. Then her hand tightened on the receiver and she realized she held in her hand the ultimate weapon.

"Oh hi, honey," she said casually, already leaving the kitchen. "Dinner's in the oven. Mind cleaning up for me while I finish this call?"

Teach him to glare at me, she thought, plopping down on the couch, the long cord stretching the coils smooth. Teach him to judge my housekeeping skills. Let him wallow around in the mess for a bit.

"I'm back, Felix," she said.

"That's fine, darling, just fine," he said in his best Cary Grant voice.

She laughed loudly enough that Mike was sure to hear from the kitchen.

Okay, so that was a little low, but she'd had *eleven* kids in that house. It'd been rainy, so they'd stayed indoors, blowing from room to room like a twenty-two-legged tornado, twisting blinds, dumping every book off the shelf, waking Sam early from his nap and putting him in a block-throwing and hair-pulling mood. And besides, her foot was throbbing.

When the oven timer chimed, she said good-bye to Felix and waltzed into the kitchen, gently clicking the receiver back on its cradle. Mike had managed to tidy up the dishes a tad, but the kitchen table still groaned under the weight of a hundred dead trees.

"We're eating outside tonight, guys," she said.

"But it's cold," Fiona said, frowning at the April night.

"Then put on a coat!"

They had to sit on towels because the patio furniture was damp from the rain. When Hyrum spilled his milk, Becky watched the white stream flow down the concrete patio into the grass and thought, *we should eat outside every night.*

"My lasagna's cold," Fiona said in the kind of high, tight voice that only an eleven-year-old girl can truly master.

"It's not lasagna; it's Pasta Chilla, a delicacy in southern Italy. To be really authentic, we should be eating it on a bed of ice. Anyone care for some?"

"I do!" Hyrum said.

Becky scooped some crushed ice from her water glass and sprinkled it over Hyrum's lasagna. He dug in, crunching and grinning. Fiona rolled her eyes, so Hyrum took another bite, chewing loudly by her ear.

"Yummy!" he said.

Normally at such times, Becky would share a smile with Mike, but she still felt like a wounded bird, so she kept her eyes on her plate. She could feel him looking at her. She knew he was parsing through everything he'd done recently, clueless and searching for fault, deciding whether he needed to apologize or whether Becky's mood was ignorable. All through dinner, he wisely kept silent.

When Becky trudged into her bedroom after tucking in Hyrum for the third time, was Mike out cleaning up the mess he so vehemently despised? No, he was reclining in their reading chair. Becky grumbled.

"You're in a mood," he said.

"Yeah, that's right." She stomped around the room, stuffing junk into drawers, ripping her pajamas free of the dresser. "I'm in a *mood*. How unaccountable, how womanly of me, must be my *cycle* or something, couldn't possibly be a reaction to anything *specific*, because all I do is sit around enjoying my life of leisure."

She grabbed the blinds' cord and yanked it too hard. She startled as the blinds snapped on the sill like the drop of a guillotine. The cord lay disconnected and limp across her palm. She had a flashback to a southern Utah vacation as a little girl when she'd made a snatch for a small gray lizard, pulling back to find the lizard gone but its tail between her fingers.

"I broke the blinds," she said quietly. "I guess I was mad."

Mike was on his feet and out the door, muttering over his shoulder, "I'll fix it."

It took a while before he returned from his hunt for some tool or other. She sat on the edge of the bed and thought about putting on her pajamas, and thought about brushing her teeth, and even thought about just lying down, but she was suddenly too tired to do any of it. She stared at the bandage between her toes until her gaze relaxed and she wasn't seeing anything at all. Zombie state. It was as close to meditation as she came, and it seemed to relax that spot in the center of her head that no amount of sleep ever touched, making her feel floaty and free, transcendent.

Then Mike was there, massaging her shoulders.

"Tough day?" he asked, and with those two words she knew that he understood and no "I'm sorry" would be necessary on either side.

"Yeah," she said, gaze still lost and falling through rings and rings of zombieness. Mike knew how much she loved zombie state and didn't try to distract her. When he finished his impromptu massage, he reattached the cord, picked her pajamas off the floor to lay them across her lap, and went into the bathroom to brush his teeth.

I love him so much, she thought. I just love him so much.

When he climbed into bed, she rolled over and tucked herself against him, their bodies touching at every point from feet to face.

"I'm sorry," she said. Might as well.

"Me too."

She breathed in his scent before falling asleep.

The next time Mike came home grumpy or was particularly obnoxious or failed to notice how hard she'd worked on looking nice that day or how many hours she'd spent scouring the house to please him, she resisted using the my-best-friend-is-Felix-Callahan weapon. But once or twice she thought about it.

Usually their marital disagreements went something like this:

"It's time to go-o," Becky called out in a tight, singsongy voice.

Mike was downstairs, watching golf no doubt. "I know-ow," he replied, his voice as tight and singsongy.

A minute later: "We're going to be late, my precious. I'm sure what you're doing is *very* important, but they'll be waiting for us."

And Mike trudged up the stairs, waving a pair of little shoes. "I was looking for Sam's shoes."

Here she could say one of two things:

1. "Oh. Sorry. Thanks for looking."

2. "Then why didn't you just say that in the first place instead of letting me think you were watching TV? Were you trying to annoy me when you know I'm already stressed to get there on time? Do you get some kind of pleasure out of seeing me upset?"

It depended on how loving she was feeling in the moment, if she'd had a good lunch, if her headache had gone away, if Mike had remembered to put his cereal bowl in the dishwasher—countless factors. But you see that for her there was no option three.

3. "Okay, then why don't you load the kids in the car. I'm just going to call Felix real quick and tell him something soooo funny!"

She really did try to be cautious. There had to be a way to balance a friend like Felix with her normal life. But she didn't realize how often the idea of Felix subtly intruded into their marriage.

For example, the night Becky was chuckling to herself as she folded laundry:

"What?" Mike said, peering over his New Testament study guide. "What's provoking the sniggering? Did I do something?"

She shook her head. "No, I was just thinking about this story Felix told me. Last night he was at a charity dinner and Matt Damon and Kiki Frie were at his table. And Charlton Heston—"

"Who?"

"What'd you mean who? *Moses.* Soylent Green is people."

"No, the other name, the one after Matt Damon."

"Oh, Kiki Frie. She's a . . . singer, I guess. You know, she wears little outfits and dances around and seems to have been seventeen for ten years now. Anyway, someone at the table—I can't remember who—said, 'Look, there's Charlton Heston,' and Kiki Frie stood up so fast she elbowed Felix in the head. Felix said, 'What are you doing?' and she said, 'Aren't we supposed to stand for the president?'"

"Felix is embellishing," said Mike. "Or the girl was kidding."

"No, she really wasn't. Felix said, 'You know that Bill Clinton is president—depending on your definition of the word *is*.' And Kiki Frie said, 'But my dad has a bumper sticker that says, "Charlton Heston Is My President," so I think he must be mine too.' Apparently Matt Damon had been taking a drink when she said that, and he started to laugh so suddenly he literally sprayed water out of his nose. Can you imagine? Matt Damon! Then right when he'd gotten a hold of himself, Samuel L. Jackson, who'd been at the next table, got up and walked behind Matt Damon humming 'Hail to the Chief,' and that was when Matt really lost it."

Becky laughed again, and Mike shook his head in amazement.

"Honestly, you wonder if some people live with their head under a rock. That reminds me, today at work the funniest thing happened."

Becky leaned forward, smiling in anticipation.

"So, Dan, a project manager, was leading a meeting, and he was projecting his computer's desktop on the wall to demonstrate this new application, but he still had an e-mail opened. Someone using the name Yosemite Sam had sent him a message with the subject line 'What up, Doogle?'"

Becky kept smiling, waiting for the punch line, realizing too late that the punch line had already come and gone. She quickly barked a little laugh. Mike nodded, as if his head wanted to encourage her that the laugh was on the right track.

"It was projected right up there for everyone to see. You probably have to know Dan to understand, because he's a pretty serious guy, but apparently he has a friend who calls him Doogle."

"Doogle," she repeated, nodding her head too and smiling encouragingly.

"And everyone lost it, I mean, really laughing, and for the rest of the day, everyone was calling him Doogle."

"Yeah, yeah, wow, that's funny, isn't it? Huh."

"Yeah."

"Yeah, it is."

She went back to the laundry. He picked up the study guide. Becky didn't even dare look at him. The silence that followed seemed to scream, "Felix's stories are funnier than yours! Felix's world is better than yours!"

Though at the time she didn't realize that Mike was hurting, she still suspected he didn't love it when Felix phoned. But part of her stiffened into stubbornness. Everything was about the kids and her husband and her church duties and keeping the house. Wasn't she allowed to be a tiny bit selfish? Once she tried to explain:

"I share everything with the kids." She was sitting on the bedroom floor, her arms around her knees. "Sam takes half of my breakfast and most of my attention, and even when the others are at school, they're in my mind, keeping most of me worrying and thinking and solving problems for them. And you're always there too. I don't have anything that's just mine."

"You should," Mike said. "You absolutely should. I didn't realize that you were feeling dissatisfied."

"I wasn't. I'm not, really. Just a little."

"I knew that, I guess, but I'd hoped that your screenwriting hobby would be, you know, fulfilling."

She shrugged. "That's just fun, like decorating for holidays. But with Felix—it's different from talking with my other friends. It's a little gift for me to laugh with him—or at him, more often than not. It's fun, but it also feels . . . important somehow. Like I'm exercising a part of my brain that's been neglected. And I feel a little more excited to live the day."

Mike was sitting on the edge of the bed, leaning forward, his arms resting on his knees. It was his "attentive" pose. He was trying, but he still didn't get it.

"It's not just for my sake," she tried. "I don't think Felix talks to anyone besides me and Celeste. Everyone should have a friend other than their spouse, right?"

"Sure. He needs friends."

"Yeah."

They smiled weakly at each other.

Mike had golfing buddies, brothers and brothers-in-law, hunting pals, and guys in the ward. Friends were easy for him, and Felix's lack thereof didn't make Mike sympathetic—it made him suspicious.

Becky didn't try to explain Felix to Mike again. She told Mike everything—no secrets from her husband, that was where she drew the line. And she never shared things with Felix that she wouldn't tell Mike. Still, there were crinkles and creases inside her that she didn't think Mike could see. It didn't make her feel lonely. It made her feel mysterious, which for Becky, mother of four in Layton, Utah, was a miraculous thing. She held on to it.

She considered later that maybe she should have tried harder. Saying to your husband "When my guy friend calls, I feel excited" had to sound so, so wrong. Mike must have stewed on those words for several weeks, until one afternoon in May when Felix called with an invitation.

In which a relationship ends

The spring weather was coy, giving flashes of warmth then withdrawing back into long-sleeve days. It teased with ideas of summer, of late light and evening walks, of heat and freedom and ice cream melting down your fingers. Soon. So soon it was almost maddening. Every day Becky pushed the kids outside, let sunlight touch their skins and air out the must and mold of winter. Everyone was laughing more than usual. Sam seemed dangerously close to exploding from pure crazy happiness. After the kids were in bed, the house quiet, Becky would stand by the sliding-glass door and stare at the luscious blue of the night yard. It was too cold to open a window, but only just.

Come on, summer, she chanted silently. Come on, you can do it.

Everything seemed to tick and tock, leading up to something big. She thought it was all about the change of seasons, until that Thursday when Felix phoned after lunch.

"I just got my call sheet and I'm off for the weekend. Three days. I bought you a ticket out here—"

"You what?"

"Don't argue, darling." He was calling her "darling" more and more often. She wouldn't admit it, but she just ate it up. "I anticipated your aversion to 'mooching' so the ticket is economy class, a measly two hundred and nineteen dollars. You leave tomorrow at ten thirty. You have twenty-one hours to find someone to take care of your children, and with an extended family your size, I can't imagine that would be a problem. My travel agent is on call, waiting to book Mike either a Friday-night or Saturday-morning flight. There's nothing to debate here."

"Where would I—"

"I booked you a room at a lousy three-star hotel nearby. I tried to shake you off, but you're like one of those pesky burrs that stick to your sock when you accidentally step off the safe, paved sidewalk into the formidable weed jungles. I don't fit in Utah, but let's give you in L.A. another shot. So."

"So."

"So," his voice got softer, unsure, "will you come?"

She sighed and said in a high, enchanted voice, "I feel as magical as a fairy princess."

"Also, there will be no princess talk whilst you're here. I was trying to be nice before, but the truth is, I've had nightmares about those *Little Mermaid* shams crawling toward me and stuffing themselves down my throat."

"You said those shams were a dream come true!"

"I know. I'm a shameless, heartless, ruthless man. Also, I miss you."

He'd never said anything like that before. Her heart jumped.

As soon as they hung up, she called her mother, who agreed to come over on Friday until Mike got home from work, and her sister-in-law Angela, who offered to take them Saturday. Becky hesitated but finally asked her youngest brother, Ryan, if he could swing watching the kids on Sunday.

"As long as you get me Felix's autograph. And a signed photo of Celeste Bodine. And an interview with Steven Spielberg."

Ryan was the only single one left in her family, his life undecided after college, but he'd always had a hankering for the movie business. She was careful that he never find any of Felix's contact information. The boy had no comprehension of the word "tactful."

"How does two out of three sound?"

Ryan considered. "Your terms are acceptable."

The way everything was falling together, the jaunt seemed divinely blessed. Despite her delight, she did have a rolling sense of unease, but she attributed that to her reluctance in accepting Felix's generosity.

She called Mike at work, full of naïve excitement. "We're going to California this weekend! Do you want to come out Friday night or Saturday morning? Felix is paying for it—I wouldn't allow it, but we really don't have the money right now, and he seems so eager. I think it's worth it to him."

"I can't," Mike said, no trace of disappointment in his voice. "I promised to help Steve with his fence on Saturday, and it's my turn to teach Sunday school."

They discussed it for some time—or rather, she discussed it and he kept asserting that, no, it just wasn't doable. In the end, she thought going alone might be for the best, giving her a chance to hang out with her pal without boring Mike to death. She was going to stay in a hotel, and Celeste was in town, so nothing shady.

She told the kids about it that night as she stuffed them into pajamas.

"I'll bring you all something. Something small—don't expect a bike or anything, Hyrum. And I'll be back Sunday night. You all mind your daddy."

Mike was brushing Sam's teeth and didn't look up.

"Felix got the three of us tickets to an opera on Saturday," she told Mike in their bedroom that night as she packed. "And tomorrow night we're going to a real Italian restaurant—not a chain. I haven't had real Italian since we went to Chicago six—what was it? No, seven years ago."

"Uh-huh."

She rattled on as she sat on the floor, rearranging the items in her suitcase—he'd need to make a trip to the grocery store, they'd all go bowling Monday night after she got back, she'd call as soon as she got there, and wasn't this crazy leaving at the last minute? How fun to be spontaneous!

Mike sat on the edge of the bed, elbows resting on knees, forehead resting on hands. His look was foreboding.

"Honey," she breathed.

"Bec, I'm . . ." He sighed. "I'm having a hard time. With this."

Becky froze, the sandals she'd been about to pack still in her hands. The air was gone from her lungs, and she actually shivered. *Having a hard time.* Mike was never tired, never sick, never hungry, never sad. Sometimes the world around him showed irritating irrationalities or inconveniences, but Mike was always a rock. So when he said he was having a hard time, he meant he was about to implode with despair.

"Tell me," she said.

"I'm trying not to. I've been trying. For months. Logically I think, why can't my wife have a friend who's a man? Then I think, a friend who's a man, a celebrity, a Hollywood hunk or whatever, the star of her favorite romantic movie, who's rich and likes to fly her out to Los Angeles for the weekend, and . . ." He looked at her again. "I'm having a hard time."

She nodded. She was still gripping the sandals. Her arms felt cold and her legs light as feathers as her body realized before her mind did that something bad was about to happen.

"I'm sorry," he said, coming to kneel beside her. "I've been trying. I'll keep trying. I want you to be happy, but I can't help . . . I worry, and I can't help thinking . . ."

She nodded.

He took her hands. His voice was very soft. "I get to wondering—am I not enough for you?"

"Oh, honey." She rested his head on her shoulder, wrapping her arms around his neck. "Oh, baby. I love you, honey. I love you so much."

"I know," he mumbled against her shoulder.

"He's my friend. We have some bizarre connection, we like being together, but it's not like you and me. You're first for me, always. You and the kids. No question."

"I don't know why it should be different. Melissa is your friend too, and Jessie and everyone. But, Felix . . ."

"I messed up," she said. "I let someone come between me and you, and that shouldn't happen no matter who it is."

"If only he were old or gay or smelled strongly of kimchi."

She laughed softly, and so did he. They rocked like that, kneeling and embracing, repeating *I-love-you*s and kissing cheeks.

"I won't do anything to make you worry again," she whispered.

"Bec, I don't want you to have to—"

"Don't even think twice about it. It's done."

They kissed and smiled at each other, and she felt the tingle of adrenaline that spoke of having survived a marital crisis. The sandals were still perched on her lap. She tossed them back into the closet.

"Go on to bed, honey," she said. "Don't wait up for me. I'll go call him."

She was in a long white nightgown, her feet bare. Usually, wearing it made her feel pretty in a Victorian heroine kind of a way—but right now, she felt ghostly. She couldn't hear her own footfalls as she walked across carpet through the sleepy house. She peeked into the boys' room, straightening a fallen blanket back over Sam's tiny body. He was so beautiful asleep. Just the sight made her heart ache. She could hear Hyrum's sleepy breathing from the dark corner. A sly light peeped from under Polly and Fiona's door, telling of at least one little girl who was sneaking in a few more pages of her book past bedtime. Becky could visualize Fiona, asleep with her face pressed to the open book, her princess flashlight burning under the comforter. Let the flashlight's battery go dead—tonight Becky wasn't going to interfere.

Hyrum made another sleepy sound, and Becky put a hand to her chest. These kids were the four chambers of her heart. She loved them so much she couldn't comprehend it, and she stood there in the dark house for some time, just feeling that inconceivable beauty.

Then she sat on the couch in the family room, staring at the buttons on the telephone. The lights were off. There was something about the anxious spin in her stomach that reminded her of waiting in line for a roller coaster. She dialed.

"Hi there," she said.

"Hi yourself, you barmy girl. Ring off and I'll call you back. You've had enough of our calls on your phone bill already."

The phone clicked. Two seconds later it rang again.

"Aren't you supposed to be in bed?" he asked.

The sound of his voice stripped away the melancholy, and she curled up on the sofa. She started out by talking movies, slyly moving the topic to lead actors, pointing out which ones were the cutest, which had the most charm, asking his opinion of Pierce Brosnan, Brad Pitt, Dennis Quaid, Tom Cruise.

"I mean, Harrison Ford, huh?" she said encouragingly. "Han Solo? You have to admit, you've given him a long look once or twice in passing."

"You're getting wily somehow, but I'm not following."

"Come on, why can't you be gay?"

Felix choked. "Gay?"

"It would make everything so much easier. You're already at thirty percent. Couldn't you just hike that up to fifty-one? For me?"

"No."

"Come on! Just a teeny bit gayer."

There was a brief silence. "This is about Mike."

"Yes."

"He's jealous."

"In a way."

"You're not coming out to visit."

"I can't."

"This is rotten."

"I know! So you see my desire for your general gayness. A little purple thrown into your wardrobe, a couple of sparkly handbags. I think you could pull it off."

"And Celeste?"

Becky sighed. "Okay, fine, you can't be gay. It was just a suggestion."

They went quiet. She hung on to the receiver, listening to his silence, soaking up all the contact that she could. She was suddenly afraid. Maybe it wasn't right to be so attached to a friend—any friend, but especially a man. Maybe this was for the best, even though it felt as wrong as swallowing chicken bones. It hurt in her throat, in her belly. She felt guilty that it hurt, that it was a sacrifice at all, and the guilt made the ache sharper.

When he spoke, his voice was quiet and a little scratchy. "When can we talk again?"

"I don't know," she whispered.

"Maybe never?"

"Maybe. I can't think about it."

"I'm going to be a tilting boat," he said. "I'm going to be taking in a lot of water, and perhaps I'll keel over or perhaps I'll sink."

"That was quite a metaphor."

"I can't talk about it straight. It hurts."

How could it hurt both of them? She'd crossed a huge line, worrying her husband, putting her marriage and family in jeopardy. This breakup was definitely for the best. But still they hung on in silence. She listened to his breathing.

Being with Felix, talking to him, having his being in her heart—it was as right as the marrow in her bones. But saying good-bye was right too. How could two opposite things be right?

"You can't let him do this," he said.

"Mike didn't do anything. It was my call. I don't know how to balance this. I don't know how to be married and have a guy friend. And I won't risk my marriage in any way. Would you risk Celeste for me?"

"Of course not. Right, so we won't talk. It's not such a to-do as all that. We'll pretend we never met. We'll just say good-bye and—wait, don't ring off yet! Don't go."

"No," she said, "I won't."

She was dazed by this moment, her whole body aching and prickling and seeming to drift as if in deep water. When had she become more to him than someone to laugh at? Still she hung on to that phone, the receiver warm against her ear.

She lay there all night. Sometimes she dozed, then Felix would say something that would wake her and make her laugh. Sometimes she'd say something and he'd be gone, then return shortly, having visited the bathroom or gone for a drink of water. Once she asked him to sing, and he did Paul Simon's "Long, Long Day." She shut her eyes and moved in and out of consciousness. It was unearthly. She stopped feeling the couch beneath her, stopped being aware of the phone receiver or the hum of the refrigerator in the next room or anything tangible. She felt buoyant.

Pale strands of light were leaking through the blinds. She realized she was cold and shivered. She must have made a sound because Felix said, "Get a blanket."

"I don't want to get up."

"You're freezing. Get a blanket."

"Sam's spare blankie is on the floor over there. Can you get it for me?"

He made a noise as though he were reaching. "No, sorry."

She hooked it with her toe and reeled it in. It fit over her torso.

"That's better," he said.

"I want to hang up before Mike wakes. I want to start the day clean for him, so he doesn't have to worry one day more."

Felix sniffed. "Do you want me to repeat my boat metaphor?"

"No, I got it. I remember every word."

"Good."

She wanted to say it, the last thing she'd probably ever say to him, to make sure he knew, even if she revealed too much, even if she took too much for granted. She said, "Felix, you were my best friend too."

He sighed, a pitiable moan, as if he hurt somewhere, and she knew she'd been right. Best friends, whatever that meant, that's what was ending.

There was nothing else. They didn't need to assure each other how they felt or make any just-call-anytime-and-I'll-be-here statements. They didn't need to say good-bye. But they did that much.

"Good-bye," Becky said first.

"Good-bye," he said.

They both hung on for a few minutes more. Becky didn't know which of them hit the hang-up button first.

She let go of the phone and lay there listening to the dial tone. Sam's blankie helped. At least she wasn't shivering anymore. She held it to her face and breathed in the homey smell of fabric softener and that other scent that was Sam, still full of babyness but also the slightly sharper smell of little boy. The scent filled her, made her smile.

She got up, rocking unsteadily with exhaustion, lurched into her bedroom, and crawled under the covers next to Mike. He rolled over and pulled her in close. He was so warm, so wonderful, she started to shiver again just to feel so good.

He kissed her head. "I love you," he said sleepily.

"I love you too."

She drifted, then dreamed. And by some miracle, the power went out, killing the alarm setting, and all the kids slept in, allowing Becky two perfect hours of sleep.

In which someone offers to commit adultery

A little hollowness sunk inside Becky's chest, a tiny wind-filled cave, reminding her of Felix's absence. It surprised and annoyed her—but it was bearable. Much worse was the heavy-as-mud sorrow, accusing her of almost compromising her marriage for a triviality.

She'd thought the hardest thing about the split-up would be missing Felix—harboring things she would've said, those fraying sentences filling her up to bursting like an attic drawer. But as it turned out, the hardest was not being able to talk about it with Mike.

He'd say, "Are you okay?"

And she'd say, "Fine," because she was determined not to hurt him again, so it was out of the question to say "Not completely. There's a pinprick in my heart, as if a thread's tied to it, and Felix is tugging on the other end, reminding me that we're apart, and that's the way it needs to be, but it doesn't keep me from wanting to let my chin quiver in pathetic gloom."

Besides, she didn't think she *should* feel so much. Felix was just a friend, she told herself. It hurts to lose friends, but there's no need to be so dramatic about it.

She didn't tell anyone about the breakup. She didn't want to make a commotion, and on top of that, in the retelling Mike looked like a jealous husband and she like a flirtatious housewife, which she thought was a little unfair to both. But when her mother asked about Felix during their monthly mother-daughters day, Becky couldn't lie. Not to Mom.

"How is Felix Callahan doing?" Alice Hyde always referred to him by first and last name. She'd never seen any of his movies. Though Becky's parents were lifelong thespians, they preferred live theater, preferably of the golden-age variety. "Oh, What a Beautiful Morning!" was Alice's personal theme song. Becky supposed it beat "The Surrey with the Fringe on Top."

"I don't know," Becky said. "I haven't spoken to him in a while. We've decided not to stay in touch."

Alice leaned back and hooted a sigh. "Thanks be for that!"

"Oh. You weren't a fan?"

"Honey lamb, you know . . ." They were sitting in Alice's trim backyard, assaulting a cheese ball with crackers and turning five hundred jigsaw pieces into a Japanese bridge under cherry blossoms. "I don't think it's ever a good idea, men and women as friends. It leads to other things."

Becky stifled a harrumph. Maybe with other people that was true, but Becky believed she was impervious to the threat of adultery, with Felix or anyone. Even if she was hit on the head and forgot that she was in love with her husband, even if all her moral convictions and sense of basic human decency were surgically removed from her brain, she always had that post-pregnancy body as a very last resort. No chance she'd allow any man to see her naked besides the one who'd gotten her pregnant four times. You broke it, you bought it, baby.

"What did I miss?" Becky's older sister, Diana, came onto the patio with her two-year-old, Robert, under one arm. He wafted the powdery scent of freshly changed diaper.

"Becky and Felix Callahan are splits," Alice said.

Diana nodded. "I guess that's for the best. I'd been worried about you."

Becky's stomach clenched, but she just asked kindly, "You had?" because she'd been working on being more humble.

"I didn't want to say anything." Diana set Robert on the lawn, and he took off after Sam. "I don't want to be the bossy, self-righteous older sister—"

"What, give up after all that practice?"

"I know, I know. But really, being so familiar with another man, I think that crosses a line."

"Steve wouldn't like it, huh?"

Diana gave an alarmed smile. "Steve? Uh, no. But how would you feel if Mike brought home some woman from work who was his new confidant? If they chatted on the phone every day, laughing with each other?"

"I think about that, and it would be weird, no question. But I like to think I'd be understanding, if they were both respectful of me."

Alice was holding a puzzle piece with some cherry blossoms and scanning the table for a match. There were approximately three hundred potentials. "Maybe it's different with men. Maybe some women can have friendships like that. But if there's a line you shouldn't cross, it's wiser to stay far away than try to get as close as possible without actually crossing."

"We know, Mom," Becky and Diana said together.

"Good," Alice said, cramming two pieces together. "Glad I raised you right."

Becky sighed. She wasn't at all sure anymore about which lines she shouldn't cross.

1. Having an affair
2. Being physical in any way with another man
3. Sharing intimate secrets with another man
4. Having a best friend who is a man
5. Having a close acquaintance who is a man
6. Being alone with another man
7. Daydreaming about fictional men
8. Having any close friends besides Mike, even other women
9. Being friendly with any adults besides Mike
10. Talking ever with anyone besides Mike

Which numbers went too far? All she knew for sure was she loved Mike, and she was going to make sure he knew it.

As weeks and then months went by, it got easier. Her addiction to hearing Felix's voice ebbed. When people (besides her sister and mother) inquired about him, her evasive answers became automatic. She avoided his movies, averted her eyes from the grocery checkout magazines splattered with celebrity photos. She wasn't numb yet, but the missing became dull and more ignorable. Why was this so hard? If her friend Melissa went away, Becky wouldn't pine like this. She no longer felt mysterious. She felt stupid.

Fortunately, there was little time to sit idly by, playing the romantic poet and taste-testing her own melancholy. Summer did come, and summer was the season of Becky Jack. The kids were free (free!) from the constraints of homework and school days. And they would go stark raving insane with nothing to do, so the Jack home became a summer camp: summer projects (raising insects, quilting, coin collecting, studying kinds of clouds, family read-a-thons), sports (swimming, rafting, hiking, Little League), field trips (zoo, amusement park, bird preserve, lakes, mountains, rivers, meadows), service projects (neighborhood widow's yard care, food bank drives), and just good hard play from sunup to sundown.

Daylight lasted for hours after Mike came home from work, and they played softball in the backyard, went for bike rides to ice cream parlors, organized neighborhood games of kick-the-can. As Mike flew Sam over his head and swooped him down to kick that can, Becky's heart nearly exploded in joy. There was no question. In Mike vs. Felix, Mike would win every stinking time.

(Here a quiet thought: Did there have to be a competition?)

Then school started and with it came that mania of reestablishing schedules, which after the loosey-goosey good times of summer felt both tragic and necessary.

September did not bloom easily in the Jack home. Polly was diagnosed with asthma aggravated by multiple allergies, requiring the house be completely cleaned of all cats, cat hair and dander, down pillows, and dust. Becky wasn't too sorry to bid farewell to Mr. Bojangles, the family's aged and diarrhetic cat, but sending Edgar Poe to a new home was traumatic for all—even Nubbin. And dust was another matter altogether. Becky and dust had maintained an affable truce for many years—she gave a cursory dusting every few weeks and the dust agreed not to draw much notice. Now that luxury was gone. What would she have to start doing next—*ironing*?

Then Sam chose this period to dabble in two-year-old tantrums (after all, the other kids were doing it, so why couldn't he?), and Fiona asserted her twelve-year-old independence by abhorring everything about her mother. Sometimes when no one was looking, Becky grabbed Hyrum and overwhelmed him with hugs and kisses just because he was the only one who remained constant. He was still his grumpy, six-year-old self, but at least he was constant.

Becky and Mike continued with their Ignorance Is Bliss silent agreement, though sometimes Mike revealed that he still thought about the missing Felix too.

"Do you regret not having a diamond engagement ring?" he asked her one evening, touching her plain gold band.

"Never. Do I look like a diamond girl to you?"

"They do say diamonds are a girl's—"

He stopped himself, as if realizing halfway through the phrase what thoughts it would dredge up. But the halting made the words even stronger, and they seemed to scream in the pause, "Best friend! Best friend!"

Becky spoke quickly to kill the discomfort. "Diamonds are a serious waste of cash. Think of the cool playset we could buy for the cost of one little diamond."

About six months into the Epoch of the Dull Ache, Becky was reading with Hyrum. He'd woken up early and crawled into her bed with the book. She didn't think what it was about until she was halfway through.

"But why do you have to go?" asked the squirrel.

"It's too cold for me here in the winter," said the little bird, ruffling her feathers. "I need sun and warm wind under my wings. But I'll be back soon!"

The squirrel waved good-bye from his tree branch and shivered under a snowflake. It was going to be a long winter.

Becky sped through the rest until the little bird returned, then shut the book and instigated a quick wrestling match. While she and

Hyrum rolled around, she pushed the book under the bed with her foot so she wouldn't have to read it again. Then she hurried into the kitchen to pack sack lunches.

Mike was leaning against the counter, holding his cereal bowl but not eating. He was looking at her in that way, those brown eyes warm and knowing, and she groaned internally, sure he could see right into her soul.

"What do you think about that book? The one you were just reading to Hyrum."

"It's great. Hey, would you mind swooping by the grocery store on your way home from work? I've got no breaks today, and we're almost out of milk."

"Sure. Honey, are you missing—"

"Oh, and some cottage cheese too, and grapes please. That's all Sam wants lately, cottage cheese and grapes." And suddenly she was washing dishes. Hand-washing cereal bowls and water cups when the dishwasher was standing there empty. Duh, Becky. Mike knew her too well—she was clearly being evasive.

She could feel him watching her. Her back tensed, and she waited for him to accuse her of secretly feeling more grief than she should for just-a-friend. Really, the pain was so minor, she didn't begrudge it. A simple sacrifice to make for her husband's happiness. But she was mortified to feel it at all. And under the pain, she couldn't bury the worry—Felix was out there somewhere. A tick in her mother's intuition warned that he needed her.

She heard Mike take a breath—he was going to speak, he was going to air out the silence of the past months, and it was going to be so uncomfortable! But then Fiona and Polly came running in, arguing about clothes. Becky didn't catch the core argument but told Fiona to let Polly borrow whatever it was, and as Fiona sulked and Polly skipped, she had apparently guessed the problem.

Then Mike was gone to work.

When he came home that evening, milk in hand (no grapes or cottage cheese), he asked, "Where is our address book?"

"The little brown one? In my side table."

He went upstairs. She saw the light flick on the kitchen phone, indicating that someone was making a call.

"Fiona, will you make sure Sam doesn't kill himself for a few minutes?"

Becky absconded to the family room, carefully removing the receiver without making a clicking noise. Muffling the speaking end with her hand, she listened. We should clarify that she did feel a little nickering guilt, but she suspected who he was calling and wild horses couldn't have kept her from that conversation.

". . . on Thanksgiving break from school next week," Mike was saying. "We had some flooding in the basement this fall, but other than that, we're doing great. Uh, how are you guys?"

"Not so great, to be honest, Michael."

It was Celeste.

"I'm sorry to hear that," Mike said. Becky could hear the discomfort in his voice and knew he wanted nothing more than to end the conversation. "Uh, is Felix there?"

"No, he is in Mexico for a week. He will not come back to Los Angeles until the end of the month. I'm lonely, but not so lonely as he is, and it is for this reason that I am so happy you called, Michael, because I've been wanting to talk with you."

Becky wasn't surprised at Mike's shocked silence. She was rather shocked into silenter silence herself.

"You . . . you have?" he said at last.

"Yes, it's about Felix. He tries to be brave. He is such a brave man! That is what first made me love him, did you know? There are so many flimsy men, so many weak men. Felix is strong. That is important, don't you think? I think so. And he continues to be so strong, but I see something new in him now. He's homesick even when we are home. Do you understand? He's homesick for his friend. And so I have been wanting to know, why must you break my husband's heart?"

Celeste waited for a response, and Becky cringed for Mike.

"I'm sorry, Celeste," he said. "I didn't want to, uh, break Felix's heart, or anyone's. It was Becky's decision. I was actually calling because—"

"So you say, Michael, but your wife made this sacrifice for you. I know women. Men are a mystery to me, a delightful mystery to be unwrapped, but women I know, and Rebecca did this for you. Why do you cause her to do this?"

He sighed. Becky thought he might be sitting down.

"So you never had any problem with it? With your husband having another woman as a friend, calling each other and planning weekend trips?"

"*Ma bichette*, of course I did! But I met Rebecca. She's a woman of large heart, Michael. She has many ways to love. She loves you, she loves her children—all four of them, somehow, and equally. I don't think the way she loves Felix takes away from her love for you, any more than her children do."

He was quiet.

"You are thinking about it, aren't you, Michael? You see truth in what I say. You see, I know women. And I know my Felix. He needs to be with her. God has made them for each other. You believe in God, don't you? So do I. God is love, Michael. Love! And so I say it—God made them to love each other. There's no other explanation. But it is still hard for you, isn't it? You are strong but you fight your strength, don't you?"

She paused again, leaving him with yet another impossible question to answer. Becky bit her lip in sympathy.

After a pause, he said, "Um, thank you . . ."

"Michael, I just had a very good idea. This might make you feel better? Why don't you and I meet? Somewhere halfway between here and Utah—in New York or Boston, it doesn't matter. We'll get a penthouse, enjoy a weekend of love, and part as friends. Will you meet me?"

Mike coughed. Becky could not tell if Celeste was teasing, and she winced for Mike's sake. Compared with this, Celeste's other questions seemed harmless chitchat.

"Uh, I appreciate the, uh, invitation, Celeste, but I'm not sure what that would accomplish."

"To make things even, you know? That's what we will do. I'll make reservations. You are a wonderful strong man. It will be beautiful."

"But . . . but Becky hasn't been unfaithful, not with Felix or anyone."

"Are you sure?"

"Yes, I am. I'm sure. Not even close. Becky would never do that."

"So Felix assured me, but when Rebecca cut off all contact, I wondered if you had discovered disloyalty of some sort."

"No, I didn't. There wasn't any. There never will be. I know her."

Becky's chest swelled.

"I believe you, Michael. But then I must ask, if their friendship has been innocent, what is the trouble?"

"No trouble. I mean, I was having a hard time with it, but maybe I was just being selfish. I was actually calling for Felix because I wanted to—"

"I see my words are already taking effect! That's very good. You think about it, Michael, yes? You sleep on it and ask your pillow. And you remember my poor Felix. He is strong. You are strong too, I hear that. And I felt it in your arms when we danced. If things don't work out with our spouses, let's still meet in Boston, okay?"

He laughed a little then. It made Becky smile. Celeste laughed too, and her laugh was light and lovely.

"Thanks, Celeste, really, but it'll never come to that. Listen, I'll just try Felix some other time."

"Yes, yes, Michael. You ask your pillow. Good-bye."

There was a click. Quiet from the bedroom. Kids calling out from the basement, laughing. Then Mike's footsteps coming down the stairs, down the hall. And there he was in the doorway. Becky still held the phone.

"I listened in," she said.

"I figured."

"So, I've heard Boston is lovely this time of year."

He laughed.

From the kitchen, Sam was yelling, "Momma! Momma! Eat, eat, eat," so Becky ran to get him a graham cracker and some milk and start dinner on the stove. Mike followed. She turned on the CD player, "Dream a Little Dream of Me," and they danced in the kitchen, Becky's head on his shoulder. By the end of the song, Hyrum was sitting on Mike's feet, clasping his ankles to go for a ride, and Sam was tugging on Becky's pants, pleading for a Popsicle.

"Always and forever, it's you," she said.

"I know. I trust you. I just forgot that I did. Or maybe I didn't trust him." He kissed her. "Give me a week. Let me get used to the idea, then let's start over again."

"I'll give you two weeks."

"Make it three."

She nodded. They kissed again. The pot of spaghetti bubbled onto the stove, but they had one more dance.

In which Becky seeks guidance from a spiritual leader

Becky made an appointment to see her bishop. His name was Andy Green, and he was a manager at a car lot. He'd only lived in Becky's ward for a year, teaching the Sunday school class for six- and seven-year-olds before becoming bishop three months prior, so Becky didn't know him well. Being a bishop was a volunteer job—Andy might be bishop for another five years or he might be released from that duty the following week. But for now, she considered him a spiritual adviser.

"But . . . why?" Mike asked, after hearing about her appointment.

"I've never met with a bishop before about anything personal. It feels like . . . like taking it seriously. I'm trying to take this really seriously."

"But . . ." Mike's frown deepened. He was no longer a bishop's counselor, but she'd witnessed how worrying about the cares of all their neighbors had weighed his shoulders and kept him up nights. "It's not any bishop's place to tell you who to be friends with. Bishop Rogers sometimes had people coming in with personal questions like that. He was a good guy, you know; he'd always listen. Some of those folks just didn't have anyone who would listen to them. But he told me he rarely gave any concrete advice because he didn't want them thinking they needed the bishop making decisions for them."

"Yeah, I see that. But besides the fact that he is a spiritual adviser, he's a man, and I want to get a male perspective on this. Someone other than you, someone who doesn't know me well, who has some distance from it all."

"I doubt he'll tell you yea or nay."

"That's okay." In fact, she was gaming on it.

Mike picked up his brown work shoe and rubbed at a smudge of rubber. "But what if he tells you it's a bad idea? What if his advice is to walk away and never look back?"

Becky swallowed. "That's part of taking this seriously."

Bishop Green was in a gray suit and yellow tie, waiting for her behind his desk at the church house. She was in her Sunday dress and twiddled with her wedding band as she told the story.

"I think I heard something about that," Bishop Green said, rubbing his bald spot then smoothing his hair back down, "about you bringing a movie star to a potluck."

"I was there with Mike. Felix was just visiting. We were all there together."

"Mm hm."

"So, at first Mike didn't have a hard time with it, then he did, but now he's fine with it. And I just wanted to check with you. I don't want to make a mistake here, so I thought I'd just ask you what you thought about my having a friendship with a married man. I know it's unusual, but it's really innocent. I mean," she laughed, "I'm not attracted to this man at all! But I want to be cautious. I did some personal study in the scriptures and past conference talks and couldn't find any official mandate about this sort of thing."

Bishop Green pressed his lips together. "The fact that you came here shows you have an honest desire to do right, and I commend you for it. I know you believe you've done nothing wrong, but there's a particular saying I like: 'Avoid the very appearance of evil.'"

She sighed heavily. "Yes, I know that one."

"So I think it's pretty clear. Even if you're behaving yourselves, this *friendship* you have with the actor looks bad. He's married, you're married. It shines an unwanted and unclean spotlight on you and your family. And besides, this is precisely the kind of action that can lead to adultery. Why even tempt yourself? Stay home, stay true to your husband."

Silence. He had a very annoying clock that insisted each tick-tick, as loud as fingers snapping beside her ears.

"So that's what you think," she said.

"That's what I think."

"But—"

"I'm frankly surprised you got yourself into this situation. From what I know of you and Mike, you're good people." His tone was stiffening, growing a little louder. "Bringing another man into your home, threatening your marriage—that's irresponsible."

"Irresponsible."

"I don't blame your husband for having a problem with it. You never should have given him reason to worry."

"Yeah. Okay. Thanks."

She left the office, her heart in tatters.

Why'd you come, you doofus? she asked herself. Why'd you have to go stir up trouble?

She didn't have to blindly obey the bishop. Like Mike said, it was really none of his business. Bishop Green didn't see all the intricacies of the situation. And she didn't like him anyway. His collars were stained, as if his neck was especially oily. How could someone with an oily neck have insight into her life? If he wasn't smart enough to use Spray 'n Wash, how could he have any wisdom about her tricky problems?

Avoid the very appearance of evil.

Ick, but that was a good one, she had to admit. She'd promised herself she'd listen to the bishop's advice, and just because it wasn't what she wanted to hear, it was bad advice? What's wrong with you, Becky? she thought. Since when did you decide to toss integrity out the window?

She stomped into the house, and when her coat fell off its hanger, she kicked it into the closet and shut the door.

"What did the bishop say?" Mike asked.

Why did men always ask the most irritating questions?

Mike was cooking dinner, but she nudged him aside and took over, breaking off the celery ends by hand. Mike sat on a bar stool and watched, fear in his eyes.

Finally Becky said, "I'm never seeing Felix again. I'm going to avoid the very appearance of evil. And I'm bitter about it. 'Choose the right'— that's a stupid maxim. It should really be 'Choose what other people *think* is the right.' How can two opposite things both be the right? Ugh! Never mind. It's over. I'm a reformed woman. I was very, very wicked, but now I've repented."

Mike gaped. "Andy called you wicked?"

"He thought it."

"I see."

They didn't say another word to each other until the phone rang. Becky answered it with a very irritated, "Hello!"

"Sister Jack? Bishop Green. Uh, how are you?"

"Fine?" She wasn't sure.

"Good. Good. Um, I've been troubled since you left. I don't know if I gave you the right advice. I think I was . . . I was responding as a husband, thinking how I would feel if my wife became friendly with an actor." He sighed heavily. "Becky, mind if I turn the tables and confess to you a moment?"

"All right," Becky said with some apprehension.

"George Clooney."

"George Clooney?"

"That's who my wife, uh, *appreciates* from afar."

"I see."

"The 'afar' part is very important here. To me. It's one thing when she goes to her sister's on *ER* night and comes home happier than usual, but if she actually met him, and became friends and was getting phone calls . . . I don't . . . I don't know how I'd react. It'd be enough to make me seriously look into striking up a friendship with Heather Locklear."

"Heather Locklear?"

"To each his own. *Ahem.* Anyway, what I'm trying to say is, I think . . . I think you're asking the right questions, and you're right to be concerned. And you *should* be very careful. And I'm still pleased with the 'Avoid the very appearance of evil' advice. But ultimately . . . if your spouse is supportive . . . I don't know. It's not right for me to tell you every little thing you should and shouldn't do, and there's no hard and fast rule. Obviously any actions or thoughts that could lead to adultery are wrong, but having an innocent friendship with a man . . . I don't know. Have you prayed about it?"

She hadn't. And she prayed for guidance when she lost her keys or couldn't remember someone's name, so her negligence here was a shocker. Why hadn't she? Because she was afraid the answer might be no?

"Uh . . ." she said.

"Ah-ha! At last, I have some solid advice to give." He cleared his throat, and his tone lightened and relaxed. "Pray about this. Keep yourself open to the guidance of the Spirit. Keep talking to Mike. You'll make a good choice."

"Thanks. Thank you, bishop."

"Well, I don't think I did much, but I appreciate your coming in anyway. I'll see you all on Sunday."

She hung up, standing over the phone for some time before she realized that Mike was back in the kitchen, chopping celery. He didn't look up as she approached, but she caught him peeking from the corner of his eye.

"Yes, it was the bishop again."

"Oh?" he asked innocently.

"He's a good guy, that Andy."

Mike smiled and knocked her with his shoulder.

That night Becky prayed about it. And the next morning. And then she kept it in her heart all day as a prayerful question, trying to keep herself open to guidance. What was most important? Her family, no question. Her relationship with Mike and the kids, that they had a home filled with love, intelligence, and fun. That those kids were safe and learned everything that they needed to know in order to have the best shot at life as possible. That was her job as their mother. And her joy, really.

So then the question became, would being friends with Felix Callahan interfere with that goal?

She spent a day imagining how their lives would be different with him in the picture. Then she spent a day imagining him gone. And she came to this conclusion: she was a happier person with Felix in her life. And as Mike often said, when Momma's happy, everybody's happy.

When the three weeks were up, Becky entrusted the kids to twelve-year-old Fiona and took Mike to his favorite restaurant, a Japanese place in Ogden. They were reading the menus in silence when Becky picked up on a conversation from the next table.

"I call her my football girlfriend, just as a joke. She's way into the NFL, and not just for show. I mean, she really knows her stuff. The wife thinks football is dull, so it's cool, you know, to have this chick who digs it too. We e-mail each other at work, and sometimes it gets a little flirty."

"Dude, you are so wrong."

"Nah, it's not like that. She knows I'm married."

"Who does she like for the NFC?"

"St. Louis."

One of them snorted. "Figures."

Becky peered over. Three men in their late twenties or early thirties. The one talking was of average cuteness with an arrogant chin, wearing a 49ers cap.

"All I'm saying is, she's hot. She wears those tight sweaters, and wears 'em just right, you know? And it's not like anything's going to come of it. But it's not too bad having a little eye candy, a little back-and-forth on e-mail. A new baby in the house isn't exactly good for the libido."

Becky's stomach turned, and she realized that the term "football girlfriend" would have incited hours of amusement for Becky and Mike if it weren't for the Felix situation.

She peered over the top of her menu. Yes, Mike had heard too. He was eyeing the 49ers guy with undisguised hostility. The guy seemed to notice, taking new interest in his teriyaki noodles.

"Is that what it seems like?" she whispered. "My relationship with Felix—is that what it seemed like to you?"

Mike glared at his menu. "I don't trust men. Felix might be in a bar somewhere with his pals swapping seedy stories about his Utah girlfriend."

"Felix doesn't have pals. Or seedy stories. At least about me."

"And there's a girl somewhere who thinks she's struck up a pleasant and completely innocent friendship with a married co-worker."

"No adult woman who regularly dons tight sweaters is that clueless."

He shrugged. "Maybe."

"It's not like . . . well, for one thing, my sweater collection is woefully baggy."

"Yeah, I've been meaning to talk to you about that."

She smiled. "I'm sorry, sweetie. I can completely see why you were worried—"

"Disturbed."

"Right. Disturbed. But you know I don't think that way about Felix, not at all, and he's never given me reason to wonder."

"Except when he thought he was falling in love with you and asked you to kiss him."

"Yeah, except for that snafu. But he didn't mean it. He was seriously confused."

"I just don't think—" Mike paused while the server placed ice water on their table. "I don't think men are ever really innocent. They always have some other plan when it comes to women. I don't think you can trust Felix."

That silenced her, and wanting to enjoy their night out, she dropped the topic until they were home again. With the kids in bed, they sat on the floor in the basement, drinking chocolate milk and watching the local news.

"You know, the root of your worry is your undying sweetness," she said. "You are attracted to me so you think all men must be. But the truth is, Felix doesn't think of me as a woman. I have no gender to him—or species, I'd wager."

"Then he's an idiot."

"Thank you. And I won't argue." She kissed Mike, then lay her head on his shoulder because she felt a little shy as she said, "I'm ashamed of myself, how I hurt you, how I was unfaithful in a way."

"Becky . . ." Mike said, meaning she was being too hard on herself.

"No, I was," she straightened up, her voice getting passionate, "because being unfaithful is ultimately about betrayal. I thought my friendship with Felix was fine, but you weren't so sure, and I should have seen that. I should have been more careful. I betrayed your love and your trust and—"

"Don't keep worrying it over, Bec."

"I need to. Because I need to be sure. There are no rules about this, so we have to figure out our own. My mom and sister think such friendships never work, so that's true for them. And Celeste and Felix . . . well . . ." She made a crazy gesture by her temple. "Still, I don't think Felix was being unfaithful to Celeste at the Valentine's Ball, because she knew his thoughts and was okay with it—though I totally wouldn't be, by the way, just in case you think you're in love with some other woman and want to test it out."

"Duly noted."

"But it's up to us to figure out what's betrayal and what isn't in our own marriage. Is having Felix as a friend betraying you? Is it wrong when my heart flutters for a character in a movie? Do I shut myself off from any romantic thoughts or any kind of intimacy with others and make the whole world just you?"

"Yes."

"Really?"

"No."

"No? So . . ."

Mike sighed. "How do you feel about it? The Felix part."

Becky was vaguely aware of the newscaster warning about Y2K trouble and she muted the television, this conversation more important to her than all the news in the world. "I've been mulling and praying and thinking, and I still feel like there was a reason Felix and I met. In some way, I think he needs me. Besides, with him as my friend, I'm a little happier, calmer . . . I can be *more*."

"You haven't seemed all there lately," Mike said.

"Lately?"

Mike smirked. "Is there something . . ." He took a breath. "Is there something I'm not doing? That I should be doing?"

"No! Heavens, sweetheart, you're perfect, almost annoyingly so. You are my eternal companion. I want to be with you in this life and the next. Felix is . . . it's like he's my long-lost conjoined twin or something. Conjoined twins can still fall in love and marry other people, can't they?"

"In most countries," Mike said.

"Right, everyone knows it's no picnic being a conjoined twin in Myanmar. So I've heard." Becky smiled at her husband. "None of my friendships should get within miles of threatening our family. If you feel remotely wrong about it, then I won't hesitate to shut that bloke out of our lives forever."

Mike kissed Becky's forehead. "It's okay, Bec. It really is. I am fully prepared to support your friendship, or whatevership, even though he's skinny and pompous. But Celeste is great and she chose him, so he must have some admirable qualities that I just can't see."

Becky brightened. "Celeste is *great*, huh?"

"Don't you think so?"

Becky raised her eyebrows.

Mike groaned. "Don't even try it."

"You know she totally digs you."

"She does not."

"She does too! And I love it. Let's both be on this marginally slippery slope together and hang on to each other for support. Really I'm in no danger of slipping. I had a chance to kiss that man and it almost made me dry heave. But you and Celeste . . ."

"Celeste is some kind of model, isn't she? And she's French, and she doesn't—"

"Why shouldn't she dig you? You're sexy and muscular and charming and kind too, and you're *so* taken, so that's just too bad, Ms. Celeste Bodine."

She kissed Mike, and they found that they had more kisses than words. Fiona came downstairs in her nightgown, rubbing her eyes.

"Mom, I can't find . . . ew. Were you guys kissing? You're so gross. Now I'm going to have nightmares."

In which Mike gets kissed a lot

The next morning Becky was going to call Felix, but Mike had a better idea.

"I haven't bought you a Christmas present yet. If you don't mind getting it early, I thought we could fly to L.A. and surprise Felix."

Becky gaped.

"Good," Mike said, "because I already reserved the tickets."

Through Celeste, Mike had learned that Felix was in Los Angeles.

"You should go see him at the studio," Celeste said. "I'll call in your names. How I wish I could be there to see his face! This is a wonderful thing. Next time I see you, Michael, I will kiss you. You should warn your wife."

"I should warn myself," Mike said.

Becky could hear Celeste's warm voice coming over the phone, and saw Mike's neck flush. When he hung up, he said defensively, "She was being nice. She does not dig me."

"She's going to kiss you."

His neck flushed darker. "She won't. She was kidding."

"She will. She's French. Kissing for her is like a genetic tic."

Mike's parents came to stay and watch the kids. They were sporting folk, both pleasant individuals who once drove past a burning twelve-car wreck without stopping to help because they hadn't noticed any commotion. That made Becky nervous, but Fiona was a keenly observant girl who was trained in dialing 911. At least the elder Jacks would be at *her* house—Becky couldn't in good conscience send the kids to her in-laws. Mike's mother had selected her countertop and linoleum patterns by how good they were at camouflaging spills and didn't change bedsheets until they emitted a noticeable odor. But, hey, they were family, and most likely they wouldn't let their own grandchildren die.

So with the grandparents in place, Becky and Mike hopped a flight, taking a bus from the airport because the taxi fare was appalling. Becky loved that bus—she felt she was having a genuine Los Angeles multicultural experience, and made sure to engage in friendly conversation with everyone around her. Mike groaned, though his fears of disaster were unwarranted until near the end of their ride when Becky spied an abomination—a little girl of about six sitting with her mother, the girl's off-the-shoulder shirt reading in sparkling ironed-on letters, FLIRT.

As a rule, Becky could not approve of children's T-shirts touting witticisms. If a little girl has to wear a shirt that says I'M SO CUTE, then how cute can she really be? Shouldn't it be obvious without the declaration? Maybe T-shirts should stick to something obvious, like I'M A GIRL or 80% WATER or LIKELY TO BREATHE. Of course Becky didn't get irritated with the textualized children themselves—them she pitied. Their parents, on the other hand, she had to scan for possible brain damage, in the way you glance at the bozo in the car next to you to see if they look as dumb as they've been driving. But . . . *flirt?* On a six-year-old girl? That was child abuse.

"You want to talk to that mother, don't you?" Mike whispered.

"Maybe."

"You're wishing you had the local number for Child Protective Services handy."

"Possibly."

"Just take a deep breath and pretend it's all a bad dream."

The textually abusive mother and child got off at the next stop, and soon after Becky and Mike arrived at the hotel. After a quick check-in and luggage drop, a second bus took them to the studio. They approached the vehicular entrance on foot. Mike put out his hands, pretending to drive an invisible car up to the guard booth. Becky slapped his hands down.

"Don't give them any reason to throw us out," she said, but there was no problem. The guard had apparently admitted stranger folk than carless Becky and Mike from Layton, Utah. He gave them directions and they were off, weaving through the maze of warehouse-like buildings.

They passed a man in Regency attire, a troupe of teenage girls dressed as fairies, a cowgirl with extraordinarily long braids, and someone in a buzzard suit who was smoking a cigarette through the beak hole.

"Nasty habit," Mike muttered. "That'll kill him."

"He'll be buzzard meat," Becky said.

"I was going to say that next."

"Sorry, go ahead."

"Nah, you said it better. I was still trying to figure out the right wording."

"Keep that up, and he'll be for the birds."

"Okay, that'll do."

They came to building #14. Becky stood outside, her hand on her stomach.

"I've got a bellyful of ice pixies performing a number from *The Nutcracker.*"

Mike rubbed her back. "We don't have to go see him. Or we can come back tomorrow."

"No, I'm fine. It's a good kind of fear. Besides, it's just silly. I mean, I'm not sure what I'm afraid of."

She could feel Mike's other hand rest on her shoulder. "Maybe that he won't want to see you?"

"Okay, yes, that happens to be precisely what I'm afraid of." She sighed gruffly. "That he'll see me and he won't care. That I've been feeling forlorn for six months because I was worried that he needed me, but he's just fine and I've been fooling myself and making a big deal out of nothing. That I made you take me to California when you would've rather gone to Dinosaurland in Vernal, Utah."

They stared at the door. The small square window had been papered over from the inside. The knob was stained with white paint. The door really wasn't interesting enough to keep staring at.

Then she noticed Mike was smiling.

"You're enjoying this," she accused.

"A little. You're never afraid of anything."

"What do you mean 'never'? You know I'm terrified of egg slicers and sharp paper."

"And stampeding sheep, and animatronic presidents, and Captain Stubing from—"

"Enough." She shuddered.

"What would be worse, that he'll be annoyed and ask you to leave, or that you'll never see him again at all?"

Becky considered. "The latter." She took a breath and put her hand on the doorknob. "Okay, shape up, Mommy. Here we go."

She turned the knob, took Mike's hand, and entered the dark. They followed the noise and came upon a set built like a studio apartment. About fifty crew members were milling around, some intensely busy, others bored and waiting for their turn. Filming was paused while electricians lit the set.

A woman with an earpiece and a clipboard was on them within seconds.

"Yes?" It was not a polite question. It meant don't-waste-my-time-I'm-not-paid-enough-to-be-nice.

Mike explained, showing the pass Celeste had arranged. Becky was searching the crowd, her hand still on her stomach.

"Ease up, nasty little frigid pixies," she muttered.

Then she saw him. He was leaning against one of the false walls, looking over a script, his lips moving slightly as if trying to memorize. She stared. She willed him to look up.

His mouth twitched, his eyes rose, looking not at her but past her, his face expressionless.

Don't look, don't look, she pleaded now, afraid beyond reason. She took Mike's hand again, was about to suggest that they flee, when the clipboard woman was suddenly at Felix's elbow, whispering in his ear. She pointed in Becky's direction, and his eyes followed the woman's hand. He saw Becky, and he didn't smile. The cold in her stomach heaved upward and froze her heart.

The script slipped from his hand and fluttered to the ground.

"Becky," he mouthed.

She smiled hopefully.

Felix looked at Mike, seemed to take in the fact that he was there as well. Then he was running. He ran the most direct route, through the middle of crew members, past the director and the gaggle of director's assistants, leaping over a sofa. Everyone looked up. Everyone was watching as Felix sprang at Becky, stopping just short of her. He grabbed both her hands. He looked back and forth between Becky and Mike, his expression wildly hopeful.

"Does this mean . . . is it over? Everything is all right?"

Mike shrugged. Becky nodded. Felix performed a brief jig, spun around, looked about to explode, his hands twitching as if not sure what to do, finally settling on grabbing Mike's face and planting a kiss on his lips.

"Alrighty." Mike took a couple steps back. "That's enough of that."

"Come here, Felix," Becky said, holding out her arms. They were shaking, she was so excited and eager and crazy to get her arms around him.

He looked at Mike. "It's okay? If we hug?"

"Yeah, of course," Mike said, embarrassed.

Felix took Becky into his arms. He shut his eyes, sighing again as he squeezed her. "I missed you. I missed you. I missed you. Also, I missed you."

"That was just icky, wasn't it?" she whispered. "We should be together, just like we decided under that skinny little moon."

"I felt that way before, but now I really know. Though I'm not happy about it."

"Me neither. Darn you."

She wondered if she should push herself away. She'd never hugged Felix like this, for so long, so tight. But Mike was right there, and it really did feel like hugging her brother. She watched Mike for any sign of his discomfort, but he put his hands in his pockets and smiled as if they were an amusing sideshow at a carnival.

"I haven't laughed well for months," Felix said, still holding her. "Say something to make me laugh."

"On demand? Not likely." She didn't let go. "You feel skinny. Are you eating?"

"No. I've been on a hunger strike until you came to your senses."

"Hunger strikes are mostly good for making you hungry." She looked around. "Everyone's staring at us."

"Let's stare back," Felix suggested, turning his head so their cheeks touched.

Still hugging, they stared back at the crew.

"Now let's look angry," Becky said.

So they stared angrily.

"Try curious," Felix said.

They stared curiously.

"Now be alarmed," Becky said.

They stared alarmingly. This finally made Felix laugh and Mike mutter, "You're a couple of little kids, I swear."

Felix had a few more hours of shooting that day, so Becky and Mike sat back to watch. It didn't take long to prove their presence wasn't going to aid the process. In between takes, Felix kept stopping to smile at Becky or to do some goofy pratfall to make her laugh or to cozy up to Mike and express his undying affection for him and for all men everywhere bearing the name of Mike. Finally the director approached Becky's chair and in a hushed voice offered use of the studio's limousine if she would just leave the set for the day. So Becky waved good-bye, and Felix waved good-bye, and they kept waving and smiling coyly at each other until the door shut between them.

Becky squinted at the sudden sunlight. "That went pretty well."

"You two are the goofiest—"

"I know, I know. It makes no sense."

Mike put his arm around her shoulders. "It was fun for me, like reuniting two little girls after summer camp."

"And I guess it doesn't hurt for you to think of Felix as a little girl."

"It helps a great deal."

A limo pulled up, and Mike and Becky stood still, staring at their reflections in the shiny windows.

"That director was serious," Mike said.

"I guess."

The driver opened the door, and there was nothing to do but settle into the leather seats, play with the radio buttons, and mutter, "We *so* don't belong here."

"Where can I take you?" the driver asked.

"Uh . . ." Mike said.

"Uh . . ." Becky countered.

They looked at each other.

The driver adjusted his hat to shade his eyes. "You want to sightsee? I could take you anywhere. There's lots to see in Los Angeles. America's cultural center west of the Mississippi."

"Why don't we go see a movie?" Mike offered.

That sounded pretty heavenly to Becky. It wasn't often they were able to just go see a film, at least one in which the characters were neither cartoons nor talking animals.

The driver clicked his tongue. "A movie," he muttered. "Cultural center west of the Mississippi . . ."

They went to an action flick, and while the lights were low, Becky snuggled up to Mike and enjoyed herself tremendously. But as soon as they were leaving, the nervous elation of Felix entered her again, and she found herself walking on her toes.

The limo driver had heard from Felix and took them to a restaurant where he was waiting anxiously, still in film makeup. Becky and Felix hugged and hugged, standing by the table while Mike read the menu and ordered beverages.

"I'm sorry about these two," Mike told the waitress. "Just so you know, I'll be embarrassed with you."

"It's just that we haven't seen each other since summer camp," Becky said.

"And we'd formed such a bond playing wily tricks on our camp counselors," Felix said.

"Remember how you replaced Miss Pepper's shampoo with liquid Jell-O and turned her hair green?"

"It was sheer genius when you stretched cling film over all the toilet seats."

"Oh." The waitress turned back to Mike, as if to address the only sane member of the group. "So, are ya'll ready to eat now, or are you waiting for your date to arrive?"

Mike played with the menu. "Actually, she's my date."

"These are my two husbands," Becky said. "We're from Utah. You know, Mormon."

The waitress stuck out one hip and gave a half smile. "You're teasing me. It's the men that have multiple wives."

Becky snorted. "You must believe everything you see on TV."

Mike rolled his eyes as the waitress left. "She's going to believe you."

"I know, but it's useless to argue."

At this point, Becky expected Felix to say something cheeky, but he was still beaming. He relinquished his hold to allow her to sit. When people slowed by their table to gape at Felix or paused to say "I love your work," Felix made an effort to smile or even thank them, but his attention never swayed from Becky and Mike. He seemed not to notice or care that in public he was constantly observed.

It must be like living in a fishbowl, Becky thought.

Throughout dinner, he kept picking up Becky's hand to kiss it, then he'd try to pick up Mike's hand to kiss it, and everything he said was completely serious if incredibly silly, like, "You two are the most stunning people in the world," and "Do you need anything? I have my checkbook. I could write you a check right now."

Becky wondered how long this giddy Felix would last and was relieved when he only made it through dessert. He had stepped out to answer a phone call from Celeste when the waitress returned with the bill. She set it down, then leaned over, resting her hand on the table, and asked conspiratorially, "You've got to tell me straight up—are they really both your husbands?"

"No," Becky said with a sigh. "This superior specimen here is the husband, the other is my best friend."

"But was that . . . was that Felix Callahan?"

"Possibly."

"You're saying Felix Callahan is your best friend? Holy—" And the waitress said a word that Becky wouldn't want repeated.

Becky did her best not to *tsk* like an old lady, but she couldn't help a pointed sniff. "Well, I wouldn't go that far."

Felix came up from behind. "I would."

The waitress turned red and scurried away. Becky glared at him.

"What," he said, "you don't think our friendship merits a few expletives?"

"That kind of language shows a baseness of mind and lack of creativity."

"Or a lust for life. You can feel your pulse beat in the harder words. Sometimes you just have to dig in and curse until you are blue." His voice was rising, audible to the tables nearby, and he raised his hand in a fist. "Go on, cut your teeth on them. Say it with me now. Holy sh——"

She put her hand over his mouth. "Enough," she whispered loudly. She removed her hand.

He picked up the bill, glancing over it casually, then whispered, "——it."

"You really are asking for it. We've talked about this—only Melissa is allowed to swear because her voice is so cute and because her life has been such that in my opinion she reserves the right. But from you it's just crass and unoriginal. And if you use that language with me again, I'm going to announce to this entire restaurant that Felix Callahan is present and eager to give away free autographs."

"You have my most humble apologies."

"Good boy."

"So, did I hear you tell our waitress that we're best friends?"

Becky looked sheepish.

Mike raised his hand. "I'm a witness. She said 'best' before 'friends.'"

"Hmm . . ." Felix rubbed his chin. "Is this upgrade going to cost me another pinky pledge?"

She sighed in exasperation. "I wish there was a better word for it!" If only she could label it, then she could treat it accordingly, and Mike and her family would understand. There were so many levels of love in this life, many more than the much-lauded Greeks had named. This instantaneously intense and evolving love she had for Felix was minuscule compared with that for her husband and children, but it was also significant and enchanting and mysterious. And she needed to give it a name.

"'Metabuddies' not working for you?" Felix said. "I suppose 'best friends' is a digestible term."

"Though it's still not right. I have other best friends, and this is different. Besides, Mike is my absolute best friend."

"Yeah, I was going to say . . ." Mike nodded with mock gravity, clearly taking this as seriously as a Saturday-morning cartoon.

"That's right, honey. Felix, you're . . . something different."

"Amen," Mike said.

"You're not like a good neighbor or a companion for Saturday shopping, and certainly not like my husband. But you are something more than what the word 'friend' can contain. Mike has my heart, completely, eternally, no second thoughts." She grabbed Mike's hand. "But you have my . . . say, my liver."

Felix frowned, pondering that. "Livers are good. Positively essential, from what I remember of biology. And good eating, if the need arises. Very well. I will be your liver, and you will be my spleen."

"No, no, no! We have to both be livers, or one of us will have two livers and no spleen."

"That's positively barbaric!" Felix exclaimed. "To think I almost sentenced us both to a horrifying death from organ scrambling."

"Yeah, I'm liking this. See, your liver isn't your heart, but you still need it. I've had appendix friends and gallbladder friends—but you're a liver friend."

Felix placed a hand over his heart. "And you said you weren't a poet."

Mike was laughing. She wasn't sure at whose expense, but it didn't matter. She loved his laugh. She patted his thigh under the table.

"You are so cool."

"I know," Mike said. "One day they're going to build statues in my honor."

Becky raised her water glass. "Here's to Mike, the Understanding Husband."

Felix raised his. "To Mike, the Nice Guy Who Finished First."

Mike followed suit. "Mike, Who Chose to Laugh."

Becky and Mike stayed in Los Angeles for two more days, sleeping in at their hotel (luxury!), walking the beach holding hands (romance!), even succumbing to the chauffeur-induced guilt by visiting an art museum (culture!). And of course, spending Felix's free time sitting somewhere, basking and laughing. Celeste was back in town their last day, and while Felix took Mike golfing, the ladies went shopping. Really, it was more of an educational field trip.

"Now explain to me why this blouse costs three hundred dollars?"

"Feel the fabric," Celeste said. "Sense how it moves through your hands like water. And the cut makes it drape just so. It will cling to you and yet hang so innocently it's almost as if you are wearing nothing at all."

"Nothing at all. Yeah, but my shirt is the same color and it cost two hundred and eighty-five dollars less."

"Rebecca, I adore you, but sometimes I think you need a friendly hit on the head."

Celeste didn't click with Becky's soul the way Felix did, finding an empty groove and fitting it perfectly. But it was the best kind of fun just to watch her move, the confidence that beauty brought to every part of her—the bat of her eyelashes, the lift of her fingers. She was a work of art in motion, a wonder of the world. Becky thought she'd rather pluck out her own eyelashes one by one than live in Celeste's world, but for an afternoon it was fascinating. And the whole time there was the knowledge that somewhere, her heart and her liver were playing golf. She kept her fingers crossed that they were having a really, really great time.

The two couples met later in front of a restaurant, and Becky did a hop of happiness to see the glow in Mike's face. He'd been golfing with Felix, and he looked happy. Progress was made!

And then Celeste approached Mike. Becky squeaked a laugh as she remembered Celeste's promised kiss.

"Hello, Michael. I am overjoyed to see you."

Mike twitched. He kept his eyes on Becky, pleading for help. But Becky was no match for a Frenchwoman with a promise. Celeste placed both her hands on his cheeks and pulled his face to her. Her eyelids fluttered closed (Mike's didn't) and she placed one very soft kiss on his lips.

"Hey!" Felix held up his hands as if to say, Am I not right here? Does no one see me standing right here watching my wife kiss another man?

Celeste still had her hands on Mike's face. "Thank you. You are the best man. The very best man."

"Hey!" Felix said again.

Celeste smiled at her husband over her bare, smooth, tanned shoulder. "Just because I am as sweet as the bee's mouth doesn't mean I don't mind that my husband has a woman friend. I mind just enough to kiss her husband." She laced her arm through Felix's. "Now I am done. Now we are all even."

Mike blinked several times. "Um . . ."

"If all it took was one kiss," Felix said, leading her inside, "I call it a bargain."

The restaurant served barbecue, but as Mike observed, it was weirdly swanky, and Felix seized the only menu and ordered for all. While Felix and Becky teased, Mike and Celeste kept their own conversation, commiserating pleasantly about having crazy spouses and even laughing a fair amount. Becky was so smug with happiness her cheeks hurt from grinning.

It was amazing to have Felix back, though it wasn't quite the same. For months after, whenever they spoke on the phone, the first thing Felix said would be, "I missed you."

He refused to forget the time they'd been apart and how his heart "was doing a fine imitation of an empty coffin." And Becky didn't forget either. Every night before falling asleep, she gave Mike six kisses—one for being her husband, one for each of their four beautiful children, and one for offering her back her best friend.

*In which Becky experiences a scare of horror
movie proportions*

Something had changed. It wasn't that "best" in front of "friend," or the
word "liver." It wasn't anything said. But things were a little bit richer.
Felix's presence didn't buoy her up only after their random and frag-
mented phone calls—the cheering idea of his existence was constant. It
was like switching from white bread to whole grain—the difference was
subtle but real and kept her from feeling hungry. Hearing Felix talk
about moviemaking got her excited about her screenplays again, and
she started working on them from time to time.

Schedule changes made mornings better than the predinner hour
for chats, and for months they never missed a weekday.

Often the calls were brief:

"Hey, it's me. What's your favorite color?"

"Am I supposed to have a favorite color? No one informed me."

"Oh, is that something adults grow out of? It's just assumed in a
household of children that every sentient creature must have a favorite
color, and I realized I don't know yours. I'm going to guess . . . gray. Or
black."

"In that case, it's pink. Bright pink."

"Polly will be thrilled! That's her favorite color this decade. Gotta
go, it's family dentist-visit day."

"Good-bye, you crazy dervish."

Sometimes they spent twenty minutes chatting about nothing,
while Becky balanced the cordless phone on her shoulder (she got a cordless for Christmas!) and folded laundry or mopped the linoleum, and
Felix did who-knows-what on the other end.

"Did I hear ice cubes clinking?" she said. "You'd better not be im-
bibing while talking to me. The mix of purity and indulgence might
explode your brain."

"Ice water, I assure you."

"Good boy! I worry you'll get dehydrated with all that alcohol
sucking the moisture from your cells. Are you taking those vitamins I
sent?"

"They have replaced all other nourishment in my life."

"Hmph. If you're steward of my liver, I don't want it returned to
me gasping its last breath."

"Simply solved—I'll never return it to you. Speaking of, I've been playing with the letters—Lovers In a Very Enlightened Regard."

"LIVER. Good one."

"Also, how about Life Invasion Via Exceptional Respect?"

"Life invasion. Like it."

"Or Lovelike Intensity Via Emotional Rapport."

"Doesn't that spell OLIVER?"

"What? Oh. Right. Well, I don't know who this Oliver fellow is, but he lays a finger on my lady friend and it's fisticuffs, mate, Queensbury rules."

Becky updated Mike that night. "'Liver' is an acronym now—stands for 'Lovers In a Very Enlightened Regard.' Hey, no wincing at the word 'lover.' It's in the original sense—you know, people who love each other. Platonically."

Mike stared.

"Isn't that kind of cute?" she asked hopefully.

"'Cute' isn't the word I would use."

But Mike got some of mileage out of the nickname, mostly by creating new and awkward acronyms (often the "L" stood for "lunatics").

Becky still thought it was a darling idea and tried it out on her friend Melissa.

"Felix is my liver. That's—"

"Did you just say he's your lover with a bad Irish accent? I didn't think that word was part of your lexicon. Besides, Ryan's the only one in your family who plays with bad accents—and look at him, living in your parents' basement at age thirty-one. The whole accent-as-humor thing clearly isn't working out for him, and I highly recommend you don't go down that road. I know that—"

"No, I said Felix is my *liver*, as in that large, glandish organ. 'Liver' is an acronym, it stands for . . . um . . ." Becky was losing her nerve under Melissa's aghast stare. "Never mind."

In her ward, Melissa had been asked to be a counselor in the Relief Society presidency, the organization for women, and had decided her purple hair wasn't appropriate for the position. So she'd buzzed it all off. Becky didn't have the heart to tell her that while the purple hair had been a little dramatic, the buzz cut was downright fierce, and offered an unfettered view to the devil girl tattoo on the back of her neck. When Sam had seen it, he'd asked, "What's that devil?" and Melissa looked back and forth, saying, "What devil? I don't see any devil." All this made Becky love Melissa even more. Especially when she spoke. Adorable.

"You're telling me that you call Felix Callahan 'liver' and that's supposed to mean something besides what my dad eats with onions?"

Becky winced. "'K, this conversation has helped me decide to never tell anyone about the liver part again."

She and Felix still kept the name for each other. For her birthday in May, she received a gold locket in a blobby shape. Felix had a matching one, though he let her know that his wasn't on a gold chain—"I wear it on a leather cord, and round my neck it looks shockingly masculine."

When acquaintances asked about the unusual charm, Becky alternately claimed it was West Virginia, the profile of Betsy Ross, or a turnip.

"Wow," her nephew Jayden said. "You must really love turnips."

So Mike wouldn't feel left out, for Father's Day Becky got him a heart pendant on a leather cord.

"It's shockingly masculine, hon. It really is."

He had the good grace to wear it that day before tucking it away "where it'll be nice and safe" in the back of a drawer.

And life was good. Sometimes in those rare pockets of calm, Becky would scratch at a creeping feeling that things were way too good and something would have to break. She ignored it. She loved her husband, she had her best friend back, and her days were filled to brimming with happily normal mommy dilemmas.

1. Do I put the Play-Doh back into the containers to save it or let it all dry out to teach the kids a lesson about responsibility?
2. Do I dare start reading that novel? If it's a good one, I'll be up late, I'll be tired, I'll be neglecting the housework until it's finished. Dang, it really looks like a good one . . .
3. Why bother to wash the sheets today? Mike won't notice until they're dirty enough to stand up and shuffle to the laundry room on their own.
4. Can I get away with unstitching the flowery border on Polly's old jeans and putting them on Hyrum?
5. I know it's Sam's favorite book, but if I have to read *Two Tired Tadpoles* one more time, I'm going to scratch out my own eyeballs. What if I just happen to misplace it?
6. How many meals can I wrangle out of a ten-pound pot roast?

These were good problems, homemade and hearty problems. And if the week was rough, she always had her nonnegotiable Friday-night date with Mike to look forward to. No matter how much Mike annoyed her (I asked him three times yesterday to patch that hole in the wall and he was always too busy, but now he apparently can make time for the important things, like watching a golf tournament on TV), she was very careful never to wield the power of her best friend against him.

Then everything changed, fast as a snap.

Mike kept rubbing his lower back, sometimes wincing, and she accused him of hiding pain until he confessed. They wasted a couple of months going to a physical therapist and an orthopedic surgeon, until Becky happened to mention Mike's pain to a neighbor.

"That's how it started for my uncle," said the neighbor. "Lower back pain. But it was cancer."

Those words could've been the most annoying, doomsdayish, flagrant scare tactic ever applied. Instead, Becky came to believe, they were an inspired warning.

Becky made an appointment that afternoon. In two weeks Mike was being examined by an oncologist. He had cancer. Cancer cancer cancer cancer . . .

She couldn't say the word aloud. It was the dirtiest, most vulgar, basest swear word imaginable. Pronouncing it seemed to scorch her lips, fill her mouth with filth. She hated it. Hated, hated, hated it, that word, that thing, that reality. She wanted to punch it. Really hard. No, worse. She was murderous. She would've taken a sawed-off shotgun to cancer's middle and pulled the trigger. She frightened herself with the hot loathing that filled her for that evil creeping disease.

But only when she was alone—in the shower, in the car after dropping Mike off at a doctor's appointment, wandering the house after the kids had gone to bed. When she was with Mike, she was a rock. She was undefeatable. She was calm and wise and meticulous and hopeful. She was Becky Jack.

"Don't worry," she said, snuggling next to Mike. "We'll beat this. Easy peasy."

"I'm not worried," he said. "Well, I'm worried about you and the kids. This is a lot for you to handle. I feel fine, I do. I'm okay. I just wish I wasn't putting you all through this."

"*Pshaw*. Don't you dare worry about me. And the kids are tough. The doctor said it would be good for you to avoid stress, so I'm creating a stress-free zone. This household is all about your constant peace. And what could be more calming, to a near-state of zombification, than televised golf? That's right, honey, you are the proud recipient of the PGA cable package! No, no, don't argue. It's the least I could do."

"Wow, you must be preparing for my death if you stooped to that extreme."

Even though she seemed to have adrenaline shooting through her body at all times and there were many nights when she lay staring at Mike's sleeping face and whispering prayers in her heart, she wasn't as worried as she thought she should be. At moments when she stopped to let herself sense for truth, there was a core of calm that ran through her, an assurance she associated with God that everything was going to be okay.

It wasn't a picnic. Mike had one kidney removed, followed by radiation treatments. Sam was three and so easygoing and stinkin' cute that Becky and Mike had toyed with the idea of a fifth child, if one happened to come along. But now there would be no more toying.

Everything was about Mike and the cancer. Everything. The entire world was turned upside down and shaken for loose change.

Imagine months of tests and treatments and anxiety over the unknown. Imagine them, because we won't enumerate. It was depressing a lot of the time, and Becky really hates a downer. But she and Mike refused to succumb to the gloom.

"Now stand sideways and put your arms up," the radiology technician said, trying to get a good angle for the X-ray. "Stretch them over, now hunch just a little . . . a little more."

"Now I want to see pouty," Becky said. "That's right, flirt with the X-ray, make it want to come back for more."

The technician cut her eyes at Becky before exiting to the booth to take the shot. After a few more poses, she left them alone while she developed the film. Mike sat on the edge of the bed. Becky sat across the room on a stool. They were waiting to hear if there was postsurgery pneumonia or (the doctor didn't say this part but they were both aware) there were unpleasant dark areas that might mean the cancer had spread to his lungs and might kill him within the year.

Becky took a breath. "I want to acknowledge the artistic choices you made in that last round. I don't know a handful of men in all the world who can pull off the sexy zombie pose."

Mike nodded sagely. "Did you notice what I was doing with my feet?"

"The parallel-with-jaunty-angled-toe? That's exactly what I'm talking about. You take the impossible and make it look easy."

Lately when Becky made Mike laugh, he sounded *grateful*—that's what almost broke her heart.

In the middle of this cyclone, Felix drifted away. There was nothing she wanted besides being with Mike and making sure those kids felt love and stability in every cell of their bodies. At first she let Felix know what was going on, but soon she stopped calling, and sometimes she couldn't answer when he called. Eventually he stopped calling too. The world outside their home seemed irrelevant. All that mattered were the test results, treatments, and the kids' happiness. Tests, treatments, kids. Mike beside her, holding her hand. Family. Oh, it was so good, that family. Pain came with goodness, she realized now as she never had before. But even inside that shocking pain, that worse-than-labor pain, that nearly frightening-to-death pain, still, her family was so, so good.

And right now, Felix just didn't make sense.

Becky was in crisis mode perhaps, and all her peripheral needs shut down. So is that what Felix had been—just a side dish? Nice to have around but nothing necessary? After the trauma of losing his friendship, how was it possible that he could slip away so easily? Becky didn't ponder it long. She just kept that household running, kept loving Mike, kept each day moving forward.

At last, the definitive word from the radiation oncologist.

"It wasn't too bad. It was localized in the kidney, and anything left we zapped to bits. Congratulations, Mike. Your cancer is officially in remission."

Remission. Remission! There should be a parade for remission, a ballad to remission—no, a marching-band number, something proud and excited and full of life. She made up a song called "Remission," sung to the *Fiddler on the Roof* tune "Tradition," and taught it to the kids.

Becky was dumbfounded by the normalcy around her. Why wasn't there a nationwide gala for remission? At the very least a bank holiday? Maybe it was the word itself. "Remission" just didn't convey the feeling for such a beautiful, graceful, hopeful thing. They should call it "rapture" or "bliss." The cancer wasn't in remission—it was struck down, decimated, defeated, obliterated!

Every day was a party at the Jack residence. Balloons and banners filled the house, carols sang out from the speakers. "I don't care if it isn't Christmastime," Becky said. "I'm in the mood for some hallelujahs." She wrote a little play that the kids performed at a family reunion. They donned armor and swords and fought a cancer monster, played by a one-eyed teddy bear that Becky had always found creepy. They slew that teddy bear. They tore its stuffing out.

Mike returned to work but was home by five each night, throwing a ball to the kids in the backyard, grilling burgers, coming up from behind and wrapping his arms around Becky for a quick kiss.

Becky was on her knees hourly, just giving thanks.

"Thank you, Father, thank you for blessing us so mightily. Thank you for curing Mike. Thank you for sparing him and keeping him here. Thank you, thank you, thank you . . ."

ACT 2

ooooooooo

Stage Kisses

It takes a lot of experience for a girl to kiss like a beginner.
Ladies' Home Journal, 1948

In which a peculiar plan becomes possible

It wouldn't be an exaggeration to say that Becky began the happiest year she had ever known. She'd never considered that she might have fallen a little out of love with Mike. When the kids came along, their relationship had just changed, their focus split. But suddenly—man, she was head over heels for that fella. He was—she even thought the word—he was *sexy*. And they had so much fun together. Had they always had this much fun? Or had surviving the horrors of the past year just helped her realize it?

Several times a week, they had cause to lock their bedroom door.

Besides this renewed love affair with her husband, the kids were at such fantastic stages. Fiona was cracking the boundaries of independence, and Becky was constantly amazed by her intelligence. Polly was ten, that unique age for girls when their personality snaps into place. She was reading, asking questions, comprehending more of the big picture, but hadn't lost that little-girl innocence. Hyrum was full of energy and began to discover how fast he could run, how far he could throw, how high he could jump. (The answer: pretty fast, really far, impressively high.)

And Sam so thrived on social interaction, Becky reluctantly signed him up for preschool three mornings each week. (Her boy! Her baby! Her littlest one, out of the house, engaging with that big scary world, on the move, never to return fully again. Aa!)

With everything perfect in her home, in her marriage, in the world, Becky was scarcely aware of the tiny void tickling her heart. At the video store, she saw Felix's photo on a movie for rent, and she felt a cold jolt run through her, an unearthly sort of fear or thrill, as if she'd just seen her own self walking down the street.

I used to know him, Becky thought.

It was a pleasant reflection, but she didn't rent the video. She might have stopped to read the synopsis, but Hyrum was teaching Sam how to do an army crawl through the Drama aisle, leaving a trail of fallen videos behind. Well, at least the brothers were playing together.

That afternoon the family drove the grueling hour and a half to Mike's sister's house because her family had inexplicably up and moved to Spanish Fork. Rounding the point of the mountain on I-15, Becky gazed down the hill to their right at the severe gray rectangles of the prison. Above the brown hill to their left was the local mecca for wind-sport fanatics. She could spot about twenty-five paragliders, bodies dangling from curved, parachutelike tops.

"Seems cruel, doesn't it?" she said.

"Yeah," Mike said, guessing her thoughts. "Floating around within view of the prison, kind of taunting them."

"Like riding your bike back and forth in front of the house of the kid who broke his leg."

"That was a pretty specific example. I don't suppose when you were a kid, you ever—"

"Me? Never."

Becky watched the wind riders, moving so slowly they appeared still, hovering in the ocean blue sky like a swarm of jellyfish. But for some reason, all she could think about was Felix.

"I wonder what Felix is up to."

"Who?" Mike kept his eyes on the road but couldn't hide a little smile. Becky found him adorable when he thought he was being funny.

"I used to feel so sure he needed me in his life, and then . . . I wonder if I should call him."

"Call him. Why not?"

"I don't know . . ."

She didn't call. The prospect of committing to something so grand was a little unnerving. She wasn't sure she was ready to be Felix's best friend again, with her soul still skinny and tired from the exertions during the illness. Mike was in remission (in ecstasy! In serenity! The cancer routed, humiliated, vanquished!), but she had been living on reserves for months, in survival mode, and she needed to beef up before she could take on so much as a PTA assignment.

A few months later when she was feeling stronger, she tallied up the time since their last contact. It had been almost a year, just after the doctor's final word. She'd come home to a message from Felix, inquiring after Mike's health. She'd called back, relieved to get his voice mail, and left the good news (if completely inappropriate word) of remission. How could she call now out of the blue? Maybe he would be upset that she had dropped him so summarily. Maybe he would be sad that he hadn't been important enough to her.

And maybe he didn't miss her.

Now her reason for not calling was that it was summer, the Season of Becky, and there was a world of playing to do. And then she didn't call because the kids were back in school and she was listless and had nothing interesting to report.

Then she started to go a little crazy.

All this time alone is a curse, she thought. A blight. An abomination. Maybe I should take up knitting.

Sam was so crazy for preschool she let him go five mornings a week and suddenly there was an entire half day free. Well, no time is actually free with four school-age children. After all, there was house-cleaning and shopping, managing the finances, getting that gum out of the carpet, locating Sam's lost shoe, carpooling to dance classes, soccer, chess club, tennis lessons, piano, co-oping in the classroom, tracking down that necklace-making kit for Polly's birthday, making dinner for a sick neighbor . . .

But there were, incredibly and increasingly, moments of stillness, an hour without panic, a time to sit and think and wonder if she was becoming unessential. How many more years would she have before she ceased to be the sun in her children's solar system? How long until she and Mike began to wither and were set aside? They talked about such things in muted tones when the bedroom lights were off. But it was not something that she would mention to Felix. Besides, how could he, in his Hollywood limo, with a whiskey sour and French model wife, surrounded by autograph seekers, understand what it meant to fear the quiet, to feel like a mother, a function, and worry that one day she would be nothing at all?

No, she was not going to call.

Instead she stuck a small television set on the kitchen counter and left it on all day. And the next. And the next. The seductive numbing was like a drug, the noise filling up the house with false energy. As soon as all four kids were out the door, on it went, always sputtering and complaining in the background. It became her routine for a week and might have continued indefinitely, but one Tuesday morning airplanes fell out of the sky.

Becky sat on the floor in front of the television watching the towers crumble again and again, her stomach plummeting with them. For some time it was all she could do, the haunting voices of newscasters repeating the same bad news all day long. She kept Mike on the phone for two hours until she couldn't stand it anymore and went to the kids' various schools to bring them home. It was a day for hugging and holding close.

They ate delivery pizza. The laundry stacked up. Becky didn't hand-wash a single dish for a week. Still those newscasters' voices crackled in the background, and the image of those towers falling and falling, mythical, like the phoenix rising from the ashes only to fall again.

Then Polly had a nightmare about an airplane crashing into their house. Becky unplugged the television.

That evening, thinking of the Blitz and darkened London homes, Becky turned on every light in the house. They ate breakfast for dinner under the blazing lamps and played Chutes and Ladders and Life until well past bedtime. Take that, terrorists.

After dropping off Sam at kindergarten the next morning, Becky entered her hollow house and shivered. It was habit to switch something on. She glanced at the television set but went instead to the office and clicked on the computer to check e-mail (yes, she'd had e-mail for almost a year now—she was *so* high tech). That didn't take up quite enough time. She needed something more distracting, something that muffled the sensation that the whole world was coming apart, something that dulled the twinge of emptiness.

She opened old word processing files and read a couple of screenplays she'd written over the past few years, rediscovering one she rather liked. During the following weeks she fiddled some more, and fussed and puttered and dabbled, until she thought, this is pretty darn good. So she sent it to Bub and Hubbub. Gypsy Annette, the producer who'd bought *Arm Candy* (only to see it languish in development hell until its option expired), had moved on to a career in convention management, but another producer named Karen read it and made an offer.

"Does this seem impossibly lucky?" Mike said.

Becky nodded, still spinning after the phone call from Karen.

"I mean, it's supposed to be really difficult to sell a screenplay, isn't it? And here you're two-for-two."

She nodded. Still spinning.

"You must be really good."

"Or lucky. You should take me to Vegas."

Karen invited Becky to have lunch in Los Angeles and talk business. Should she call Felix? Just in case he was in town?

She didn't.

Becky exchanged the deliciously cool sweater weather of Utah for sunglasses and a T-shirt in the City of Angels. It was faux-summer, but Becky couldn't relish it, because summer didn't mean heat—it meant kids out of school, the zoo, the amusement park, a household run like a summer camp. She was determined not to enjoy this trip; it was business. She would suffer through it then hurry back home to endure non-summer with her family and tuck herself in beside Mike and smell his wonderful smell.

But from the moment she met Karen, Becky felt a tickle of hope that this experience would outshine the previous Bub and Hubbub meeting—no pretentious high-rise office this time, no jangling bracelets or expensive bathroom with no place to perch a purse. They met instead at a café near the production office and sat outside in the sunshine, barely talking business at all they were so enjoying each other's company. Karen was darling, skinny and tall with strawberry blonde hair and the sweetest freckles just so across her nose and cheeks.

The meeting wasn't totally necessary, Becky came to realize. Karen had recommended Becky to an agent, a white-haired, bug-eyed woman named Shelley, whom Becky had met that morning over breakfast. Shelley and Karen would hash out the details and make official counters and addendums. But Karen liked to meet the writers she signed, so they sat and lunched and chatted, and were just easing into the topic of movies when Becky heard someone call her name.

Across the crowded sidewalk, leaning against the waist-high fence that enclosed the café's patio, was a man in a baseball cap and sunglasses, wearing a very familiar, very wonderful grin. Her blood rushed from her belly outward, tingling her toes and feet, making her face feel hot. She stood up, her napkin sliding off her lap and onto the ground.

"What the hell are you doing here?!" he called.

"What the heck are *you* doing here?"

"I live here, you beautiful thing. But I'm in Sydney this month— I'm just in town overnight for a meeting."

"Australia? Is that why you aren't as pasty as a true Englishman? You'd better get over here right now."

"Can't. I'm already late for that aforementioned meeting. Stay here until I get back."

"I'm leaving from here for the airport. Don't make me swear at you. Get over here."

"Hang on." He ran off.

"Was that—" Karen started.

"Felix Callahan. He'd better come back. He'd better." Becky couldn't look at her food. Her stomach had gone hard and small. Now that she'd glimpsed his face, she needed to see him, she needed to hug him this instant. How had she ignored that pull on her heart for so long? It was such a strong tug now, and it made her tremble with impatience. She forced herself to sit, but she kept scanning the crowd while trying to pay attention to Karen's conversation.

Finally she interrupted. "Sorry, Karen. That man's my lost puppy and until I know he's okay, I can't concentrate on anything but fretting."

"Sure," Karen said, taking a bite of salad and giving Becky that knowing look she'd received so many times in the past when it came to Felix.

"He's my best friend," Becky explained, and realized that it was still true.

"Wow," Karen said. "I mean—wow. I didn't know Felix Callahan had best friends. That's— Wow."

Then there he was, sprinting back to the café. Becky squealed and ran toward him. Without slowing his stride, he put a hand on the fence and vaulted over, landing before her. He picked her up and swung her around while she screeched, putting her down again only to hug her more fiercely.

"Don't leave again, ever," she said, her face smooshed against his chest. "I won't either. I promise. I'm sorry."

"Mike is okay?"

"He's perfect."

"How old is our Polly now?"

"She's eleven, the sweetie pie."

"Eleven! So . . . wait, how old does that make Sam?"

"Four."

He squinted. "That's impossible. How could you let that happen?"

"I know. We've taken him to the doctor, but there's nothing they can do."

Felix couldn't stop hugging her. "Can I eat you for lunch? Nothing crude, I assure you. I just want to swallow you whole so you can't get away."

"Please do," she said against his chest. "Aah, I hadn't realized my heart had been torn in half. We weren't supposed to be apart anymore, remember? You're a terrible heartbreaker and I hate you."

"I hate you too," he whispered against her head, then kissed her hair.

She wondered if she should feel bad for hugging him like that. She'd had such careful rules about physical touch with Felix. But hugging him felt about as smutty as *Sesame Street*. Besides, she was so outlandishly in love with Mike, and Mike was healthy (Remission! Remission!), and all was well.

Still, last time they were together, in Los Angeles and hugging, Mike had been there too. To stay on the safe side, she shimmied out of his hold.

"What's with the hat and glasses?"

"I'm in disguise."

"As what, a famous actor?"

"I have to shield myself from my fans lest they swoon at the mere sight of me."

"You are such a dork."

"And as ever, my lady, you are a poet."

He put his arm around her as they walked back to the table. Karen was staring. So was the lunch crowd. Becky flushed.

"Karen, do you mind if Felix joins us?"

"Not . . . at . . . all," Karen said, hitting each word with delighted emphasis.

"I'm sorry," Becky said. "I'm so rude to interrupt our lunch like this. But at least I'm not a shameless show-off. He pretends he wants to be anonymous, but really he's a ham around any audience. Did you see how he hurdled that fence? Flaunting his manly fitness, trying to pretend he's still twenty. Look at those eye wrinkles. Does this look like the face of a twenty-year-old to you? I bet he pulled a muscle performing that jump, but he'll never admit it."

"My pride is shocking," Felix said, shaking Karen's hand and taking a seat. "As is my incivility. But I can't be blamed. Some force in the universe makes it unbearable for me to be away from this woman. I mean, look at her. Does it make sense to you? No scientist in the world can explain it. And believe me, I've hired dozens."

"It's pretty simple, actually. I drug his tea. He's English—*and* he drinks tea. It's so cliché. I tried to tell him, but he insists."

"I eat crumpets too."

Becky rolled her eyes. "I ask you, Karen, is this to be born?"

"Don't make me tell her about you."

"*And* he has his eyebrows waxed. Professionally waxed. I know this for a fact. I saw the receipt."

Felix rested his elbows on the table, leaning toward Karen, getting enthused. "Let's talk about cliché—she lives in Utah, she's Mormon, *and* she has four kids. And she makes zucchini bread."

"I love zucchini bread," Karen said.

Felix waved his hand in the air. "You're all freaks."

Becky pulled his hand down and examined the fingernails. "You see these white marks here? These are signs of vitamin deficiency. You're not taking multivitamins anymore, are you? I'm going to have to call Celeste about this. You know I will."

"I know." He leaned back to look at her. "Stay longer."

"Impossible. I can't stand to be away from Mike since . . . Besides, tomorrow is laundry day, and if I miss that, our system takes weeks to recover. Come stay with us. I could dig *The Little Mermaid* comforter and matching shams out of storage."

"Storage? No more Ariel fascination for fair Fiona?"

"Hardly. Fair Fiona is into indie rock, and Polly . . ." Becky flinched, anticipating his reaction. "Polly is enamored of a certain bow-wielding elf."

"No! Not Polly too!"

"I know."

"If only . . . but I can't. The Sydney movie resumes shooting in two days."

"Oh, Felix, when are you going to give up that ridiculous fantasy?" She turned to Karen. "It's sad, really. He wants to be an actor and he has reasonable talent, but you need more—a certain charm, an indefinable handsomeness. And look at him!"

Karen looked. She nearly drooled.

Felix started to pick through Becky's salad, eating the nuts and celery. She pushed the plate toward him, instructing, "But not the beets."

He plopped a cubed beet into his mouth.

"Not the beets, I said. Hey, drop that beet!" She slapped his hand.

"Ow."

Karen picked up her purse. "Well, maybe I'll go and let you two catch up."

Felix and Becky started to protest at once.

"No, no," Felix said.

"Let's just pretend he isn't here. It's easy—I've done it many a time."

"I should really—" Karen started.

"Don't you dare leave," Becky said. "Alone, we're liable to sit around saying stupid things trying to get the other to laugh while drinking carbonated beverages. It's embarrassingly immature. Besides, you're far more important." She turned to Felix with a smug smile. "Karen's interested in buying my new screenplay."

Felix snorted. "Claimed it was hers, did she? You can't believe a word Becky says."

"Well, it's mine now," Becky said. "I won the eBay auction fair and square."

"Becky couldn't write a screenplay to save her life."

"Felix can't act his way out of a box."

"Boxes are tricky," Felix said, frowning. "And sometimes they're taped shut."

"Felix," Karen said slowly, as if an idea was just emerging, "I assume you've read Becky's script?"

"Me? No, of course not."

"Ha! That's as ridiculous as the thought of me going to see one of his movies. They're all rated R lately. He has *such* a potty mouth."

Karen wet her lips. "I just had the most scrumptious thought. Felix, what would you think about playing the male lead?"

"Certainly not. I assume it's another romantic comedy."

"Wait, wait, I haven't finished." Karen scooted forward in her chair. "I can see you playing the male lead, Felix, and Becky playing opposite."

They stared at Karen, both quiet for some time. Then, as if on cue, they laughed.

"I'm serious," Karen said.

"Wait, wait, tell me the plot," Felix said.

"This gorgeous guy falls in love with a woman over the telephone, you see," Karen explained. "But he knows she'll be suspicious of him and won't believe he really loves her, because she's self-conscious of her own looks and had been played by an attractive man in the past. So when he starts to woo her, he pretends to be blind."

"And what is it called, *Love Is Blind*?"

"Of course not." Becky said. She took a bite of salad. "It's called *Blind Love*."

Felix began to wheeze with a laugh.

"There are excellent supporting characters, witty dialogue, lots of opportunity for physical comedy," Karen said. "This part was made for you, Felix. Becky must have been hearing your voice in her mind when she wrote the part. One romantic comedy every ten years can only improve your career. You're brilliant at it. You're the king of this."

Felix shook his head. He was still laughing.

"And Becky, you've acted before."

"I've played background scenery in made-for-TV movies and done a little community theater. I'm no motion picture star. I mean, look at me!"

"This part is about an ordinary gal who captivates a gorgeous man."

"Hm, that's very interesting." Felix rubbed his chin and slitted his eyes at her.

Becky sighed. "It's *not* about us."

"Perhaps not. Or perhaps you're expressing your pent-up desire for me."

"Yes," she said dryly, "that's what I'm doing. Expressing pent-up desire. For you."

"Seriously," Karen said, "the way you work off each other! Becky, you know Hattie is more of a supporting part while the Lionel character carries the story. This is more about relationship and chemistry than complicated acting. You know this script. Now, can you imagine exchanging those lines with Felix?"

"Seriously, Karen, what studio is going to let me star in a film?"

"If it meant they could have Felix Callahan?"

Becky turned to smile at Felix and share the joke, but his face had gone serious.

"You're actually considering this," she said.

He shrugged. And she knew that he was. So did Karen, by the way her eyes lit up.

"But my family . . ." Becky started.

Karen leaned forward, getting really excited now. "A rented house in Los Angeles will be part of the package, peaches. Your hubby can telecommute or, with the extra dough you'll be bringing in, take a leave of absence."

For a minute, no one spoke. Becky became conscious of the cacophony of conversation all around her. Every table on the patio was filled. How many of those sunglassed, tight-jeaned people were negotiating movie deals as well? It was unnerving. She didn't belong here.

Becky sighed. "But—"

"Plan on about three months for the shoot," Karen interrupted. "And the money you make could go in a college fund for your kids."

Becky's sigh became a moan. "But—"

"Before we talk numbers, let me just pitch this to you: one location. No exhausting globe-hopping. A rented house for Becky's family. And when the movie is released, all publicity will be joint publicity— that means if Felix is asked on a talk show, so is Becky. We'd pitch this as a friendly romantic comedy acted by best friends. The media will eat it up."

It was ridiculous. But they'd been apart for so long, and the idea of working with Felix, of seeing him every day, was filling her chest. She looked at him. He was looking at her. He'd started to smile.

"What do you think?" he asked. "You and me on set together? A nice two-month slice of liver time?"

She couldn't help smiling back. "I think it'd be bloody great."

He gasped. "Mrs. Jack, you swore!"

"Not really. Did I? I mean, it's a British word. Does it count as swearing if I'm not British?"

"Karen, I have to apologize on Becky's behalf. She has such a potty mouth."

"I didn't think it counted. I was just . . ."

Felix patted her shoulder and whispered over her head to Karen, "We're getting her help."

"I mean, 'bloody' just means—"

"Let's run up to my office and film you two talking together," Karen said, gathering her things and tossing some bills on the table. "It'll take an hour, Becky, I swear, then I'll have a car take you to the airport. Once the execs see you two together, I'll have no problem pitching a newcomer opposite Felix Callahan. Oh, this is going to be so great!"

Felix gobbled up the remaining beets from Becky's salad as they rose from the table.

They started after Karen, weaving through the tables, but Becky had to grab the back of a chair to keep upright.

"Whoa, easy there," he said, catching her arm. "Are you okay?"

Karen was waiting at her black SUV, gesturing for them to hurry.

"I think I nearly swooned. Swooned! Honestly, this is too crazy. I can't be in a movie. With you. With anyone."

Felix put her arm in his and walked her to the car. "Don't worry, darling. The odds are astronomical. Thousands of movies are pitched for every one that actually gets a green light."

Two months later, *Blind Love* got a green light.

In which a Hyde family dinner isn't fun (for some)

Becky and Mike talked about it for hours, making a list of pros and cons. He ran the telecommuting idea by his boss and agreed to fly home for one week a month.

"But are you sure, Bec? Do you want to do this?"

"Be in a movie? I think it's a grandly stupid idea. But I'm sure that I missed Felix. And I'm sure that this is going to be an adventure of epic Jack family proportions. But I'm only sure so far as you're game."

He winked and clicked his tongue, pointing at her with his gun finger. "I'm game, baby. I am so Hollywood."

"Oh, thank goodness you're so not. But really, can we pass this up? It seems ungracious to be given this crazy chance at a fantasy and throw it away."

"It's like if I was asked to play the U.S. Open."

"Sure, kinda like that."

"Yeah, okay."

They sat the kids down and gave them the scoop.

"It would be for the entire summer. Uncle Ryan wants to stay with us, so he'll hang out with you, take you to the beach and other cool places, while Dad works from home. I'll be pretty busy. Still, we can do Disneyland and other fun stuff during my free time. You'll have to leave your friends, but you'll get to know a new place, and there will be times when you can come on set and see the workings of a Hollywood movie. So, what do you think?"

Fiona: "Whatever."

Polly: "Oh."

Hyrum: "Cool."

Sam: "Will we get to go on an airplane? Will there be ice cream? Like, an ice cream store by our house? Or a 7-Eleven I can walk to and buy Slurpees with my allowance? Can I make new friends there and have them over and can we play video games? Can I go play a video game right now? Aw, come on, Mom! Aw, come on, just for a minute. Aw, Mom, come on, just for one minute."

Mike and Becky weighed their children's responses and determined that they qualified as a resounding "Yes, let's do it, dear parents. We're elated about the upcoming exploits." After all, children were barely fluent, so wasn't it the parental prerogative to interpret what they were saying?

It was settled. And Becky was unsettled. Time to take some aggressive preemptive action.

First she wrestled with the script. She made sure she and Felix were always together, trimming herself out of scenes opposite the talented supporting cast. Her character didn't make a journey, didn't require range. Becky would only need to be a little funny, to have some chemistry with Felix, and to help move the story along. She thought (hoped!) she could do that much.

She sent it to her agent, Shelley, who passed it along to the director. He approved but went a step further, employing a script doctor to "punch it up a notch." It came back with a new subplot: Hattie (Becky) had been a young mother, her husband good-looking but a scoundrel. He'd left her with a baby and never come back. Now said baby was grown into a gorgeous young woman, creating a romantic subplot as Hattie's daughter falls for Lionel's (Felix's) attractive assistant. It was a good addition, Becky thought. Audiences didn't seem to have much patience watching a less-than-dazzling woman for too long, so the gorgeous daughter and attractive assistant magnified the film's eye-candy quotient. And the subplot whittled even more screen time away from Becky.

Next, Becky started working out. Yes, she was going to play the "ordinary" woman, but that didn't mean she had to sport a mother-of-four kangaroo pouch. She was going to pump up, tone up, get fit and fine and in the best shape of her life!

Then it turned out, to get into the best shape of her life, she had to give up her secret stash of caramels and stop making snickerdoodles and go to the gym practically *every* day. After a month and no change to her belly, she buckled down and hired a personal trainer. Justin the Jazzed put her through twenty intensive weeks that felt like boot camp, but it did the trick. She'd thought that biceps were a muscle unique to the male anatomy, but there they were on her arms, pushing through her shirt in a pleasing little arc.

Even fifteen pounds lighter with noticeable biceps and a diminished belly-pouch, no one could mistake Becky Jack for a movie star. She'd lie awake imagining being on set, trying to speak lines, the director and the crew laughing at her, or worse, looking away in uncomfortable horror. Some nights she nearly panicked herself into a fetal position.

She called Felix. "Ack. Ack. Argh. Ick, help, no."

"Deep breaths," he said. "That's it. Now find your happy place and . . . well, would you look at that? Your happy place is with me! Ten weeks of uninterrupted best-mate time."

"Help," she said, drifting off into incoherent mumblings.

"Come now, you're the kind of woman who walks into a room and knows that she's the most capable person present."

"But this is . . . this is . . . for Pete's sake, what am I doing? I can't act."

In truth, she could, a little, enough to know how much she didn't know. At least that boded well for her. She watched films, practicing her favorite scenes with the television. Actors rarely blink, she noticed. Don't blink, she told herself. Hold the audience's attention with the mesmerizing power of your gaze! But just thinking about it made her eyes sting and she'd need to blink all the more.

This movie would be made or broken not by her acting ability or unblinking stare, but by her chemistry with Felix. It was all she could bank on. So she watched her favorite romantic comedies and studied the lead couples.

Becky's top ten:

Notting Hill
Baby Boom
When Harry Met Sally (edited for television, of course, since it
       had been rated R)
Rattled Cages
While You Were Sleeping
Groundhog Day
Much Ado About Nothing
Philadelphia Story
Bringing Up Baby
Moonstruck

She couldn't approve of the sexual content in many of these movies, of course. But she tried to look past it and just enjoy the story. She wasn't so discriminating as her sister, Diana (who wouldn't watch an R-rated movie even if it was edited for television), but that Cher in *Moonstruck* did make her a little uncomfortable. Going to bed with her fiancé's brother, and the first time she met him even? No, she could not approve. But she still watched it.

And she signed up for a local film acting class taught by a former soap opera actor.

"You're always aware of the camera," the instructor said, holding a lens in her hand and circling the acting students, coming within inches of their faces. "You're aware of it, you turn yourself to it, you perform for it, but you never acknowledge it. This is your audience, this little glass disc is your entire audience. Don't look. Close your eyes and sense them."

Becky closed her eyes. She tried to feel the presence of the camera, to know where it was, to turn herself to her tiny audience.

"But I can't see anything with the blast shield down," she muttered.

After three sessions, Becky gave up on the class and showed up at her mom's door.

"Would you take on a private drama student?" Becky asked, looking as bedraggled and pathetic as possible.

Alice squealed and pulled Becky into one of her bone-cruncher hugs. "Ooo, I would love, love, love to. You're naturally brilliant anyway, Becky. Let's just polish you off. My own girl, Hollywood-bound. I'm so stinkin' proud!"

Becky met with her mother once a week. They sat in the basement, going over her lines in the script, doing character exercises, and just laughing. Alice glowed, and for the first time, she began to refer to Felix by his first name.

And Felix spoke to Becky daily, talked her through all the movie-making lingo, describing a typical day on set, the functions of all the different crew members, how best to work with Wally Lamotte, the director, and detailing the kinds of treats that would be offered by craft services (that last bit was particularly inspiring). Once she could imagine her life as an actor, she found she could rein in some of the terror.

In all honesty, the best thing she did in preparation was the dental whitening. She began to flash her brilliant smile at the least provocation. Sam thought it was hysterical. Mike began to call her Mother Shark.

"Check out these choppers," she announced to the whole Hyde family one Sunday dinner at her parents' house. "Come on, feel my biceps," she invited her brothers one by one. "Huh?" she'd say proudly. "Huh? How about that? Pretty toned, right? And I lost fifteen pounds. Not too shabby."

"Let me check out those pearly whites," her mother said, holding Becky's face still while she examined her like a horse. "Aah, I'm blinded! They're glorious!" And she began to sing something from *Starlight Express* while dancing Becky around the kitchen.

Her sister, Diana, was the most encouraging, reaching across the patio table to feel Becky's bicep and exclaim, "Wow! That's amazing. And you look great too."

"Well, hopefully I look ordinary," Becky said. "But maybe ordinary-great rather than ordinary-frumpy. I had to lose fifteen pounds since the camera adds ten, so I'm left five pounds skinnier."

"You're all muscle, sister. You're going to wow them."

Dinner was mostly over, the kids already scampering off to attack their grandparents' playset or sneak into the basement to watch television. Becky's mother and a few other adults, including Mike, disappeared, most likely to use the bathroom, check on the kids, or eyeball dessert. But Becky and her five siblings remained, along with some of their spouses, creating the ideal environment for the Hyde family's staple game, Fun for Some. It was a simple concept: pick the victim and roast 'em.

"Maybe they'll let it slide today," Laurie whispered to Becky. Laurie was John's wife, and about as cool a person as Becky had ever known. She'd been thirty-five and a highly regarded speech pathologist when she married a much younger John. Unable to have children, they decided to adopt older children with special needs, and Laurie quit work to take care of their three kids. She had a huge toothy smile, a short sassy hairdo, and a sense of humor that never turned ugly. Fun for Some was *so* not her cup of tea.

Growing up, Fun for Some had been a brothers' game. As a girl (and a nice person besides), Diana was immune. But Becky's gender could not protect her after she began to participate in the attacks. How could she help it when she thought of just the right zingers? And in turn, she paid her dues. As a teenager, her times being "It" left her convinced she was as attractive as a bloated frog. In truth, she was prettier than she thought, but what girl isn't who has four brothers?

Her brother John leaned across his wife to tell Becky, "Mike sure left in a hurry. Isn't he up for a little Fun for Some?"

"Johnny, I don't think any of us are today," Laurie said, serious despite her huge grin.

"Is someone worried?" John raised his voice so everyone at the table could hear. "Maybe Becky's worried someone might point out that her newly whitened teeth make her eyes look yellow."

"Ooh!" Ryan said, offering a high five.

"Fun for Some has begun," Greg said. "And it looks like Becky's It."

Laurie sighed and left the table, patting her husband's shoulder in passing. Becky wrinkled her nose. She'd pinned her hopes on Greg being It. He was wearing a purple shirt with a shimmery sheen to it that was just begging for a good trouncing. Now she'd have to save her lines for another day— "What do you call the color of that shirt, Greg? Nightclub grape? Glitter bruise? Please insult my manhood, steal my wallet, and leave me curled up and crying on the pavement?" Hm . . . maybe it was good she'd have time to work on that last one before he wore the shirt again. Regardless, she wouldn't be gibing him today. She was in the hot seat, and her job was to sit there and take it. That she could do. She'd had over two decades of practice.

Her youngest brother, Ryan, started them off. "'I'm *so* strong, everybody! Let me show you my impressive biceps—just look through this magnifying glass . . .'"

Laughter. Becky nodded. It was a fair hit.

Jerry, the eldest brother, piped up. "'I'm Becky, and I smell as sweet as rose—as long as I stay downwind.'"

Laughter. Becky shrugged. Accusing a sibling of smelling wasn't terribly original, but it was a classic.

Next was Greg. "'Be nice, guys, your insults are *suffercating* me! I'm *suffercating* to death!'"

Laughter. Becky pointed at Greg and winked. She'd mispronounced "suffocate" into her early teens and wouldn't be surprised if on her hundredth birthday at least one of her brothers would be there to remind her of it.

Then Carolyn piped up.

Before we hear what she said, some background: Becky and Greg were the nearest in age and had been close growing up. Then he'd married One-Eyed Carolyn. That's how Becky thought of her, because Carolyn had this habit of shutting one eye and squinting at you when she thought you were being stupid. Which was often. One-Eyed Carolyn, terror of the seven seas. *Arrr!*

But it wasn't the one-eye thing that bothered Becky. When Greg first brought Carolyn home to meet the family, Carolyn put her feet up while others set the table. During the washing up and dessert prep, Carolyn sat on the floor doing yoga poses. Fiona, three at the time, brought over some Go Fish cards and plopped down beside her, asking for a game. Carolyn sighed, but she did play, a move that made Becky (who was spying from the kitchen while pretending she was drying dishes) smile with relief and say a silent prayer asking forgiveness for having judged Greg's pirate-yogi fiancée too harshly. Until . . .

"No, Fiona, you can't play that card. I asked for this card. This one. Can't you see the difference?"

"Fiona, I told you to go fish. That means you draw a card, *one* card, not start sifting through the deck for what you want."

"Ha-ha! I got the tortoise! That's what I asked you for and I drew it! Let go of those cards, Fiona. I get another turn."

"Count up. You got four pairs, and I got eight. That means I win. No, *I* win. Just because you're little doesn't mean you can cheat."

Recall that Fiona was three.

Becky had expected marriage would smooth Carolyn's rough edges. Then she had hoped motherhood would do the trick. Three children later, Carolyn was still the terror of the seven seas. Arr.

"My turn, my turn," Carolyn said, sitting up in her seat. There was a visible cringe from the listeners. She adopted a high, squeaky voice in mockery and said, "'I'm Becky, and I think I'm better than everyone because I have a movie star as a friend who I'm secretly in love with, and everyone in the family knows it except my husband, because he's clueless.'"

Greg winced, Jerry groaned, Johnny stared at his plate. Becky's father and two other sisters-in-law stood up and began clearing the table. Carolyn grinned, looking around. "Who's next? Who's next?"

Greg patted his wife's shoulder. "I think we're done with the game."

Becky grabbed a stack of plates and made sure she walked at a casual pace to the kitchen. She was hand-washing when Diana joined her.

"Hey," Diana said quietly.

"Hey."

"You upset?"

Becky shrugged.

"I think Carolyn means well, but she—"

"I don't care what Carolyn thinks." Becky faced Diana, letting slug-sized bubbles slide off her hands and onto the kitchen floor. "I care what you think. Are you worried?"

"Not like she said, but the movie . . . I've read the screenplay. I mean, are you going to do it all, even that last scene where Hattie and Lionel kiss?"

"No, no, real actors never do their own kissing. The director hired Uma Thurman as my stunt kisser."

"Becky . . ."

"It's just acting. It's harmless."

It was true, they would have to kiss, but Becky hadn't thought much about it. Her first screenplay, *Arm Candy*, had been more romance than comedy. But *Blind Love* was more comedy, the romance a device to bring out the laughs, so the prospect of being Felix's love interest hadn't troubled her. Truthfully, she'd barely considered that final scene. The screenplay simply said, "They kiss for the first time."

"Don't you think this could be dangerous? I know you're not in love with him now, but don't you think that pretending to be in love could needle those feelings inside you?"

"I would *never* risk my marriage and my family if that was the remotest possibility."

"But how do you know?" Diana asked. "What if you don't know until that moment? And even if it's totally innocent, how will it look to your kids to see you in a movie kissing someone other than their father?"

"We've seen Mom and Dad kiss other people onstage."

"Yeah, and it always bothered me. But even so, they were stage kisses, you know? They look more innocent than those love scenes in movies. It seems risky, to pretend you're in love with Felix, to kiss him like that."

"Professional actors do that all the time."

"And look at their divorce rate."

Becky set her jaw. Hot words waited on her tongue, but she couldn't speak them to Diana—the only girl in the world who at age thirteen would turn down an offer for her own room so she could keep sharing with her little sister, who would claim fault for any calamity to keep her siblings out of trouble, who still remembered everyone's birthday and sent homemade fudge. Curse her, but Becky adored fudge.

But she did say, "Mike and I will never get divorced. Never. There's no possibility. Come on, Diana, you know me."

"Yeah, I do. Which is why I'm so surprised by all this. You're not the kind to get bedazzled by a movie star."

"Ha! I'm not bedazzled by Felix, I promise."

"I'm sorry." Diana took a soapy dish from Becky and began to rinse. "I'm just trying to think of a reason you'd act this way. I've made myself sick thinking that I should be speaking to you about this instead of worrying behind your back. It's not just me who's concerned. Jerry bet that your friendship with Felix Callahan would lead to a broken marriage, and Greg said—"

Becky was storming out of the kitchen before her mind caught up to what her body was doing. Her brother Jerry was sitting on the couch eating gingerbread cake on a plastic plate. She caught him by the collar and yanked him to his feet, walking him out the door while he protested, the cake squashing against his sweater.

"Yo—what—whoa—wait . . . Bec!"

Greg was on the patio retying his shoe. She grabbed him by his belt and pulled him along with her other hand.

She didn't let go of collar or belt until they'd reached the tire swing in their parents' yard. Jerry grabbed the tire and held it before him like a lion tamer's chair. Greg put both hands up as if to ward her off.

Greg was the cute one in the family. He even had dark, wavy hair like his Brady namesake. As a teenager, he'd been intolerable when his friends were around; but alone, Becky couldn't have asked for a better brother, funny and fun and even kind most of the time. So his betrayal especially felt like a punch to the gut.

"Carolyn didn't mean—"

"Forget about Carolyn, Greg. Worry about yourself." Becky glared at Jerry. "You bet everyone that I would be unfaithful to Mike?"

"What? I didn't bet anyone! I just said . . ." Jerry blinked.

"Said what?"

Jerry sighed. He was six foot four and wiry, but in the past few years he'd grown a round little potbelly. It rose and fell with his sigh. Becky often had to resist the urge to pat it.

"Okay, let me explain." He glanced at Greg before folding his hands under his belly and taking a deep breath. "When I was bishop, I saw a couple of marriages torn apart because of infidelity, and no one set out *intending* to commit adultery. It was heartbreaking to watch, Bec. One of those guys—he was the last guy on earth I'd thought would betray his wife. But he let his guard down. He traveled for business and he started to be more friendly with a female co-worker, started to confide in her things he didn't tell his wife, eventually convincing himself that he'd fallen in love. He sobbed in my office, he was in so much pain, realizing what he'd done. Now he lives with the misery every day, trying to earn back his wife's and kids' trust. I've come to believe there are lines that married people just can't cross, and one of them is friendship with members of the opposite sex."

"I can appreciate that, but my friendship with Felix is different."

"Maybe, but is it worth the risk?" Jerry blinked some more. This wasn't surprising. His eyes were always either opened wide or blinking. It made him seem confused, or when he smiled, a little dim. The truth was he'd built a transistor radio from scratch at age eleven. He'd earned an engineering degree in three years while working full time at the local Radio Shack. His brain was a buzz saw—but that darn blinking . . .

"I mean, of course I trust *you*, Bec. I know you wouldn't do anything. But I don't trust Felix."

"You don't even know him."

"Well, you said yourself he's an atheist and—"

Becky made an outraged expression. *She* was allowed to mock Felix's heathen ways, but Jerry certainly wasn't. "So you think people who believe in God have the inside track on morality?"

"Well . . . I just mean . . ." Jerry sighed again, his little potbelly rising and falling. "Who told you what I said? Diana? I bet it was Diana."

"No more betting."

"I never bet—argh! I'm sorry. I really am. You have no idea."

"Wait a minute. What do you mean you bet it was Diana? How many people have you talked to about this?"

Jerry and Greg exchanged looks again. They were getting really good at it.

"So, what, the whole family has been talking about this behind my back, taking bets on my infidelity and—"

"No, we—"

"—no one had the decency to talk to my face except Diana?"

Jerry shrugged. "We knew you wouldn't decapitate Diana."

"So . . ." Becky was afraid to ask. "Mom and Dad were part of the discussion too?"

"No, not Mom and Dad."

Becky tried to hide her enormous relief by putting her hands in her pockets. "But *you* thought I would leave Mike for Felix."

"No." Jerry looked defeated, his head bowed over his chest as he glumly picked cake crumbs off his sweater. "I just thought you might be caught up in the . . . I don't know, the glamour of it, and were being careless in a way that could lead to trouble. Growing up, my friends' sisters were always gooey about the popular guys and cute guys, but you and Diana were never that way. So with this movie-star business, I haven't known what to think."

"And like he was saying," Greg said, nudging Jerry and nodding with an I'm-on-your-team expression. "It's not you we're worried about. It's Felix, because he's a guy, and we know how guys can get. He may say he's just a friend, but there's no way he'd even be your friend if he wasn't a little attracted to you."

Becky put her hands on her hips. "You think a man has to be physically attracted to a woman in order to be friends with her?"

"No, no . . ." Greg said.

Becky reflected on Greg's former "just friends" girl friends—pretty, pretty, gorgeous, not bad, pretty . . . "What about Diana's friend Hannah?"

"What?" His look got cagey.

"You know, Hairy Hannah. She's a nice lady, smart, not terribly self-aware, but nice. Could you be friends with someone who looked like her, mustache and all?"

"Uh . . ." Greg glanced over his shoulder in the general direction of his wife, who was too far away to hear, head-down doing yoga poses on the lawn. "Uh . . . I don't know."

Becky gasped. "Admit it! *You* couldn't be friends with a woman you found unattractive!"

He leaned over, whispering. "Yes, okay? Yes, fine. That's true. Which is why Felix makes me suspicious."

"Well, not every man is as shallow as you, Gregory Ulrich Hyde. But even if Felix isn't completely grossed out by my appearance, which would be a nice thing ultimately, that doesn't mean he's having impure thoughts about me."

Greg shrugged. "Maybe."

"I don't believe that men secretly want to sleep with every woman they meet. It's a load of hooey, and that kind of thinking practically gives permission to some men to be lewd and morally lazy. Felix has been happily and faithfully married for eight years."

Greg shrugged again. "Okay, maybe I'm wrong, but maybe I'm not."

Becky shuddered in her bones. She was not having a good time. "What about you, Jerry?"

Jerry startled, as if hoping she'd forgotten about his presence. "I . . . uh, I'm not attracted to anyone but my wife."

"Would you have to be attracted to a woman in order to be friends?"

"Absolutely not," he said staunchly.

That didn't answer much. Jerry never even approached any non-related human females. Becky had often wondered how his wife had managed to get close enough to score a date, let alone an engagement ring.

"But regardless," Jerry said, "you shouldn't take this all so lightly, not when your marriage is at stake."

Becky waited for the rising growl in her throat to calm before responding. "Jerry, know that I haven't taken my friendship with Felix lightly. I've thought about it a lot, Mike and I talk often, we've been very cautious, and I really believe that Felix should be a part of our lives."

Jerry nodded, and had the grace to look shamed. "You're right, we should all just trust you. But you be careful too, okay? Mike's my favorite brother-in-law."

"You only have two."

"Yeah . . . don't tell Diana, but Steve's boring."

She laughed a little because it was true—good as gold, that Steve, but as exciting to talk to as a bowl of oatmeal.

"Are we good then? A little hug?" Jerry held out his long, skinny arms.

She brushed the gingerbread crumbs off his sweater before submitting to his bony squeeze.

Greg rubbed the top of her head. He wasn't a hugger.

"Come to me next time," she said against Jerry's chest. "If you've got a worry, tell me, not Diana, okay?"

"Sure thing, little sister."

"You got it, puny arms," Greg said. "Careful there, Jer, don't *suffercate* her."

"Hmph."

Mike watched her warily on the drive home.

"You okay? You haven't flashed your choppers for a couple of hours."

"Later," she said, because she could see the glints of Fiona's all-seeing eyes from the rearview mirror. That girl was way too observant for her own good.

After the kids were all tucked in, Becky and Mike sat on their bedroom floor with two forks and half a mixed-berry pie.

"You're sure it's okay?"

"I'm sure Carolyn needs professional help. And I'm sure I'd like to have a talk with Jerry and Greg," Mike said, taking an extra-large fork-ful of pie in emphasis. "They both crossed a huge line."

Becky took a very tiny, berry-sized bite. Losing the fifteen pounds had been way too hard to gain it back in one sitting. "Yeah, they did. But Greg isn't so . . ." She tapped her head. "Sweet and fun, but not so . . . And Jerry's my big brother. He was great at monitoring bullies for us on the playground—a horribly nerdy kid, but tall, and that blinking confused the enemy. I don't think he grew out of wanting to protect me, in his own bizarre way."

"Mumph," Mike said, his mouth full of pie.

"Yeah, I agree." Becky skewered a blueberry with one fork tine. "But you just think for a minute, just close your eyes and explore that aerodynamic brain of yours, and see if there's any lingering doubt, any concern, any left-out feelings. And if there is, I'll pull the plug right now and never point a finger of blame."

"And you just prod around inside that huge heart of yours and down into your *liver*—"

"Cutie," Becky couldn't help saying—he usually couldn't speak that word without wrinkling his nose as if smelling skunk three-days-dead.

"—and see if you have any complications when it comes to how you feel about Felix."

Becky thought. She aimed to take it seriously and use that time to make sure she was being brutally honest with herself, verify that her liver wasn't taking over her heart. She felt perfectly healthy in all organs. And there was Mike, so darling with berry pie smeared on his chin, making little liver jokes, his not-so-little hand resting on her leg, and . . . okay, she pounced him, right there on the floor of their bedroom. They did move the pie out of the way first. We don't need to go into details, but the pie filling on Mike's chin was soon all over Becky's.

No further discussion was needed. It was as good an exercise as any to make sure all collective organs were feeling fine.

The next morning they packed for California.

In which Becky plays the role of karma

Eight months and two days after the lunch with Karen, Becky found herself at the cinematographer's house in Beverly Hills with the cast and crew of *Blind Love*. Wally, the director, said, "For the next few months, we're all a family," and insisted on a family party so everyone could meet their cousins. Becky adored Wally—his huge round midsection, his huge round glasses, the squeak in his voice when he got really excited, which was often. "An ensemble film," he kept repeating. Ensemble was a lovely idea, though who was anyone kidding? This show was all about Felix.

Mike decided to stay at the rental house with the kids, some sporting event on television more enticing than finger food and hobnobbing with strangers. Becky and Felix went separately, which she now regretted because he hadn't arrived yet, and here she was alone, shuffling around the edges of the mostly glass room in a khaki skirt and teal blouse, while most everyone else was wearing highly fashionable jeans. Who knew jeans could look so flashy, so expensive, so skinny? She was feeling backwoods and bogus and tempted to hide behind a planter, so she scolded herself and got to work learning names and faces. Nine times out of ten, she was able to guess cast from crew purely by the whiteness of their teeth.

She felt a lot more cozy around the crew members, who dressed down and leaned back. She tried to make friendly with the cast too, but . . . well, here was one conversation:

Becky: "Have you worked with Wally before?"

Supporting Actor 1: "Wally? No, no, no . . . he's a little too gamey."

Becky: "Gamey? Uh . . ."

Supporting Actor 1: "I took the role as a favor for a friend of mine, Matthias, one of the producers. You know Matthias of course?"

Becky: "I—"

Supporting Actor 2: "Bonnie's partner, right? What was all the fuss about last—"

Supporting Actor 1: "In *Variety*? Oh that, you didn't know?"

Supporting Actor 2: "I heard about Bonnie and the other one . . ."

Supporting Actor 1: "Well, if you know a doctor who can treat schadenfreude, I could refer at least one potential patient . . ."

Supporting Actor 2 (laughing): "That's barbaric! But sure, that's how it'll be."

Supporting Actor 1: "Mmhm . . . and then it was all over the boards that she only got eight."

Supporting Actor 2: "But it's likely an affected leak, don't you think?"

Supporting Actor 1 (stirring his drink and looking coy): "That's not what Edith said . . ."

Supporting Actor 2: "No!"

Supporting Actor 1: "That's the word. And I don't doubt Edith. She was part of it all since—"

Supporting Actor 2: "Since *Chinatown*, I know, I know . . . Wow, that *is* news."

Supporting Actor 1: "Not that you heard it from me."

Supporting Actor 2: "Mum's the word."

Becky: "Sure. I won't tell a soul either. About . . . it."

And four years after the ward potluck, she felt belated sympathy for Felix.

After half an hour of exhausting chitchat, she took a break to investigate the food table. As she suspected, not one item in the spread would be approved by her personal trainer. So she loaded up her plate (after all, Justin the Jazzed was hundreds of miles away) and turning around, bumped into a young man with an affected hat-hair-do.

"Oh, hello! I'm Becky."

"Yeah, hi."

"What's your name?"

No answer.

"Uh . . . I'm sorry, what was your name?"

His gaze slowly took her in. "Scott. S-C-O-T-T."

"Hi Scott. Are you going to be working on this picture?"

"Mmhmm."

"Great." She was a little put off by his manner but tried again. "I hope this whole experience can be great for everyone. I'm trying to learn names, but you know how that can be! There are so many crew members especially, I don't know how I'll—"

"Look, I'm not really interested in chumming it up with the script girl or whatever, okay?"

Script girl? Couldn't he see how white her teeth were? She smiled a little more broadly so he would get the hint. But he wasn't looking at her anymore. Her smile began to wilt.

"Okay. Scott."

"I'm looking for Felix Callahan, if he bothered to come. So kindly bug off for a minute."

She gave him a glare that was turning from aghast to blazing. "I don't make a habit of *bugging off*, so I think I'll decline. I'm starved. I'm going to camp my mother-of-four rear end by the snacks table and plan on staying here most the night. Scott."

He gave her a smarmy smile. "I know one of the producers of this flick *very well*, so—"

"Who, Matthias? Oh, I know all about that, and Bonnie and *Variety* and only getting *eight*. Very hush-hush but fascinating too, huh? Really? Isn't it?"

She raised her eyebrows and smiled encouragingly. Scott didn't laugh. Well, it'd been a long shot.

"Are you crazy or something?" Scott looked around as if for security, his eyes lighting up at the sight of Felix.

"There you are!" Felix bounded into the glass-walled room, owning the space at once. He was wearing a white button-down shirt with jeans—casual, simple, and yet he seemed to bury everyone around him in the shadow of his brilliance.

Scott straightened up. "Mr. Callahan! It's such an honor to meet you. Do you have a free moment? I have a thought I'd like to—"

Felix waved politely at the young man, but his eyes stayed on Becky. "Look at you! I don't care if you're wearing the most absurd costume I've ever seen—you're still gorgeous to behold. Good enough to eat. You belong on a platter."

She made noises of protest as he picked her up and set her on an empty platter. He leaned against the table beside her.

"Do you have any idea how tedious these things can be? Celeste stopped coming to any parties that didn't include media, and I can't blame her. But you are the sun in this gloom."

"The sun?"

"Well, at least a planet."

"Hey, I lost fifteen pounds!"

"And you look smashing." He turned to Scott. "Doesn't she look smashing? Let me warn you away from her or you're likely to fall in love. And it's a most inconvenient thing to be in love with this woman. She winters *and* summers in Utah."

"I'll, uh, I'll keep that in mind."

"You better."

"When can I get off the table?" Becky asked.

"Becky," Felix said with lips nearly closed, as if what he was telling her was too embarrassing for others to hear. "It's a common custom at Hollywood parties to sit on platters. Don't protest or you'll look the novice."

Scott was now standing even closer with a hopeful grin plastered to his face.

"And you're still here," Felix said. "Was there something you wanted?"

Scott straightened his tie. "I just . . . I had an idea for another scene between our two characters. I play Buddy? The busboy? You know? Anyway, I think it could be showstopper funny and I wanted to pitch the idea to you, maybe over lunch this week?"

Felix stared at him in silence for so long that Scott took a step back. Felix leaned toward Becky and whispered in her ear, "What do you think?"

"Do I get to be karma today?" she whispered back.

"Of course."

"Then, no."

"Was he rude to you?"

"Don't blame him. He probably had a miserable childhood."

Felix's eyes narrowed but he still spoke under his breath. "No one belittles you, not in my town. Except me. Those are the rules. Shall I ask him to audition for a stunt role and you can display your right hook?"

Becky looked over Felix's shoulder to see the young man glance around as though unsure whether he should leave.

"Poor kid," she said quietly. "Maybe you should at least hear his pitch."

Felix leaned in closer as if they plotted something illegal. "Not a chance. Maybe he should have treated my best mate better. Karma's a bitch."

"Hey, I thought *I* was karma."

"Bitch in the very best sense of the term."

"Like a dog, you mean. A female dog of good breeding and a lovely, glossy coat."

"Exactly, a best-in-breed bitch, a real show bitch."

"Let him down easy," Becky begged as Felix began to turn.

"What was your name? Buddy the busboy? A quick tip. You never know who in this town is important, so it's best to assume that *everyone* is important. Do you understand me?"

Buddy the busboy nodded, looking a little afraid.

"I want you to repeat it back to me," Felix said.

"Uh, everyone is important."

"Without the 'uh,' Buddy the busboy."

Scott's eyes widened in genuine fear. "Everyone Is Important . . . sir," he said, his voice cracking over the last word as if he just hit puberty.

"Very good. And since Becky forgives you, I will too, and you may keep your current role. Now do us a favor—run to the kitchen and see if they can't drum up a hot chocolate for this movie's star."

Buddy skedaddled. Felix turned back to Becky, smiling proudly.

"See how easy I was on him?"

She patted his head. "I am so proud. But it's going a bit far to say I'm the star."

Felix blinked innocently. "Oh . . . did you think the hot chocolate was for you?"

She slugged his shoulder. "Stop that."

"At any rate, don't think you can hide in this movie. Anthony Hopkins was only in *Silence of the Lambs* for seventeen minutes. You still have enough screen time to steal the show."

"Ack! No, I don't want to steal it, stealing is bad, thou shalt not steal a show and take any focus away from Felix Callahan and promise me you'll steal it instead so no one will even be watching me when I'm on-screen—promise!"

Her hands were gripping the front of his shirt in panic, and she realized it wasn't cotton like she'd thought. She fingered the cloth.

"Ooh, silky."

He removed her fingers from his shirt, smoothing it flat. "Are you calmed?"

"Did you promise?"

He sighed heavily. "Not that I have any choice in the matter. Everywhere I go, I simply dazzle."

"You simply dazzle . . . Yeah . . . okay, that did the trick. I'm calmed."

"It really is wonderful to see you . . . even though I have no idea what you're wearing. Is that a . . . skirt? Never mind. Mostly I'm happy because the fact that you're here means you're not going to back out."

"Did you think I would?"

Felix examined a tiny quiche shaped like a heart then put it back on the tray. "After all those panicked phone calls? Yes, it crossed my mind."

"I'm terrified, Felix. But there's no question about backing out. My teeth are just too gorgeously white. Besides, I lost fifteen pounds, and I didn't even sniff a snickerdoodle for six months. That kind of sacrifice can't be wasted."

"You're going to be beautiful," Felix said.

"I hope so."

"You are. You already are."

He sounded so sure. Either he believed it or he was an excellent actor.

They wandered into the enormous sitting room with a full-sized bar and six separate sofas. Some of the crew had set up a karaoke machine on the raised fireplace. The first song was "I Will Survive," performed by many of the women and some men who weren't afraid to shake their groove thing. A couple of soloists followed, performing a slow Elton John and an off-key Lisa Loeb. Someone hollered for Felix. He shook his head, content to sit at the bar with Becky while she nursed her hot chocolate.

"Go on," she said. "They probably don't even know that you can sing. Put them all to shame."

"Not in the mood."

"Of course you are."

"No, not drunk enough."

"That's a lousy excuse. Go on."

Felix's expression turned sly. "Only if you perform a duet with me."

"Nooo," Becky said, shaking her head. She still had nightmares about auditioning for musicals, and there was that whole incident where her brothers caught her singing to the mirror. "I don't sing—I warble. I croak. And I don't know everyone yet, and Buddy the busboy thought I was too lowly to contemplate, and I still feel a little vulnerable and I'm not anxious to make everyone hate me. And besides, it would be a bad idea."

The sly expression evolved into mischievous. Felix went to flip through the list of songs while one of the producers (not Matthias or Karen) screeched a Céline Dion song. At the end, Felix hopped up on the brick stage, to the raucous pleasure of the audience.

"This is a duet, but since she won't join me, I dedicate this song to my best mate, Becky."

She hid behind her hands. The song was "Islands in the Stream." There was no way she was going to squawk through any song in front of all those strangers, but especially not that one. She thought it was kind of lame.

She was wrong.

Felix sang both the Dolly Parton and Kenny Rogers parts, and Becky could objectively say that the bouncy country tune became a little sexy with his British accent. He looked at her as he sang, making pleading motions. Soon everyone was staring. Some prodded her, saying helpful things like, "Go on, go on . . ." Her bar stool was becoming more awkward than a stage.

"I can't stand being serenaded," she said, jumping up there and grabbing a spare mic.

On the fly, Becky changed the word "lover" to "liver" and realized that Felix had done the same, and after a few bars, she was having fun. Felix didn't leave her alone, still singing the Dolly Parton parts so Becky never had to go solo. With a little bit of hot chocolate in her system, she relaxed, letting her body do the karaoke sway. The really delicious part was joining her own voice with Felix's, hearing how he made her sound better. It gave her chills.

She wondered, Is this what it'll be like to act with him?

She hoped. She even crossed her fingers behind her back.

Let this be it, she prayed. Let his talent pull me up higher, rather than my amateur self pull him down. Let it be good. Please let it be good.

There was wild applause when they were done, and someone stuck in "Summer Nights," so they stayed at the mic. Felix really hammed it up this time, forcing a severe John Travolta accent and improvising some semi-impressive lunge moves. Wally laughed so hard he kept having to remove his glasses and wipe his eyes. Several women and men joined them for the chorus parts. Someone tossed up a pair of pink underwear. It was one of the weirdest experiences Becky could remember. She grabbed Felix's arm when they were done and said, "You're a wild man."

"You're my lady."

"Don't you dare sing that Kenny Rogers number to me."

The music cued up.

"Felix," Becky said like a warning.

"Lady," he sang.

She left the stage, returning to her bar stool and her cold hot chocolate. He really could be exasperating.

She was staring into the milky brown goodness when she detected a change in Felix's tone. He wasn't playing with the song anymore, he was digging into the words, finding beauty in their resonance, laying meaning on every note. It became sultry, tangy, heart-stopping. She felt a cold pitch in her belly and kept her eyes down. Was he looking at her? Singing like that and looking at her? What should she do? Laugh and pretend he's kidding, glare and scold, or run away?

He took the notes up, rising with passion so inappropriate that running away seemed her only option, and then the crowd began to hoot and applaud midsong. Becky glanced up. Celeste had arrived. She was approaching the karaoke stage in slow, lingering strides, her eyes on Felix. And his eyes were on her. He was singing to his wife, and no Kenny Rogers number had ever sounded so heated. All they did was look at each other, but Becky was prepared to book them a hotel room and call them a taxi.

Celeste kept moving forward, timing her strides so that she arrived within touching distance just as the song ended. Felix put one arm around her waist and pulled her in, planting his mouth on her neck. Her arms rested at her sides, her smile turned to the room, and she said, "Hello all. I hope I am not crashing the party?"

No, no! everyone assured, offering her drinks and hors d'oeuvre platters. She would have resembled a gigantic heavenly body pulling all the lesser bodies into her orbit, except that she was so thin.

Felix gazed at his wife as she gazed at her audience, and his complete adoration emanated out in nearly tangible waves. Becky sighed a happy sigh. Love was good.

A new song started up, and Felix and Celeste crossed the room to Becky. Celeste sat at the bar, and Felix stood behind, his arm over his wife's.

"You came," he said.

"Mmhmm." Celeste leaned her head against his chest. "I was home and thinking, where do I want to be now? I want to be with my husband. It has been a long time since you filmed so close to home, so I have decided I will stay close too. This summer, I am everywhere."

Her eyes flicked to Becky. The tiniest arctic breeze blew between the two women, hardly worth mentioning, but that it gave Becky goose bumps.

But the moment passed, and Celeste was all adoring graciousness, introducing Becky to anyone she didn't know, hooking her arm through Becky's and enveloping her in her warmness. And Felix stayed near Celeste.

Becky watched him and remembered what Diana had said. She was going to have to kiss that man. And not just kiss him, but *kiss* him.

She'd think about it tomorrow.

In which Becky tries to find her Hollywood legs

There was a read-through the next day, with the cast sitting around a conference table at Bub and Hubbub (no gypsies spotted). Becky had the entire script memorized, but she held on to her copy, her gaze clinging to the words on the page. It saved her from having to look at Wally or Felix, in case they were frowning. She was pretty sure she sounded like the lead in the junior high school play. But Felix was next to her, and his voice was so warm, and he was so funny! Soon she relaxed, and it seemed to go okay. More or less.

She'd already gone through the preproduction hullabaloo—screen tests, haircuts, wardrobe tests, the long debate about whether, as Hattie, Becky should wear glasses (in the end, it was decided yes, in some scenes). And with her hair short and perky, and new clothes on her body, Becky found it was easier to feel like someone else, someone who might have business being in front of a camera.

Before her first day on set, Felix came to the Jacks' rented ranch house and rehearsed in private. At least, in as much privacy as anyone can have in a house with four children. While they went over lines, Sam and Hyrum wrestled at their feet.

"When I pin you like this, you've gotta swish your legs around. That's how you get *leverage.*"

"Okay, Hyrum. Okay."

"See, I'm heavier and stronger than you, so you've got to use your size and speed as leverage against me. You can't move your upper body, right? So you need to get moving with your lower body and create leverage."

"Okay, Hyrum. Okay. I'll do leverage."

Polly lounged on the couch, her pink-panted legs straight up in the air, pointed toes swishing back and forth in an upside-down ballet move. She was on the phone with one (or more) of her friends back in Layton, and her side of the conversation went like this:

"Yeah . . . yeah . . . yeah . . . Oh? . . . Oh. . . . Yeah . . . yeah . . . Yeah? . . . Cool . . . Okay . . . No . . . Sure . . . But . . . yeah . . ."

Fiona was in the kitchen listening to some fairly loud music, and from the slight quaking of the floor, it seemed, practicing a dance that involved a lot of stomping.

The noise didn't bother Felix; he had an actor's focus. And it was easy for Becky to tune them out, a skill she'd perfected long ago. When her children were in trouble, she had dog ears, picking up a cry for help from a mile away. But let them be muddled in a nonlethal sibling spat or a tirade of whining for something they couldn't have, and Becky might as well have been relaxing in the countryside, no sound but the wind clicking through the sycamore leaves.

The only hitch was Ryan, who couldn't decide if he wanted to be in awe of Felix or rib his big sister. It didn't take her long to banish him to his bedroom.

Mike came in from the study to perch on the fireplace and read the newspaper, occasionally looking at the duo with an inscrutable expression.

"How's it look, honey?" Becky asked.

"You're great, Bec, but your partner sounds a little . . . British."

Felix gave a wan smile. "That is a tragedy."

"Don't beat yourself up," Mike said. "It takes a lot of practice to achieve our level of hick and make it sound natural."

Becky laughed. She couldn't get enough of Mike being smart with Felix.

The rehearsals helped, but the next morning she arrived on location at the deli where her first scene would be shot, and she panicked. Her legs wobbled as if her bones considered dissolving, her heart raced so much that she found herself looking around for something life-threatening to face.

Felix patted her shoulder and shook his head with a casual, friendly frown, as if to say, "It's nothing. Don't spend a moment worrying. Everything's fine."

She nodded, as if to say, "Sure, okay. Everything's fine. You're right."

It wasn't, so she had to pretend it was. That was the real acting.

She straightened and faced the room, robing herself in her persona of Mommy of Four. If there was a problem (and there would always be a problem), then she could fix it. She couldn't do everything, would never know everything, but there was no sliver of doubt in her that she was the best person on this earth to be her children's mother.

I'm the best person in this room to play this part, she told herself. So stop trembling and moping and just do it, Becky.

She began to do it; she began to feel it. Felix made it easier. Acting with him was like dancing with him—he led lightly, casually, so that she barely felt his hand on her back, and yet when he led, she didn't miss a step.

"You're a master," she whispered to him after their first take.

He smiled with just a touch of the smug. "You may be able to clean a house, raise four children, bake zucchini bread, and whistle Rachmaninoff at the same time, but this"—he waved a hand around him—"is my world."

"Oh, you are so lucky I'm trying to be on my best behavior and can't laugh at you right now."

"I'm sure you'll make up for it later."

That first shot took twelve takes, but at last the director called, "Print it."

Felix whispered, "See, I said you would be beautiful."

They wrapped for the day before dinnertime, and Becky rushed home to her family, spilling into the sofa and exhaling loudly.

"Call off the search. I survived."

In moments Sam was on top of her, burrowing into her arms till she hugged him tight. Mike sat on the edge of the couch, lifting her feet onto his lap.

"How'd it go?"

"It went. Okay, I guess. Have you eaten yet?"

Mike shook his head, and his stomach squeaked.

"Hello, empty belly. Did you forget to have lunch?"

"No, I . . ." Mike shrugged. "I've been fasting for you today, praying it'd go well. You know."

"Aw, hon." She reached over burrowing Sam to grab Mike's hand. "That was the extra push I felt. Your prayers were floating all around me, like the birds in *Cinderella* that help her get dressed. You have bird prayers."

He shrugged again. "I try."

"Thank you." It made her feel a little misty-eyed, so she didn't say much else until dinner: take-out Chinese.

After the first couple of weeks, Becky relaxed into this new, strange, but still wonderful kind of summer. The kids were having a blast going to the beach every day with Uncle Ryan and taking excursions to all the Los Angeles places they'd seen in the movies. And on Becky's days off the whole family celebrated enough to shame a decade of summers.

One Saturday Celeste and Felix sailed the whole Jack family to Catalina, while Uncle Ryan took the day off to meet some indie filmmakers Felix had introduced him to. Celeste was magical, tanned and lovely in short-shorts and a striped shirt, her chestnut hair aflame in the wind. Becky wondered if it got tiring, being so beautiful all the time, if Celeste ever wished to take a break and just be normal. She was darling with the girls, sitting on the bow with their legs dangling over, bare feet tickled by ocean spray.

Mike was always eager to learn something new and manly, so he and Felix ran the boat, chatting about sails and rudders and chutes and ladders and who-knew-what. She made a mental note that the two men could in fact carry on a conversation, if supplied a practical topic.

As they traveled over heaving waves and under hard blue sky, Becky hid behind sunglasses and pretended to steer so she could watch her little boys undetected. The moment Hyrum suspected his mom was observing him and his brother play—and worse, approving!—would be the moment he called it quits, returning to doleful ways, muttering with old anger about being forced away from his friends all summer. But for now, Hyrum and Sam ran around with kerchiefs on their heads, yelling "Ahoy!" and "Thar she blows!" The sight was chocolate on her tongue that never melted.

They ate fresh seafood at a restaurant facing the bay, and eight separate people passed by their table with the express purpose of saying to Felix, "I love your work." That was what everyone said, not just on Catalina, but at Disneyland and at restaurants and walking down the street helping Polly find chic souvenirs for her friends back home: "I love your work." Why those four words? Sure, there were also the "I'm a huge fan" people, and the flustered "I can't believe it's really you" people, but 90 percent of the time, if words were spoken, they were "I love your work."

"Is that the official celebrity-sighting motto?" Becky wondered aloud.

"Must be a new fad," Felix said. "Usually all I hear is, 'My baby kicked when I saw you! It must be a spiritual sign. Be my best friend,' that sort of thing."

Really, the "I love your work" people were the least annoying. Felix was regularly accosted by young filmmakers as well as seasoned filmmakers, philanthropists wanting money or to use his name, and of course the autograph seekers and tourists with eager cameras.

"Everyone wants something from you," Becky said. "Not *you*, the real you, but the superstar Felix Callahan. It must get tiring. It seems like they don't care about you—they just want what you can do for them."

"Everyone but you, darling."

Her tear ducts stung, and she blinked rapidly and turned away, wondering if it was true.

Sometimes Felix groaned at the attention from fans, sometimes he pretended deafness, but more and more often, he managed to respond politely.

"Take a look at our boy, Celeste," Becky said. "It's getting so we can take him out in public."

And they did go out quite a bit, with Celeste and Felix slipping into the Jack family without much fuss. The couple was a real boon to outings—they got seated quickly at restaurants, and family games of soccer were much more sporting.

So days off were great, but days on set weren't too shabby either.

Becky hadn't worked outside the home since Fiona was born, and so much time away from the kids was worrying (Uncle Ryan let you do what?!), but then again, she got to work alongside Felix.

"Hello, passably talented," she'd say as soon as she ran into him on set, and give him two cheek kisses—Becky was a pro at this now, no lip contact, just the barest grazing of cheeks.

"Hello, darling," he'd say.

Then they'd be über-professional, talk only about the upcoming scene, sit as quietly as church mice, listening to the director, waiting their turn. But as soon as they were released on a lunch break or filming wrapped for the day, it was like school was out for the summer.

The set was a petri dish for practical jokes. A live donkey awaited Felix in his trailer, thoughtfully nibbling on a towel. The wardrobe mistress showed Becky her outfit for an upcoming scene—a bustier and stilettos. Becky blushed and stuttered until she heard Felix snickering behind the dress racks. At Becky's request, Lorraine in craft services baked a muffin filled with mushed anchovies especially for Felix. The following week a handsome young police officer showed up on set looking for Becky, which was alarming until he pushed Play on a CD player and began to sing "Happy Birthday."

A singing telegram! she thought. It's not my birthday, but what an unusually sweet prank for Felix to—

The music dipped with some heavy bass. The officer removed his jacket. Becky put it over her head and waited in blindness until the performance was over. She was only a little sorry to miss it. From their hoots, the female crew members had sounded sincerely entertained.

But mostly Felix and Becky were model children, who sat quietly and made faces at each other behind the director's back. There was plenty of time for this. Wally liked to have Becky on hand as the screenwriter, ready for a powwow or to rewrite a line, so even though her acting part was small, she was there as much as Felix.

"You are more than just my liver now," he said as they ate lunch in the dining tent. "You're also my spleen."

"Spleen? Which stands for . . ."

"Seriously Platonic Lovers and Emotionally Empathetic Neologists."

"Neologists?"

"Because we're creating new words. Look, it wasn't easy to come up with something for 'N.'"

"*Seriously platonic lovers* . . . How long did it take you to come up with that one?"

"Fifteen minutes and an online thesaurus."

"It's good. I like it."

"Be a good girl and I'll make you my pituitary gland."

One time the script girl asked Becky, "So, what's the deal with you and Felix?"

"We're bestest chums," she said.

The script girl shook her head as she walked away. "That is so friggin' cool."

Becky nodded happily, not because she thought it was *that* cool, but because she was pleased with her use of "friggin'."

Felix returned to his star chair, his eyebrow arched meaningfully. "You shouldn't look so satisfied, Mrs. Jack. Do you know what *friggin'* stands for?" He answered his own question, tossing out a word even Melissa wouldn't use in Becky's earshot.

"Watch your mouth, young man. What would your mother say to such language?"

"'Pish posh,' probably. She used to say that a lot."

Used to . . . Becky knew Felix was an only child—his father had left him and his mother when he was a boy and died a few years later in Spain. Since his mother was his only family, Becky assumed she must be more precious to him than scones. Her death would be appalling. "I'm sorry, Felix. She passed on?"

"No—at least, I don't think so."

"Oh! Oh? But you used the past tense there."

"I don't know what she's saying currently, as I don't see her anymore."

"Anymore what? Anymore this year?" Becky felt a small earthquake rock her chest. "Felix, when is the last time you saw your mother?"

He didn't answer.

"Felix . . ." she said with warning.

"I'm counting . . . fourteen, fifteen—"

"Please don't tell me those are years. Assure me that those numbers aren't years."

Felix groaned. "This isn't going to end well for any of us."

"But she's your mother; you're her only little boy. She must be devastated! This is catastrophic. How could this happen? What happened?" She was on her feet, clutching her heart.

"Nothing. Sit down. We had a row when I was at university, that's all."

"Felix . . ."

He grabbed the arm of her shirt and pulled her back into her chair, his gaze mindful of the watching crew. "Calm, quiet, silence, I beg you. Anyone could be a tabloid spy."

This was not the sort of thing they usually discussed, but still Becky asked, in a whisper now, "Will you tell me?"

Felix glanced at the crew setting tracks for the camera, as if judging how much time he had left.

"We had a spat, and after she remarried—"

"No, start from the beginning. Or Celeste will tell me her version. You know she will if I ask—she can't help herself."

Felix groaned. "Right. But—fine. So. My mother was intense. Piano lessons, singing lessons. She was always there, hovering over me, constant. Until I was ten, we slept in the same room."

"Oh, Felix." Becky's heart was aching for this mother somewhere.

"Don't be dramatic. She cared less about me than how the neighbors saw her, determined to prove to them that she was a good mother even without a husband. Despite the forced culture and odd home, I did all right in school, mostly because I was a decent footballer. But she didn't know how to mother a teenage boy. I attended Cambridge and she'd call me several times a day. When she came to visit for the fourth time in the Michaelmas term, I . . . well, I fought with her. I was nasty. I wanted to knock her away."

"What did you say?"

He shrugged, his eyes on the director of photography, who was helping secure the camera to a dolly. "It wasn't so much 'what' as *how*. She claimed I was being ungrateful, listing all the things she'd given up for me, including marriage. There'd been a bloke by the name of Herbert, a real pillock. She said she would have married him, but I hadn't liked him and she always put me first. So I told her to let off and go marry Herbert, and I'd be happier if she did."

"And then? You made up and lived happily ever after?"

Felix chucked Becky's chin with mock gusto. "That's right, princess."

"Did she marry him?"

"Yes, she married the pillock. They came to opening night of a play I did in London. Herbert wasn't impressed. I had a cast party to get to and couldn't stay. Herbert hates London, it turns out. So I stayed in London for many years."

"And you didn't visit home? You didn't call?"

"After a time, neither did she. It was the best for both of us."

"Felix—"

"Mom!" Sam came running for her, flinging himself onto her lap, his arms around her neck. He was the number-one most snugly kid she'd ever known, and she needed it right then; her insides were roiling with the thought of a mother somewhere, for fifteen years missing her son. Becky nestled her face into Sam's hair and breathed in, smelling chlorine.

"You've been swimming?"

"Yeah, there was a floating alligator and me and Hyrum made it attack Polly, and she swam all around screaming, but she was just teasing. Do you think we could get a real alligator?"

The rest of the Jack family was right behind, Mike done working for the day. Several crew members (the ones Becky was particularly fond of) shouted hello to their regular visitors. Fiona went off immediately to confer with the wardrobe mistress, who let her leaf through costume design books and try on dresses. Felix greeted Polly, transparently relieved for the diversion, and the two of them sang a duet for a crew member's personal video camera.

Becky sat Mike in her "star" chair and gave him a shoulder rub while he and Wally talked golf, making a tee-off date for Wally's exclusive country club. Mike couldn't stop beaming about it.

"Hey, you weren't this excited about the time we went golfing," Felix complained.

"Are you kidding?" said Becky. "He made a 'My Day with Felix' album, and taped in his scorecard and a blade of grass that had stuck to his shoe."

Mike shrugged. "It's just that I figure Wally actually knows a five iron from a putter."

That made Felix laugh. Becky smiled to hide the pain—or rather, the plotting.

She was on the phone with Celeste that evening.

"How do we reunite Felix with his mother?"

"Rebecca, it's a lost cause. But . . . perhaps not for you."

Biddie Callahan-Coxhill was living in Devon, Felix's hometown, married to the aforementioned pillock Herbert. So Becky wrote a letter:

Dear Mrs. Callahan-Coxhill,

My name is Becky Jack. I'm a friend of your son Felix and his wife Celeste. I am also a mother. I've had the honor of knowing Felix for about six years, and I know he has a very good heart.

I was aghast to learn recently that he hasn't been in communication with you for a number of years. At the risk of meddling, I have hopes of reuniting you two again. Slowly might be best for Felix, would you agree? I'd thought if you could write a

letter to him, that could be a start. If you felt so inclined, I think
he might be ready and happy to hear from you. I'm attaching his
mailing address in Los Angeles.

I don't know the details of all that has transpired, but I
hope you can forgive Felix. Every boy needs his mother.

With many hopes,
Becky Jack

She told Celeste to keep an eye out for a letter. Celeste reported a
few weeks later.

"It came! And he opened it. I watched him read. Once he muttered
your name."

"Was he angry? Amused? Annoyed?"

"Annoyed, I would say. But he did not tear up the letter. And he
does tear up things sometimes, so that's good?"

"That's very good."

Becky didn't inquire further, proving a restraint that Mike called
"legendary." But Celeste suspected that Felix did write back.

Felix gave Becky some knowing looks, smoldering with accusation,
but besides that, nothing really changed—at least, not for the worse.

The fourth week in production, Becky was in makeup. Cynthia,
the makeup artist, was dusting Becky's face with an unseemly amount
of powder when Felix hopped onto the counter and began to twiddle
with a brush. In the mirror, Becky caught the brief look of happy longing in Cynthia's eyes before she pretended Felix wasn't there, giving the
star the illusion of privacy that all makeup artists apparently learn in
the trade. It made Becky smile. At her best guess, all the women on set
were a little in love with Felix.

"So," Felix said. "I just heard from Larry. They offered me the lead
for a new picture, *One Thousand Bedrooms*. Seems the story of my karaoke performance spread about town."

"Ooh, there's singing? What's the story?"

"It's a biopic, but Larry says the script is good, puts a real twist on
the story, doesn't get bogged down in covering every detail. Says it's
funny too. It's about Dean Martin."

Becky inhaled sharply then began to cough out powder while exclaiming, "Yes! You have to do that. You are so loungy. And you'll get to
sing. Felix, what a perfect role for you. If you don't take it, I might
punch you. Again." Becky looked at Cynthia in the mirror. "I hit him
once, and he assured me that it actually hurt."

"Oh yes, she has a mean right hook. Don't buy the innocent-
housewife act."

Cynthia smiled politely.

"Felix, I'm really excited about this one. You'll be so great. You can do impersonations, you can do comedy and drama, you can sing. It'll be a Felix Callahan showcase."

"Or it could be disaster."

"Not a chance."

He rubbed the brush back and forth across his fingernail. "Would you take a look at the script? Give me your professional opinion?"

"What?" she said, replaying his question in her mind, searching for buried sarcasm.

"Your professional opinion, as a screenwriter."

She stared. Cynthia had to press a finger against her cheek to make her turn her face back around. "You want my opinion?"

"Of course I do."

Something had changed. He'd never considered her a real screenwriter before and never asked her opinion on anything. She knew he adored her in a with-a-side-of-onions way, but there were areas in each other's lives they just didn't poke at. This was so startlingly new that Cynthia had to stop working with her blush brush until the color faded from Becky's cheeks.

"Sure thing," Becky said casually. "I'd love to. You bet."

Felix hopped off the table and said, "I'll call Larry. See you on set."

"Okay."

Becky glanced at Cynthia's expression in the mirror. She wished the incident had happened in private. Curse those observant makeup artists!

That night she read the Dean Martin script while Mike snored in bed beside her. It was brilliant. She knew it was brilliant because she couldn't wait to turn each page and not one line irritated her and begged for rewriting.

She handed it back to Felix the next day.

"Do it," she said.

He flipped open his cell phone and speed-dialed his agent. "Larry? Felix. Becky says go."

And that quickly, he was resolved to it? Becky thought. All he needed was her opinion?

Something had changed.

But she didn't ponder it. Becky wasn't much of a ponderer in any case, not when there was so much to do. Days off with her family were one long, wonderful vacation. Days working were scores of hours with her best friend.

Every day when she got her call sheet outlining the schedule for tomorrow, she felt relieved that the last scene wasn't up yet. She was preparing on the sly, hoping a rush of confidence would overtake her and she'd look back and laugh at her anxiety. What, me, worried about kissing Felix? Ha!

Time ticked forward.

In which Becky readies for the kiss

Becky had thought she had been as prepared as possible for moviemaking, but some things took her by surprise.

- She had a stand-in, basically a professional doppelgänger whose job was to represent Becky on set while the crew set up lights and cameras. Her name was Barb, and she looked a lot like Becky's reflection in a fun house mirror. Becky always smiled and said hello then hurried on her way. Barb had a lazy eye and a snarly smile. Barb was creepy.

- The waiting! The time to set up a scene, do the take, do it again for a different camera, and again and again. And then waiting while the crew prepped the next scene. She'd never hung around so much in her life. She played a lot of cards. Also, we mentioned the donkey in the trailer. The donkey's name was Earl. It's not as difficult to rent a donkey for a day in Los Angeles as you might think.

- The food was really good. And that meant more gym time. Dang.

- Whenever another actor joined her and Felix in a scene, Becky had to reapply deodorant every hour. Acting opposite Stockard Channing? You've gotta be kidding! Four years with Uta Hagen wouldn't be enough preparation.

- Acting with Felix was even better than singing with him. He was brilliant. He carried her, he relaxed her, he made it fun. But what would prove her greatest challenge was creeping ever closer . . .

One Friday evening, the assistant director gave Becky Monday's schedule—they were shooting the finale, out of order, as moviemaking often required. They hadn't yet filmed the scene where Hattie discovers Lionel's lie and decides to leave town, or the sequence of Lionel racing through the city trying to find her and stop her, leaping over tumbling fruit stands, buying a little girl's bicycle to race down the sidewalk (that sort of thing), finally hopping a train to discover Hattie absent but her daughter and his assistant running away together to SeaWorld. So he rushes to her apartment and finds her torn between what her mind and her heart are saying, but she lets him in to see what might happen next. What happens is—they kiss.

Why, oh why, did she write that?

Of course back when she blithely composed the script, she never dreamed that she herself would be the one doing the smooching. And when she rewrote some scenes to lessen her part, she didn't even think to touch the kissing scene. It just felt right.

Becky believed the kiss was the magic moment a romantic movie reaches for, works toward, finally achieves. Sure, there were the love stories where two characters were jumping into bed the first half hour, sucking each other's toes, removing clothing to reveal glistening skin. Becky preferred the story where two people connect, there's the electricity, there's the compatibility, there's everything there that should make them the happiest couple in the world, except for . . . [insert insurmountable obstacle here]. And because of that obstacle, they grow, they change for each other, toward each other, until in the end, all it takes is that final symbolic climax, an exquisitely simple physical manifestation of their love, their surrender to each other, their union—the kiss.

She'd angled the entire story to lead to that kiss, so it had to be just right. She could appreciate those directors and screenwriters who like to play with the formula to see what they could make out of it. But there was something so lovely, so perfect, about that classic ending that when done well was enough to make even the hard-hearted sigh and believe in the kind of love that promises to go on after the credits roll.

The kiss not as flirtation but realization. Kiss as epiphany. Kiss as completion.

That was the goal, anyway, the lovely vision she'd had when typing on her computer. Actually carrying it out was another matter. Acting, she'd discovered, was so much harder than just showing emotions you're not feeling. Merely speaking lines in a convincing way was a trial. Not to mention being interesting to watch. The toughest thing to do? Laugh. Laughing for real. Tough.

The second hardest thing to do? Kiss beautifully.

Have you ever watched real people make out? Saliva, tongues, teeth clanking, noses rubbing—*blech*. Becky was not at all confident that she could kiss on film and allow it to be a beautiful moment instead of a wince-fest. So she'd been preparing for weeks. First she made a list of her favorite movie kisses of all time:

- *One Fine Day*, when, after the actually quite horrible day, Michelle Pfeiffer and George Clooney finally find each other in a scrumptious kiss.

- *Willow*. That's right, *Willow*, when Val Kilmer kisses Joanne Whaley in the tent, leading up to her kissing him in the middle of a sword fight. Even that long black wig couldn't diminish Mr. Kilmer's appeal.

- *Spider-Man*. The upside-down kiss just looks so yummy.

- *Empire Strikes Back*, between Han Solo and Princess Leia. "I like nice men," she says. "I'm nice men," he says. What girl wasn't in love with Han Solo?

- *An Officer and a Gentleman*, at the end when Richard Gere carries Debra Winger. Say what you will, but it's a classic.

- *A Room with a View*, when Julian Sands rushes upon Helena Bonham Carter in the meadow, seizes her, and kisses her without a word. Loosen my corset so I can breathe.

- *It's a Wonderful Life*, while they're trying to converse with that other guy on the phone, all the while staring at each other, touching, trying to ignore the heat building up between them. Talk about a smoking hot first kiss!

- *Rattled Cages*, of course. Let that umbrella fall away—a kiss so tender, so passionate, they didn't even feel the rain.

Becky watched those kissing scenes again and again, studied the techniques, analyzed what changed them from nasty germ-fest into weak-knees splendor.

She kept notes:

- No tongue.

- No lip sucking.

- Mouths shouldn't be open wide unless it's a hugely dramatic, desperate kiss.

- Hands are very important. Too much touching can take focus away from the kiss itself. Around waist and back is good, or on neck and face. For hesitant kisses, hands on chest, as if half pushing away, or held up and not touching the other person at all.

- Hungry kisses are yummy.

- Sweet, slow kisses are a relief to watch.

- To be powerful, a kiss should make a journey, be its own story—begin with hesitation, move to realization, then melt into bliss.

The night before D-day, Becky put Uncle Ryan in charge, pulled Mike behind a locked bedroom door, and showed him her collection of quintessential kisses. Then she practiced on him.

It was an odd exercise. She and Mike had kissed so many times over so many years, they'd fallen into a pattern that felt absolute. So instead of approaching each other with noses to the right, they tilted heads the other way. They tried the old fashioned movie kisses, long moments of lips stuck together with no movement. They pretended it was their first kiss, hearts jackhammering, unsure where to put their hands. They mimicked a sudden rush of passion to see what that does to lips, then followed with a kiss that was a kind of dance, one person leading, the other following, lips moving together. Mike started laughing, the laughter made him seem all the more toothsome, and they got sidetracked into some marital good times. So when Becky reported on set the next day, she was feeling a little tired.

Still, she looked pretty good, maybe her best yet. In this scene more than any other, wardrobe wanted her stunning. She wore an amber silk turtleneck, the color bringing out the more interesting tones in her eyes (and under that . . . ah, the wonders of the right bra!). Her skirt was long and flowy, somehow managing to look casual but in reality a dry-clean-only number. And she wore knee-high brown boots, the heels giving her a lift so Felix wouldn't have to bend down in the kiss. Her hair was flipped out and sassy, and her makeup superheavy and yet natural. Feeling nice helped calm her squeamish middle, and she'd almost convinced herself she was fine—until she started to mess up her lines.

"You do look a little dreary," Becky/Hattie said.

The script girl called out the correction, "You do look a little *dreamy*."

"*Dreamy*? Who wrote these lines?"

There was some polite laughter from the crew, and Felix said, "That'll make it on the DVD extras."

She smiled at him and realized with an achy jolt that fear of messing up the kiss wasn't the only problem. Could she admit it? She tried to recognize the problem slightly, just squint at it, not look at it straight-on. (The other issue was Felix. She was kissing Felix. Her best friend.) The ice pixies in her belly began to perform a full-blown Capades.

She wished Mike were there; his grounding presence would make everything seem okay. But he'd had a conference call he couldn't miss.

Diana was wrong. Becky knew she was in no danger of unlocking some buried desire for Felix. And ever since Mike had said, "I'm having a hard time," she'd tried to take such care, check in with herself, maintain a balance. She hadn't kissed anyone else since falling for Mike eighteen years ago. Could she even do it?

After they filmed the dialogue leading to the kiss, Wally called a break to reset the cameras. Becky caught her face reflected in a window and scowled.

This won't do at all, she told herself. I look way too cute to waste this moment on fretting. I need a plan of action.

Felix was standing still while Livie, his makeup artist, touched up his eyes. He winked at Becky and asked, "You ready to snog?"

For that alone, she would make him pay.

"Lorraine," she said, hustling over to her craft services friend. Becky had often thought, let others kiss up to the director or the producers—I say, get a friend in craft services and you're a made woman.

"Lorraine, what do you have on hand that's terrifically stinky? In the next scene I'm supposed to kiss Felix."

Lorraine bounced with joy as she rummaged through her fridge. "Ah-ha! Minced garlic."

"You're a genius. Smear some of that on a cracker, will you? A lot of it. On second thought, just give me a spoon."

Becky fed herself a couple of teaspoons of minced garlic and bit off the bulb of a green onion for good measure. It made her eyes water and her saliva glands protest, but it would do the trick.

Creepy Barb was waiting on set while the electricians adjusted the lights. She looked at Becky with her active eye while her lazy eye slid away. Becky shivered.

At last Becky and Felix stepped up to rehearse the blocking for that scene while someone marked the floor with tape. They didn't rehearse the kiss, just stood close and faked it, smooching the air dramatically. Becky made sure not to breathe on Felix.

"Okay, let's do it for real," Wally said.

"Quiet on set!" the assistant director shouted.

The bell rang, then everything hushed. Becky's stomach performed a 360-degree flip.

She'd heard the crew give those same wind-up phrases dozens of times that summer, but there was something frightening about them now, a doomsday countdown to the point of no return.

"Roll it."

"Rolling."

"Speed."

"Forty-one, take one."

"Action."

Felix put his hands on her shoulders. She tipped her face up to his. She ignored her nervous belly, thoughts of George Clooney and Michelle Pfeiffer, and worries of slobbery messy kisses. She pretended not to know that when you write a romantic movie that culminates in a kiss, it must be a good one, had better sum up the entire story, wrap it with a bow and sell it to the audience as a thing of beauty. She disregarded memories of Calvin the sexy pet shop owner kissing wild child Katie in the rain. All she thought was garlic, garlic, garlic.

His lips touched hers. He winced and pulled back, making a gagging noise.

"Whoops, I may have had a *little* garlic for lunch."

The sound mixer called for a check, pausing to adjust levels.

"Two can play this game. Wally, give me a click?" Felix jogged over to craft services. Becky heard Lorraine laugh.

They set up the scene again. The anticipation was incredible, props people clutching their props, grips gripping things. Becky gave her lead-in line, Felix responded. Then he put his hand on the back of her head and slowly leaned in for a kiss.

She tried to kiss him. She felt bad for the crew waiting while they fooled around. If only she hadn't breathed in through her nose.

"It's like . . ." She coughed. "It's like kissing a herring. A . . . pickled herring, was it?"

"I did have some for lunch."

"Obviously."

"And when you imagined kissing me, there was no herring flavor about?"

She considered. "I guess I thought it'd be more like bass or cod."

"One of your larger sea fish."

"Exactly."

"I wonder what's worse, kissing a fish or an Italian buffet."

"Yeah, sorry about that. Lunch was pretty garlic-intensive. Was it a mood killer, do you think?"

"Just a tad."

"Hm."

"Yes."

The crew was snickering. The director yelled, "Cut."

"This is good, surprisingly," Wally said. "We just might keep this."

Felix blinked. "Really?"

"Yeah . . . What if right here we cut to you two in the bathroom, both brushing your teeth and your tongues? Then you'll come back to the balcony again. And take it from there, as if you've both just freshened up and are ready to try the kiss for real."

"So, Wally, we don't actually get to freshen up before the next take?"

"We're rolling, Felix."

"Right. We just won't breathe in through our noses."

Felix took Becky's hands. He smiled at her, that warm smile that made her feel snug at home. "Shall we try this again?"

She nodded. Her heart was drumming so loudly she wondered why the sound guy didn't ask for a break to readjust the microphone levels. She was going to have to kiss Felix. For real. Could she do this? Really do this? The cameras and all these people watching, waiting, the money and time and equipment, and Felix himself. He was a professional. He could do this. But could she?

You have to act now. Right now, Becky.

Felix brushed his thumb over the corner of her mouth. He looked at her, into her eyes, his gaze so delicious, his whole being exuding a palpable love.

Man, he was good at this.

Suddenly she wasn't Becky with her best friend. She was the fantasy version of herself, magically transported into a romantic moment, the kind that would make her sigh on the edge of her movie theater seat. She was with a drool-able gorgeous man who was looking at her as if she was the most beautiful being in the world. As if he wanted her.

He moved in closer. Slowly. Her breath trembled, her leg bones considered liquefying. She closed her eyes. A wave of panic washed over her, and she scrambled for something safe to grab, anything to survive the moment—she imagined she was with Mike. It was Mike's hand on her face, on her waist. It was Mike who pulled her closer, whose lips touched hers. And she kissed Mike, the man who stole her heart at age twenty-one. The man who raised four children with her, who cleaned up her morning-sickness mess off the bathroom floor, who washed her car after rainstorms, who knew her every look, who loved her so powerfully he never had to say it and yet he did anyway, every day, in a dozen different ways.

These lips on hers didn't feel like Mike's—they were unfamiliar, slower, soft in a different way.

We're playacting, Becky thought. We're in our bedroom, trying a new way of kissing.

She could do that. She kissed him back.

It was so easy to kiss Mike and mean it. She was in love with Mike. She loved his touch and smell and mind and laugh. Eyes closed, she put her hands on Mike's face and let the kiss become more passion-ate, telling him with her affection how much she loved him, how much she wanted to be with him forever. The kiss was as rich as a black-and-white movie, but she ached for more. Her hand went into his hair, his hands were on her back, pulling her in closer.

"Now pull back," Wally whispered, "and look at each other."

Becky opened her eyes and saw Felix before her. He was smiling, his eyes a little wet. Her own felt the same, and when she blinked, a tear dropped to her cheek. She took a breath. She felt shaky.

He's Lionel, remember? You're Hattie. Be Hattie now.

She smiled, then laughed with joy, sure at last that this man, Lio-nel, though impossible, was truly hers.

"And . . . cut!"

Felix and Becky both exhaled relief at the same time, right into each other's faces, then turned away to cough at the stench. The crew laughed.

"Did we get it, Wally?" Felix asked.

Wally wanted them to do it two more times, making it a little more hesitant at first, stopping to look at each other, then falling in deep. She wasn't able to spark a tear as she had the first time, but the kissing wasn't as hard as she feared. Becky found the flow: eyes closed pretending it was Mike, eyes opened remembering to be Hattie. Felix was professional, re-spectful, guiding her through it, never taunting or teasing. Even so, her stomach wrenched as if she'd been on a roller coaster for an hour, forever climbing impossibly high slopes, then falling so fast her breath was torn out of her. She sighed with relief when Wally called for a break while he reviewed the tape.

Felix put his arm around Becky's shoulders and led her to her chair. One of the production assistants was standing within earshot. Felix glared at him until he scooted away.

Felix leaned in close to speak. "You all right?"

She shrugged. "I'm not used to kissing anyone but Mike."

"I know. I was worried for you, but you did great. Really great."

"Thanks, you're sweet." She knocked him gently with her shoulder. "I'll admit, I was scared."

"No more pretending you're not a real actress, I'm afraid, because you were acting up a storm just now."

"No, I just tricked myself. When I closed my eyes, I pretended that you were Mike, and I was okay."

"You pretended I was Mike?"

"Yeah. It seemed the easiest way to get through it. That's probably cheating. I should've been channeling the Hattie character the whole time, not pretending I was Becky with Mike. Or maybe that's a trick you real actors know. Do you always pretend you're with Celeste?"

Cynthia came to touch up Becky's lipstick and Felix didn't respond.

"Looked great, guys," Wally said, squatting before them. "That's going to be a gorgeous closing for the movie. We're lighting the bathroom now for the toothbrushing scene and then we'll wrap you two for the night."

"Wow, an early night! What a treat." Becky closed her eyes as Cynthia brushed on eye shadow. "You want to come over for dinner, Felix? Fiona is taking a turn cooking tonight. Should be adventurous. She's so—"

"Um . . ." Cynthia said. "Becky? Felix isn't here anymore."

Becky opened her eyes. No sign of the man. "The trickster. I owe him one for that."

"I know a guy who could rent you a llama," Cynthia said.

When Becky met Felix in the bathroom for the toothbrushing take, he wasn't in a teasing mood, and she ended up not asking him to dinner after all. For the best. Fiona had experimented: avocado lasagna and spaghetti squash salad. She called it "California cuisine." Hyrum called it "inedible." Becky couldn't scold him—he'd aptly applied a four-point vocabulary word. Becky and Mike praised Fiona, then after the kids had gone to bed, sneaked bowls of cold cereal and ate it in the bedroom with the lights out.

"I was thinking about you a lot today," Becky said.

"Oh yeah?"

"Mm hm."

"Does that mean I'm going to get lucky two days in a row?"

"Just let me finish my Raisin Bran."

In which Becky gets fancy and Felix is an alien lawman

After a couple more weeks of filming, Wally announced, "That's a wrap, people!"

There was cheering. Felix hugged Becky, which was nice because he'd been acting a little distant. Wally hadn't called her on set as screenwriter as much lately. She'd only had a couple more scenes with Felix, and he hadn't spent any time at the Jack House o' Fun. Despite the tiny nag of worry, Becky had been glad. She'd had a chance to dive back into family, roll around in the hot joy of summer and freedom.

Mike decided to attend the wrap party at Wally's house, and he and Becky found a way to waltz or two-step or fox-trot to any music the DJ could play. After a while Mike went off with Wally to check out his in-house movie theater, and she and Felix danced. No waltz this time, but an incredibly silly cha-cha that kept Becky laughing through the entire song. If Becky were the type to gloat about her own good fortune, she would have looked around the room and counted all the women of the crew and cast (and a couple of the men) who stared at her with Felix, exuding palpable envy. As it was, she just barely glanced—and she certainly didn't count.

"I missed you," she said.

Felix folded her into his arms. "I'm sorry. I have been a wanker lately, haven't I?"

"I wouldn't go that far—I have a feeling that's a dirty word. But I worried you were avoiding me because you were humiliated by my acting."

"No! I'm so proud I'm puffed up and crowing. I was just knackered, the end of shoot and all. Now you've seen me at my worst."

"Hardly. Your worst is the way you eat breakfast. Any time sausage is involved, your table manners are appalling."

"Can I be blamed? That mix of meat and spice is an intoxicating concoction, but banger skin is not to be borne. Surgery must be performed."

"Hello, Mr. Callahan. Hello, Ms. Jack," said Scott/Buddy the busboy, pleasant but eager to pass out of their line of sight.

Felix twirled her around, out and back in, and then dipped her to the rhythm of "Mony Mony." When he pulled her back up, she couldn't hide her watery eyes.

"Hold on," he said, tipping her chin up. "What's all this about?"

"This song always gets to me. It's just so beautiful."

He stared. She poked him in the ribs.

"It's 'Mony Mony' not *The Messiah*."

"I never know with you."

"I'm just sentimental. It's been bordering on spectacular to be with you so much, and now—"

"Don't sign my death certificate yet. We'll have a break, and then there's bound to be some reshooting and looping before the parade of publicity begins."

She'd forgotten about that. But Karen the producer hadn't. She was obvious in the crowd, wearing a black pant suit, her pale skin and strawberry blonde hair practically glowing in contrast. As soon as Becky waved to her, Karen pulled her aside.

"Becky, I don't want this to be awkward," she said, thereby making it nothing but awkward, "but some of the others are worried about you . . . well, about your wardrobe. You should, you might want to . . . why don't you go shopping and get yourself a dress for the premiere? And a wardrobe for press junkets and talk shows? It's looking like there will be a couple of talk shows, and it'd be nice if—"

"If I didn't look like a lower-middle-class mother of four?"

Karen smiled sweetly. "Go to Rodeo Drive before you head back to Utah. Splurge. Have a heyday. You've earned it."

"Sure thing," Becky said oh-so-casually.

Then when she and Mike were ensconced in the car, she gripped his arm. "Shopping for a 'wardrobe' terrifies me more than the first day of shooting. More than labor."

Mike nodded and offered the best advice he could. "I think you should call Celeste."

Two days later, Becky and Fiona were wandering Rodeo Drive with Celeste. The mother and daughter wore jeans and one of their nicer T-shirts. Celeste wore—well, Becky didn't even know what kind of fabric that blouse was, and didn't suppose she could really refer to Celeste's denim trousers as "jeans."

"Oooo," Celeste squealed, "this is divine. Rebecca, you were right to phone me. This is my world, and you're going to flower in my world."

"Yeah, I'm a bit uncomfortable. I don't want to be dishonest about who I am. I don't belong here; I know I don't. And dressing up like the natives feels—"

"Come on, Mom, you should totally get something fancy," Fiona said. She'd aged five years over the past three months, leaving the teen-age whine behind in Utah and suddenly becoming a woman. She even looked taller, and older, with her brown hair up in a pretty ponytail. "What're you gonna wear to your movie premiere—your church dress? And while we're at it, we should get me something too."

"Listen to your daughter," Celeste said.

"It feels so vain. I can't help but think, every penny I spend on clothes takes away from my kids' college funds."

"Don't think of this as a frivolity. For you now, a fine wardrobe is a necessity. Besides, you are with an expert, *ma puce*. For the premiere dress, at the very least, I will get a designer to lend something gorgeous to the star of the new Felix Callahan movie."

"You can do that?"

Celeste made a beautiful pouting gesture. "This city bends to my will."

"I believe it," Becky said.

"Me too." Fiona was staring at Celeste as if at Aphrodite riding an oyster shell.

And there she goes, Becky thought. She felt a twinge of regret that she was not her little girl's idol. Of course, she hadn't been Fiona's epitome of fashion since Fiona had learned to dress herself. Still, it was a loss, and Becky the Mother felt each one as they came, keeping them close like charms on a bracelet.

But after about five minutes with Celeste, Becky couldn't blame Fiona in the least. The woman was magnificent.

It was all very *Pretty Woman* as they entered boutiques, Celeste at-tracting the sales attendants like wasps to raw meat.

"We have precisely five hundred dollars to spend in your store," Celeste said, running her hand over a turquoise blouse. "Please help this woman look as fabulous as she deserves. If you manage to dress her bril-liantly from blouse to toes and still have money left over to buy some-thing for my darling Fiona, I'll send you an autographed glossy to hang on your wall. You understand?"

And so it went all afternoon. One thousand four hundred and fifty dollars later, Becky stepped into a cab with her bagged wardrobe: a sweater, slacks, two blouses, two skirts, a dress, a pair of black boots, and a pair of heeled sandals. Becky nearly administered CPR on herself at the sum, but she also realized the price would have been much higher if she'd been shopping without the goddess of fashion. And Fiona made off with a couple of shirts and a scarf, which she promised faithfully to share with Polly. She was clutching her bag with white-knuckled hands, her gaze far off, as if imagining how her life would magically change from mundane to majestic whenever she donned her new attire.

No premiere dress was found, but Celeste pooh-poohed any worries. She would get a designer to provide one on loan. "It will be good publicity for the designer, as you will be photographed at the premiere."

"The dress can't have cleavage or a low back," Becky said. "No sleeveless or spaghetti straps, no see-through spots, and the skirt will need to be at least as low as my knees."

Celeste looked as if she would protest, then changed her mind. "Fine. It will be a delightful challenge to find the right dress for you, and all the more rewarding when I see you dressed perfectly."

"Thanks. Thank you so much. I'd be—well, you can imagine what I'd look like without you." She tugged on her nice T-shirt, which seemed thin and drab. "Hey, do you know if anything is going on with Felix and his mother?"

Celeste shook her head, but her eyes were hopeful. "He doesn't talk, and I don't ask. But I think there was a phone call. There is very, very good work there, Rebecca. Very, very good. We will see someday."

The Jacks returned home in time for the kids to start school. Becky had loads of laundry, a house to put in order, dance lessons and Little League practices, church responsibilities, and a scrapbook to update. Life was busy but blessedly normal, and the California summer shifted in her head to a dreamlike memory. She was so accosted by daily living that she rarely phoned Felix or thought about him at all. The pining had just started to pinch when the time arrived to meet again.

"Sometimes I forget how much I miss you until I see you," Becky said, hugging him at the LAX baggage claim.

"I never forget," he mumbled into her shoulder. "Not for a second."

"How come you're so sweet?"

"Because you are."

She poked him in the stomach. "What's going on? Are you up to something?"

He shrugged and wouldn't answer as he shouldered her bag.

First they had to shoot a couple of pickup scenes, replacing ones that hadn't gone over well with test audiences. There was some looping, recording audio over lost lines or scenes with sound problems. Celeste was in town, so Becky stayed at the Callahan-Bodine home in Beverly Hills.

"Ten thousand square feet? Do you really need ten thousand square feet? You both take up about ten square feet with your arms outstretched, spinning in circles."

Felix said, "The west wing is for Celeste's wardrobe."

Celeste said, "And the east wing is for Felix's ego."

Back home again, the Jack household seemed much louder than Becky had remembered, and she noted for the first time that they had somehow neglected white carpet and stainless steel furniture in their home decor. She only had time to clean and kiss and noodle and love and bake and sleep, and then it was on the road for publicity.

First Becky met Felix in Chicago to appear on *Oprah*. (*Oprah*!) Most of Becky's friends and family thought it was pretty cool, if strange, that she was in a movie. But the fact that she would be on *Oprah*—that's what catapulted her to superstar in their minds.

Becky wore a sage green silk blouse with black slacks and black boots and the pearl earrings Mike had given her last Christmas. Thankfully, she didn't have to do her own hair and makeup. She walked onto the set feeling prettier than she'd ever felt. It didn't hurt to have Felix holding her arm. The sleepless night she'd spent racking her brain for clever things to say quickly proved unnecessary. She was just with Felix. They were just chatting.

"Doesn't she look great?" Felix said to Oprah. "Usually she wears some ridiculous T-shirt with her children's faces ironed on."

"I love that shirt!" Becky said.

"Yes, but should children be decoration? I ask you."

"Never was there a straighter man more concerned with wardrobe." Becky leaned closer to Oprah. "And he gets manicures. Seriously. I've never had a manicure in my life."

"If only she would. Backstage, Becky chipped a nail and you know what she did? Filed it down against a brick in the wall. I would not lie to you, Oprah."

"No, that's true." Becky held up the nail. "Bricks don't do a fine job, but it smoothed the nail down enough so it wouldn't snag my blouse. That would've been a tragedy. This blouse cost more than my car."

"I should clarify," Felix said, "that explains more about her car than the blouse."

"Just because I'm not Mr. Fancy with his . . . weird, I don't know what kind of car you have."

"I have never driven a car in my life."

"Seriously? You never have? Ever? Well, I'm speechless."

"And yet you cover up the infirmity admirably."

"Thank you, Felix. You see, Oprah, he really is a nice boy when he gives it a shot."

"Now you've got to give us the dish," Oprah said. "Are you two really best friends or is it a publicity stunt?"

Becky and Felix looked each other over.

"Yeah . . . he's okay," she said.

"I'm growing on her."

"Like a mold."

"All right, all right, you want the truth? As painful as it may be? I adore this woman."

"Six years now. It was best-friendship at first sight. And nothing more, mind you. I had to kiss him in the movie, and I won't be repeating that experience, thank you very much."

The audience made sounds of doubt and sorrow. She'd had the chance to smooch Felix Callahan and hadn't enjoyed it? Say it isn't so!

"Easy now," Becky said. "Imagine it this way—it doesn't feel like kissing Calvin the sexy pet shop owner as much as, say, your older brother."

Oprah made some suggestive comments, wondering if there was more going on than they admitted. It was a setup question, allowing Becky to bring out her prearranged props.

"This here is me." She held up a blown-up photograph of herself in a swimming suit, taken at a neighborhood pool a year before the movie shoot. It was a grandma suit with the little ruffle around the hips, in a shade of pink that made her skin look extremely white—not Nicole Kidman peachy-white but old woman bluish-white. "And this," she brought out a photo of Celeste in a red bikini from a magazine, "this is Felix's wife, Celeste Bodine. If there's any doubt which of us is Felix's best friend and which is his wife, just shut your eyes and visualize these images."

Felix grabbed her photo for closer examination. "Truly, that is a horrible picture of you. I don't think I've ever seen you in a swimming costume. Did you alter it somehow to make yourself look worse?"

"Nope, I'm just that pasty and soft. Mother of four, baby. That's what a real body looks like."

"Come here," he said, wrapping his arm around her shoulders and pulling her closer to kiss her cheek. "Show all the unflattering photos you like, you can't fool me. You are stunning."

Oprah gushed. The audience applauded.

Becky said under her breath, "You're such a ham."

"I mean it," he said. And she believed him now. She wondered how he conceived of her, what genus he filed her under. Perhaps she was gorgeous to him the way a crocodile was gorgeous to Steve Irwin.

The next day they were off to New York for the *Today* show then back to Los Angeles for *The Tonight Show*. The latter one made Becky's heart pound so hard she was afraid it would rip her new sweater. Backstage was tense, with dozens of crew members and assistants with headphones scurrying around as if preparing to protect the queen ant from hostile intruders. But when Becky walked out into the bright lights and ocean of applause, Felix was beside her again. And sitting beside him anywhere felt so normal, so comfortable, that she forgot to be nervous.

The next morning they had a press junket, where Becky and Felix sat in a hotel room while reporter after reporter came in for private interviews, four minutes apiece. Almost every reporter asked a variation of the same three questions: "What's the movie about? Are you two really best friends? Any funny incidents from the filming that you could share?" The first forty times Becky and Felix told the garlic and herring story, it was still mildly funny. By about Telling #53, Becky was fantasizing about putting a spike through her own temple. Soon they gave up altogether.

Reporter: "So, what's this movie about?"

Becky: "It's a western . . ."

Felix: "A sci-fi western."

Becky: "Yeah, that's right, a sci-fi western. I play the harlot with the heart of gold."

Felix: "And I'm an alien lawman. I wear a hat."

Becky: "A white hat."

Felix: "A big white hat."

Becky: "With holes cut out for his antennae."

Felix. "A huge white hat with holes. Also, my character doesn't have ears."

Becky: "Or a nose."

Felix: "Or a nose."

Reporter: "Um . . . are we talking about *Blind Love?*"

Becky: "Or eyes. He hasn't got any eyes."

Felix: "And we fall in love. But it's doomed."

Becky: "Because my character is a shady lady."

Felix: "And because of my enormous white hat with holes."

Becky (jabbing him): "Don't spoil the ending!"

Felix: "Right. Sorry. Forget I said anything about the hat."

Becky: "Also, there's a musical number."

Felix: "Becky's brilliant in it."

Becky (smiling shyly): "Stop it. You steal the show with the tap dancing."

Reporter: "Tap dancing?"

Felix: "My mum taught Little Clodders tap school. I re-create one of her signature numbers in this film. It's quite emotional, given that my character doesn't have any eyes."

Becky: "Or a nose."

Felix: "Or a nose."

Reporter: "I see. Uh, sounds like fun. So, moving on . . . um, are you two really best friends?"

Becky and Felix: "No."

Reporter: "Alrighty then. Um, any anecdotes you can tell us?"

Becky: "You tell it, Felix."

Felix: "Okay, okay. There was this time when—you remember this, Becky?—when I was in my trailer and I was opening an envelope, and I got a paper cut."

Becky: "A paper cut right on his finger! Can you imagine?"

Felix: "I had to wear a bandage, and there I was, about to shoot another scene!"

Becky and Felix laughed heartily. They paused and looked at each other, and then broke out into a second round of guffawing.

Reporter (trying to laugh): "Wow. Such fun. Guess my time is up."

The next reporter came in.

Next Reporter: "So, tell. What is this movie about?"

Felix: "It's a disaster flick."

Becky: "That's right. I play the plucky young scientist who sees it all coming."

Felix: "And I'm the world-weary sheriff who saves the day."

Becky: "After he kills me with molten lava."

Felix: "It's irony. You don't expect it, then, *wham*! A nice twist."

Becky: "A disaster flick with a twist."

Felix: "And no special effects."

Becky: "Also, it closes with a Broadway revue."

And then, at last, the premiere.

Celeste was true to her word, and Becky had a fabulous gown. It was black, with elbow-length straight sleeves, the neckline and skirt reminiscent of a 1950s housedress, the fabric not clingy, sparing too much detail of the shape of her hips and butt. She'd pulled her hair back in an elegant bun, wore silver hoops in her ears and new black heels, and felt as pretty as she had any right to.

She and Felix (in his five-thousand-dollar tuxedo) arrived together in a chauffered Rolls-Royce. They pulled up to the theater and someone in a headset opened the car door, muttering into the tiny microphone, "Felix Callahan is here. Repeat, Felix on the red carpet. Also his co-star."

Felix stayed in the car a moment, squeezing Becky's hand.

"Did I tell you how happy I am that you're here?"

"You did, but you can tell me again."

"I lose myself in these things."

"I know, sweetie."

He smiled. "You're not going to be able to pull off the unattractive, frumpy housewife after tonight. You look stunning."

She was wearing a girdle. She didn't confess this to Felix, but it should be mentioned—she was wearing a girdle.

"You look fairly photogenic yourself, Felix Callahan."

Fans outside were screaming. Through the white noise of hollers and hoots emerged a rhythmic shout. Becky strained to understand.

"Felix, they are chanting your name."

Felix nodded. "You see, this is exactly why I need you here."

"To tell you what they're chanting?"

"To laugh at it, darling. Or I might take it seriously."

He helped her out of the Rolls. Cameras were flashing. Not a lot of cameras—the romantic comedy was a small release, by Hollywood's standards, and the premiere was no circus. Still, there was a line of entertainment television reporters to pass through, and the mob of fans behind barricades.

Becky and Felix moseyed through the polite chaos, answering questions, stopping for photographs. When Celeste pulled up after the more famous of the supporting cast members, everyone wanted photographs of her with Felix, and Becky stepped back. And back. And a little farther back.

Occasionally one of the reporters would ask her, "What was it like working with Felix Callahan?"

"Splendid," she'd say, or sometimes, "Wonderful." She made a game of it, tapping into her mental thesaurus: "Terrific, amazing, astonishing, startling, staggering, shocking, appalling . . . also, really nice."

Her own family arrived in a rental car at the tail-tail-tail end of the motorcade, and Becky grabbed Mike's arm. He was wearing his best church suit, dark blue. Fiona and Polly strolled down the carpet, selfaware and trying fiercely not to grin. They were holding each other's hands as they hadn't since they were little girls. Hyrum and Sam ran about until a production coordinator asked Becky to rein them in. She put her arms around their shoulders and whispered promises of ice cream cones.

"Are you okay?" Mike asked.

"Oh yeah. I'd be a lot more uncomfortable if they pretended to be interested in me."

"Really?"

She watched Felix working the crowd, shaking hands, signing autographs, posing with Celeste. "Yes, really." She felt no desire to sign her name or (of all ridiculous things) hear it chanted. And she felt proud of him, so gallant and adored. Although she had been just a little surprised by how easily he'd let go of her arm once the cameras started flashing.

As if in answer to her thought, Felix rushed over. "Don't leave me again! I'm drowning out here. I need you on my arm. Do you mind, Mike?"

Mike stepped aside, taking hold of his two boys. "It's your night. You camp girls go crazy."

Soon the production coordinators were shooing everyone inside the theater. Felix and Becky entered last, her hand on his arm. The auditorium was filled with cast and crew, their family members, friends of the producers, big shots and their kids. And they applauded for Becky and Felix as they walked down the aisle.

"Wow," she said. Her feet had an airy feeling, as if she were floating on the applause.

"You get used to it," he said.

"Stop it. You can't possibly."

He looked around and grinned. "No, I suppose not. Not if you don't want to."

"I know it's not for me, but it's still pretty amazing."

She waved at everyone, felt her skin shiver under the gaze of hundreds, and prayed silently, Please like the film. Please, please, please.

She'd seen the movie before at a private viewing with Wally. She thought it was funny. But would they? And was her performance winceworthy? Did she shame Felix? Would she look bloated and unhealthy on a really big screen, like the corpse of a sea lion washed ashore? Or even a seal or otter or a smaller animal, but still bloated with the pallor of death about her? And flies too . . . flies buzzing about, angry buzzing flies laying eggs in her bloated—

"What are you thinking about?" Felix whispered as the opening credits rolled.

"Flies," she said.

"You're imagining the whole you-as-whale-corpse thing again, aren't you?"

"Absolutely not." The title lit up the screen. "Sea otter."

"Hmph."

At the movie's first funny incident, the audience chuckled. At the second, more chuckling, though on the laughter continuum, it was much closer to "polite" than "uncontrollable." She gripped the arm rest to resist hiding her face in her hands.

"It's funny," Mike whispered from her left side. "It really is."

She leaned over to catch sight of her kids' faces. All four were turned up to the screen, eyes wide and serious, lips slightly parted, or in Sam's case, mouth completely gaping. No smiling, no laughing.

Mike whispered, "But what do kids know, huh?"

"True," she said, taking a small comfort. "Sam thinks Japan is a company that makes computer games."

Then Felix's character started in on the blind charade, and the chuckling turned up to a real laugh. And then they roared.

"You hear that?" she whispered to Felix. "You hear? They love you! You're brilliant."

Felix kept his eyes on the screen, but a small smile curled his lips. "That was really fun. Those weeks with you. Thank you."

"Tell me I don't look like dead beached whale. Please, just one more time and I promise I'll never ask you again."

"You don't look remotely like a dead beached whale."

"Or sea otter?"

He studied the screen, evaluating. She elbowed him in the ribs.

In which a tabloid attacks the home front

After starring in a major Hollywood movie that opened at number three at the box office, after appearing on national talk shows and seeing her face in *People* magazine, and after spending so much time in dry-clean-only clothing and wearing enough makeup to kill a warren of rabbits, returning permanently to normal life was surreal for Becky. And also absolutely necessary.

Felix's agent, Larry, phoned, saying he'd had inquiries about her for future projects. She declined.

"I may write more screenplays, but my acting days are done."

She'd had a couple of funny moments in the show and otherwise played a respectable straight character to Felix's comic genius. The kissing scene had turned out surprisingly un-wince-worthy and maybe even a little bit lovely. But if she tried any other role, acted opposite any other man, she was certain she'd fall flat on her face. Besides, she didn't want the actor's life.

And after her third viewing of the movie, she was also quite happy that her real life was not a romantic comedy, a story where the first kiss reigns supreme. It had taken a year of marriage to realize marital felicity had little to do with the heart-shaking, cloud-walking craziness of falling in love. She'd had a friend, Heather, who after five years decided her marriage was belly-up, mostly because she didn't feel that head-over-heels sensation anymore. She divorced and moved, and Becky had lost touch, but at last report, Heather was divorcing for a second time, perhaps still on her quixotic quest for permanent infatuation. Becky understood the need for a little romance reminder from time to time, to experience the thrill of it through a character on a screen or in a book. But after leaving the movie theater or putting down the novel, she always felt oh-so-glad to be Mike's wife, even when all they did before bed was talk about how to exterminate their ant infestation.

Marriage was good. Home was best. Becky snuggled into the couch next to Sam to read another book while the tangy, garlicky scent of cooking lasagna filled the house, and felt quite certain that this was her place.

Mostly she tried to pretend the movie had never happened. That wasn't always easy—she had been on *Oprah* after all. Some news was welcome: she had worried that the story line might offend sight-impaired communities, but Felix's acting had pulled it through. He found the humor in the situation and pointed it at himself.

Felix warned her, "Do not read reviews. Ignore them. Avoid them. Abstain with every gram of that indomitable Mormon willpower you possess."

For two weeks after the release Becky walked around in a brilliantly blind haze of ignorance. Then she got an e-mail from Darci, a high school acquaintance now living in Virginia:

> **Becky! I saw a review of your movie in our local paper and I couldn't believe it! You're starring in a movie with Felix Callahan!!! I told Craig it was you, but he said it couldn't be, but there was a photograph too and even though your hair is different and you look older I just knew it was you!! LOL! You always were so talented!**

[Actually, in tenth grade Darci had called her an "alien-faced kill-joy."]

> **Next time we're in Utah, we should totally go out to Nielsen's Frozen Custard like old times!**

[For the record, there had never been even one "old time" when Darci and Becky had gone together to Nielsen's Frozen Custard. Also for the record, Nielsen's Frozen Custard is delicious.]

> **I'm so proud of you! I'm telling everyone I know that I'm friends with a famous movie star!!! Give Felix a big smooch from me! LOL!!!**
>
> **Darci :$**

Becky spent some time staring at the "emoticon" after Darci's name and trying to make sense of it before deciding it must be a typo and letting her eyes continue on down the e-mail to the next block of text. Becky had read half of it by the time her brain caught up and warned her that Darci had pasted in the review. But it was too late. Far too late.

> **In *Blind Love*, Felix Callahan returns to frothier fare as Lionel, a handsome lawyer who is so desperate to prove his love to an ordinary woman, he'll fake blindness. Even with this painful premise,**

Callahan proves once again there's no part he cannot play, no joke he cannot deliver, no female movie-goer he cannot make swoon. The object of his affection is played by newcomer (and Callahan's real-life best friend) Becky Jack, who has as much screen time as Lionel's German shepherd. While Jack is occasionally convincing as the unattractive baker who eschews love, she is clearly out-sparkled by a deep supporting cast including Stockard Channing, Jim Broadbent, Missi Pyle, Jennifer Garner, and Ryan Reynolds. Romance is tepid at best in this pleasant little movie, but the friendly chemistry between Callahan and Jack is often playful. It purports to be a romantic comedy, but forget the date and take a pal to this flick.

She sat very, very still, as if a bee had landed on her nose and all she could do was stare at it encouragingly ("You don't really want to sting me, do ya, little fella? Feel that inviting wind? Go take a flutter. You deserve it.") Then she read the review again—why not? The damage was done, might as well roll around in the muck. She read it a third time. Then she began to reread the adjectives—*ordinary, newcomer, occasionally convincing, unattractive, clearly outsparkled, tepid at best, pleasant little* . . .

She became aware of Polly, reading over her shoulder.

"Mom, you okay?"

"I wondered how I did. I saw myself up there and I wasn't sure, but now I know."

"You were really good, Mom. You really were."

"I was 'occasionally convincing.' That's not bad for a freshman effort, huh? And if I didn't expect to be outsparkled by the likes of Stockard Channing, then I had another thing coming, indeed I did. Didn't I? I did. Very much so."

Polly wrapped her arms around her mother's shoulders. "I love you, Mom."

"Thanks, honey," Becky said with a little laugh. "I shouldn't need comfort. This is all very expected. At least my novice performance didn't make Felix look bad. That was my only concern." She heaved a breath. "It's good. It is."

It wasn't the only hug Polly would be giving her mother in the coming weeks. It must have been a slow celebrity-news week, because a tabloid television show premiered "Exposé: The *Blind Love* Affair."

Footage of Felix Callahan and Celeste Bodine
holding hands and smiling for photographers at a
red carpet event.

                         NARRATOR
Felix Callahan and Celeste Bodine—one of
Hollywood's most glamorous couples. And one of the
happiest?

Bad photo of Becky Jack, squinting in the sun.

                         NARRATOR
Not if *she* has anything to do with it. Will one
woman's secret love tear two marriages apart?

Photo of Becky and Felix on *The Tonight Show*,
laughing with Jay Leno.

                         NARRATOR
Felix Callahan and Becky Jack claim they are
nothing more than friends, despite having starred
together in a steamy romance. But Hollywood
insiders tell a different story.

                       TONIA JEANU
                 Writer for *Exclusive!* magazine
It's painfully transparent that Becky Jack, a
married mother of four, is very much in love with
her so-called best friend Felix Callahan. She
writes a screenplay about an ordinary-looking
woman and a handsome man who falls completely in
love with her. Is she fooling herself, or does she
just think the rest of us are clueless? Is Callahan
clueless too? Watch out, Celeste Bodine, or a nasty
little Cinderella just might steal your husband out
from under you.

                         NARRATOR
                        (mockingly)
Despite overwhelming evidence, friends of Jack
refute the claims.

                  RUSS "THE WIG-MAKER" NIMAR
                    Blind Love Crew Member
Becky's family was on set all the time. She and her
husband are very close. There was never anything
but a friendly relationship between Felix and Becky.

Music: dramatic cello. Zoom in and move back on a
copy of *Blind Love* script, vertigo effect.

> NARRATOR
> (in ominous tones)
> But skeptics claim one need look no further for
> proof than in the screenplay itself, penned by
> Jack's own hand.

A script of *Arm Candy* lying on a desk.

> NARRATOR
> And insiders report that Jack wrote a second
> screenplay called *Arm Candy*, the story of an actor
> and a model who fake a relationship to increase
> their celebrity status.

People magazine open to a spread of Felix and
Celeste under the title "Hollywood's Hottest
Couples."

> NARRATOR
> Through this supposedly fictional story, was Jack
> actually revealing secret information about one of
> Hollywood's most photographed couples? Is Felix
> Callahan and Celeste Bodine's marriage a sham?

Felix and Celeste pause to be photographed on a
red carpet.

> NARRATOR
> Is his displayed affection for his wife simply a
> show for the paparazzi . . .

Felix and Becky laughing together on set of *Blind
Love*.

> NARRATOR
> . . . while his true love, a married woman, can
> remain secret?

It got to be a minor Hollywood flurry. Becky was answering awkward questions from neighbors, ducking from glares at the grocery

store. So she fought television with television. Nothing like a heart-to-heart with a beloved local news anchor to quell the storm—at home anyway. Mike joined her on the air. The interview was repeated on all the local channels. She talked with newspaper reporters and was a guest on radio programs. Her friends sent letters to the editor scandalized by the bravado of sensationalism among so-called journalists.

But the hassle—the stares and the explaining, and the questions her kids faced at school . . .

Avoid the very appearance of evil, Becky thought grimly.

If she hadn't gone and found a famous guy friend, none of those accusations would have been possible, and some mornings she believed it wasn't worth it.

At the first Hyde family dinner after the exposé, she winced in anticipation of dark looks and *I-told-you-sos*, but surprisingly, her siblings took up verbal pitchforks.

"I can't believe those unscrupulous bottom-feeders!" Jerry slammed his fist into his hand. "It's all a bunch of lies. Boy, it makes me want to—"

"You'd already written *Arm Candy* when you met Felix," her sister, Diana, said. "They don't even check facts, do they? It's unethical."

"And *Blind Love* too," said John's wife, Laurie. "Didn't you come up with that premise years ago?"

"Yeah, I remember that one from when we used to play Original Movie Plot on road trips," Greg said.

"They were too caught up in their splash titles and thrumming music to actually investigate," Ryan said.

"I'm writing a letter to the show, and the network," said Diana.

"So am I," her father said. "They owe you an apology, Becky, and a retraction at the very least."

"How dare they?" Jerry hit his fist against his hand. "It makes me want to—"

"You don't deserve this, sweetheart." Becky's mom wrapped her arm around her daughter's shoulders. "I'm sorry."

"*They'll* be sorry," said Jerry, who had never hit anyone in his life and still held the record for the fewest fouls committed in Davis High basketball history. "They attacked you. It's slander. And it makes me want to—"

"You should sue," Greg said, who had taken the LSAT before deciding to work in landscaping. "You should sue them to kingdom come."

Becky wasn't the litigious type, and suing sounded less a panacea and more like a fine way of protracting the ugliness. Besides, the ickiness that poured from that exposé and stuck to her was abating. Her family was on her side.

"Hey, Jerry." She sidled up to him in their mother's bright yellow kitchen as he refilled his ice cream bowl. "So, what changed?"

He looked at her with those wide open eyes, his stare as befuddled as always, then the blinking started, and she knew he understood. "I ran into someone the other day—Augie Beuter."

"Augie! How is he?"

"Fine, I guess. He's got three kids; they're living in Draper. I hadn't seen him in years, then our families ended up seated next to each other at the BYU game. Anyway, I was remembering you and him in high school. We all thought that you really were secretly . . . you know . . . for each other and would end up married. But you didn't. You knew all along. It wasn't that kind of a thing—you two really were just friends. How come you didn't stay friends?"

She shrugged. "His girlfriend Jen—now his wife—she was uncomfortable with me. And I was head over heels for Mike and didn't want any reason to scare him away. And that was it. I missed Augie for a long time and I felt guilty about missing him. But I don't regret it. At the time, backing away and giving our spouses more space in our lives felt like the right thing to do."

Jerry's eyes were blinking rapidly, then they stuttered to a stop. "And Felix?"

"I'm going with my gut. This time I don't have to lose my Augie."

Jerry swatted her on the shoulder. "Okay then, Bec. And if you need some muscle to take out those tabloid folk . . ." He brandished an ice-cream-stained fist as he walked away.

"Thanks, Jerry."

In grade school, all he'd had to do was stand behind her to scare away those meanie kids. She wasn't sure Jerry's potbelly and dumbfounded expression would have the same effect on cable channel corporate lawyers, but it was nice to know she had an ally.

"Tom Cruise." The whisper was sudden in Becky's ear. Becky startled. It was Diana.

"Tom Cruise. That's who it would be for me. Not the real Tom Cruise—I mean, I don't know if I'd actually like him in person or if we'd have anything in common. But that face . . ."

It took a while for Becky to remember to breathe again. Diana had never kissed anyone besides her husband, Steve—*after* they were married. She was an "altar girl," as they say, and still averted her eyes when characters kissed on-screen.

"Tom Cruise, huh?"

"Yeah. I just had to admit that to you. So I wasn't being hypocritical. Tom Cruise."

"Would you ever kiss him?"

"Of course not."

"If he fell in love with you and begged you to leave your husband and go away with him to a chalet in Switzerland—"

"Never, don't be ridiculous."

"If you were alone in a big city and he was kind to you and offered to buy you dinner so you could chat—"

"No. No! Maybe . . . no. I don't know. Never mind. That's all."

Diana hurried away without a backward glance.

Wow. Tom Cruise. For Diana, that was like admitting she'd killed a puppy for fun. Becky put down the ice cream, much less interested in dessert than in finding Mike. She had news to share.

In the end, Felix took care of "The *Blind Love* Affair"—they'd defamed him as well, and he had a lawyer on payroll. There was no suit, but the cable show agreed to never re-air the exposé and published a retraction, which no one paid the least attention to.

The brouhaha died more quickly than Becky could have hoped. A singer was implicated in the murder of an ex-girlfriend, and Becky Jack, husband stealer, was forgotten. Besides, as it turned out, the public at large had never taken the story seriously. They looked at Celeste Bodine, they looked at Felix, they looked at Becky—it was obvious who belonged with whom.

"You okay about all this?" Becky asked Mike.

"No way. Stupid tabloid journalists. I'd like to hit someone."

"If you and Jerry are both threatening physical violence, this really is Armageddon."

"You should watch out. I'm unpredictable." He pretended to look away then hurled a small, plush duck at her butt.

He was okay about all this.

And Becky was left with the memories, some expensive outfits, and a chunk of change. She decided to get rid of the money right away. Her cut for acting and screenplay combined was a fraction of Felix's paycheck. Of course he offered to split his share fifty-fifty, and of course she refused.

She and Mike created college funds for the kids, replaced the fritzy air conditioner, and paid their mortgage down to a nice manageable sum. They wanted to include their families in their windfall, so they shelled out the remaining cash for a four-day vacation at a large cabin in southern Utah, inviting the entire extended family. There were high points— all her kids had a blast with their cousins, her mother organized a family talent show that was a sidesplitting good time, and each evening Mike's sister Virginia supervised a simply glorious dinner.

And there were low points—on day one, a few nephews, a brother, and a sister-in-law began to murmur. On day two, the murmurers whined, and by day three . . .

"You must've made a buttload of cash on that movie, and all you can buy for breakfast is cold cereal?"

"Bunch of ingrates," she told Felix on the phone. "Did they think I'd waste my kids' college money on caviar?"

"Can't stand caviar," he said. "Lumpy balls of salt. They pop between your teeth, and you know you're killing baby fish."

"Ew."

"Yes."

"I should go back." She was on the porch, cradling her brother's borrowed cell phone against the wind.

"Aunt Becky," shouted one of her nephews out the window. "Can we have some cash to go rent a few movies?"

"Oh for cripe's sake," she muttered, storming back into the house. "Listen up, people. Can you hear me in the kitchen? Pipe down, I'm giving a speech! Thank you all for attending our family bash. There's been some misunderstanding about the state of our funds, so let's clear it up. We are not wealthy. I did not get a million dollars. In fact, the money is depleted. I'm going to give each one of you five bucks, and that will dry me out. Use it for video rentals, pizza orders, or save it to pay your phone bill. Complain about what we eat for breakfast or ask for more money, and I'm giving Mike permission to throw you in the lake."

The room was tense. Even the toddlers stopped toddling. Mike seemed capable of tossing any one of them a respectable distance, and the expression on his face promised he might enjoy it. For a moment, the only sound was muffled, tinny laughing, and Becky realized that Felix was still on the phone.

"Did you catch all that?" she asked, holding the receiver back on her ear.

"Bravo, my lady. And I'll let you go to deal with the aftermath."

He hung up. Everyone was still quiet.

"Any questions?" she asked.

Matt, her eighteen-year-old nephew, raised his hand. "So, are you going to give us a fiver or can I get mine in ones?"

Becky very slowly walked out of the room.

"Money's a curse," she whispered to Mike, who was at her side.

"You're my hero," he said.

And basically, that was that. Polly and Fiona gave her a *Blind Love* scrapbook for Christmas, with frames from the movie and publicity shots, as well as family photos of their summer in California. It was the best thing she got out of the experience—except for the time with Felix. To be honest, the way you can only be honest late at night and in your own head, the whole thing had been pretty cool. She'd been in a movie. She was Felix Callahan's bosom friend. She was painfully in love with her husband, and her kids were awesome. Life was very, very good.

This time she didn't even stop to wonder if everything was going to turn ugly, so when it did, she was unprepared—her spiritual windows weren't boarded up, her emotional sandbags weren't in place. But perhaps the unexpectedness of this tragedy was a gift in disguise; preparation for something far worse.

In which Becky receives a midnight call

The phone woke her, and she was too bleary-eyed to read the clock, even though its huge orange numbers were so bright she often considered wearing an eye mask.

"Hello?"

Felix's voice. "Are you asleep?"

"Hold on," Becky whispered.

Mike rolled over and muttered, "Something wrong?"

"No, just Felix. Go back to sleep."

"K . . ." and he snored.

Becky crawled out of bed, walking the familiar path to the family room with her eyes closed, feeling for obstacles with her feet. She hadn't bothered to stick on her glasses, since she was too sleepy to focus anyway. She dumped herself onto the couch and asked, "What's up?"

He sighed. She heard a lot in that sigh, and she realized with a jolt that opened her eyes that she was lying in the exact spot as the last late-night call. The night Mike had said he was having a hard time. The night Becky had said good-bye to Felix. It was still the same couch, pale beige with embroidered flowers, which had been a thoughtless choice for a home with four children—with any children, really. Colorful splotches created by spilled food and careless markers had become permanent features of the design. Upholstery stain removers were the biggest scam since snake oil.

"Are you going to ask me to try to be gay?" she asked.

Felix didn't laugh. It was a bad sign.

"Oh no. It's Celeste?"

"She said seeing us in the movie, seeing me and you together on the talk shows, she said I looked so happy. She said it made her realize that she can't make me as happy. And that I'm not making her . . ." He choked on the words.

"Was it that exposé—"

He cleared his throat. "No, no one takes those seriously. She said . . . she said something is missing between us, that it's always been missing. That we haven't been growing together for some time. That we need some space. Those very words—*we need some space.* I never imagined that our relationship could be so poorly written."

Becky lay down, resting her head on the stained armrest. He was saying good-bye. Her heart curled into her chest like a snail in a shell.

"I need . . ." He paused as if gathering strength. "I need to not talk to you anymore. Or see you. To show Celeste that there's no one more important. More important than her."

"Of course. Good for you." And she meant it, though her voice faltered.

"I need to go now," he said. "I can't linger. I'm . . ." His voice cracked again.

"Okay, sure, I'll . . . I mean . . . take care of yourself, Felix. Bye." She spoke quickly and hung up.

She lay on the sofa for an hour or more, still clutching the phone, still holding the hang-up button. She only knew she was crying because there were warm lines of sensation running sideways down her face. After a time, the armrest felt a little wet.

This is silly, she told herself. You're forty-one. Buck up. You'll survive losing your friend again.

Putting down the phone, she folded her arms and, still prostrate, said a prayer for Felix and Celeste, for their marriage, for his pain, for her understanding. And while she was at it, she prayed for her family—that Mike could land a new position at work where he'd be happier, that Fiona's heart wouldn't break over her current boy love, that Polly could be bold with her manipulative little friends, that Hyrum could feel more confidence in school, that Sam would be spared the life-threatening accidents he seemed determined to tumble into. She didn't pray for herself.

When she returned to the bedroom, she could tell Mike was in his delicate stage of sleep, where the least disruption might wake him and spark insomnia. She gently closed the door, went back downstairs to the kitchen, and stayed up until three making pies. She couldn't send one to the person who needed comfort the most, but at least the world didn't feel as heavy and hopeless when there was pie.

Months crept by without a word from Felix. Becky avoided reading Internet entertainment sites. She didn't see his new film, even though it was rated PG-13. Mike knew the whole situation of course, but she didn't tell anyone else, which made it awkward when she got the common "How's Felix?" inquiry.

"Fine," she'd say. Lying wasn't her cup of herbal tea, but she couldn't very well divulge Felix's private business to anyone who happened to ask.

"Hey, how's Felix?"

"Fine, he's fine."

From what she could see of the magazine covers in line at the grocery store, his marriage trouble hadn't yet hit that fan. That was good. Maybe they were working it out. She wrote Celeste a letter illustrating how much Felix loved his wife and no one else, then spent a week agonizing over whether or not to send it, going back and forth with Mike on pros and cons. In the end, they decided she'd be wise to hang back, be invisible.

It wouldn't have made a difference. Celeste's mind had been made up for months.

"Hello?"

"It wasn't you and me," Felix said, his words slurring together. She could nearly smell the whiskey wafting through the fiber optics. "It wasn't me. It's not me . . ."

"Tell me," she said, walking into the kitchen to put some distance between herself and the rowdy pounding that was Hyrum's piano practice. Felix's voice after all this time, mixed with the wild music and the fact that all she'd eaten that day was a bowl of Yogurt-Zapped Breakfast Rings, was making her head spin.

"Celeste is seeing someone else. She's in Florence. His name is Alfredo. Alfredo!"

Becky's breath was yanked out of her. She squeaked, "Is it serious?"

"Someone sent me an Italian tabloid. That's how I found out. There was a photo. They were in their bathing costumes on the beach, kissing. On a beach. Kissing on a beach. I don't have—isn't there a list of the top ten worst clichés? And that's one? That has to be one. Apparently he's a musician, though he looks like a complete drip. I called her. She didn't deny it. She's in love, she said. She's sorry she didn't tell me first, she said. That's the bit she regrets, she said, but she can't regret being in love. With Alfredo. Alfredo the Italian musician."

"Where are you?"

"In New York. Doing a play. I took the rest of the week off from rehearsals."

"Are you alone?"

"Yes."

"I'm coming out."

He paused. "Okay."

It wasn't until Mike came home from work that Becky realized what she was about to do.

"Could you come with me, honey?" she asked.

"I've got a client meeting tomorrow. Are you having second thoughts?"

"Sort of, but I think he needs me. He sounded horrible. I booked a seat on the red-eye. But . . . but we'd be alone, and he's separated from his wife, and I can't remember where the lines are anymore"

Mike stared at her as if trying to determine her species. "What do you mean, 'lines'?"

"I've been trying to keep track of all the lines that abhor a crossing, you know, since Felix is a guy and he's not gay and doesn't smell strongly of kimchi. And it was the night before I went on a trip alone to meet him that you had a hard time, and I don't want to worry you."

He still hadn't figured out her species. "Bec, it's Felix." He said "Felix" like he might've said "Twinkie" or "miniature golf."

"Yeah."

"So . . . I'm not worried."

"The airfare was steep last-minute."

"That's a bummer, but if he needs his best friend, I wouldn't expect anything less of you."

"Thank you."

He was right, and she knew she should go, but she still felt a heavy ball of unease in her belly. She dismissed it as sorrow for the end of one of her favorite marriages. Celeste—how could Celeste . . . it didn't make sense. They were so much in love. She was such a genuine, warm person. How could she do this? How could she hurt Felix, allow herself to fall in love with Alfredo, break apart their marriage, toss away something so sacred?

The thoughts hounded and scorched her. Becky didn't sleep on the plane.

Felix wasn't waiting at the airport. When the Jack family had first arrived in Los Angeles for the movie summer, he'd been waiting at baggage claim in his chauffeur's hat, holding a sign that said "Jack," scanning the crowd as if he didn't recognize them. Of course now he was navigating some rough seas. He wouldn't be in shape to get up early and haul out to the airport. But as she watched the baggage carousel rumble by, a wave of something dark rushed over her. She called it foreboding, but it might have been exhaustion. The spinning carousel was hypnotic in her sleepy state and it took her several minutes to remember she hadn't checked a bag. All she had was a carry-on, her purse, and a homemade apple pie.

She took a taxi to his apartment on the Upper West Side, the pie perched on her lap. One of her weekly give-away pies had been claimed already when Felix had called. But another had been waiting patiently on the counter for an unknown sad soul who needed comfort, and she hadn't hesitated to find a box and bring it along. Two thousand miles she'd schlepped it, careful not to let it get smooshed through security and turbulence. Then she set it on the cab seat while she paid.

She was standing on the curb watching the taxi drive away when she realized aloud, "Felix's pie is in that cab." She was too tired to wave or shout or run after it. Maybe the cab driver was having a lousy day. Maybe he really, really needed a homemade apple pie.

Twenty minutes later, Becky was still on her feet, standing in the building's lobby while the doorman tried to reach Felix. He buzzed, he rang. No answer. Becky tried Felix's cell phone. She tried the apartment phone. Finally Felix came off the street through the glass doors, a bag from the corner drugstore in hand. He stared at her for several seconds before seeming to recognize her face.

"You're here," he said blankly.

His under eyes were purple, his face pillowcase pallid. He was wearing shorts and one of Celeste's sweatshirts. It was too small, and he reminded Becky of a growing boy, last year's shirt rimming his belly, cuffs a couple of inches from his wrists. He'd never looked more pathetic, or frankly, adorable.

"Hi Rufus," she said.

She held out her arms. He blinked again, and a little life returned to his eyes. He stumbled over, wrapped his arms around her, and lay his head on her shoulder. She heard him sigh.

"Thank you," he said into her hair. "Thank you, thank you, thank you."

They stayed in all day. He didn't smile, but a glint of his normal self would occasionally catch in his eye. He'd had Chris Isaac's "Wicked Game" on repeat, which was making matters worse in these circumstances, so Becky took possession of the CD and hid it in a book when his back was turned.

He hadn't been eating well—her well-trained eye could spot that in a moment—so she put Aretha Franklin on the stereo ("because the Queen of Soul knows heartbreak and makes it feel good," Becky said) and made a big breakfast. Biscuits, bacon, poached eggs with cheese, chunky hash browns—she scavenged whatever she could find in the kitchen and transformed it into comfort food. It was her motherly superpower, and she wielded it obscenely well.

He ate, and that seemed to help. Then she pushed him into the bathroom, forcing him to take a shower by threatening a sponge bath if he didn't comply. He came out, red faced and glistening in his bathrobe. She turned on the ocean-sounds machine and tucked him into his bed. While he napped, she puttered around, taking anything that might remind him of Celeste and stowing it in the closet.

When he emerged from the bedroom a couple of hours later in pajama pants and a Boston Marathon T-shirt, she was cleaning the fridge, throwing out soft carrots and spinach that had begun to leak a brown liquid.

Becky beamed at him. "Good morning, bedhead."

He put a hand to his hair, feeling the postmodern mess that sleeping on wet hair had done to him. "It's fashionable."

"So I hear. But I think I'll stick to the suburban mother look that's such a rage with all the kids."

He didn't quite smile, but his face softened. Then he saw Celeste's protein shakes in the fridge door, and he put his hand over his eyes.

She led him to the couch, tucked a decorative throw around his legs, and let him talk. He seemed ready to spill it out, though his voice carried the slow, monotonous heaviness that characterize the zombified or extremely bored. He spoke about how he and Celeste had met, he spoke about the promises they'd made, how he'd never been unfaithful, how he'd always told her everything, even the time he'd kissed a woman at a pub in Ireland. He talked about how much he hated Italy. The entire country—it's history, culture, food, and street names.

"She called again yesterday. She wanted to apologize. She said she understood that I would be angry, and if I threw out her clothing, that I would be justified, but please be kind to the necklace on her dresser with the golden flower pendant. It had been her grandmother's." He paused for so long Becky wondered if he'd forgotten he'd been talking.

"The flower pendant?" she asked, prodding him.

"I ate it."

She gulped. He almost smiled.

"I put it in her closet. I'm not to the anger stage. Yet. I am still stupefied. She said she'd like me to meet him. Alfredo. Isn't that a kind of a sauce? She wants us to have dinner. She wants to bring him, Alfredo, to New York. The man, not the sauce. She'd like for the three of us to have dinner in New York—Celeste and I, and Alfredo. The Speedo-wearing drip of an Italian musician. Having dinner. She said she thinks we'd get along. Me and Alfredo. Alfredo and I."

That was when Becky nestled in beside him following her instinct to comfort. She put her arm around his shoulders, drew his head onto her shoulder, rubbed his arm, kissed his forehead, as she would have cuddled Sam after a fall off his bike. At least, she thought that's what she was doing. Looking back, she wondered if her motherly touch had felt very different to the heartsick Felix.

"I'm glad you're here," he said.

He held her hand. And they sat like that for a bit, snuggled in next to each other, holding hands. His warmth began to mingle with hers until she no longer felt chilly in that unheated apartment. She could smell the soap he'd used—it reminded her of hotel soap. She wondered if that was what he was using, soap picked up at hotels, and that thought made her sad. She was mentally planning a shopping list of things she'd get for him during her stay when something happened.

He lifted her hand to his mouth and kissed the back of it. Then he kissed it again. He closed his eyes, he turned her hand over, and his lips lingered on her palm, kissing slowly. She stared at him, a shock of cold running through her. He was running her fingers across his lips. His lips parted. His breath was warm and hinted that he was just beginning, and she imagined him kissing her fingers again, sucking her fingertips, moving to her wrist, her neck . . .

She gently pulled her hand away and set it on her lap, leaning slightly away from him. His eyes were still closed, but his brow furrowed.

"The music stopped," she said casually. "I'll put on something else."

She gave his shoulder a friendly, casual rub as she stood and went to the CD shelf, looking for something upbeat and unromantic. She thought Smash Mouth should do the trick. Then she went to the kitchen, calling back to see if he wanted something to drink.

"I'm good," he answered, his voice raspy.

Out of sight, she leaned against the fridge, pressing her hand to her pounding heart, and tried to breathe slowly. Her hand still tingled.

What had just happened? What did it mean? What should she do now?

Smash Mouth sang out some advice. None of it was relevant.

The best thing was to pretend it hadn't happened. He'd been drinking, she thought. She wasn't a good judge of how drunk a person was or how clearly they could think and remember things. So she decided to believe that he hadn't been really aware, that he would forget about it soon, that it was harmless and meaningless. He was sad, he was achingly lonely, he'd reached out to her for affection and hadn't realized that he'd crossed a line. Their friendship would remain unscathed.

"Good," she whispered to herself. "Fine. Good. No problem. Everything's okay."

She poured herself some water, and when she came back, Felix was filling another glass of whiskey. He glanced up and smiled. It was a passionless smile, a pleasant smile, a Hey-there-glad-to-see-ya! smile. She let out a relieved breath.

"So I was considering," he said, staring at his drink, swishing the liquor around in the glass just enough that it would graze the glass rim without splashing out—a practiced gesture. "What do you say we go out for dinner?"

"Yeah? Would that be good for you? Absolutely. Let's blow this depressing park-view high-rise luxury apartment, get out there and paint the town a reddish-orange."

"Persimmon?"

"I'd imagined more of a burnt sienna."

They went into separate bedrooms to get changed. Happily she'd packed a prettyish summer dress, with big yellow flowers, short sleeves, the hem just below her knees. It'd been warm spring weather in Utah, but New York was breezier and her dress not quite right. So she stuck a white cardigan over it. She tried not to look at herself too closely in the mirror as she put on makeup. She'd been on the red-eye after all, hadn't showered that day, and wasn't feeling particularly ravishing. But it didn't matter, because she was with Felix, her best friend. It just didn't matter.

They both came back to the sitting room at the same time, and when she saw him, she nearly gasped. He looked devastating.

"New rags?" she asked.

"Going-about-town garb." His modern-art hairdo was now a naughty-boy kind of messy. He was in one of those black suits that had something different about it, something her untrained eye couldn't specifically define but that let her know this was not an off-the-rack number. His shirt was blue, open two buttons from the top, no undershirt, no tie.

"All that ensemble needs is a liver pendant on a manly leather cord," she said.

He smiled. Things might be turning around. They took a cab to an Indian restaurant in midtown and had an uneventful dinner despite two autograph seekers. Felix dismissed them without insult.

On the cab ride home, Felix gave the driver a different address.

"It's a little club I've wanted to see," Felix explained. "We can go hear some music, sit in the semidark, you can nurse a Shirley Temple. Doesn't that sound brilliant?"

No, not really, she thought. Her limbs were already feeling waterlogged with sleepiness. But Becky didn't argue. He needed distraction, she reasoned.

There was a line of beautiful people waiting around the block. They all looked younger than twenty-five. And the women were dressed as if it were high noon in July. Felix paid the cab driver and got out.

"You don't want to wait in a line, do you?" she asked.

Felix laughed at her. She'd heard that laugh out of him before, directed at people he thought were stupid. He'd never laughed at her that way. She took a step back.

Felix was shaking the muscled doorman's hand and whispering something in his ear. He opened the door. Felix motioned to Becky and disappeared. Becky nearly didn't follow until he reached back and took her arm.

The lights were dim and bright at once, the music scorching. Becky tried to recall the time in her life when this atmosphere had been heart-pounding exciting. When noise had made her feel more alive, not tired and old.

"This will be good for you?" she half-yelled to Felix.

He smiled his knowing smile.

The hostess gave him a round booth near the stage, where a band made up of various electric instruments, brass horns, and tribal drums were insisting a song. Drinks magically appeared before them. Becky's looked suspicious, pale yellow and heavier than juice, so she didn't touch it.

Felix was staring at the band, his thumb keeping time on his glass. Honestly, she didn't know how he found any rhythm. When had she gotten so old that contemporary music became a foreign language? And how did Felix manage to slip into a younger culture so easily?

"You're amazing," she said. "You fit in anywhere."

He nodded, but she realized it was in response to the beat, not to her.

So they sat quietly inside that can of clamor, Felix's eyes scanning the band, the room, the women who would pass by. She'd never seen Felix look over women like that, at their bodies without shame. It made her frown. But he was having a hard time, she reasoned. He had cause. She waved down their waitress and asked for a mineral water, then stared into it, counting bubbles.

He turned to her for the first time since they'd come in. "Do you want to dance?"

"Dance?"

True, there were some people sliding and bumping in a mysterious fashion on the dance floor, but their movements were as puzzling to Becky as the melody of the song. She was relieved none of her kids were there to see her, awkward and old in her flowered sundress, or any coolness she'd gained from being in the movie would be flattened.

"Truthfully, I'm bushed, but if you want—"

"Excuse me." A perky blonde no more than twenty stopped at their table. She leaned over so Felix could hear her, and the neck of her dress gaped, opening a tunnel view to her navel. "Are you that actor?"

"Felix Callahan," said her redheaded friend. "He's Felix Callahan."

"Have a seat." He stepped out of the booth, gesturing the blonde one in. He had on his suave smile. "I want one of you on each side, if you don't mind. I'm feeling a bit chilly."

They didn't mind at all. They sat on each side. The blonde bumped into Becky, forcing her to slide to the end of the booth.

At first Becky smiled politely and tried to contribute to the conversation. Before long she was back to counting bubbles.

"Do you dance?" the redhead asked. "Let's see if you can shake the British right out of you."

Becky played with her straw and watched Felix shake out his Britishness, never spilling the drink he balanced in one hand. The girls slid up against him.

He needs this, she told herself. This is his way to relax, to forget. He needs to have fun, let go, feel attractive again.

She did a good job of convincing herself for an hour or two. But it kept getting later. The waitress gave her hot glares when she wouldn't order any more drinks. One o'clock in the morning and still the club seemed to have no intention of closing. Becky pulled her heels onto the bench, held her knees to her chest, and rested her head. The glaring lights and glaring waitress were hurting her eyes.

I'm ugly here, she found herself thinking more and more the later it got. I feel so ugly, so soul ugly, so fat-pants-and-dirty-hair ugly, so washed-out, wilted-mushroom, discarded-wrapper ugly.

She wanted Mike. She wanted to be home, Sam snuggled up on her lap, Mike bringing her a doughnut, Fiona playing a hymn on the piano. Bedtime at ten P.M. Flannel pajamas. Her down pillow wafting fabric softener. Home. For a pair of ruby slippers to click together. For a hot-air balloon headed west. For even a cell phone. She really needed to invest in a cell phone.

She put her head on the table and closed her eyes. Despite the music, there were moments when she dipped briefly into sleep. It was like dozing with a dog standing on the bed, barking an inch from her face.

Three A.M. and Felix was sitting at the bar with an entourage of young ladies. He had another drink. He was smiling at a blonde, his hand on her knee.

What about Celeste? Becky couldn't help thinking. How could Felix and Celeste be over? This is wrong, wrong, wrong!

She hated seeing him there with other women, his eyes spilling over their draping tops, his hands finding reasons to touch their shoulders, their waists, their hips. It was a Felix she'd never seen before. Her stomach sickened, and she felt crazy desperate to have her friend back. If he turned just a sliver, he would make eye contact with Becky. She stared, willing him to look at her, wishing it. Praying.

He didn't look.

Exhaustion and alienation were making her feel wobbly and confused. She didn't have a key to Felix's apartment and didn't remember the address anyway. Her address book was back at his place with her luggage. She trolled through her wallet, counting twenty-two dollars in cash.

There was a line of taxis waiting outside the club. She leaned into the window of the first one.

"Would twenty-two dollars be enough to get me to a hotel near JFK?"

The driver rubbed his eyes and shook his head. "I can take credit cards, lady. You have a credit card?"

She got in. "A chain hotel, if you please. Something clean and safe but not too much money, okay?"

The driver rolled his toothpick to the other side of his mouth. "And here I took you for the Ritz-Carlton type."

He peeled out. Becky looked through the back window just in case. Felix didn't emerge.

Forty-five minutes later, Becky was sitting on a droopy-flowers bedspread at a Howard Johnson. The room was cold. She didn't have any pajamas or change of clothes or toothbrush. She stared at the mottled wallpaper, not moving for some time. Then she started to cry.

Kicking off her shoes, she crawled under the sheets and called home.

"Hello?" a sleepy Mike asked.

"Hi honey."

"Bec, you're crying. Oh baby, what happened?"

"Nothing. I just—I miss you. I love you. I don't want to be away from you anymore."

"Come home, honey."

"I will. Tomorrow. I'm sorry about the money I spent on this trip. I know I've put a real dent in our plans to take the kids to Oregon this summer. I was impetuous. It was wrong."

"You were helping a friend. You were being Becky. You did just what you had to do."

"Okay" was all she could say because she'd started crying again.

"What happened? Did Felix do something?"

"Not really. It's not that big of a deal. I'll tell you tomorrow—I don't want to cry anymore tonight."

"I think I had news for you . . ." Mike said, as if he wanted to distract her. "Oh yeah, Sam lost a tooth. He tugged and tugged at it all day, he was so set to get that sucker under his pillow by bedtime. I've never seen him more determined."

Becky laughed quietly. It was happy news. Sam had just begun losing baby teeth while Hyrum famously lost his first at age five. Sam didn't like feeling like a baby. He'd potty-trained himself at two and a half after Hyrum had said, "Baby Sammy poops his baby pants." He'd taken off his diaper, emptied all the new diapers in his room into the kitchen trash, and never worn one again.

"What did the tooth fairy bring him?"

"A Susan B. Anthony dollar."

"Oh, he'll be so happy. He thinks she's a good-hearted witch who grants wishes."

"I thought we could take him to the dollar store, let him spend it."

"I'll fly home in the morning. Do you think you could get off work early, pick me up at the airport?"

"You bet. You're due a foot massage, by the way."

She sighed. "I love you, Mike. I'll call you in the morning with the flight details and the Felix details. None of it really matters. I'm just happy that I'll see you soon."

"Me too. I love you."

"Good night." She hung up the phone without lingering, because she knew the hotel was going to charge her brutally for the call.

Now she could curl up. Now she could shut her eyes and find some comfort in the pillow. Mike's voice stayed with her as she fell asleep.

In which Becky stews, boils, and bakes

While she was in the air, Felix called Mike.

"He asked if I knew where you were," Mike reported as he drove Becky home from the airport. "I said you were flying home. He said he was glad you were okay. That he'd send your things back. That he was sorry he hadn't had a chance to say good-bye."

"'Hadn't had a chance'..." she muttered under her breath. "What else?"

"That was all." Mike paused. She could tell that he was considering whether or not to tell her the rest. "I heard a woman's voice in the background and he said he had to go. He said, 'See you round.'"

"'See you round.'"

"Yep."

"You wanted to tell him off, didn't you?" she asked.

"Of course I did! He abandoned you. He was acting like a complete putz."

She couldn't argue with that.

"But his voice was kind of pathetic," said Mike. "I guess he's not himself right now."

"No, he's not." She gave Mike a weak smile. "I need a bath."

"You really do. I can smell you."

"Hey! I've had a rough couple of days!"

"You still smell."

For several days, Becky was good about the whole situation. Poor Felix, she said to herself. He'd never have done that to me if he'd been in his right mind. This is incredibly stressful for him. He feels so lonely.

Then her overnight bag arrived on the doorstep—a week later. She'd figured it was lost or something, but no, Felix had actually sent it third class. And she found herself thinking, He makes several million dollars each picture, and he couldn't overnight it?

He didn't call. And he didn't call.

A woman's voice in the background, she thought.

Perhaps he'd gone home with the blonde. Or the redhead. (Or both?) So, he had escaped into a stranger's embrace. He'd been lonely, devastated, he needed that comfort. She had no right to expect him to live by the same morals she believed in.

But the thought of it began to irritate her, like an itch at the back of her eyeballs.

At first she didn't say a word about her internal rumblings to Mike. She was going to be good; she was going to let it roll off her. And she managed to stick to that oath of silence for two whole weeks, while the idea of those voluptuous girls fermented inside her, until she broke down and declared, "You should've seen them, Mike. What are girls like that doing in a club? Don't they have better things to do? Shouldn't they be in college at that age and home studying?"

Mike shrugged. "We used to go dancing in college."

That wasn't the response she'd been hoping for. So she brought it up again later from a slightly different angle.

"He's forty-four years old, Mike. Why would young girls go after a man that old? Don't they have friends their own age? There's something wrong with a twenty-year-old who can't find dates her own age. Maybe something certifiably wrong."

"It happens," Mike said as he made some grilled cheese sandwiches for the boys. "And besides, we don't know all the particulars."

Mike was being infuriatingly reasonable. He would.

When she read that Felix's play was panned and closed down, she actually felt a small twist of "that serves you right." Then in a supermarket line she saw Felix's photo in a magazine she'd stopped to flip through. He was dapper. He looked younger (plastic surgery?). He was walking on a boardwalk somewhere, holding hands with Jessica Bedecker, a twenty-six-year-old actress with perfectly gorgeous flyaway brown hair and a build right at home in a V-neck sweater.

Becky began to boil.

"He's forty-four, Mike. Did I mention he's forty-four? What's he doing?"

"Are you worried for Celeste's sake?"

"Not anymore. She's made her choice with Alfredo, the saucy Italian musician."

"Then I don't understand why this upsets you so much. You know he's going through a public and difficult divorce. I'd think you'd be happy for him to be dating again."

"You don't understand," she said.

"Why not?"

So she had to think of a reason. "Because you're a man."

"Oh."

That wasn't the end of it. A few days later:

"The point is, he'd been crying about Celeste a few hours earlier, then he went to a club and hooked up with two bouncy girls."

"They were adults, weren't they?"

"Yes, yes, bouncy infantile adult girls. Why are you defending him? He probably slept with one of them that very night! Or both! Don't you see, Mike? I mean, what is he doing?"

Mike sat down on the edge of the bed and said carefully, "Becky, what are *you* doing?"

Becky stopped pacing. The tone in his voice stilled her. She had some words she'd like to shout, none of them rated G. But she couldn't bear to fight with him when he used that tone—the sweetly reasonable, the concerned, the loving Mike tone. It wasn't fair.

She waited for him to speak again.

"I can't figure it out. You're acting funny. You don't usually get riled up like this—not about other people's decisions, not unless it affects the kids somehow. It's almost like . . . you're jealous. But I don't think you are. Are you? Jealous?"

She let that question bounce around the quiet room. Then she whispered, "That was too far," and walked away.

Things were a teensy bit tense in the Jack household. Becky and Mike spoke like business colleagues, comparing to-do lists, engaging in stilted small talk that skirted anything emotional. Mike didn't give Becky hugs in the kitchen, and Becky didn't laugh much. Hyrum acted out more, playing trouble for trouble. Sam said things like, "Why's everyone being weird?" Fiona looked at her parents askance and was double quick to do as asked.

Polly was the only one who didn't seem to notice. The week before, on her fourteenth birthday, she'd been allowed to start wearing a second item of makeup (in addition to lip gloss). She'd chosen mascara, and it took up a lot of her attention.

It took a week before Becky and Mike rolled toward each other in bed and touched each other again. It was a white flag, an "I still love you even though I don't want to talk about this right now" event. And it made the coming weeks a little more bearable.

Still Felix didn't call.

All through May, Becky boiled. She made her prayers inconsequential. She read her scriptures nightly without allowing the words to sink inside her. In many ways, she felt liberated, as if she'd thrown off her bra and taken to wearing large purple hats. She'd always been so careful to guard herself, to live and let live, to not criticize others, to not use her own faith as a measuring stick for anyone else. And now—ha! She was giving the entire world the evil eye. Felix was wrong! Those bouncy girls were wrong! Everyone was wrong but her, and it was a thrill like she'd never experienced before, a rush like sledding down a black-diamond ski slope.

Even so, she was aware that the rush couldn't last forever. That she'd hit the bottom. That she'd have to sit still eventually and feel the world spinning beneath her.

She held it off until summer.

They spent five days at Mike's parents' cabin on Bear Lake, and Becky found it impossible to put up defenses against trees and water and wind moving over water. She sat on a rock, her feet dabbling with the lake. The rush of the ski slope stopped, her feet hit ground, and she had to think.

The lines of light on water winking at her, the gray blue sky in the lake looking back up at itself, the way the cold began to feel warm on her toes—it was raw and unflinching and perfect. And she couldn't hide from it. She took a breath and had to admit that she'd been out of line. And she knew why.

Mike came walking along the shore, his jeans rolled up to his knees. He had big, muscular man calves. She'd always thought that he would've been a hit in Shakespeare's time, when men wore breeches and tights to show off their legs. Those forehead-shaving dames would have gone mad.

"Romeo, oh, Romeo," she said.

"Yo, Adrian."

She smiled. "The kids okay?"

"My mom's watching Sam and Hyrum. The girls are cutting up magazines."

He stood behind her, waiting for an invitation. She offered it by saying, "I'm ready to talk about it."

His eyebrows went up, but he didn't say a word as he sat beside her. He dipped his feet into the water, breathing in through his teeth when he felt how cold it was. Stoic Mike, never complain Mike, never even mention a headache Mike, but he was such a wimp about the cold.

"Okay, here it is. I'm not jealous. Not about Felix flirting with bouncy girls or hooking up with young actresses. I was a little afraid that I might have cared, and that made me cranky because I so badly didn't want to. If I'm going to be absolutely honest, I'm glad he's been seen with other women so publicly—it means the tabloids won't be digging up that old story and pointing to me as the homewrecker."

She tossed a pebble into the water and watched the rings roll out, letting that thought sink in before she jumped to her blame.

"But I *was* jealous, in a way. I was resentful that those puerile strangers were more interesting to him than I was. That he could toss me away so easily. That my company alone wasn't enough to cure his depression. I wanted to be that important to him. Not just privately, but publicly. It's gross to admit, but it's true."

These thoughts had peeked inside her the past couple of days, but only while speaking them did she really see and understand. And Mike was the only person on earth to whom she could reveal those ugly parts of herself.

"I've always felt that the Lord put me in Felix's life for a reason, and there would come a time when he'd need me to . . . to save him. And when I got the call and went to New York, part of me thought, this is it. This is why we met in the first place, why this friendship has seemed so important all along. Because he needs someone now, and he hasn't allowed himself anyone close besides Celeste—and me. With Celeste gone, I'm all that's left. Now I can save him, and it will all have been worthwhile; it will all make sense. But instead . . ."

"The puerile strangers."

She nodded. "I was close to useless. I'm not as important as I'd hoped. Not only didn't I save him, but I lost something. He's Felix Callahan, and his attention used to make me special." She winced. "I thought I was immune to that. I'm not. I feel so stupid about this, but that's the truth. I should have made allowances for his grief. I should have understood and given him space. Instead I've sulked because I realized I'm not as *special* as I thought."

At first, Mike's expression was full of humble sympathy, but he began to smirk and then said in a high-pitched, mocking tone, "I'm Becky, and I like to be special."

She laughed, as he knew she would. She attacked him, lunging for his soft underbelly, and he let her knock him back. They wrestled there on the stony beach until they were panting, Becky allowing the physical activity to push the last of the resentment out of her body. Just to seal the deal, she let Mike throw her into the chilly water, pulling him in after her. It was a desperate baptism and made nothing more important than the warmth of a home. They shivered and laughed, and scurried into the house drenched and beaming.

From her post on the couch, Fiona tilted her head, a questioning look, and Becky winked. The tension in the family crumbled away.

In which Polly walks the red carpet

Now that she'd forgiven Felix, Becky was ready for their third reunion. He didn't call, though nearly every time the phone rang she wondered whether it was him. He didn't drop by, though when the doorbell chimed unexpectedly, she expected to see his face through the screen. She considered contacting him, of course, but in her best, quiet, post-prayer state, she felt she needed to let him extend the olive branch. Waiting made her anxious, even stung a bit, like trying to light all the candles on a birthday cake before the match flame reached her fingertips.

Months ticked by and the memory of her anger had been worn down to sand when she got the flowers: a huge vase of sunflowers, her favorite. The note said, "Forgive me?"

She called him. He didn't answer his cell. She phoned his London house and his Los Angeles house, but she didn't want to leave a message. She was about to call Celeste to get an update before her memory caught up, and her heart tore anew for the loss of that marriage. At last she just e-mailed him and said, "Of course I forgive you."

He called the next day.

"Hi."

"Hey."

"Are you all right?"

"Yeah. You?"

"Pretty good." He paused. "I'm sorry."

"I am too. I'm happy to hear your voice."

"Yours is nicer."

"How's Jessica?"

"You heard about that? She's good. We're in Houston now. Her family lives here."

"How long will you be in Texas?"

"Another week, and then I'm back in L.A." He cleared his throat. "We're about to release the Dean Martin movie."

"You are? That's wonderful!"

"Yes. Thanks."

A pause.

"This is awkward now but next time it'll be easier," she said.

"Just a matter of getting used to each other again."

"Exactly."

"And that's why I'm going to have a layover in Salt Lake City next week. I'd like to see you."

The following Tuesday she picked him up at the airport and they had lunch at the Red Iguana, ten minutes away. She ordered the mole negro. He had the "Killer Nachos," a huge, heaping, sweating plate of tortilla chips covered in cheese, beans, meat chunks, chile verde, guacamole, and sour cream. He ate three of the chips.

"You look well," she said.

"I've been in the sun a lot lately. And Jessica is good for me."

"I'm glad. You deserve someone good for you."

"Also, I'm taking a multivitamin."

"You see? I knew they'd help!"

He smiled.

Now what? Were they going to talk? Did she need to tell him how she'd felt? Would she confess her boiling months, her jealousy, her spiteful thoughts? And how the lake worked it out of her? Would he reveal the tortured machinations of his brain that led him to abandon her at the club and ignore her for months? Or would they stay silent and pretend it never happened?

"I've been an a—" He paused, altering his word choice. "I've been a *stupidhead*. I won't overexplain, for fear of making excuses. The plain truth is I've been a big, fat stupidhead."

Relief surged through her. Until he'd said it, she hadn't known how much she needed him to admit that he'd been an—whatever naughty word he'd been about to use. And in truth, she was almost as pleased with his substitution of "stupidhead" as she was with the apology itself. Felix just sounded so darling speaking that Hyrum-ish word.

He was looking at her shrewdly. "I was, wasn't I? You're not going to argue?"

"Oh no, you hit that one right on the head."

"And you forgive me?"

"Completely, I think. I've missed you, Felix, more than I've even realized. I've missed me with you."

And it was good. And they smiled. But by the time she had to take him back to the airport, they still hadn't laughed.

She kept the radio off for the drive home and spent that rare hour of quiet wondering if they would ever laugh together again. Mike would've told her she was being fatalistic. She hoped that was all. But the silence felt permanent, as if she'd never hear anything but the drone of the car's engine again. She always feared silence and scratched at it until the next wave of chaos rolled over her again and buried her in sweet normalcy.

Felix called her that night. And the next. Just a few days later, after a sum total of four hours of postcrisis talking, the icy space between them thawed just enough and they shared their first laugh of the new era. It was timid. It came from their throats rather than from their guts, was more an auditory expression of a smile than an irresistible guffaw. But it was a start.

It took a few weeks before they were engaging again in typical Becky-Felix conversations.

"Hi there."

"Hey, hoser. How's the movie release going?"

"Good. Busy. I have precisely thirty-two seconds left."

"Well, that's not nearly enough. Do you want me to talk to your people and finagle more time? I can be terribly convincing."

"I would even say frighteningly convincing. Shockingly convincing. Horrifyingly con—"

"Or maybe I can win your director over with love. I'll FedEx a loaf of zucchini bread."

"It only took thirty seconds to confirm the fact that you're still absurd."

"I love you too. Hoser."

After the publicity tour, he came to Layton for the first time in three years. He stayed at a local hotel and complained endlessly.

"That's quite a shiner you have there, Sam. It's the exact color of the wallpaper in my room. Is that an open sewer we just passed? A similar odor was leaking from my minifridge."

"Quit your whining or you'll be set up in the Jack family *Little Mermaid* Suite."

"Shutting up."

He took the whole family out for miniature golf and pizza. At the ninth hole, Mike walked him aside for a private chat, and Becky imagined the scoldings and mild threats her husband might be expressing. For Felix's part, he seemed to take it well; at least, he shook Mike's hand and didn't cut his trip short.

She didn't need Mike to defend her. Felix didn't need to hear what Mike thought about his behavior to know that he'd been a stupidhead. But all the same, Becky loved Mike for it. To be frank, it made her feel all gooey and affectionate.

After his Layton trip, Felix and Jessica broke up.

"She wants a family one day. She wants children. It's more important to her than her career is, than I am. And I'm not interested in being a father."

"Felix . . ." she used her motherly tones. "You would be a wonderful father. You really would."

"No. I wouldn't. And I don't care to be. Besides . . ." His voice was sad, and he didn't say any more.

"Oh, sweetie," she said, hearing in the silence, *Besides, Jessica isn't Celeste. Besides, no one will ever be.*

He began a series of relationships with other actresses, makeup artists, singers, all significantly younger than him. Some he mentioned to Becky; some she discovered by paging through the celebrity magazines.

Becky missed Celeste.

But he was between women when he was nominated for a Best Actor Academy Award.

"You were so brilliant, Felix," Becky said. "If you hadn't been nominated for this movie, I would've marched on Hollywood. Do you know I saw it five times in the theater? I can't leave my children unattended without worrying Hyrum will burn down the house or Sam will crack his head open. Can you imagine then the pains I went to just to view you as Dean Martin five times? This is what I'm trying to tell you. You were that good. Five-times good."

"It was a decent flick. I did it because of you."

"Then you'd better mention me in your acceptance speech."

"I find myself flying solo just now, and not having a date for the Oscars I—"

"Want me to attend with you? That's so sweet! I've always wondered—"

"Er, no, sorry. You had to return the dress you wore to our premiere, didn't you? And I don't trust what hideous getup you might deem appropriate."

"Oh. What a relief. If I had to watch you pretending to be humble while the crowd chants your name, I might—"

"Right. So I was asking about Polly. I'd hoped you might allow me to fly out your family for the before and after hoopla, and then at the awards Polly could play the part of my goddaughter and spare me inquiries about my current dating. I never forgot how she glowed at the premiere. I think she really enjoyed stepping into that world. Do you think Fiona would be heartbroken?"

Becky spoke with Fiona. Her first question was, "Will Celeste be there?"

"No, honey, I think they burned their bridge pretty thoroughly."

"Oh." Fiona thought. "Can I still get a dress?"

"Sure. He's invited us all to a couple of parties where you could wear something nice."

They were sitting on the couch, Fiona's feet on her mother's lap, and as the conversation turned to dresses and fashion, Becky detected a rare passionate tone in Fiona's voice.

"Honey, do you think you'd like to design clothing?"

Fiona smiled shyly. "I'd been trying to keep it a secret. I was afraid it was silly."

"The only silly part is keeping it a secret. You'll be fabulous."

So Polly was to be Felix's date, and in compensation, Fiona got to design and make hers and Polly's dresses. Becky dug out an old e-mail address for Celeste, sent her a quick line asking her to phone, and crossed her fingers.

The same day, she got a call.

"Hello, Rebecca. I had been expecting to hear from you for some time and am only surprised that it took you a year to come after me. Listen, there was much to our relationship that I am certain Felix never informed you, and before you begin to tell me what a wicked woman I am for leaving him, you should know that."

"I . . . uh, Celeste, sorry, that's not why I wanted to talk—"

"Then you wish to inform me that you and Felix are lovers? Are you trying to hurt me? I may not have gone about the end of my marriage in the best manner, but nevertheless, it *was* for the best. I am happy and can't be wounded by that information. Go and enjoy each other, and I hope you can live with what you have done to Michael."

Becky considered that Celeste was the most difficult phone conversationalist in the world.

"No, uh . . . no, not that either, Celeste. Mike and I are still married and very happy. No, this isn't about Felix at all."

"No?"

"No. I—well, this is even more awkward than I thought it would be. *Ahem.* I just wanted your opinion on something. You remember Fiona? She has a passion for fashion design and I'd love for her to be able to pursue it and just wondered if you had any advice—"

Becky was cut off by laughter.

"Advice? You're calling for fashion-world advice for Fiona? And I attacked you and accused you—*que honte, mon lapin*, you see what a monster I am. I am a pile of rubbish to be swept into the yard and buried under sand. Rebecca, my darling, of course! Advice and more and the world for dear Fiona! She is practically my niece. She is nearly my own flesh and blood. If you and Michael are killed unexpectedly I demand full custody of that child. How divine!"

They exchanged relieved compliments before hanging up. Becky stood by the receiver, staring at it for some time. Celeste had thought Becky had left Mike for Felix. Becky felt a little ill, as if she'd eaten a fast-food combo meal, and she went to find Mike and kiss him and tell him she loved him and always, always would. It seemed the best thing to do. It usually was.

Celeste called Fiona and soon they were regular e-mail correspondents, and Fiona began to stand up straight for the first time since she'd started puberty. Becky said a silent prayer of thanks for Celeste, considering that mothers are so important everyone needs more than one.

"Ouch," Becky said aloud as a long-forgotten worry bit her—Felix's mother. "Estranged" and "mother" were two words that should never go together. She called him at once.

"Polly is ecstatic about going to the awards and it's very sweet that you asked her, but isn't there someone else you might want to take?"

"We already had this conversation, and I don't know how nicely I can tell you that your entire wardrobe deserves to be burned at the stake."

"Not me. Family."

Silence.

"Is this the bit where you confess your meddling?" he asked.

"Don't think about her," she said. "Or you. Think about Hyrum distancing himself from me for years, and one day accomplishing something amazing, and how I would feel all those years later if he called and asked me to come. You know how I would feel, right?"

More silence.

"I'll think about it," he said at last.

The next day, he phoned to say he'd booked a flight for his mother.

"I won't crush poor Polly's spirit, however," he said. "She will still be my date on the red carpet, and my mother will join me inside."

"Bless your heart, Felix Paul Callahan! Just bless your fuzzy little heart!"

"Enough."

"Okay. Sorry. No more blessing. No more fuzzy hearts." She couldn't silence a little squeal however, and he groaned and ended the call.

The phone rang a few seconds later, and Becky assumed it was Felix calling back to throw out some snarky comment he'd thought of too late, but instead Celeste's warm, syrupy voice asked for Fiona.

"She's not here now, Celeste. I'll tell her you called."

"Yes, thank you."

"Thank you for what you're doing for her." Becky cleared her throat. She didn't know how to talk to Celeste. As Felix's best friend, she thought she should be angry, resentful, protective. But just then, she felt shy. "How are you and, uh, Alfredo? Doing?"

Celeste sighed. "Alfredo is gone. He is a passionate man, so passionate, and he burns and burns and consumes and then believes he must rage on elsewhere. I don't hate him. It's just as well—I grew weary of the burning. But I'm not left alone."

And that's when Becky heard it—the tiny hiccup cry of a newborn.

"Celeste, do you . . ."

"Yes! Yes, yes, Rebecca, I know what you are to say because we're both mothers and mothers have powers of intuition. Yes, I have a baby here in my arms, my own baby. His name is Bellamy, and he is divine."

"Oh, Celeste, I'm so happy for you. I really, really am."

"Yes, I am too. And Rebecca, I tell you, I'm surprised by the power of that yes. Yes! Yes! I say it, I—shhh, Bellamy, shh. I'm too noisy. *Maman* is so noisy." She made some humming noises, some cooing noises, and her voice softened. "Felix didn't want children, Rebecca. And I wanted Felix. I thought I didn't need the children. I thought Felix's love was enough. But years passed by and I began to realize I didn't know what I wanted. That's when I met Alfredo, you see. He yearned for children, dozens of them, desperate he was, so impassioned, so warm and vibrant. I saw a different life I could have." Her voice softened even more. "Now Alfredo is gone, but the baby . . . Oh, Rebecca."

"I know."

"I had no idea. I didn't understand."

"I know."

"I never understood love or what it means to live, to have cells inside me splitting and forming new ones, to have blood rushing through me. I never understood anything until my baby. He is everything."

"He is," Becky agreed. "He so is."

"I'm sorry for what I did to Felix. I'm sorry for how it ended. But it had to be so, you see? It had to be. So Bellamy could be. God stood beside me and pointed the way. I took the wrong path getting here, I know, *mon lapin*, but here I am now with this baby in my arms. *Grâce à dieu.*"

After the call, Becky wandered the house for an hour, looking for something useful to do, but each time she began to fold laundry or tidy the family room, she got distracted and wandered off again. There was a buzzing in her bones that made her need to keep moving, a tingling in her legs that begged motion. She was happy. Celeste had a baby. Little Bellamy. Becky ambled back to the kitchen, disappointed to find no dishes to wash. Regret stung a little in the glow of goodness—she wished it could have been Felix's son. She wished Felix could be a father, that Celeste hadn't broken his heart, that there could be a family where family was needed.

But the sting of regret couldn't kill the glow. She had heard in Celeste's voice just how smitten she was with her little guy. Somewhere in France there was a boy who was as loved as any creature in this world. It was a reason to rejoice.

Not sure how Felix would feel about her contact with his ex, Becky decided not to mention it to him until the stress of the Oscars had passed. But at the pre-party in Los Angeles, he took one look at the girls and said, "Been in touch with Celeste, have you?"

"How did you know?" Becky asked.

"Come now, who would have helped Fiona have that dress made? You?"

"Oh, okay, fine." She took a breath. "Did you know she had a baby?"

He stared hard at the ground. "I knew."

"She and Alfredo are quits. She's raising the baby alone, living with her mother in France for now. I was thinking, if there was a time when amends could be made—"

"Becky." He held her hands, his eyes clear and hard. "You want to mend the whole world, but some things are best left alone. I'm not being bitter when I say I don't want to see Celeste again. We changed. There is no us to reunite. She's happy; I'm happy. It is quite over. As it should be."

Becky nodded. This one she would let be.

So Polly and Felix walked the red carpet. The family watched from Felix's living room and screamed when they saw Polly, her sweet, shy smile picked up by hundreds of cameras. She was so beautiful, so beautiful, Becky's heart teetered between bursting joy and shrinking fear to see her baby girl fourteen and nearly grown, dressed for a ball and out in the world.

"That midnight blue is the perfect color for her," Becky said.

Fiona gazed at the screen. "It works with her skin tone, and it's the exact color of the outer ring of her irises. With her build, she'd do better in patterned tops, but for this I wanted a single tone—more elegant. So I offset the plainness of the color by creating more interest around her neck and shoulder, with the folded fabric there and the gathering on the one side."

"Wow. You are so much smarter than I am."

Fiona smiled with more shyness than was her wont. "I'm trying to impress you."

"Baby, you don't even have to try."

On camera, Felix introduced Polly as his adopted goddaughter and they sang a short duet of "That's Amore" for the camera. The family applauded so loudly Becky thought Polly might hear a few blocks away. Even Hyrum hooted for his sister, as loud and urgent as the last Who yelling for Horton.

Mike went down to the theater to wait for Polly, plucking her out of the crazed chaos and bringing her back to Felix's place. She stayed in her dress all night, sitting carefully on the sofa to watch the televised awards show, smiling so hard Becky worried her cheeks would give out.

The show was painfully long, but Becky couldn't tear her eyes from the screen, even during commercials. She put both hands over her mouth and held her breath when at last she saw what she'd been both yearning for and dreading—Felix on camera with his mother.

Biddie Callahan-Coxhill was perhaps seventy years old, her white hair dyed brown in a clumsy job that even Becky's eye could spot. She was wearing a purple taffeta gown, the frills doubling her girth, and no jewelry except a heart locket. Becky had been with Felix when he'd purchased that locket a couple of years before, not knowing then whom it was for. Biddie had a look about her—cunning if somewhat simple eyes, disapproving mouth—that made Becky think she might not be the most relaxing person to be around. But Felix had a hand atop hers, and she was gazing at her son. Smiling. Beaming. Actually glowing, so that Becky wondered if she could read a book by the light of her face alone.

"Good boy," Becky whispered. "Good, good boy."

Jamie Foxx won the Oscar, but Becky was certain Felix must have come in a very close second and declared it often. Mike chose to go back to the hotel with the boys while Becky and the girls attended an afterparty. Felix took them to a relatively quiet gathering hosted by a director who had small children, guessing that it would be decent for the girls.

Felix was in great spirits, no matter that he didn't win. "It's over. I'm a free man. Hallelujah."

"Is your mother here?" Becky asked, looking around.

He shook his head. "She was knackered and went back to her hotel."

"Mm," said Becky.

"You want to know how it went."

She shrugged.

"You want me to tell you how I feel about it and what Biddie thought."

She lifted one shoulder and looked away coyly.

Felix sighed. "It was not unbearable having her here. And Mum was . . . happy. So, thank you."

That was when Becky attacked him with a ferocious momma hug.

Even her meddling couldn't dampen his mood after being freed from the shackles of waiting-on-Oscar. He danced with Fiona and karaoked with Polly. He and Becky did a reprisal of "Islands in the Stream," then the four of them shared the microphones and sang "We Are Family." Felix was spry and joyous, dancing foolishly, plying them with handfuls of candy stolen from various bowls. It wasn't until the end of the evening that Becky realized she hadn't seen him drink anything but water.

On the cab ride back to their hotel, Fiona said, "I like Felix."

"Me too," Polly said.

"Yeah, but you always have. I used to think he was mean, or just cold or something. But he was fun tonight. I think he's a good guy."

On the phone a few days later, Becky told Felix what Fiona had said. He laughed.

"You see? Children are wonderful once they grow into adults."

"And so are you, Felix."

"Well said, Mrs. Jack. Well said."

ACT 3

○○○○○○○○○

Last Kisses

How far away the stars seem, and how far
Is our first kiss, and ah, how old my heart!
William Butler Yeats

In which we waste no time, because Becky would abhor dwelling on the sad parts

Remission. Becky loathed the word. It sounded bland, clinical, passive, innocuous even—oh, sinister, ugly word! Insidious, corrupt, malicious word. Hateful. Lying. Duplicitous. Evil lurked between the letters, waiting to pounce. How had she ever rejoiced in it? When had it seemed full of hope? *Temporary*, it was really saying. This joy is temporary. The illness is still there, waiting for its time. And this time the attack will be much, much worse.

They discovered it at Mike's yearly checkup. He had no symptoms. He was feeling fine. But the doctor worried about the urine sample results. They did follow-up tests. Becky left the boys in the care of Polly, who was almost fifteen and becoming less flighty and more reliable. Becky and Mike sat in the leather armchairs at the doctor's office, holding hands, and waited for words of comfort. The doctor sat down. His cushioned chair wheezed as it settled and sounded remarkably like passed gas. So Becky was on the verge of laughing when the doctor said,

"It looks like it's back."

The laugh fell away, replaced by a sensation like being belted in the stomach. He didn't prepare them at all. He didn't ask them to think of happy thoughts or make sure they were sitting comfortably. He didn't say, "I've got some bad news." Just, "It's back."

And then, "Let's get a plan for how we're going to eradicate it for good."

Okay. Plans were good. Becky liked plans. They gave her things to do, ways to use her hands, keep busy, fight for that end result.

So they planned. And they fought. Tests and tests and treatments. Back to radiation. Go, fight, win.

Mike was a rock. Besides the cancer, his body was in great shape, and the doctors kept saying, "He has an excellent chance. He's young, healthy, with a happy, stable home life. The cancer is serious, but his odds are better than most."

The worst was dragging the kids through it again—because Becky was certain it would all end well. She had that deep-rooted sensation of comfort, almost as if a small voice were whispering, everything will be well. Everything's going to come out fine. She just hated for those poor kids to have to worry about their dad again. So she didn't let them worry. She was up, up, up all the time. Happy, calm, hopeful.

"Bec, you're working too hard," Mike would scold. "Why don't you go out tonight, see your sister or Melissa, do whatever girlie stuff you do when I'm not around. Like catch a Felix Callahan flick."

"What, those cavalcades of smut? No thank you." She lay next to him, fitting her hand around his jaw. "I like being with you."

"Because I'm so fascinating."

"You have your moments, but mostly, I just like to look at you. Your momma knew how to make a fine-looking laddie."

When Mike was asleep (she made his bedtime nine-thirty—he needed his strength) and all the kids settled, she would talk to Felix. Never for long. She needed her rest too. Just a few words, just to touch voices with someone who was moving out in that bright, untainted world.

"It's not until I'm alone that I realize how tired I am."

"I can come out. Tomorrow."

"No. I'm so busy I'd feel guilty that I wasn't paying enough attention to you."

"I don't need attention."

"Ha! That's a good one, Felix. You always were so witty."

"I'll disappear into a corner. You won't even know I'm there."

"Then I'd be sad. No, stay where you are, off in fantasyland making moving pictures and dating lively young impossibilities. It makes me happy that life is going on normally somewhere."

"If you need something impossible and you don't call me for help, I will get very angry."

"And I won't like you when you're angry."

"No, you'll still like me. You can't help it. But it's a messy scene—sometimes I throw things, like milk. And pens."

"I'll call."

"Good."

Again at the doctor's office—*wham.*

"The radiation is having less effect than we'd hoped."

What? That wasn't supposed to happen. It was going to be a repeat of their last treatment adventure—hard times, icky procedures, ultimate victory. This cancer was not playing by the rules. It was enough to infuriate Becky—but she was calm. She strapped on more armor, determined to pull them all through.

She read. Books, medical journals, scores of Web sites. She counseled with the doctors about every procedure, every symptom, every test. But she was nice about it. She brought them cookies.

Postsurgery times were the closest Becky got to cracking.

"In order to feel the least bit normal," she told her friend Melissa, "I need Mike home in his own bed."

Melissa put both arms around Becky's shoulders. "You're Wonder Woman. You can do this."

Becky nodded. "I can."

"But you don't have to go it alone."

Becky hesitated.

"You don't," Melissa said like a threat.

Melissa knew the many secrets of the hospital routine, having seen her father through six years of chronic illness.

"Don't fight the hospital," Melissa said. "Claim it as a second home. Own it."

She showed Becky the best and most often available parking spaces, and divulged the hours she could leave for lunch and still return to find a place. She introduced Becky to the volunteers at the information desk, and soon Becky knew not only their names but also the names of their grandchildren. Melissa took her on tours of the cafeteria, pointing out which foods to ingest and which avoid, and revealed a booth in the corner where one could go to have a private cry. Together they decorated Mike's hospital room with relics from home and made alliances with the nurses. One invited Becky to her wedding.

Four months later, the disease was taking a visible toll on Mike. It was frightening to see that big, strong man lose weight, lay so small on his side, curled up on the hospital bed, more of a question mark than a person. She stood in the hospital room, watching him as he slept, her arms folded. This wouldn't end badly. She wouldn't allow it. Strength and fierceness poured through her and she was sure she could wrestle a Herculean beast into submission, if only one would be so gracious as to terrorize the hospital.

Mike's cure wasn't progressing. The doctor laid out new plans. They involved lots and lots of money.

Becky had barely mentioned it before Felix arranged to pay for a cutting-edge treatment that their insurance wouldn't cover, and Becky didn't argue with him about the money. The plans were failing one by one, the fight was getting nebulous, her hands were feeling weak. It was starting to get difficult to think clearly. She felt haunted. This thing, this infected phantasm, was clinging to the family, whispering in their ears, making the whole house feel drafty and prone to collapse, their lives thin and chilly. With each sliding moment she realized more fully—she was living in a horror movie.

Don't go down those stairs, Becky! Don't open that door!

If only she knew which door was the one that would unleash the killer, she'd board it up for good. Instead every moment seemed to inch by as if a creepy soundtrack played in the background, the eerie kind of music that is designed to speed up your pulse, make your skin hurt in anticipation of attack.

She took deep breaths. She fitted herself with more armor. She would not succumb. You hear that, foul cancer beast? I won't give up my husband! You won't take any of us!

She kissed Mike a lot. She kissed the kids a lot. She made buckets of snickerdoodles.

The night before they found out the results of the new treatment, their bishop (not Andy the car lot manager—a new one) and a neighbor came over in suit and tie to give Mike a blessing of healing. They anointed his head with olive oil, placed their hands on his head, and began the prayer. Mike had had several blessings so far, and Becky fully expected it to go like the others, full of lines like "We bless you that your body will heal and you will experience a complete recovery."

But as the bishop was speaking the prayer, he paused. He started to speak again then hesitated again, finally saying, "We bless you, Brother Jack, to feel your Savior close by you, preparing you to return home. We bless you that your pain will decrease, your mind will remain lucid, and you will be able to fully enjoy the time you have left with your family in this life."

Becky's eyes opened. Take it back, she wanted to say. But she couldn't get her mouth to work.

The bishop's eyes were wet. Mike was crying quietly, as was the neighbor. Becky didn't cry. She felt dried-up, a fallen winter leaf ready to crack underfoot. After they finished the blessing, everyone was silent, motionless. Finally the bishop spoke.

"I'm sorry. I wanted to bless you with remission, but I felt impressed to speak the words that I did. I think the Lord has other plans for you, Mike."

Mike nodded. He didn't dare speak, Becky knew, for fear that he might sob. The kids were all there, staring, eyes wide, Polly's chin trembling. Becky cursed herself. She should have hidden them away, plugged their ears, spared them from this tragedy. From all tragedy. Or maybe not? Maybe they needed to hear it all to be prepared, hear the "I've got some bad news" parts before the bad news really struck?

It was going to strike. Becky felt that now, prowling on the edges of her forced calm.

After the bishop and neighbor left, the six Jacks sat in the family room. Even Sam, the youngest at age eight, seemed fully aware of what had just happened. A stunned, icy silence vibrated around them, as if the air were frozen solid and shaking under the blows of a hammer. The kids kept glancing at their mother, waiting for her to speak the comforting words, make it all better. Where was she going to get those words? She took a deep breath, hoping that they rested deep within her, that if she just started to speak, somehow the tiny grains of hope still left inside would multiple into loaves of brilliant comfort that would feed the entire family.

Mike spoke first. "It's all right. It doesn't matter. Whether I'm going to experience a miracle and be completely healed, whether I'll get sicker before I get better, or whether I'll die—it's out of our hands. We don't have to worry about it. Whatever happens will happen, and it won't change the fact that we've got the best family in the world, and we'll be a family forever. So what that it stinks? We've been through stinky times before. Remember that summer Hyrum had the foot fungus?"

Sam and Hyrum chuckled.

"Talk about a stinkfest," Fiona said.

"I used to wipe my feet all over your pillow," Hyrum said, between maniacal giggles.

"You did? That's gross! Mom, did you hear that?"

The next day at the doctor's, they heard the news—the cancer had spread to his liver, his lungs. There was no more treating the disease at this point, only the symptoms.

"Time," Becky said. "I want to know how much time."

The doctor sucked in his breath. He was considerably less spunky than usual. The potted plant behind him was drooping. The whole world felt sluggish, malaised.

"It's hard to say . . ."

"Say," Becky insisted. She'd supplied him with a steady stream of snickerdoodles over the past months—that should buy her one sentence of truth.

The doctor pressed his lips together. "Weeks. If you would take my advice, Mike, live them. Live each one."

"What do you want most of all?" Becky asked that night, curled up beside him in bed.

Mike's face was tired, but his jaw didn't clench. There was some peace to be had in knowing that he didn't have to fight anymore. "Just the family. Let's get away, the six of us, somewhere quiet and beautiful, somewhere we can be alone together."

Mike's parents' cabin was too far away. Thinking was becoming hard for Becky. Since the unhappy blessing, she couldn't arrange a bouquet of flowers let alone a family vacation. In all her life, she'd never met a challenge that had stripped her of all confidence and left her feeling so small and useless. It was time to crack and ask for help.

She had her parents and Mike's parents, her siblings, Mike's siblings, a combined total extended family of 126 people, besides friends, neighbors, ward members, all begging for ways to help, all waiting for her call.

She called Felix.

"Tell me," he said.

"Mike doesn't have long. I need—"

"Anything."

"I need to take the family away. Where we can be alone. People are constantly calling and coming by and the kids can't relax and just be with their father. We need to get out of this house, but we can't be more than an hour from the hospital. I can't think, I can't—"

"I'll take care of it."

"I don't want to bother you, but Mike, all he wants is to be with the family someplace quiet and . . . and beautiful . . ." Her voice broke.

"Did you hear me? I said I'll take care of it. If you waste your time worrying about it for another second, I'll fly out there just to paddle your bum."

She sighed in relief. Felix would take care of it.

Four days later the family took possession of a house on a mountain lake twenty minutes from the hospital. They found the fridge and pantry fully stocked, fresh sheets on the beds, flowers on every table, stacks of board games in the living room, a six-person boat waiting on their private dock. Nothing cumbersome or unnecessary, like televisions or computers or neighbors. A nurse checked in on Mike every afternoon, but otherwise they were alone. It was quiet and beautiful, and afterward Becky supposed it was among the most blissful weeks of their lives.

They boated. They ate. They played games and laughed. Mike couldn't sit on the sofa without at least one child snuggling up next to him. And at night, he held Becky in bed, held on to her as if she were a buoy in a tossing lake. His most casual touch was hot with significance. Each word he said, each expression, she fought to keep with her as if remembering them meant saving the world.

"You're memorizing what I'm saying," he accused her one night.

"I am not."

"Every word I say. You get that look of concentration, then later when you think I'm asleep, you go scritch scratch in your journal."

"I do not! I mean, I'm just recording thoughts, I don't remember every—"

"Poo."

"What?"

"Poo. I'm saying poo. Poop. Poopy poop. Poo everywhere. Poo on your head, poo between your toes, poopy poopy poo."

She started to laugh, and that laugh broke into another laugh, and she stuffed her face into her pillow to keep laughing without waking the kids, and soon he was laughing, quietly, in that tight way he did to keep from being in pain. She put her arms around his neck.

"You're right. And I'm going to remember every word."

"Mmhmm, that was the plan." He kissed her forehead.

"What's the difference between poo and poop anyway?"

"Poo is what goes in the toilet; poop is what you find on your front lawn."

"So is poo determined purely by its maker, or does it refer to its semiaquatic state?"

"Uh . . . all I got is poo. You'll have to ask Felix about the details."

"He is the poo meister."

"Is he?"

"Naw, I just liked the way it sounded."

They lay there, foreheads touching, staring at each other's eyes. It was enchanting to see what the dark and the closeness revealed about Mike's eyes, how the familiar became strange, alien even. And beautiful too. So complex. Rings and marks and colors, roundness and flatness and intricacy. Eyes were the most amazing things in all creation, she thought. Mike's eyes especially.

"Bec," he whispered after a time, breaking her transcendent contemplations about eyes, "when I'm gone, it's okay for you to fall in love—"

"Don't—"

"I want you to hear this now and remember every word and go scritch scratch in your journal. You're forty-four years old—that's only half your life. If you have the chance to fall in love again, I want you to take it. If you find someone who could be a good surrogate father to the kids, don't turn that down. I'm giving you permission."

"I don't want—"

"Well, I'm giving it anyway."

He stroked her hair. She let him. She wasn't going to argue. If he needed to believe that she could move on, so be it. But she knew her own heart. And there was no possible chance.

She'd met her Unattainable Crush (Felix) and had the opportunity to fall romantically in love with him. How many people get that chance? Their number-one choice, their sigh-and-dream fantasy man, their tip-top unreachable ideal? He'd asked to kiss her, and she'd laughed. It had been unthinkable, unintelligible, unimaginable that she would ever choose Felix over Mike. So if her fantasy man fell so far short when compared with her husband, how could there be anyone else even remotely adequate?

No, Mike was all she'd ever want. The memory of him would be enough to sustain her in a desert. She had bonded with him, merged into one, half of her contained within him. That couldn't happen twice in a life. And besides, he was still very real, very warm and near, and she breathed in his smell and pulled him in tighter.

They'd been lying like that, foreheads pressed together, his hand on her hair, her arms around his neck, for minutes or hours. Maybe they'd both fallen asleep for a time and woken again. Even after that long space of silence, their conversation still hung about them, like spiderwebs dangling from the trees, tickling her face, reminding her that there were creeping things about.

"I love you," she said, meaning, only you, only ever you.

He said, "You want to argue with me still. I can tell. What are you holding back?"

She grumbled.

"What?"

"You said I was forty-four. I'm forty-three."

That made him want to kiss her. And he did, until they both fell asleep.

Becky didn't argue with him about the future. And he didn't need to bring it up again—just as he suspected, she did remember every word. There was no need to squabble. They just tried to live each moment perfectly.

The paradise in limbo lasted exactly three weeks. Then overnight, Mike worsened. They sped away from the cabin on the quiet lake and back into the valley, back into the white hospital room with constant watching and things that beeped. Two days later he died in the night while she slept beside him, holding his hand.

Untitled

The family had been prepared. Not that it mattered. There's never enough preparation. There's always the last-minute miracle, after all— God's unexpected hand, an experimental cure, Superman zooming to catch the meteor and hurl it back into space. Becky considered that the difference between sudden and anticipated death was more time to hope for the miracle that wouldn't come.

"I miss Daddy," Sam said, as he curled up tight in his bed, his forehead to his knees. Becky's insides were sliced by those words. She lay beside him as he fell asleep, her belly against his back, her arm over him, tucking his hands into hers.

She couldn't talk to her kids without touching them, holding their hands, petting their hair, rubbing their backs. She had an instinctive need to feel them, hold them, almost afraid that if she wasn't tangibly aware of their presence, they would cease to exist. Sam needed the touch, Hyrum tolerated it, Polly melted into it, and Fiona gave it in return.

Of all the kids, Becky worried most about Hyrum because of his silence. The others talked to her and to each other, could say words like "I miss" or "I'm sad" or "Why?" and "What now?" But Hyrum rolled up and shut off.

"Hey, sweetie."

"Hi."

"We're going to Uncle Greg's for dinner. They got a new Play-Station and Aunt Carolyn is making that chicken casserole with the potato chips on top."

"No thanks."

"Honey, we're—"

"No thanks."

There was no time for Becky to grieve. She was grieving for her kids, she was praying and working for the kids, her heart beating for Hyrum. And for the first week, she was a rock. Family was everywhere; she never had a chance to be alone and think.

Melissa made herself present, doing a fine impression of a bulldog whenever she thought people were bugging Becky too much. Neighbors came by to deliver meals and flowers, but if they lingered, Melissa was on her feet and walking them to the door.

"They need to learn—they're here to give, not to get," Melissa said as she locked the door.

Diana drugged her sister at night to make her sleep, alternating various sleep medications so that "you won't get addicted." And in the daytime there was the funeral to arrange and Mike's life insurance and pension and the bills and the kids. The kids, the kids. And writing countless thank-you cards for all the dinners and flowers. It hardly seems fair that she should be expected to fulfill that task at such a time, does it? But she did. She never even considered letting it slide.

Felix was there for the funeral. When he came through the front door, she toddled to him, and he swept her up and held her for a long time. She didn't cry. She just let herself be held. It was the most relaxed she'd been all week. Usually she was the one holding others. Melissa was right in a way—when the neighbors and friends came to offer condolences and hugs, they really wanted something from her. They needed to feel that they were helping somehow, making her feel better, and so asking for their own comfort. She was constantly giving her energy over until it was peeled away layer from layer. Sometimes, she felt like raw bone.

Except with Felix. He just held her.

But soon she was pulled back into family and food and planning, and he was swept into the corner. She barely spoke to him, and he didn't insist himself on her. Sometimes he sat on the couch and sang with Polly or read books with Sam. Once she looked out the kitchen window and saw him kicking a ball around with Hyrum. That sight gave her heart a happy spark.

She wasn't sure when Felix left Utah, but a few days after the funeral, a landscaping service showed up to weed and mow the lawn, saying they'd been paid in advance for the next two years. They also planted perennials in ecstatic colors. Nice mute fall colors would've been appropriate for September, but her yard was roiling with bright pink, yellow, and orange. The landscaper left a card that read, "In lieu of flowers. Call for ANY reason. FC."

Postfuneral, things were calming down, visitors slowing, the house emptying, the scores of bouquets on every table or countertop in the house wilting at once as if on cue, the air thick with a sticky sweet miasma of decay. Polly, who had seemed okay for a couple of days, splintered suddenly and wept through dinner over her bowl of minestrone soup.

"Can you put it into words?" Becky asked. "Are you angry, are you in pain? Confused or heartbroken, exhausted or sick to your stomach? It helps to stick words on it."

"There's a pain here," she pointed to her chest, "like I'm on my back and a boulder is pinning me down."

Fiona nodded, absently rubbing her own chest.

"And I keep thinking," Polly said, "about how Dad asked me to come out in the garage and help him restring his fishing pole. He didn't really need my help, I could tell. He just wanted some company. And I said no because I was watching TV."

"When was this?"

"When I was in third grade."

"Oh, honey. That was so long ago, and he knew you loved him. You had so many good hours together, that one time doesn't matter."

"It feels like it does," Polly said, chin quivering.

"I know, sweetie. Let's put a name to it—guilt. That one will get you too, just as nasty as heartbreak and anger, but sneakier. It'll skulk up behind you and bite your ankles."

"Like a hyena," Sam offered. "That's how they down their prey. They bite their ankles so they can't run away."

"Hamstring 'em," Hyrum said, his eyes still on his soup.

Becky was careful to keep her voice even so Hyrum wouldn't suspect how happy she was that he'd spoken. "Exactly. That's perfect. Guilt is the hyena that'll lunge from behind and hamstring you."

"And hobble you so you can't walk," Polly said.

"Or even stand," Fiona said.

Becky nodded. "Sam, if you were lost in an African night and you saw the glint of hyena eyes in the brush and knew they were coming for you, what would you do?"

Sam scooted up taller. "I'd kick 'em! I'd keep kicking back until I heard their yelps. Hyenas are the cowards of the animal kingdom, you know. They only attack easy prey. One good boot . . ." Sam kicked at the air. "Oof!"

"That's my boy. Will you do it for Polly?"

Becky pulled Polly, still on her seat, away from the table and Sam circled around, kicking at imaginary hyenas.

"Yay! Hi-yay!"

Fiona joined him (she was such a good sport) and Becky too, and the three of them did a pagan dance around Polly, kicking and hollering. Polly giggled once. Hyrum watched from his chair, arms folded, but he didn't leave for his room.

Becky's heart was eased a tiny amount by the sound defeat of the hyenas, and so her guard was down. When she was brushing her teeth that night, she looked at the mirror and an unbidden thought leaped into her head: *I won't have to clean Mike's toothpaste spittle off the mirror anymore.*

The thought caught in her throat like a fish bone. Defiantly she thought, *Or hang up his coat, or remind him to return his library books,* or cook his eggplant—his stupid, slimy eggplant. She went on, count-ing fifty things she'd never have to do again, ticking off each one as if jabbing herself with a needle. Because it was her fault, somehow. She should have been able to keep him alive, somehow. She'd failed him; she'd failed the whole family. And she wanted to feel all the pain she deserved. All the pain in the world. Let it press down on her, let it crush her under its hard heel, let it burrow inside her bones, sputter and seethe and burn bone to ash.

She repeated this ritual each night and went to bed feeling chafed and bloodied and hopeless. Some days she toyed with the idea of blam-ing God, but it was futile. Becky had always believed that God had a master plan, an understanding beyond her ken. Blaming him for any suf-fering in life made as much sense as Hyrum blaming her for a scraped knee. "You brought me into this life, so any pain I feel is your fault!" There was some attraction to this philosophy, but neither her logic nor her faith would allow it. Darn it. No, that wasn't satisfying enough.

"Damn it," she said aloud. Then she got bolder, using words only Melissa said in her hearing, shouting phrases even Felix avoided. She swore and spit and cursed till her face turned red.

It didn't help.

But for the kids, she was still a rock. At dinner each night, she had them name the zoological onslaught of their pain. Sorrow, they decided, was a raven, dark as night, that perched on your shoulder and ate away at your heart. Grief, as opposed to sorrow, was a crow that sat on your other shoulder and pecked at your eyes so you couldn't see clearly. Anger was a rhinoceros that gored you from behind, spurring you to holler and run.

"What are you feeling today, Sam?" Becky would ask.

"Angry," he'd say. Sam was mostly angry, because he liked to fight the rhinoceros, which involved imaginary weapons. Though one night he admitted that he was sad—an enormous toad sitting on his head, mak-ing him feel wet and cold and too weighed down to move. The only way to fight the sadness toad was with lots and lots of hugs.

Hyrum's patience couldn't withstand the sadness toad. Hyrum went to his room.

Sam played along with his mother's ritual, and Fiona did too. Polly mostly did. Usually Hyrum watched. Sometimes one of the kids would ask, "What about you, Mom?"

So Becky said, "The anger rhino is goading me because in this life my kids don't get to see their father anymore," or "The worry scorpion has got me tonight, crawling under my clothes and stinging, because Hyrum is so quiet," or dozens of other worries and sorrows about her kids. That's all she would allow herself.

During the daylight hours, her sole concern was their comfort. But at night, with the kids asleep, she entered her bedroom and faced her old nemeses—silence and solitude. That's where the smoldering grief flared up and consumed her to ash over and over again. She had a great deal of sympathy for Prometheus and wondered how often he wished that liver would just stay eaten.

With blaming God not an option, of course she blamed herself. She shouldn't have bought Teflon pans or served bacon on Saturday mornings or allowed the million other innocuous carcinogens into their home. Or she should've sensed Mike's illness earlier. Or loved him enough to prevent anything bad from ever happening. Mike's death was her fault, so she wasn't allowed the honest pain of grieving. She deserved nothing more than being turned into a pillar of salt.

Please, God, turn me into a pillar of salt.

And so she hardened, and stilled, and while others might not have found her any more savory than usual, she felt the crackle and shift in her bones, the numbness settle into her skin. And she fancied if she moved too quickly or felt too much, she would crumble and fall apart.

"You should talk more," Becky's mother said, nestled close beside her on the couch. She came over almost every morning now, so Becky wouldn't be alone while the kids were at school. "I'm afraid you're not taking care of yourself."

"I showered today," Becky offered.

"Your hair is still shiny, even at your age." Alice smoothed her daughter's hair, her blue eyes wet. "Mine went dull at thirty. You are so pretty."

"Mom . . ."

"You are."

She pulled Becky into her, hugged her, pressing her lips to the top of her head. And Becky sighed into the embrace. It was good, a touch that she needed. Alice comforted that Becky who was still a little girl, soothed her tender part, her innocent part. But the Becky who had failed her children and let her husband die would not be comforted. That part closed up, a fist tight with guilt.

Her guilt was unquestionable (yes, she was on a first-name basis with those yipping hyenas). For example, Mike had loved golf. But it was an expensive hobby, and he didn't want to leave the family for hours on a Saturday. Watching TV golf had been his way to keep up with his passion and still be a good father. But so many times over the years she'd scolded him for it. Why? Why hadn't she let him just enjoy it? Because she was wicked, unforgivable refuse. Clearly.

Each night, Becky lay on her her huge, empty bed and let the hyenas go to town.

She was sorely tempted to replace the king bed with a smaller mattress, one that didn't seem to scream, "YOU SHOULDN'T BE IN HERE ALONE! HOW DARE YOU LIE HERE ALONE!" She wanted nothing larger than a twin, or a sleeping bag, or maybe a bassinet. But she wouldn't risk alarming the kids. So she stacked pillows on Mike's side, enough to push against her while she slept, leaving her a narrow strip, her arms and knees hanging over into space.

"I'm pathetic," she muttered.

She was not one easily crushed by the problems of life—Polly's asthma, Mike's layoff in 1994 and those eight months when they lived on savings and unemployment checks, Hyrum's fight-you-every-step-of-the-way-ness, even Mike's illness. She could always deal. We're a family. I am Warrior Mother. Everything will work out.

It was shocking to face herself de-shelled, the limp worm of a snail.

The weeks that followed the funeral, when things (horribly, inexplicably) returned to normal, Becky nestled into numbness. She stopped taking sleeping pills, and the lack of rest turned her into a zombie. She pushed through each day. For the kids. Smiled and cooked and cleaned up. Took dinner to neighbors when someone had a new baby or the flu. Put on a content face. She detected a quiet tug on her soul, and interpreted it as a reminder that if she sought divine help she could feel some peace. She refused it. The numb pain Mike's death left behind was the most tangible part of him she still possessed, and she refused to let go.

Later she supposed she'd been throwing a spiritual tantrum. I want to suffer! You can't make me not suffer! You think you can comfort me? Ha! I will hold my breath until my soul turns blue—see if I don't!

When people inquired after her, it was easy to divert attention.

"How's my Becky today?" Melissa asked on their now biweekly lunch date. Her brown hair was long and straight, free of purple streaks, and she'd recently taken to wearing nonprescription cat-eye glasses as a fashion accessory.

"Good. The kids are perking up even faster than I could've hoped. Sam's—you know Sam. Can't keep him down for long. And Hyrum," she sighed with a little relief. "His cousins are teaching him to snowboard and that's all he talks about. But he's talking. Polly and Fiona are blessed with oodles of friends, lots of outlets to talk about the loss."

Melissa nodded. "That's all great. But I didn't hear how *you* were."

"I said 'good.'"

Melissa nodded again, chewing her stuffed grape leaves very slowly, her eyes suspicious.

With the kids on the mend, the intimate family dinners fighting invisible monsters petered out, so Becky switched tactics and made sure the house was full of noise and energy. Almost every night for dinner, someone was there—the grandparents, one of her brother's families, Uncle Ryan. She wanted surrogate fathers in the house. She wanted laughter and light.

She worked tirelessly to keep that house running as if all was well, but there were things Mike had always taken care of that she just forgot. Like the garbage. A couple of weeks went by, and she noticed the cans around the house overflowing (mostly with used tissue), so she did manage to dump them in the garbage can outside. Garbage day was Monday. Each Tuesday the outside cans were empty again. She never dragged them from the driveway to the curb. She never even realized she was supposed to. But each Tuesday, they were empty and waiting for more tissue trash.

On a cold, bright morning after a night completely devoid of sleep, she was lying on her bedroom floor trying to count her eyelashes when she heard a sound she couldn't name—a bumpy, rolling sound, like someone dragging something across gravel. She peered through the blinds. It was her neighbor Charles, dragging her garbage cans out to the curb, as he must have been doing ever since Mike's illness.

Becky had to choke down her cereal that morning, her throat was stiff with unshed tears.

In general, her ward members mobilized like an army of angels. People didn't just ask that lame question "Is there something I can do? Just call if you need anything." They didn't ask—they did. Garbage cans for starters, but also shoveling walks each snowfall that winter, dinners kept coming for a month, and then after that once a month two men assigned by the bishop arrived at her front door with a toolbox and said, "If we wouldn't be a bother, Sister Jack, we'd have a blast puttering around your house and seeing what we can patch up." Other single women began to include her in their girls' night out on Fridays; other fathers in the ward began taking her boys ice fishing or snowshoeing.

But there were the sour moments too.

Becky told Melissa over baba ghanoush, "Yesterday at church, a lady took me aside with the express purpose to tell me, 'Don't feel bad. When God closes a door, he opens a window.'"

Melissa choked on some pita bread.

"I kid you not. What the heck does that mean anyway? That I'm supposed to climb out a window now? Or is the window just to air out the house, which is stinking to high heaven, given the fact that the door has been shut indefinitely and NO ONE CAN GET OUT?!"

"Okay," Melissa said, fishing scrap paper and a pen from her purse, "I want name and address. Tonight I'm going to board up her doors."

To be fair, Becky wouldn't have been comforted by any idiom that fits onto refrigerator magnets. If you want to see Becky seethe, just suggest that she take the lemons life has given her and make some lemonade.

And there was Joann, a well-meaning neighbor.

"I'm sorry about your husband."

"Thanks, I appreciate that."

"You know, my husband left me when I was thirty-three and had four small children. Just be grateful that didn't happen."

Becky stared. Only with superhuman restraint did she keep from asking, "You're saying I should be *grateful* my husband died?"

"Experts say that divorce is a harder trial to bear than the death of a spouse." The woman nodded to herself. "Hard stuff. Hard times. Yep, hard, hard times. Well, sorry!"

The worst thing about this exchange? Becky couldn't call Mike to tell him about it. The ache of that reality was briefly too much to bear, so she e-mailed Felix, describing the exchange.

Apparently, if only Celeste had died, you'd be better off.

He responded:

I couldn't agree more. This Joann shows some sense, though I suspect she is a demon dressed in human skin. I'd like to shave her head next time I'm in town, though I know you won't let me, so perhaps we could schedule one evening to park near her house and stare at it menacingly.

The e-mail helped some, imagining Joann as a demon in human skin was distracting at the very least, but Becky still felt overturned by the comment. She reasoned that it didn't matter whether or not that woman's divorce had been harder than Becky's loss—both were hard, and trying to weigh one against the other invalidated Becky's pain. She knew that, in a tight, angry, buzzing sort of way. But she got to wondering: Would it have been worse if Mike had chosen to leave her rather than been forced out of life by that nasty, cell-sucking disease? Definitely not, because the kids would still have their father, no matter how much being betrayed and cast off would have stung Becky. But what if he'd been a lousy father? What if he hadn't loved the kids, or been abusive, or had a thousand-dollar-a-day cocaine habit?

Becky passed much of the evening imagining scenarios that would have been worse than death. It didn't help any more than the swearing.

And she woke up the next morning feeling the same as always, as if it were the antithesis of Christmas. The morning was tacky with hopelessness, nothing to look forward to, and no marvelous anticipation would ever exist again. Because Mike was gone.

Months pulled by, and while the kids got stronger, Becky, so slowly she barely noticed, was plunging deeper and deeper. Mike's side of the closet was full. She didn't change the sheets on the bed, hoping to retain his smell. She still turned to him to say something funny and had to rediscover again that he wasn't there. She was reminded of amputee victims reporting that they still felt sensation in the missing limb. She still felt Mike beside her. Some days it was an empty comfort. Some days it made her flat-out angry. Once, she punched a wall. She bruised her knuckles and didn't even leave a dent. How irritating is that?

She was a pillar of salt. If she could just keep standing, pretending to be the same solid mother, everything would be fine. No one would know her truth.

The real question was, that first year, why didn't she just break? Later she reasoned that she must have been walking on the prayers of others, she must have been surrounded by angels. She certainly wasn't trying to survive on her own. No, she'd get through each day, each moment, for the kids, but really, she'd crossed her spiritual fingers and hoped to self-destruct.

She moved through her year of grace like an ant through a drop of honey, until those powers of perseverance pulled back and nudged her to stand on her own. It was on the one-year anniversary of Mike's death. There she was, left to her own strength, and of course, she collapsed.

It hit her like a piano falling ten stories. The best part of Becky, the most brilliant and confident part, was the mother part—and what kind of a mother can't keep her children's father alive? She felt the cracking as she made Sam his peanut butter and sliced grape sandwich.

"You okay, Mom?" he asked.

"Uh-huh." She didn't think she could use real words.

She clung to her fraying ends as she hunted down Hyrum's shoes before he missed the bus.

"Why're you being weird?"

"Mm," she said.

The moment the front door clicked closed and Becky was left alone, she lay facedown in the family room and imploded. She cried, letting eyes and nose run into the carpet fibers, too defeated to hunt a tissue, too broken to lift her hands.

Pretty much everything all her life had come easily—friends, school, pregnancy, birth, all the crooks and crannies of motherhood, housekeeping, even selling two screenplays and acting in a movie, things mundane and things extraordinary. She'd never really been challenged.

Until now. She didn't know how to go on, didn't know how to be Becky anymore.

How was a woman who'd been sawed in half expected to keep standing? How could she survive with half of her gone? Mike was yang to her yin in every aspect of her life—the kids, the house, her thoughts, her spirituality, her very being. There was no space within her that he didn't share.

Except that Felix part of her. Except her liver.

The phone rang.

The cordless was lying on the carpet a couple of feet away. She didn't want to answer it. But what if it was one of the kids? What if they needed her?

She reached, clicked the Talk button, rolled it to her ear. "Hello?"

"Becky. Are you all right?" It was Felix. They'd spoken a few times over the past year, but she'd mostly avoided him. Probably because he was a comfort, and she didn't deserve comfort.

"Sure," Becky said. All she said was "sure."

He must have understood everything in that word. He was in Chicago. He said, "I'm coming."

In which Felix wears tourist shorts

Fiona found her mother splayed on the carpet.

"Honey . . ." Becky had forgotten Fiona was coming home from a summer study in California that day. She tried to remember if Fiona had asked her for a ride from the airport—no, a friend was going to pick her up. That was a relief, at least.

"Let me get you a snack," Becky said, hauling herself up to a sitting position. "I'm fine. I'm just—don't worry. I'm fine. We have some apples and cheese, and there's some banana bread . . ."

"Mom," Fiona said with such tenderness it made Becky's eyes sting.

Fiona didn't ask what was wrong, didn't panic to see her indestructible mother in a heap on the floor. She just helped her stand, walked her to her bed, and tucked her in.

Fiona melted cheese on crackers and made fruit and yogurt smoothies. She hauled the small family room television set into the bedroom and lay beside Becky, watching soap operas with the sound muted, making up her own dialogue to try to get her mother laughing.

"'And that is why, I say, that is why, I intend to turn myself into a dog.' 'If you think I'll rub your ears, then you have another thing coming.' 'Oh no? Then I will glare at you. You see me here, glaring at you? I am the master of the glare. I have a Ph.D. in glare.' 'Well, I can glare too! Watch me glaring. Tremble at my glaring.'"

Becky wanted to laugh, but mostly she stared at Fiona, pondering with a sublime ache how beautiful her daughter was, how kind and precious and clever. With the floodgate so recently opened, Becky had little control and that set her off again.

"Sorry," Becky said through sobs.

Fiona fetched a box of tissues and lay on her side, looking at her mother matter-of-factly. "I've heard it said that it helps to put words on feelings. What's it feel like, Mom?"

"A whole zoo on my chest." She was breathless with sobbing. "Noah's ark, boat and all."

"First step, we drown them." And Fiona drew her mother a hot bath.

Around noon Fiona made a couple of calls in the kitchen, then marched back into her mother's room and commenced packing a suitcase.

"Honey, what's—"

"Everything's taken care of."

"But I can't go anywhere. It's the year anniversary. We should be together as a family and—"

"They're fine. Grandma and Grandpa will keep them for a week."

"Sweetie, I—"

Fiona shushed her, stuck her in the car, and drove her to the Salt Lake Airport. Felix was there, wearing a bright blue sweater that looked wonderfully soft. Becky hadn't seen him since the funeral. She barely had time to notice how blue his eyes looked before his arms were around her. She tucked her head against his chest, softening into new sobs. The sweater really was delightfully soft. Fiona kissed her good-bye and before Becky fully realized what was happening, she was flying first-class to Mazatlán.

"I'll pay you back my half," she squeaked.

Felix laughed. He was going to win this one.

"It was about time you left the country," he said. "You don't know how your domestic-bound life has haunted me. Without a passport, this was the most exotic location I could take you. Well, there was Puerto Rico, but they didn't have available first-class seats."

"We could've flown coach."

That made Felix laugh.

They settled back to watch the in-flight movie. Unbelievably, it was a clever if overwrought thriller called *Run Cannibal Run!* starring one Felix Callahan. This set Becky into a fit of giggles. The laughing felt strange in her throat, raw and thick, scratching her as it came out. She wondered when the last time was that she'd had a genuine laugh. She wondered if laughing was a betrayal to Mike. She was certain she didn't deserve it. But it was hard not to relax around Felix; it was hard not to fall into the old Becky, the Becky who laughed, the Becky who didn't ache everywhere. He pulled that Becky out of her as easily as he'd waltzed her on the dance floor.

"I never saw this one," Felix said. "The premiere conflicted with Mike's funeral. Bless his heart, he saved me that day from the red carpet torture."

"Yes, in those last moments, your premiere was foremost in his mind."

"See what I mean? A gentleman's gentleman."

They wore the ear jacks in only one ear so they could whisper to each other through the movie. There were some tense moments, some clever lines, but despite Felix's brilliant character part, the clumsy post-production meddling of a dozen separate producers had put a crimp in the overall appeal.

"See how handsome you look in gray," she'd say. "Ooh, you're so *serious* there!"

Felix groaned a lot. The people across the aisle kept staring.

It became easier and easier to fall into a laugh with Felix, in part because he hadn't been around during Mike's illness and the year after, her relationship with him untainted by the crippling gloom. Suddenly, she was four years younger sitting beside Felix on the movie set and giggling into her script to keep quiet. Besides the giggle, Becky discovered other forgotten friends popping up—a carefree tone of voice, a relaxed right shoulder, a twitching smile in the corner of her mouth. It felt good, like pressing heat on a strained muscle. But she was also afraid. Being with Felix was keeping that hulking slobbering beast of mourning at bay—temporarily. Soon her reprieve would be over, and she'd fall back into that horror story again. Hitting bottom was sure to hurt so much more than if she'd never crawled up.

The lady at the resort check-in said, "All right, I have a nonsmoking suite with a king-size bed—"

"No, no, we should have two rooms," Felix said.

"Oh for goodness sake, yes, two rooms. Felix snores like an elephant. Or so his ex-wife assured me. Though I was never clear on how she'd come to hear elephants snoring . . ."

"But with connecting doors."

"Oh yes, connecting doors. I don't want to have to go into a hallway to see him. But with locks on the doors. I can't have him barging in while I'm dressing."

"It's for my protection, really. She wears the most ridiculous smalls."

"You wish you've seen my 'smalls.'"

The lady stared. "Um, I've only been working here for a couple of weeks and I have no idea how to respond to that. Would you please pretend that I replied appropriately? Great. Here are your room keys."

Becky thanked her and felt certain that if they'd been neighbors, she and the check-in lady would've been friends. The thought tingled inside her that this world was full of wonderful people.

And then she felt it again like a slap—*but Mike is gone.*

Her breath caught and she stopped walking. Felix took her arm.

"Hey, hey there, are you all right?"

Her chin trembled. As much as she tried to ignore the thought, it was there, the elephant in the room. The huge, attention-hungry, snoring elephant—Mike is gone, Mike is gone . . .

"I can't have this. I can't have you unhappy." Felix picked her up under her knees and carried her to the elevator as if across the threshold of a honeymoon suite.

She squirmed. "You can put me down. Never mind, I'm fine. It was just momentary panic."

He hefted her as if testing her weight. "Either you weigh near nothing or I'm terribly strong. I think it's the latter. Definitely the latter. I had no idea I was in such excellent shape." He caught his face reflected in the elevator's polished chrome. "And so indescribably handsome. You are one lucky lady."

They went into their separate rooms and Becky might've been inclined to sit on her balcony and feel melancholy, but Felix had unlocked his side of the connecting door and was already rapping.

"Hallo?" he said in falsetto. "Housekeeping. I bring you fresh towels and chocolates. And an indescribably handsome man to do your bidding."

She opened up. He was wearing a towel over his head, giving him the look of an awkward Madonna sans child.

"Let's do dinner followed by a pedicure," he said. "Isn't that what ladies like to do to indulge? Come on, I'll let them paint my toenails whichever color you choose. It'll be fab-u-lous!"

"I'm not going to let you pay for everything, you know," Becky said.

Felix removed the towel. "You have no choice, darling. Fiona and I conspired on every detail, including the surreptitious removal of all your credit cards."

Becky rushed to her luggage and checked her wallet. Empty slots stared back. She watched it, waiting for the cards to reappear, wondering if she should insist or declare something or be willful and stubborn. She sighed defeat.

"In that case, for dinner I want filet mignon."

"I love it when you're bloodthirsty."

Six days they spent in Mazatlán. Mostly they ate.

The mornings they communed by the water, finding hammocks or beach chairs, reading paperbacks or just talking in that leisurely, oceanside way, the push of water and wind cleaning all worry and hurry out of them. Nothing seemed really important or devastatingly sad on the beach. The rhythm of water rushing and slapping the sand trumped the rhythm of days and years, and all of time seemed enfolded into the present moment.

After a rest and shower, they would meet up again for lunch. Felix emerged from his room, the tip of his nose bright red.

"You got Rudolphed," Becky said with a laugh.

"Explain."

She pointed to her nose. "The sun kissed you here, my friend. You must have been a good boy."

He nodded slowly. "Rudolph. I am often compared favorably to the noble caribou. No, of course you were referring to Valentino. He could learn a few tricks from yours truly."

Through the hot afternoon, they sat on the floor of Felix's room and played whatever games the hotel concierge could supply—Sorry, gin rummy, Candy Land. Their favorite was a board game called Zombies Attack!, which they played for hours on end, ordering room service and partaking of it on the rug so as not to interrupt their last stand against the tiny plastic zombies plaguing the board.

"I'll show you, you brain-sucking deadhead," Felix shouted. "Eat my shotgun!"

They went shopping at the faux-markets and challenged each other to look the most like a tourist. Becky did well with a Hawaiian shirt, sarong, huge hat with fake mums, and grass purse. But all it took was seeing Felix in some well-chosen Bermuda shorts pulled up over his waist for her to gracefully concede the contest. They wore the outfits whenever they went out, especially to nice dinners. No one asked Felix for an autograph.

Becky phoned home every day. Fiona was fine. Polly and the boys were fine. Grandma and Grandpa were fine. In fact, they all seemed to be enjoying the holiday. Her mother said, "Don't rush home!"

In the absence of anything to worry about, Becky teetered between panicking at the hostile entropy of the world and actually relaxing. If alone, who knows what madness might have consumed her. But Felix was there, wearing Bermuda shorts pulled high.

On their last evening, they were standing on the hotel balcony and watching the ocean. There was something about large bodies of water that tugged everything out of Becky's soul and left her clean and floating. So she floated, watching the waves curl far below, letting her gaze try to spot the point on the horizon where the ocean disappeared. At the moment, she couldn't feel any invisible animals gnawing on her flesh—not so much as an unease mouse nibbling her toenails.

She looked at Felix. He was staring at the ocean too. It looked like a movie shot, the light outlining his face so perfectly it seemed artificial, the breeze playing in his hair, his expression wonderfully conveying the peace of the moment. He turned, saw her looking, and smiled the sweetest smile, a smile for a best friend.

It wasn't a movie.

She started to cry. She didn't even know why. Felix put his arms around her, pulling her into his chest. She cried on his flowered tourist shirt. He rubbed her back. He kissed her hair. There was a loosening in her heart, an unclenching. They didn't say anything for a long time.

When they finally let go, night had begun to recline over the ocean and the breeze was wet. She shivered. She hadn't been cold inside his arms. He ducked into his room and came back with a sweater, draping it over her shoulders.

"Thanks," she said.

But when he looked at her, there was something different in his eyes. She didn't think about what it was then. She only knew that it made her stomach squeeze as if she were about to go on a roller coaster and was shying in anticipation.

They decided to go to dinner and chose a noisy, seaside jazz club that served huge fish sizzling on wooden boards. The music, the people, the fish sizzle made it almost impossible to talk. Which seemed to be what both of them wanted that night. She leaned against him in the booth to watch the musicians, her body positioned so that she couldn't see Felix's face. His arm draped around her shoulder.

She said a prayer. Thank you, Father, for this man. And help me know what to do.

She realized that the new look in Felix's eyes was hope.

In which Felix plays Santa Claus for the first time

After Mexico, Becky no longer felt pianos dropping on her head. It's a shame we can't say she was all better forever; but heartbreak is a wily, vigilant rodent always finding a new hole to hide in, a new way to burrow through. The heartbreak rat still scratched at her, woke her up at night, provoked sudden tears, and perhaps would for the rest of her life. She loved Mike. He loved her. He was gone. Yes, she believed his spirit lived on, that they would be reunited in a very real way after death. But what about now? What about the growing-old-alone part and the nine-year-old-boy-without-a-father part?

"I hate death," Becky would mutter to herself.

Nevertheless, the weight of the grief lifted, just a little, just enough to let a breeze into the room. It was a miracle in Becky's eyes, as much as water turning to wine (though water would do just fine, thank you). Of course, getting better also meant growing a new half of herself so she could stand upright again. That hurt. A lot.

So she began to grieve in earnest—not in the fold-herself-up way, not as a pillar of salt, but grieving as a way of putting names to her sorrows, understanding them, and yet still choosing to live. It was as if she'd broken all her bones and untreated they healed wrong, so now she had to rebreak them and set them right.

Looking inward made her want to howl, so she tried to look outward. The Sunday after she returned from Mexico, she made three pies, a tradition she'd put on hold for a year and a half. Mike wasn't sitting there across the counter, talking to her while she baked. She hoped her bitterness wouldn't infect the pastry.

The kids ate one pie that night, and per usual, Becky kept the other two for giving to persons yet unknown. She waited, but no names popped into her mind. Monday afternoon passed, then Monday night, and still she had no ideas. She leaned against the counter and said a prayer. Who should I give these to? Who is hurting and could use a pie?

You.

It was the warm, quiet kind of thought she'd always believed didn't come from her own mind but from God. Not a word or an image, but an idea, simple and sweet, and it made her heart burn.

You, Becky. You.

She felt noticed, and that both sang and stung. She sat on the kitchen floor and cried. Then she ate half a pie.

Over the next few months, Becky cried so much she feared she might sustain permanent water damage. Hyrum as a baby had been constantly wet—drooly, weepy-eyed, runny-nosed, his chin and nose covered in red prickly rash from the constant moisture. She'd kept him in a cloth bib so she could wipe him down at will. That was how she felt now. If only she could find an adult-sized bib.

Between the sobbing and breathing, sobbing and healing, she found a new sensation entering into her hollowed parts—mystification.

But I wasn't supposed to be alone, she thought. The kids keep growing up and they'll have their own lives, and I'll be alone. I'll always be alone until I die. That wasn't supposed to happen.

Noise, chaos, ruckus were Becky's lullabies. Mike's snoring had soothed her to sleep. Now she was standing in the hurricane-swept desolation of her life and wondering how on earth she had ended up there.

"What haven't you taken care of that you should?" Alice Hyde asked Becky during their now-weekly lunch. It had been ten days since the Mexico trip, and Alice was looking over Becky with a shrewd expression.

"Nothing, I'm doing better, really."

"Rebecca Louise, I'm asking you again as your mother. What do you still need to take care of? What's hanging over you the heaviest?"

"The bedroom," Becky said. Even as a child, she couldn't lie to her mother.

The bedroom had been the site of her companionship, her quiet love with Mike, where they met up and checked in with each other after the kids slept and the house was still. "I hate being there. Alone. I detest it. I . . ." She choked, surprised to discover a sob in her throat.

Alice nodded. "Let's reinvent it."

"I don't want to disturb anything that would upset the kids."

"Nonsense. It's been a year. This won't bother them."

"Mom . . ." But Becky didn't argue. Her mother's gaze was distant and calculating, and Becky well knew there were no words to bring her back now. Besides, her other reason for leaving the bedroom intact was too horrible to speak. (I need to keep it as-is, just in case it was all a mistake, just in case Mike's alive and coming home any day.)

They bought a secondhand bedroom set and painted it deep purple. The walls they redid in lime green, Sam and Polly lending a hand. Alice got one of her theater friends who painted sets to create a forest scene on one wall. Alice made a quilt and shams in garish colors. The new bed was a double, the king gone, leaving room for a love seat, chair, and coffee table. They ripped out the old, dark curtains and put in new light-permeating blinds. The room was brighter, inviting, felt more public than private, and Becky kept magazines on the coffee table and little bowls full of candy to lure in kids and visitors.

It became a ritual to gather in Becky's room before bed. Sometimes it was just Sam and Polly, who were still a little more tender and apt to weep, a little more eager for their mother's embrace and voice. Sometimes Hyrum joined them for family prayer, followed by snacks and chats in the love seat.

"Better?" Alice asked, inspecting the room one clear winter morning.

"Yeah . . ."

Alice put an arm around Becky and pulled her into her soft chest. "Tell me."

"I miss him."

"Of course you do."

"And . . . I don't know how to be a mother anymore. I thought I was good at it. But so much of the parenting was really Mike—we talked about everything, and his surety gave me confidence. Now I feel like a fraud."

Alice kissed her daughter's head several times. "It'll come back. Your confidence. You'll find it again."

"I don't know . . ."

"You're a good mother, honey lamb. I know it, and so do your kids. Just promise me when that confidence comes knocking, you'll let it in."

Becky gave in to the spiritual proddings poking soft fingers at her heart, began to pray more, and allowed herself to feel the comfort that she was accustomed to feeling after her prayers. She dreamed of Mike nearly every night. Dreaming of him helped her believe that Becky and Mike hadn't ended that day in the hospital, that they would go on forever. He didn't carry important messages from beyond. He was just there, they were together, and the feeling of it would linger with her in the morning, the way the smell of cookies baking hangs in the air even after they're all eaten.

And there was something else. A quiet buzzing of anticipation whenever she thought of Felix helped drone out the pain of loss, just a little. It helped give her something to wonder about instead of the constant questions: Will my kids survive the loss of a father? Will my heart hurt this much for the rest of my life? Will we ever be okay?

Right about two years after Mike's death, the extended family began to talk to Becky about "moving on." It was a sudden attack from all sides, like those ants that crawl up your leg then send out a chemical signal to all bite at once.

"One of my co-workers, Paul, he's a really great guy, a widower himself . . ." her brother Jerry said as they cleared the table from Sunday dinner.

"Time to get that meat back on the market," her brother John said, slapping her backside. He was always the tactful one.

"It wouldn't mean you love Mike any less," her sister, Diana, said as they planted bulbs in the backyard, five of their combined twelve children chasing each other with worms.

Becky buried her face in her dirty hands. "Shut up," she said, because that was a forbidden phrase growing up in their mother's house, two words that would send them to bed without supper. And Becky was feeling like a cornered animal and wanted nothing more than to lash back as if for her life.

"Becky . . ."

"Are you telling me that if Steve died, a couple of years later you'd be over it and out dating again?"

"Let's be honest—I have eight children. Any man who would have me would be insane, and I couldn't marry an insane man. But yes, personally, I would be ready. I could get married again."

Becky nearly called her a liar, but she supposed that Diana and Steve had always had one of those professional partnerships, where both knew their responsibilities and kept the family running. They didn't seem to laugh together. And when Steve was out of town, Diana didn't speak as if she missed him. Not like Becky and Mike. There was that flare of pain in her general heart region again.

"Diana, some animals mate for life. You don't tell a goose that lost her mate, 'It's time to move on.' No moving on for a goose. In fact, a goose doesn't even appreciate the insinuation. Try to be all cute and helpful with a goose and just hint at the moving on advice, and that goose will up and bite you on the tush."

Diana knocked the dirt off her shovel. "How about we just pretend I didn't bring this up?"

"Sounds good to me."

At least one Jack was open to new love. Polly had a boyfriend named Theo, a pale, sad-eyed, floppy-haired ghost of a boy who was never without his black trench coat, a beaten-up paperback of Sartre's *Nausea* peeking out the front pocket.

For weeks he'd wandered the Jacks' front yard or sat on his bike staring at Polly's window before Polly ever invited him in. Becky wasn't sure how they had any relationship, both just sitting in silence, sometimes listening to music, sometimes not. They would lounge in Polly's room (with the door open—house rule), studying together. When Becky passed by, Polly's eyes would be on her book and Theo's eyes would be on Polly. Eerie? Still, the girl seemed happier than she'd been in two years.

Good for her, Becky thought, and better her than me.

While Diana had backed off the Move On harassment, her brothers and parents kept the parade going. Becky didn't tell Felix about it. They spoke a few times a week, but she couldn't even consider leaving her kids to visit him, and Felix was busy, having started a production company.

But he did come for Christmas—two years, three months, and five days since Mike died. Felix had arranged a hotel, but the first night he and Becky stayed up so late talking that he ended up sleeping on the sofa. The next day he brought his bags from the hotel and took over Fiona's room. Fiona was in Los Angeles, having finished a one-year program at a design school in New York and was now fulfilling an internship Celeste had helped set up. When she arrived on December 23, she insisted she wanted to bunk with Polly, leaving the basement room to Felix.

Becky couldn't find *The Little Mermaid* comforter in their storage room, but she did dig out the matching shams and put them on his pillows.

Felix jumped right into the Jack Family Christmas Week Extravaganza, which included caroling, attending a production of *The Nutcracker* and *The Christmas Carol*, a *Messiah* sing-along, strolling the Christmas lights at Temple Square, wrapping presents, and baking herds and herds of reindeer cookies for neighbors. And he was introduced to Loki, the family's hairless cat.

"The kids wanted another pet," Becky explained as Felix stared in horror at the creature beside him. "But with Polly's allergies . . ."

"You are lying to me. You borrowed this creature from a zoo to play a prank on me. This isn't even really a cat, is it? This is some sort of rat and opossum hybrid. This is a lifelike Japanese robot that can dance to disco music."

"Funny. They're called sphinx cats. Come on, feel her skin. Like peach fuzz, right? Isn't she sweet? Give her a good rub. She's very affectionate."

"Ah-ha, yes, isn't that just . . . er, what is coating my hands?"

"It's . . . it's like a body wax. I should've bathed her before you came. The hairless cats, they ooze this waxy stuff to protect their skin. 'Cause they don't have hair. To protect them. So the waxy ooze helps. You see."

Felix stared at her for several seconds, his hands held up like a doctor about to perform surgery.

"I'm going to wash my hands now. And I'm going to try very hard not to run out of this house screaming."

Besides that, there was no drama during his visit, unless you count a minor (and mostly pleasant) fuddle when they took the three kids to the movies.

"I'll pay the admission," Becky insisted.

"Fine, as long as I can buy the concessions."

That seemed fair until Felix, Hyrum, and Sam came back from the concession stand loaded with five jumbo popcorns, bucket-sized sodas, and a heap of enormous candy bars.

"Look what he bought us, Mom!" Sam said.

"Felix, are you planning to supply the Russian army?"

He schlepped his provisions up the stairs to their seats, spilling popcorn in his wake. "Er, the boys assured me it was the typical fare for a family movie night."

"I bet they did. Now at last we have inventory to open that concession stand of our dreams." She sighed. "Better set aside half that candy for later, 'cause that'll be the last movie treat you boys get for a year."

"Mom!" they both whined.

"I'm kidding. It's Felix's treat, so I can't complain. Go ahead and make yourselves sick."

"Sweet," Sam said. Out of his ten-year-old mouth, that word sounded so cute Becky just had to kiss his cheeks.

"Oh," Polly said sadly. "Everything has chocolate."

"Boys, I'm surprised," Becky said in a so-not-surprised tone. "You know Polly's allergic to chocolate, and usually your snack food motivations are purely selfless."

Felix gave Hyrum a bill and asked him to be a gentleman and go buy Polly some licorice, then sat next to Becky. "Since we're on the subject, how are you managing? I mean, financially?"

"Are we on the subject?"

"We are now. So, how are—"

"Fine," she said.

"Tell me."

"No."

"If you don't, I might get rough."

"Do and it'll be Momma's smack-down time."

He picked her up, right there in the movie theater, gripped her around her waist and turned her upside-down. "Tell me or it's the dirt nap, baby."

"Put me down, show-off!"

He really was a shameless show-off, though even upside down, Becky thought to be impressed that he was so strong, especially as he was only a couple of years from fifty.

"Promise."

"Okay, fine. I'll talk, I'll spill the beans, I'll crow, whatever you want!"

Upright again, she straightened her sweater, turning to explain to the gaping spectators behind her, "I had a coin stuck in my pocket and he was trying to shake it out."

The couple behind them smiled politely. Polly and Sam were laughing when Hyrum returned with the licorice.

"Felix picked up Mom," Sam said.

"Upside down!" Polly said.

Hyrum scowled. "Crap, I miss everything."

"Tell me," Felix asked again in a quiet voice.

Becky whispered back so her kids wouldn't hear. "The life insurance paid off the mortgage, and thanks to the movie windfall we have the kids' college money put away. We had some retirement savings, but I'd rather not dip into that for another twenty years. So, it's just a matter of paying the day-to-day stuff . . ."

"And can you?"

"Sure."

"Becky," he said like a warning.

She sighed. "I have a degree in early-childhood development, and I haven't worked outside the home in nineteen years. I don't have a career. I've tried to sell a couple of other screenplays I'd been writing, a family comedy and a teen comedy, but Karen passed, and Larry looked them over and didn't think he could make them fly. I've made a little money doing technical writing by contract, but it's not quite enough, so I've started working on my real estate license."

He looked at her a long time. Her look back was defiant.

"Let me—"

"No."

"Just—"

"No."

"Sod it, you stubborn, stubborn woman!"

"Shh . . ." said the couple behind them. The previews had started.

"Yeah, shh," Becky whispered. "I swear, sometimes you can be so inconsiderate. I mean, talking in movies and offering to pay a widow's bills—geez, some people."

"Please," he said, a little ache in his voice.

"No."

He pushed his fist against his mouth to still a smile.

"What's funny?"

"You are. I can't think why I love you. Eleven years I've been wondering and I'm no closer to—"

"Shh . . ." said the couple behind them.

"Yeah, shh," said Hyrum. "You guys are worse than little kids, I swear."

"How old is he again?" Felix whispered.

"Fifteen. Which makes him only slightly more mature than you."

"Oh really? Is he mature enough to pull off the yawn-stretch maneuver?"

Felix yawned, stretched, and settled his arm around Becky's shoulder.

There they were, she realized, watching a movie, eating popcorn and sipping sodas, his arm around her shoulder. Mike wasn't there. Celeste wasn't there. She hadn't meant to ask the question aloud, but during the opening action sequence, she found herself whispering, "Are we on a date?"

"Yes," he whispered.

"What?" she said, surprised by the response.

He turned to look at her, and his eyes assured her he meant exactly what he said. "Yes, we are."

"Oh."

There was a plunging sensation in her middle.

Behind them, a cell phone rang, chiming the theme to *The Godfather.* The guy answered it in full voice. "Hello?"

Felix turned very slowly, looked at the guy, and raised one eyebrow.

Becky laughed, a piece of popcorn flying out of her mouth and hurtling over the seats before her.

Christmas Eve, Becky decided to stay home and keep it simple. Since Mike, she'd taken every opportunity to drown holidays in family and noise so the kids wouldn't notice who wasn't there. But this year, Becky wanted candles and music, dinner at home, kids in pajamas playing games, hot cocoa and cookies, photo albums and popcorn. Felix had made a reservation at some bed-and-breakfast up a canyon, saying he didn't want to interfere with the family and that Christmas meant nothing to him. But then the heavens opened, and snow filled the earth. The streets were white, the air was white, the tree branches balanced inches of fat flakes. So Felix sat down to the ham dinner and just stayed. And stayed and stayed.

He played Boggle with Polly and Fiona, who let him get away with British spellings until he claimed b-a-u-g-x was the way all English children were taught to spell "box." He put new logs on the fire and read Christmas books with Sam, doing accents for all the characters. And after the kids had gone to bed, Becky grabbed him by the hand and pulled him into her bedroom. She locked the door behind them, giggling.

"Usually in such circumstances," he said, "I have a pretty good idea of what's going to happen next, but right now, Mrs. Jack, I am stumped."

She rolled her eyes. "Get your mind out of the gutter. I just want you to help me play Santa Claus."

She pulled bags of goodies out of the closet and instructed him in the fine art of stocking stuffing. Then they tiptoed with excruciating quietness to the family room. The filled stockings were too heavy to hang back up, so they placed them on chairs and on the sofa, arranging the larger gifts around them.

"Don't they all know by now . . ." Felix whispered, "you know, who is putting out the gifts?"

"Of course they do."

"So why the secrecy?"

"Because *what if* . . . what if they were wrong? I mean, what if they thought there was no Santa, but there really was? They've never actually seen me or Mike put out the gifts, so there will always be that tiny hope, that little piece of the child in them that believes there is some magic, and Christmas morning will make all their fantasies real."

"What a load of rubbish. The truth is, you just have fun doing it."

Becky giggled some more.

Felix said, "Shh." And he arranged Sam's new sled at a different angle.

They crept back upstairs, shut the door to her room with an almost silent click, looked at each other and sighed relief.

"Made it. One more year."

Felix dropped into a chair as if he'd just run a race. He wore a goofy grin. "Can we do that again?"

She sat on the floor and pulled her knees to her chest, still feeling bouncy and charmed from the family room adventure. "When is the last time you had a good family Christmas?"

Felix shut his eyes. "Mmm . . . nineteen seventy-one."

"What?"

"Every Christmas after Mum and I had our own little celebration, I would go to a mate's house—Mark Taggart. Mark's mum was fond of me, a real blaze of life, reminds me of another woman I know. And she loved a good holiday. The phrase 'deck the halls' can't describe the state of that house. Five children, a mother and a father, loads of food and gifts and music, candles and fire blazing, tree and holly and mistletoe. It was . . . perfect." He shook his head. "I ran over every Christmas Day, happy as anything. By the time I got back to our bleak, empty little house, I felt whittled down to the core. The Taggarts moved house when I was thirteen, and I was honestly relieved to have them gone. It wasn't pleasant having that comparison."

"And you haven't celebrated Christmas since."

"Not so much."

"Felix . . ."

"Hey now, this is not a tragic night. You showed up the Taggarts, didn't you?"

"You better believe it. I doubt the Taggarts supplied you with *Little Mermaid* shams."

Felix shuddered. "Now is an appropriate time to apply the word *tragic*."

"It is, actually . . ." Becky felt weariness wash over her, as if all of a sudden her body realized the late hour. She laid her head on the love seat. "You know in the real story, the non-Disney one, the prince marries someone else, the Little Mermaid dies and is doomed to turn into sea foam but instead becomes a daughter of the air."

"That doesn't really make sense. Are you half asleep?"

"You know, I think I am . . ." Her eyelids fluttered.

Felix picked her up and settled her into bed, sliding the comforter over her shoulders. She meant to say good night, but the lights blinked off and the door clicked shut, so she sank into her pillow and set about dreaming of sugarplums.

Felix was the first one up in the morning. He was as giddy as a little kid, watching everyone unload the stockings, exclaiming at each gift as if it were the first time he'd seen it. Then he brought out gorgeously wrapped gifts of his own, leaning forward with anticipation as each was opened. When he unwrapped the Jacks' gifts to him, even the purple socks from Sam, Felix gushed.

"Purple socks! My man, this is precisely what I wanted this year. You have made me one happy bloke."

Later, over cinnamon rolls, Felix asked her, "Is this what Christmas morning is like every year?"

"Pretty much."

He stared into his mug of hot chocolate, and in Sam tones said, "Awesome."

The rest of Christmas Day was a flurry with Mike's family and Becky's family. For his own sake, Felix absconded to some private club in Park City. When Becky and the kids returned home late that night, he was still gone, but there was a new leather sofa set in the family room, replacing the mangled flowered couch.

"How did you get those delivered on Christmas Day?" she asked him the next morning.

"Me? I'm not responsible. And frankly, I find it appalling that the police don't do more to protect the honest citizens of Layton. Reckless thieves, breaking into homes, pilfering chesterfields and leaving behind these disgusting totems wrapped in dead animal skin. Egregious!"

Felix left on December 27, New York–bound for a couple of days, then on to Devonshire.

"Mum and I thought we could ring in New Year's together. Herbert promised to spend a lot of time at the pub. Noble of him."

Becky squeezed his arm. "You're such a good boy."

Felix shrugged.

"She needs you. She needs you desperately. No matter what happens and how useless it feels, know that she needs you. You're saving her just by being there. It's the best Christmas present you could give a mother."

The visit seemed to go well—at least, Felix didn't complain about it. Much. It wasn't for weeks after he returned to London that Becky discovered diamond earrings in her jewelry box, because she rarely opened the thing, only stumbling over them when she did because she'd been hunting for a safety pin. She gasped. They were round and huge, sparkling like lit fuses.

When she called to thank/scold him, he said, "I've been wondering about those. So . . . did you read the card?"

"There was a card?"

"Check on your dresser."

She didn't find it immediately, and fearing it contained something obnoxious, like a check, she put it off. Then one day while hunting for her keys, she found a red envelope fallen beneath her dresser. She opened it. No check. Just a note.

Dear Abby,

I am madly in love with my best mate of eleven years. It is a tricky maneuver to change from best mate to lover, and I know she will have bounteous objections, but I must tell her how I feel. Do you have any suggestions?

Signed,
Devilishly Handsome in Devonshire

"Holy crap," she whispered after she'd read it a dozen times. She was clutching the letter so hard, it ripped. "Holy crap. Holy. Crap. Holycrapholycrapholycrapholy—"

"What're you doing, Mom?" Hyrum was standing in the doorway in his basketball uniform, squinting at her seated on the floor.

"Nothing. Nothing. I just . . . I sat down for a second. Do you need something?"

"Uh, *yeah*. I've been waiting in the kitchen for like ten *minutes* to leave for my basketball game. You *said* you were looking for your *keys*."

"Yes, right, that's right. I'm coming. Here I come." She looked at her hands. All she was holding was the letter. "Where are my keys?"

Hyrum groaned.

It wouldn't be amiss to say that Becky was a bit spacey all day. Once, she even accidentally cheered when the opposing team scored a basket. On the court, Hyrum rolled his eyes.

She kept one hand inside her purse, gripping the letter in private.

What . . . what . . . should I . . . I mean, I can't possibly . . . what should I do? Should I . . . I can't even . . . is he serious? No, he can't . . . we're not even . . . this is . . . I mean, me and Felix? It's a joke. Isn't it?

She knew it wasn't. Why would he say this now? How long had he been feeling it? Or was he just being noble and making a sacrifice so he could pay her bills and take care of the family?

At three A.M. she wrote a response, sealed it, and went out into the freezing March night in her slippers to mail it before she could reconsider.

Dear Passably Handsome,

I'm sure your best friend loves you, but there are too many obstacles:

    1. You live on different continents for half the year.

    2. She has a large family who needs her.

    3. She gave her heart to her husband and it will never be fixed and whole again. It just won't. It's scientifically impossible.

    4. You have very different religious beliefs.

    5. You're British, and she doesn't drink tea.

    6. It's just a harebrained idea anyway, and if you actually had to spend more time together, you'd drive each other crazy, and after all your twenty-year-old girlfriends, the sight of a naked forty-five-year-old mother would throw a chilly bucket of water on the old libido, and then you wouldn't get to be best friends anymore.

Felix phoned a few days later.

"Hello gorgeous."

"Hi." She could hear her own voice was tight.

"Do you really mean it? What you said in the letter?"

"I do."

"I mean the bit where you say you love me?"

"Yes, but—"

"Because I—"

"I can't, Felix. I'm not over Mike. I'll never be over him, and I don't want to be."

"That doesn't matter. I won't try to be Mike. You know I'd have no hope. We'll just be us but closer."

"Yes, that whole 'lover' stuff . . . You know I don't live that way. I've never been with anyone besides Mike, and we waited until we were married. The idea—"

"That's beside the—wait. You're telling me you've never slept with anyone but Mike? No little romp in college, some postparty spontaneous slap and tickle with a bloke you never saw again?"

"Ick. Seriously—ick. I don't know how people can do that. I don't *enjoy* using public toilets—why on earth would I . . . would I *romp* with someone I don't know? The germs, the disease, the awkwardness, not to mention the immorality, the social depravity, the—"

"The reckless abandon, the freedom, the sexiness of giving over to the purely sensual, the rush of—"

"Felix, I'm going to stick with 'ick' on this one."

"Yes, I rather thought you might. Well, if you've really sworn to be chaste, then . . . I'll chase you."

"Oh gag. That was a bad line."

"Really? I'd been saving it up for a special occasion." She could hear some tapping, as if he were scolding a countertop with a pen. "But I don't understand. How could you know if you and Mike were compatible enough to marry if you'd never—"

"Ha!" she said.

"I don't think I'm going to let you get away with just 'ha.'"

Rats. She'd hoped he would, because the question had nicked her guilt gland. She had often thought the same thing about her sister, Diana—how could she have known Steve was the guy without even kissing him? It was crazy! A kiss was the answer to a question, a kiss was a portal into the soul. She'd always thought Diana was loony not to test her future husband first with at least one kiss.

Oh ye hypocrite, she thought. So she tried to answer as honestly as she could.

"I knew . . . I just knew. We were compatible in every other way. And I suspected that in that aspect . . . you know . . . we would be too, because of his . . . well, his smell."

"He must have smelt pretty good."

"His pheromones practically danced down my gullet and straight to my ovaries. I was so attracted to his scent that I knew we'd have beautiful babies. Our eyes met, and our genes sang arias to each other. That's what makes me suspicious about Internet dating—what happens when people fall in love without smelling each other first?"

"I never knew you were so feral."

"I'll tell you what—a lot of people procreating with incompatible genes, mutant children flooding the earth."

"So," there was a definite eyebrow-wag tone to his voice, "do you find my scent compatible?"

That stumped her. "I . . . don't know. It doesn't matter. It's not as if we're going to be having children together."

"That's right, darling. Just some old-fashioned, highly compatible lovemak—"

"Aah! Don't say that! I cannot think about you that way and retain any shame. Besides, I don't believe in sex outside of marriage."

"I'm talking marriage here, sweetheart."

The wind was knocked out of her as hard as if she'd fallen two stories onto her back. "Marriage? Are you serious?"

"Becky, are you going to make me beg? Is your reluctance based on real trepidation, or are you just trying to torture me?"

"Mike and I," she paused to take a breath. "We were married in a temple. It wasn't just till death do us part. We believe our marriage was sealed for time and all eternity, that we'll be husband and wife forever."

"So that means you can't marry anyone else?"

"No, I can marry again, just for the 'time' part and leave off 'all eternity,' but—"

"Then it's settled. I don't believe in the 'all eternity' anyhow. I only want to be your fellow for the rest of this life, till death do us part."

"No, Felix, it won't work. It just won't. I'm sorry."

He was quiet. Her heart squeezed.

"Felix? Sweetie, are you okay?"

"In that case . . ." His voice twanged with wickedness. "In that case, I'm going to have to romance you off your feet."

She gasped. "No you don't . . ."

"Yes, I'm afraid so. Becky Jack, may I woo you?"

"No."

"Ha! That 'no' was so weakly spoken I'm going to ignore it entirely." He chuckled. "This is going to be fun."

"No it's not! No you're not! Don't you dare, Felix Callahan."

"Maybe I will, maybe I won't. You'll have to wait and see."

"You're so aggravating! I don't know why I let you hang around."

"Because of my swoon-worthy looks?"

"You're tolerable, but you're no Cary Grant."

"He was milquetoast compared to what you're going to get. I'm going to woo you until your knees go soft."

"Argh!" She hung up the phone.

In which Becky Jack gets romanced

It started with flowers. Delivery vans showed up hourly, handing over an indecent number of overflowing vases, turning her home into a Thomas Kincade painting. Soon every flat surface sported a bouquet—not sunflowers this time but roses, lilacs, gardenias, lilies, jasmine, all fragrant varieties so there was no corner of the house where she could escape their rich scent.

She came home from the grocery store and discovered a CD player on her front stoop, Kenny Rogers singing "Lady" on repeat play. She wondered who in Utah was doing Felix's bidding—some hired assistant, a concierge service? It was a little bit creepy.

Two days later, she woke to a second CD player outside her bedroom window playing "Islands in the Stream." She let it play, listening with her eyes closed, her big toe wiggling to the beat. She was really changing her mind about that song being lame.

The next day, it was "Short People." She put her face in her pillow to stifle the laugh. She was trying to pretend none of this was happening, but she was running out of places to put the CD players. All the flat surfaces still held flowers.

That sort of thing went on for a few weeks—songs, flowers, chocolates in the mail, a housecleaning service showing up and explaining that they were paid through the end of the year. All that time he didn't return her calls, which was so irritating, because he was the one person alive in the world she would have liked to tell about a ridiculous wooing. Instead, she was showered with distant attention but kept from speaking to her best friend. And she missed him.

Then she started running into the man himself.

First at the grocery store. She was pushing a cart down the cereal aisle, searching for Hyrum's favorite brand of raisin flakes, when she collided with another cart.

"Excuse me," she started to say, until she saw who it was. "What on earth are you doing here?"

"Oh, hey there, Becky," he said, speaking with a suburban mother accent. "Do you shop here too?"

"You're not serious."

"Well, this is my first time in this store. I only just moved into the neighborhood."

"Moved into the . . ."

"Mm hm." He picked up a box of cereal, pretending to be very interested in the list of ingredients. "I'm renting a flat over on Fort Lane. One bedroom, but I *love* the location."

"You're lying. Are you lying?"

"Nope." He emphasized the "p" noise, popping the word in his mouth, and smiled wickedly before his faux-normal demeanor returned. "Well, I should go. I have quite a shopping list to fill. You know how it is. See you round!"

He winked as he left.

It was weird how hard her heart was pounding.

On Friday, the kids came home from school with Felix stories.

He'd been a guest speaker in Polly's twelfth-grade English class, explaining the process of making a movie based on a book.

"When he left, Mrs. Elkins called after him, 'Come anytime!' and then batted her eyelashes. Then all the girls were swarming around me saying, 'He's so hot!' And I was like, 'Ick. He's like my uncle.'" It was a big, bold paragraph for Polly to speak, and it made Becky extremely proud.

Then he showed up in Hyrum's social studies class, prearranged with the teacher, to give a British perspective on current world events.

At lunch period, he met up with Hyrum and Polly. He brought a large take-out lunch for them to share, and they sat on the school lawn and ate and talked.

"What did you talk about?" Becky wanted to know.

Polly shrugged. "Just stuff. He asked us about stuff, school, friends, you know."

"Did you talk about me?" Becky asked.

"No, Mom. We were just hanging."

"Everyone was staring at us," Hyrum said. "It was pretty cool. I mean, I knew Felix was famous, but I didn't know he was *cool* famous. I thought he was, you know, snooty famous, like old-people famous."

That afternoon, Felix made an appearance at Sam's fifth-grade class. "He was our phys ed teacher for the day. He knows all these cool soccer moves. He calls it *football*. And he told us stories about how in England people kill each other over football. Killing people over soccer! That is *so* cool."

The next encounter was at Sam's soccer game on Saturday. Felix was wearing a purple shirt, the Tigers' color, and had a purple megaphone. At least he hadn't painted his face.

"All right, Sam!" he'd holler from the front row of the bleachers. "Great block! Come on now. Don't let him get away. Go Tigers!"

Becky sat on the other side of the bleachers and tried not to let her Felix-glaring interfere with her Sam-cheering.

The Tigers were down several goals, and Sam was looking glum. When they had a break, Becky expected her boy to come over for some cheering up. Instead, he went to Felix.

Felix gave some sort of soccer advice that involved using shins and knees, and Sam nodded, his mouth open as if he were literally eating Felix's every word. When Sam left to run back to the game, Felix rubbed the boy's head in a fatherly fashion. Sam was grinning.

The Tigers lost in the end, badly in fact, but it didn't matter, because in the second half, Sam scored a goal. Becky had never imagined that Felix could yell so loud, jumping about, shouting Sam's name and pounding the air with his fist. You would have thought his team had won the World Cup.

She invited him to join them for some celebratory ice cream, and he spent the entire time absorbed in Sam and recounting details of his inspired playing.

"Did you see how you used your shins to keep the ball away? It was a bloody brilliant move. Tell me what you were thinking when that redheaded kid tried to steal the ball from you."

"I was thinking, no way! This is my ball. You'll have to wait your turn."

"I knew it. I knew you had the warrior spirit. A champion in the making."

Sam positively glowed. "The British *know* football, Mom. It's in their blood. Felix has met Pelé *and* Beckham, and he says I have the same wild look of a champion."

"Of course you do, sweetie."

Felix barely paid any attention to Becky until they'd gone back home. Sam ran into the house to tell Hyrum about his game, while Becky and Felix stayed out under the April afternoon sky, leaning back against the car and staring up into blue.

"He's a good kid," Felix said. "I like him much better now that he can talk."

"Are you doing all this to show that you could play the part of his daddy?"

"No. He already has a daddy. I'd just like to be his mate and his mum's husband."

"Felix—" she started to say, but he took her hand, kissed it, and walked away.

"I have a date with another woman. Don't be jealous—she's eighty-two."

He pulled his bicycle out of the back of her minivan.

"I wouldn't put it past you," she called after him as he rode off. "And you really should learn to drive a car!"

The next day was Sunday. Becky was in sacrament meeting when she felt someone sit on the bench beside her and turned to see a very stoic Felix Callahan in a black suit and white shirt. He looked outlandishly debonair in that Layton, Utah, congregation, even though he'd clearly put on a conservative striped tie in hopes of blending in. He stared straight ahead at the speaker.

"Don't you dare pretend to convert just for me," she whispered.

"Of course not. I'm here because I want to be here. With you."

She stewed for a time.

"If this is—"

"Shh," he whispered. "Don't you know it's rude to talk in church?"

After Hyrum and other boys his age passed around the bread and water of the sacrament, after Becky's friend Jessie gave the first talk, the bishop returned to the podium.

"Now we'll have a special musical number given by a friend of the Jack family, Felix Callahan."

Becky gripped his arm. "What are you doing?" she hissed.

He just smiled at her before going down the aisle to stand by the piano. The pianist, eighty-two-year-old Ginny Castleton, played an introduction, and Felix began to sing.

It was the children's hymn Hyrum had sung at the ward potluck over nine years before—a simple melody, no sharps or flats, no trills or grace notes, just a steady, innocent tune. But somehow Felix's voice lent it depth, gave the words wisdom.

He didn't look at Becky as he sang about being a child of God, about having a family on earth, about pleading for guidance so he could go home again one day. He took in the whole room, kept the entire congregation rapt with his voice. They'd heard that song sung a thousand times, but never like that. Polly was smiling sweetly, as if at a very dear friend. Hyrum was resting his head on the pew in front of them, but Becky could tell that he wasn't asleep. Sam was mouthing the words.

When Felix returned to the bench, Becky wiped her wet cheeks.

"I'll never understand why you cry at that song."

"I'm crying because you're so aggravating."

"I don't believe it."

"No, you don't believe it," she whispered. "That's part of the problem. You don't believe that you *are* a child of God."

"But I believe that you believe it," he said.

"Felix—"

"Shh, I'm listening. Don't you know it's rude to talk in church?"

He came over for Sunday dinner. She'd made a Crock-Pot roast with potatoes and carrots, and the smell and the animated talking and laughing felt so Sunday-ish, so natural and wonderful, that she kept expecting to see Mike at the head of the table. She saw Felix instead. It hurt her heart, but not as much as she'd supposed. Felix could never replace Mike, but he was there, and he was there because he wanted to be.

He was pretending to be a stodgy old Englishman, calling for the butler and declaring the outing "rather jolly, pip-pip and all that," and the boys were laughing too hard to eat. How could she feel sad when her boys were so happy?

In which Felix risks it all

Felix came over Monday night to help Hyrum with his history report, and Becky hung back and watched. Of all the children, Hyrum had taken the loss of his father the hardest, going quiet, hunkering down in his fifteen-year-old body, speaking in outbursts of anger. But there he sat at the kitchen table with Felix, chatting about Charlemagne, and if he didn't smile most of the time, he also didn't storm off. Sometimes, when Felix was reading from the book, Hyrum would look at Felix in a way Becky had seen before—the way he looked at his baseball coach, the way he had looked at Mike, that I-care-what-you-think-of-me way. In waves it delighted her and terrified her.

As soon as they took a break, Becky yanked Felix's arm and dragged him onto the back porch.

"Tell me what's cooking in your sinister little brain."

"Can't a fellow—"

"No. A fellow can't."

He combed his hair with his fingers as if he were distraught, but it also made his hair stand up in a rakish and adorable way, and Becky suspected he was aware of that. She pretended not to notice.

"Your children are your world. If I want to live in your world, I need to know them better, and they need to want me around."

"Yeah, well . . . what about me?" She glared. "I miss you. I miss talking with you."

"I hoped so."

"That was part of your plan?"

He shrugged. "What can I say? I'm devious, cunning, *and* unscrupulous. I will do anything to win your heart and hand."

"No you won't."

"Oh but I will," he said matter-of-factly. "I really will. Try me."

"Yeesh, I'd rather not."

"I don't know how you persist in being so stubborn—"

"It's a superpower. I was bitten by a radioactive mule."

"—but you're going to succumb in the end."

"I have no choice?"

"Oh, you have a choice. And you will choose me."

He leaned in, and their bodies were inches apart, his face close to hers. Then he bent and kissed her bare neck. She got goose bumps up and down the entire side of her body and thought angrily, He shouldn't be able to make me feel this way.

"Come to New York with me," he said, now touching her shoulder. "One weekend, the two of us."

Her breathing was shallow. "If I do, will you stop stalking me and return to being my friend?"

"Yes. If after the weekend that's what you want, then yes."

"Okay."

She stuck out her hand to shake, because he was still leaning in that way, as if he wanted to kiss her more on the neck, or elsewhere, and it was making her toes curl. He took her hand, shook it, and said, "Agreed," then grabbed her and kissed her neck one more time, slowly, before returning to the house.

She stood on the porch a few minutes, feeling a sensation that started on her neck but slithered inside her, curling into her gut. Why was she feeling like this? Was it really possible that she could love Felix in that—no, no. No! No, that was wrong. She never had, she never could, she was halved and there could be no one else.

Then why was she shaking? Or maybe she was just imagining it. She held out her hand to see if she could see the tremble. And there was her wedding band. Usually she didn't even notice it, but now the sight of it stung.

"Ouch," she whispered. "Ouch, Mike. It still hurts."

She heard Felix and Hyrum laughing inside the house and thought she couldn't go to New York with this man. She couldn't be alone with him. She felt stretched between two men, both impossible to have, and the pain seemed empty and cruel.

I promised to go, she thought. I even shook his hand.

Well, it would be the end of the wooing, she was certain of that. She'd have a wonderful weekend with her best friend and then find a way to make him understand.

As the date inched closer, she panicked and tried to find an excuse to skip out on the trip, double and triple checking with her children, carefully watching for any sign of sorrow in their eyes. She couldn't even detect a glimmer of melancholy.

"Are you sure it's okay if I leave?" she asked.

Hyrum blew air through his lips. "Geez, Mom, it's three days. Give me a break."

But then Felix's carefully planned "Weekend O' Wooing

Extravaganza" began, and she forgot why she'd been dragging her feet. First off, they flew first-class. She'd never admit it, but she could really get used to first-class.

And second, it was Felix. It was impossible to do anything with him but relax and laugh. He didn't lean. He didn't kiss her neck. He just took her arm and led her in a dance.

They stayed at the Plaza (which she discovered has *great* break-fasts, the number-one factor in her opinion of any hotel), and stayed up late in their connecting rooms laughing and talking.

By golly, she thought, but I love to laugh with this man.

Felix knew the city, and he didn't bore her with Broadway revivals or excursions to the Statue of Liberty. Instead it was plays at the Circle, hole-in-the-wall Italian restaurants, downtown walking tours of hidden architectural wonders. Becky had never seen New York like this, and she strolled around and around the Frick Gallery in awe, color and brushstrokes filling her with an oceanlike rhythm.

Felix held her hand. And she held his, even though she knew he held it not as a friend, but as a . . . (gah, could she really say it?) . . . as a *boyfriend*. Yes, she was in New York with her potential boyfriend. He really was more than just a best friend now. So she became con-scious of every touch, every embrace, every time his arm was around her shoulder.

Once, as they left a restaurant, a photographer raced up to snap a few shots. Felix didn't shy away. With his arm encircling Becky's back, he turned toward the photographer and smiled. The flash flared in her eyes.

She stared at him as they walked away, mystified by his fearless-ness, the pressure of his arm still around her shoulder.

"Hi there," he said and kissed her forehead.

"You let them take a picture."

"With pride. It does my career good to be seen with a tasty nugget of arm candy."

"Yeah right." She flashed him a goofy smile, but he wouldn't budge. "I always thought you didn't consider me a . . . uh, a human woman."

"Perhaps at first. But you changed, or I did, or everyone else did, because now I think you are more of a woman than any other woman I've known."

He began to sing "More Than a Woman" in a falsetto-perfect Barry Gibb as they walked, stopping to do a fancy spin. In truth, she was so impressed she had to keep her mouth shut or she'd gush. Who can do a dead-on Barry Gibb? Felix was a genius.

The last night he took her to one of those ridiculously fabulous restaurants named after its own chef where each menu item was a para-graph of description: "Mustard dry-rubbed and slow-roasted free-range bantam breast, paired with crisped organic loin of rabbit, green parsnip butter, black truffle and butterbread porridge, red corn panisse, smoked strawberries, and three-year-old Moroccan olives, simmering in a candied shallot broth." After asking the server for an explanation, Becky said, "Oh, so it's chicken? But then why isn't it fried?"

The server was not amused.

"Uh, I'll have the third item there, the one that has the longest description. That's gotta mean something fairly hearty."

She had very little idea what exactly she was ordering, and actually seeing the food on the plate didn't clear up the issue—there was a tiny strip of some kind of meat, artfully arranged with a greenish paste and a yellow crumbly substance, garnished with some vegetable curled like ribbon. It was a museum of different tastes and left her feeling more intrigued than full.

"Mike would've taken one look at this plate and said, 'Could you ask the chef to mush it all together and stick it on a bun?'"

Felix chuckled. "I would have paid to see that."

Becky smiled as the thought of Mike's absence, for the moment at least, didn't sting.

For dessert they shared "avocado and olive oil ice cream on a cornbread wafer drizzled with mulberry coulis and topped with sugared rose petals." And Becky learned, add enough sugar and cream to anything, and you can call it dessert.

After dinner, instead of returning to the hotel, the limousine pulled up to the last place Becky expected to be—a certain club with a line out front, bouncer, and neon sign.

She scowled. "The Blue Note."

"Oh, right, we've been here before, haven't we?" Felix asked, his tone casual.

"I'm not going in there again. You may think this is funny somehow in your sick little mind, but I'm not reliving that—"

"We're going back to the scene of the crime, just for an hour."

"I hate that place. I was so ugly in there. And tired. Man, I was tired. And you . . ." She glared at him. "You were a stupidhead!"

"Please, Becky." He was standing beside the limousine, holding out his hand, his eyes pleading. "Please come in with me."

She made a show of resisting before taking his hand and stepping into the pleasantly chill May night. The doorman let Felix and Becky right in, and a young woman in go-go boots escorted them to a reserved table by the dance floor. Immediately a waiter brought over a plate of cheesy potato skins and two Shirley Temples.

Felix sipped one, watching the band. "Mm, nothing like a Shirley Temple to curl the hair on your chest."

Becky rolled her eyes. He held her hand under the table.

Two girls came over. Bounced over. One was a blonde, one a red-head, both in their early twenties—not the same two as before, but there was a remarkable resemblance in all the right places. They wore little halter tops, butt-tight jeans, high heels. And they wore them well. Becky sniffed.

"Hi, aren't you Felix Callahan the actor?" the blonde chirped.

"I am."

"Wow, I love your movies. Isn't he cute, René?"

"He's so cute," René agreed with pouty lips. She rested her hands on the table, and parts of her gushed forward. "Very cute."

The blonde leaned against Felix's back, wrapping her arms around his neck. "Why don't you come dance with us? We'll have lots of fun. I promise."

Felix's eyes were bored as he said, "Please disengage yourself from my neck. Can't you see I'm already with the most beautiful woman in the room?"

The girls tottered off, disappearing into the crowd.

Becky felt a sly smile curl her mouth. "You paid them to do that."

"I don't know what you're talking about," he said as he sipped his Shirley Temple, his lips tense to keep from smiling.

"You actually hired a couple of models to come here tonight and play out that little scene."

"I don't need to pay admirers. I have to beat them off with a stick. But now that you mention it, wasn't it serendipitous that I met with a nearly identical situation and responded the way I should have the first time?"

"Miraculous even."

The band began to play "A Kiss to Build a Dream On." Felix looked up, acting surprised. "Why, this is the song we danced to the day we first met. What a coincidence."

"Yes, amazing."

He stood and offered his arm. "May I escort you onto the dance floor?"

"I'm a pretty good dancer, you know."

"I know."

As they stepped out, the rest of the dancers withdrew. A blue spot-light drenched them and the bandleader announced, "Ladies and gen-tlemen, the legendary Becky Jack." The watchers applauded.

She almost slugged him then. But he wasn't laughing.

"You *are* legendary," he whispered.

He put his hand on her lower back and swung her out, spinning her back in and against his side. He was adept at leading, and she felt as if she floated across the floor. His hand was so light on her waist, and yet so firm that she always knew which way to turn. It was no flashy tango or jaunty fox-trot—just a gentle two-step, a dance that knows exactly what it is and doesn't pretend to be anything else, a dance that keeps a steady movement and yet allows a bit of spinning fun.

"Tell me that you weren't a little tempted by those young beauties."

"I was not tempted, not a little, not a lot. I'm nearing fifty, and I'm knackered trying to keep up. I sought out the taut young things after Celeste because I didn't want to get entangled with a woman who had children or wanted them. Then I realized there was one woman and four children I did care about a great deal. It's time for me to settle into my adult skin. It's time for me to be happy, and I'll be happy when I'm with you."

"But I'm no bouncy girl, you know. I don't look like the women you've been dating these years."

"I'm quite eager to gaze upon your naked body and confident that the sight will thrill me—"

"Oh stop it!"

"—to no end, but I know I can't convince you of that, so here's a thought. What if I went blind? I could lay my hands on some sulfuric acid, splash it round. Just think of the made-for-telly movie they would make about us one day. I can only dream that it will be titled *Blind Love*."

"I wonder who will play me. Probably Gwyneth Paltrow. Ooh, or Penélope Cruz!"

"If only Lucille Ball were still alive . . ."

"Felix . . ." She paused, aware of his hand holding hers, his other hand on her back. The touch felt nice, but doubt swam through her. "Felix, how can we possibly—"

"We'll buy a house near Layton, so you can be close to your family and Hyrum and Sam can finish school with their mates. When I'm filming on location, you can be home. We'll have a house in Los Angeles, and as Fiona seems to have settled into the City of Angels, we can let her live there and take care of it when we're away. We'll spend the summers and some holidays in England. I am impatient to see the entire Jack family with passports, and won't it be good for the boys to grow up knowing another country?"

"Wow, you have thought it through."

"I have a real estate agent in Salt Lake City awaiting your call."

There was no floor beneath her feet. Felix held her up, and they danced on solid air. It gave her a queer, tickly sensation, dancing so high above the ground. Freeing in one way, and yet frightening too, because the ground was still down there, hard and unforgiving.

It's not a prank, she realized. She'd let herself believe that this was some silly game Felix was playing, a joke on her, something to distract her from her mourning, so she never had to take it seriously. But he meant it. All of it.

Could I be with him? Could I really? Maybe I could, really really?

He spun her, and even when she was back in his hold, she was still spinning.

She kept right on floating and spinning for the rest of the next song, soaring back to the limousine, hovering over the seat as he held her hand, sure that her eyes were sparkling. She didn't remember entering the hotel, getting into the elevator, but the upward pull made her feel so light she thought she might keep going up forever. He was still holding her hand, keeping her with him, stopping her from rising right through the roof.

We could be together. I wouldn't have to be alone. The kids like him. Mike wouldn't mind. It could be true.

He walked her to her room. They stopped before her door, and he took both her hands. He was looking at her, in that way that meant he'd like to kiss her, as he had at the Valentine's Ball eleven years ago. But now there was a decade of friendship between them, his face as familiar to her as her own, and she loved him so much, and there was nothing to prevent her. She could kiss him, and she wouldn't betray anyone. She could be with him.

He smiled, so kindly, so sincerely, though there was a fire of longing in his eyes too. "Marry me, Becky." He put his hand up, cradling the side of her face, his thumb brushing the corner of her mouth, as he had on the movie set years ago. And then he came closer.

There were no cameras, no gelled lights, no director to yell "action!" No bite of garlic on her tongue. This was not a prank. This was the kiss that would change her world, this was the kiss of no return. This was the part of her story where she could let go, move forward, forget the past and become happy and carefree again.

She wanted to kiss him so badly. She wanted to lean in and feel his lips on hers and melt into him and let Felix become her new half so she could be whole again. She closed her eyes. She felt his breath on her lips, and for the barest moment she thought the man leaning toward her was Mike.

The weight of reality brought her slamming back down to the ground. She took a sharp breath.

Mike. I love Mike. Mike is mine forever. I'm married, aren't I? I'm still married. "Widow" doesn't mean anything. Death isn't a divorce. If it were my choice, I'd still be with Mike. I've never loved anyone else but him. And I can't, I'm afraid. This is wrong. It would be a lie, a horrible lie, a lie I could never undo. No, no, no . . .

"No," she said. It hurt to say it. There was an actual physical pain in her heart that radiated down into her stomach, but there was no *yes* inside her to speak.

Felix winced, as if he could tell that this "no" was different. The unforgiving resonance of the word still thrummed in her head. She meant it. She started to cry.

"No. I don't know what I was thinking. I'm married to Mike. I can't. I won't ever be able to. I'm sorry. I'm sorry. I'm sorry."

Felix let go. They were still standing in the corridor outside her hotel room, and a couple of men in basketball jerseys walked past, talking about hamburgers. Felix and Becky froze, turning their backs to the intruders, waiting with exhausted patience until the men entered their room.

Felix leaned his arms and head against the wall. When he spoke, his voice was muffled and low.

"I risked it all."

"I know . . ."

"Becky, if you mean this, then I can't . . . I crossed over these past months, and I can't go back."

"I know," she said, though it was only at that exact moment that the truth of it crashed down on her. "I know, I know, dammit."

"You swore," he said without looking up.

"I did not." She paused. "I did. I meant it. I'm sorry. I'll miss you so much, but this in-between, this pulling back and forth between you and Mike, it's killing me. It's like he's dying all over again."

"Then it would be best if we parted ways."

He was formal as he took her hand, his face like a rock—no sadness, no regret. The look terrified her. She wanted to slap him, just to see some emotion there. Worse than having Felix hate her or explode in anger was to see him turn to stone.

His face may be stone, she thought, but not his heart. Please, Father in Heaven, save him from the misery of my mistake. Don't let his heart turn to stone.

"Felix, I'm sorry."

Felix kissed her hand. "Good-bye, Becky."

He went into his room and shut the door.

In the morning, a hired car waited to take her to the airport. Felix wasn't in it.

In which Becky claims her miracle

That was a second bad time for Becky. She was accustomed to feeling a flood of calm after doing the right thing, even when it had been a difficult decision to make. But there was no peace now. Instead she felt beat-up and tired. But that couldn't mean that she'd made the wrong choice—she knew she and Felix couldn't change their relationship to *that*, she was certain she couldn't be a wife to anyone besides Mike. Surely that anxious gnawing inside her wasn't a reprimand for a bad choice, but rather just the misery of a post-Mike world.

"I'm going to be alone," she realized in the shower, speaking the words aloud to the drowning sound of water. "I really am going to be alone for the rest of my life. And my children will never have another father."

She cried into the pouring water until her throat ached, and even when soaking wet, she felt dried-up and crumbling. Her husband was gone, her best friend was gone, and now she knew just how miserable she would be.

She stuffed all her DVDs of *Blind Love* under the sofa and stopped going to movies with the other single neighborhood ladies because they tended to pick romantic comedies. It seemed such a farce now, such a grotesque mimicry of actual love. The very idea of those plots—the plying of two individuals who are gorgeously compatible but kept tragically apart—were so flat, such a joke, so meaningless. That game, that freak show, it had nothing to do with love, not companionship love, not the partnering of two people, the creation of family, the essence of home. What was the use? Why had she wasted a single moment on those stupid screenplays? How had she let fictional romance abduct her mind for one moment away from Mike? Just the memory of sitting in a movie seat and sighing over a handsome character made her physically ill.

"You're moping," her friend Melissa said as they waited in line for movie tickets (a screwball comedy with no romantic subplot whatsoever).

"What do you mean, I'm moping? I'm just standing here."

Melissa fixed her with a stare. The devil girl tattoo on her neck was three years gone, her brown hair was twisted into two innocent braids, but Melissa's stare was just as intimidating as ever.

"I miss the purple you used to put in your hair," Becky said, fingering one of Melissa's braids.

"Don't change the subject. A little girl about six years old just walked by in a T-shirt that read, 'Eat your heart out, boys.'"

Becky couldn't hold back a shudder.

"I knew you saw it! But you didn't even wince, let alone haul her parents downtown for questioning. You've lost your spunk, Bec. It's scary."

Becky stuck out her bottom lip. "I'm still spunky."

Melissa shook her head. "You seemed to be better. The last few months you were like a half-dead plant that was getting watered again. But now . . . what's going on?"

Becky was counting how many women in the theater lobby didn't have a man beside them. Twenty-six. That seemed like a lot. She felt Melissa sidle up closer and hook her arm.

"You're allowed to grieve, Becky Jack, but you're most definitely not allowed to go away. Come back to me."

Becky realized how in many ways she and her oldest friend had changed places. Melissa had spent the past four years working with a phenomenal therapist, and the difference in her expression alone was remarkable. Her smile seemed so new and genuine, Becky wondered if her lips had been smile-less for years. A few months before, Melissa married a widower with three children and found a dazzling kind of peace and purpose as a stepmother to teenage boys. Her existence had lost that constant wail of pain. She was the one offering an arm of comfort.

Becky pulled Melissa closer and lay her head on her shoulder. The least she could do was make Melissa believe she was helping. But nothing seemed to touch that hollow ball filling her chest.

"I've been thinking about putting in hot pink highlights," Melissa said.

Becky nodded against her shoulder. "That sounds nice."

Besides the sadness, things were ugly and tight with her checkbook. Hyrum couldn't go to soccer camp because there was no money, and Becky thought it typical that she would go into real estate right before the real estate market imploded. Everything in her life seemed cursed.

Polly kept asking why Felix didn't come around anymore. So did Hyrum, to Becky's surprise. Sam especially noted the change, mostly because Felix had promised Sam a helicopter ride and still hadn't come to deliver.

"Will he come tomorrow, Mom?"

"No, not tomorrow."

"Next month? Is he in California or England now?"

"I don't know. Sweetie, it's possible that he won't come again ever."

Sam looked at her with wide, horrified eyes, then his face relaxed. "Nah, he'll come. He promised. He took a pinky pledge."

Becky flinched.

Polly was listening and later asked her mother in whispered voice, "Did you guys break up?"

"We were never together, honey. We were always just best friends."

Polly looked like she very much doubted that. "But . . . so are you still friends?"

"We'll always be friends, I think. But from . . . afar. We probably won't be in each other's lives so much."

"Oh." Polly's face was very pale. "Oh."

Becky squinted as she washed the dishes—the ache in her heart was traveling to her head. She'd always had the tendency to fall into happiness. Even on the worst days, she'd had enough natural delight to dance while making dinner or smile sympathetically at herself in the bathroom mirror. But mourning Mike sapped all her spare energy. She didn't know if she could keep it up much longer, and if Polly's spirits were crushed, Becky might as well lie down on the linoleum, shut her eyes, and hold a flower in her crossed hands.

That evening, she overheard Polly on the phone with Fiona say the name "Felix." Her tone was concerned.

A few weeks later (a few long, gray, fraying weeks), Fiona came home for a visit. The whole house lightened. Fiona drifted in swathed in colors and fabrics Becky couldn't name, looking like a grown woman, smart and saavy and as content as she'd ever seen. She took Becky's breath away.

"You are stunning."

"Thanks, Mom," Fiona said, shrugging.

"Thank *you* for coming home. You lift my heart, my girl. I didn't realize how much I missed you."

"I feel the same. I actually didn't know I missed home until I walked in. I've been so busy, but happy too."

"Bless you, you wonderful girl! Nothing you could say would make me happier myself."

"I love what I'm doing, and I love California. But it's good to come home too. I walk into this house and the smell makes me feel like a little kid again. Except that I keep expecting to see Dad."

Becky nodded.

Fiona glanced at the family room where Sam was reading a fantasy novel almost too heavy for him to hold. He was too far away to overhear. Her mannerisms softened, as if she were tending to a sick child.

"Mom, do you remember when Bronson broke up with me my junior year? And you found me in Hyrum's tree house crying? You climbed up and didn't ask me any questions; you just sat beside me and hugged me. And after a while you said, 'Fiona, you deserve to have someone who sees how truly fabulous you are.'"

Becky had forgotten. There was no greater gift in the world than when one of her children thought she'd done something valuable, offered evidence that she'd been a good mother.

I *was* a good mother once, Becky thought.

She turned away because her eyes were stinging. Handily, she was in the kitchen, so she began to wash dishes.

Fiona leaned against the counter. "Well, I've been thinking about you and Dad, and I feel like I've had a little inspiration, I guess, though you know I've never been very good at that stuff."

She did. While Becky used to come upon little Polly on her knees, praying for help to find her stuffed elephant or missing headband, Fiona had seemed hesitant spiritually. She didn't rebel or even doubt, but just stood back, observing instead of doing.

"Since I was little, the knowledge that you and Dad would never split up has been my greatest source of security. I knew you would stay married and in love all your lives. And after, too. Dad wouldn't have remarried if you'd died first, and I know you feel the same way. You still wear your wedding ring. If you met Felix right now, you wouldn't even be friends with him, would you?"

Becky lowered a dish into the water and looked at her daughter, but didn't speak. Everything Fiona was saying was true, and she wanted to keep listening.

"Well, here's the inspiration bit. What if God knew that? What if he arranged for you and Felix to meet all those years ago, so that you'd be best friends, so that he'd be here for you after Dad's death, and it'd be too late for you to shut him out? So that you could have someone to be with now, so that you could keep feeling loved, so that you don't have to be lonely. I think that's something God would do."

Becky's eyes were burning now, and she pressed the back of a sudsy hand over her face before she could cry in front of her little girl. She felt Fiona stand behind her, wrap her beautiful arms around her mother's waist, and lean her head against Becky's back. Fiona's voice, still confident and fearless, softened to a near whisper.

"You still deserve to be with someone, Mom, someone who sees how truly fabulous you are. And I think Felix does. That's all I wanted to say."

That night Becky had another Mike dream. They were always doing something simple, like grocery shopping or sitting on the porch swing and talking. Those dreams were a clean, well-lighted place where she felt her relationship with him continue to grow. This time they were sitting on the cabin steps in the Colorado Rockies, where she and Mike had spent their honeymoon. He was whittling a stick. He claimed it would be a whistle, though she couldn't imagine how he'd hollow it out just right. But Mike had a knack for doing things he'd never done before. She was leaning back, just staring at him, marveling at his arms and chest, the glorious shape of him.

She said, "I miss you."

Mike said, "I'm right here. Let's get some lemonade later."

She said, "Okay," and forgot why she'd been missing him.

She said, "How are you feeling?"

Mike said, "Me? I'm fine. Never felt so fine."

"You used to be in pain, didn't you? I can't remember now."

"Was I? I can't remember either." He leaned back, looking up. "That's about the prettiest sky I've ever seen."

She said, "It is," submerging herself in the forget-me-not blue. They watched clouds float back and forth like kelp, dream wind moving like water. They held hands.

She heard a trill and looked to seem him playing the wooden whistle. "You're amazing. I didn't even see you finish it."

He placed it in her palm and stood up, bending down to kiss her cheek. "I'd better go. I've been pretty busy lately. You'd be surprised."

She said, "Wait, there was something I was wanting to ask you . . . what was it? Something about Felix, I think."

Mike had started to walk away, but he stopped and turned back. "Felix? He's skinny, isn't he? And fussy sometimes. But he's improved over the years. I like old Felix better than young Felix."

She said, "Do you think I should stay his friend? Do you think it's good for me to be with him until I'm with you again?"

Mike said, "I think he's good for you, Bec. And what's good for Momma is good for everybody."

He leaned down to kiss her again, on the lips this time, a kiss that sizzled and dropped down through all of her, warm and electric.

For the first time, when she awoke and realized it'd been a dream, she didn't feel sadder.

Fiona believed. Felix believed. And then the dream—for three days after, Becky's skin still tingled, her whole self wrapped in wonder. But Becky couldn't believe. She wasn't capable of loving someone else the way she'd loved Mike. She wasn't. It'd been nearly three years, and she wasn't remotely recovered. No chance she ever would be. She was a goose, and that was that. And second, it was Felix. Falling in love with him was a leap too great to take without falling down a Wile E. Coyote ravine.

Which was a shame. It was a shame when she slept with her bedroom lights on and the door open, to keep that hulking isolation at bay. It was a shame when the kids were out and she was home alone, the solitude palpable, pressing like four tight walls and feeling as permanent as a coffin. It was a shame when she thought of her children's weddings, the photos where she would stand alone, everyone conscious of that empty space at her side.

She wanted Fiona to be right, in those moments between seconds, in those thoughts that she didn't mean to think, that surprised her when she was tired and her gaze had gone soft. She wanted to have that whole aching matter settled, to not be alone, to not only have her best friend back, but also allow him to become more and vanquish the loneliness.

But it was impossible. Ask a fish to grow lungs. Ask a bird to give up the sky.

Then again, there was the Mike dream, and that cold spot on her already-Mike-achy heart that told her she was missing Felix, and Fiona with her perfect wisdom . . . Night and day, Becky tossed and turned with the question, never finding rest.

One morning, with the kids gone to school and no real estate appointments for several hours, she sat at her computer and opened her word processing program. She started to write notes, just so she could see the problem put into words. Then taking it a step further, she pushed the words into story. It wasn't long before she was writing a screenplay.

```
                 THE ACTOR AND THE HOUSEWIFE
                        By Becky Jack
        FADE IN:
        INT. Bub and Hubbub PRODUCTION OFFICE      DAY


        ANNETTE and BECKY sit opposite a cluttered desk in
        a cramped and lived-in office. ANNETTE looks
        incongruous with her workday surroundings, dressed
        like the Halloween version of a gypsy.


                           BECKY
        Would it be better if I found an agent?


                          ANNETTE
        No need. We'll deal woman to woman, shall we? Now
        just look over the contract and sign on the bottom
        line.
```

```
Annette slams a Bible-thick stack of papers on the
desk before Becky. As she begins to thumb through
it, in walks FELIX. He is in his midthirties, and
every inch of him is the Hollywood dream hunk.
```

Thoughts about the screenplay stuck to her constantly. Even when she wasn't at the computer, she was writing dialogue in her mind and tweaking the order of scenes—at night before bed, in the morning if she woke up early, any minutes she could snatch from laundry or errands or work. Never had any story so haunted her. As she fiddled with which details to include and omit, she discovered the bulk of the story focused on Felix, Mike and the kids playing supporting cast. Which certainly wasn't historically accurate. But, she reminded herself, this wasn't a true tale of her whole life, only the part of her life that was Felix.

Of course, she couldn't remember the exact words that had been spoken ten years ago, or last year, or even last month, so it became "based on a true story," and some of the scenes she consolidated, making one phone call conversation stand in for an entire year. Still, she nailed the essence of it, even if she might have made herself just a little bit wittier in memory than she deserved—but that's a writer's prerogative.

Every scene built up to answer those questions: Could Becky the character love again after Mike? And fall romantically in love with Felix? Not just love him but *love* him, be his lady, let him be her children's new father, keep him as close as her own soul?

She lay down the skeleton of the story, except for the final scene, having no idea how it would end. Then she went back over the script and began to massage the details, put in the texture, endow it with that spark of life that turned a outline into a full-bodied story. And that's when the magic part happened.

It was a Friday night. Polly and Hyrum were both at sleep-overs with friends, and Sam, feeling left out, went to spend the night with his cousins. Becky was alone, and that huge empty bedroom in that maliciously empty house was a drooly monster threatening to gobble her up. So she turned on the television for company, curled up on the sofa (the leather one) with her laptop, and worked all night. The pieces started to link. She saw for the first time the profound randomness of their relationship, the obvious coincidence. How did she not notice it at the time? Again and again, the improbable occurred. She began to list these events.

1. Against all odds, she sold a screenplay. How is it possible that a Layton, Utah, mother of three (and a half) with no Hollywood

connections or professional writing experience would sell a
screenplay? Without an agent, without a contact, and not only
that, but be flown out to Los Angeles to seal the deal?

2. Felix Callahan just happened to come into Annette's office
while Becky was there. Then she had to use the restroom and so
approached the elevator just as he did. His apartment was being
renovated so he was staying in a hotel—the exact same hotel as
she was.

3. The mere fact that he was Felix Callahan to begin with! If he'd
been any other actor—Jude Law, Denzel Washington, Antonio
Banderas, Brad Pitt, Tom Cruise, Will Smith, Kurt Russell,
Pierce Brosnan, Johnny Depp, George Clooney—then Becky
would have been amused by their verbal tussle and relished
retelling the story back home, but she never would have gotten
into that limo, never let him look over the contract. Or dined
with him. Or danced. (They'd danced!) Only because it was
Felix Callahan, her one weakness, was she tempted to bend her
personal rules and see what might happen next.

4. Felix had a layover in Salt Lake City the *exact* time she was
presenting at the film conference, enabling yet another
encounter.

5. And that autumn day in Los Angeles when she was lunching
with Karen and selling *Blind Love*. If she'd phoned Felix to say
she'd be in town, she would have met up with him before or
after her Karen meeting, and so the movie idea never would
have been broached. Instead, in a city of nine million people,
they just happened to be in the same place at the same time.
They hadn't spoken in over a year and the friendship might
have dissolved for good—instead, they ended up starring
together in a movie, the friendship intensifying and solidifying.

6. He called on the one-year mark of Mike's death just at that
piano-drop crisis and saved her. He really had saved her.
Looking back at the moment from inside the story, she had no
doubt now. Every molecule of her had been half Mike—
mother, wife, person, woman, she was halved when he left.
Only the Felix's-friend part of her had never mixed, preparing
that separate Becky. So only Felix could have reached down
and pulled up the fragment of her that could survive until
Becky could make herself whole again.

Movie plots depended on some amount of coincidence to stick
together. Real life was just too huge and haphazard to create a tidy
hour-and-a-half romantic comedy without leaning on a happenstance

meeting or two, a misdirected package, a misheard conversation. But real life, her life, couldn't possibly be so stuffed with serendipity, could it? Not unless there was some other power at work.

It was four A.M. and she read the script again, marveling at the events that had brought her to Felix. Sleepiness and the strangeness of an empty house were making her feel ethereal, drifting from thought to thought, half in her body and half hovering over her own head. For her, it was like examining a human cell under a microscope and discovering a tiny signature inked in the corner—*God*. It was like getting a huge, warm, divine hug. It didn't make her cry; instead, it made her sleepy. She wanted to curl up in bed, cozy under the covers, and feel the warmth of that discovery rock her to sleep.

The wonder of the realization didn't fade with morning. It was even more brilliant by daylight, all the edges and textures of the miracle gaining clarity after she'd stretched and showered and had a bowl of cereal. She imagined the past eleven years like a map in her head, and saw too that in this garden of forking paths, she hadn't been yanked along, kicking and screaming. At so many times, she could have jumped off and gone another way. But she hadn't. Becky Jack did not believe in Destiny with a big ol' capital "D." But she did believe she was guided a certain way by a divine hand, and she'd chosen to follow.

But how would it end?

She phoned the kids to check in (because since Mike, she had to speak to each of them every morning—their voices were her morning caffeine) then curled back up with that laptop. There was the story, almost finished, everything leading up to the final scene, to the part of the story that hadn't happened yet. There was only one real option for her: a kiss. Their first real kiss.

A kiss wasn't a magical orb of insight. But in matters of love, she considered, nothing else so simple had such power to cut to the quick. A kiss woke up Sleeping Beauty. A kiss brought Snow White back to life. A kiss changed Mike from person of interest to future spouse. So it had to be a kiss. But beyond that one detail, Becky was still in the dark. She started to write, trying to discover what would happen next.

```
INT. JACK KITCHEN        DAY


                   BECKY
                 (on phone)
Hey, Larry. I need to talk to Felix in person.
Today. Do you know where—he's there now? Okay.
Okay, I'm coming out. Don't tell him I'm coming,
okay?
```

INT. AIRPLANE, ECONOMY CLASS DAY

Becky sits next to a large man who overflows a
little into her seat. He nods rhythmically as she
blathers on, as if he's agreeing with everything
she says. She focuses on her bag of pretzels and
doesn't turn completely to look at him.

               BECKY
It's just, we were friends for so long. And if it's
possible that we could be in love, I mean, really
in love, now, then what about before? All that
time, I was best friends with a man that I could
marry? That would mean that I was unfaithful to
Mike in a way. I hate that thought. I hate it. And
I don't believe it. I . . . no, I just don't
believe it. But am I letting my fears keep me from
being with someone I could love? I don't know. And
I don't know if Felix has already moved on. It's
been three months since our New York trip, he
might be with someone else now, and that would be
the answer. That would be fine. But . . . oh,
sometimes it just hurts. The loneliness. The
what-ifs. The . . . the not knowing. It's still
not settled. I just need it to be settled. You
know?

Man removes an earbud-style earphone and turns to
her. He hasn't heard anything she's said, he was
just nodding to the music.

             LARGE MAN
Sorry, ma'am, did you say something?

Becky stares at him, blinks, then points at the
window.

             BECKY
Look, clouds.

             MAN
      (thinking Becky's a nutjob)
Yeah, how about that? Clouds. In the sky.

She waits until he puts his earbud back in and
isn't paying attention to her anymore, then she
starts in again.

                         BECKY
I mean, it's not that I'm blind to his
attractiveness. I'm definitely not. Please, he
was Calvin the sexy pet shop owner. But there's a
huge leap from liver to lover—HUGE. And the chasm
is very, very steep. I know. I've peeked down.

EXT. LAX   DAY

Airplane whooshing into Los Angeles.

INT. FILM STUDIO   DAY

Becky, with a VISITOR tag around her neck, takes a
deep breath as she passes from the brightness of
outside into the studio. Felix is on the set of a
subway car, facing off with a black-haired mob
villain in a nice suit. Becky stands back and
watches.

                         FELIX
Tell me where the bomb is, and you might walk away
from this train in one piece.

                         VILLAIN
               (in an extreme Russian accent)
You are for talking big now, *Gospodin* Arthur. Soon
Ivan will be marinating your eyeballs in his
martini.

Felix and Villain engage in a choreographed fight
sequence. Without sound effects, the fake punches
seem very silly.

                       DIRECTOR
Cut! We're getting a glare off that window.

                     ASST. DIRECTOR
Take five, everybody! We need to reset the lights.

Felix comes off the set while electricians move on
to fiddle with the lights. He notices Becky.

> FELIX

What are you doing here?

> BECKY

Hi.

Felix looks at her for a long moment, as if
tempted to go to her. Then he heaves a breath and
busies himself getting a bottle of water.

> FELIX

Becky, I can't see you.

> BECKY

I know. I wouldn't have come back if I hadn't
changed my . . . hadn't realized that I . . . if I
didn't really believe that it would work.

> FELIX

What would work?

He steps back onto the set. She follows while
trying to explain. Becky is so focused on Felix,
she doesn't notice that as they talk, all the crew
and cast members slowly disappear, leaving Becky and
Felix alone on the set.

> BECKY

Our story. I didn't believe in it as a story, I
thought it was doomed to fail. And I didn't believe
I could be that person, the heroine of that story.
But I was forgetting the important part—the fact
that . . . that I love you. I love you.
Goshdarnit, I love you so much.

They stand looking at each other for a few beats—
Becky wanting Felix to speak, some sign that he
still cares, and Felix as if he is considering
turning away. Then the motion of the subway car
starts up, at a pleasant amble. The screen behind
the windows changes—they're no longer rushing

through a subway tunnel but meandering through a
typical green English countryside. The lights
soften. Sweet pastoral music plays.

                    BECKY (CONT'D)
Where . . . what happened?

                    FELIX
I'm taking you home, at last.

                    BECKY
Wait . . . you knew I'd be here . . . How did you—

                    FELIX
Larry spilled the proverbial beans.

Becky shakes a fist in the air.

                    BECKY
Larry . . .

                    FELIX
You should praise his name. Otherwise you would
have blurted those awkward declarations in front
of a room full of gawkers.

                    BECKY
          (realizing they're alone.)
Hey, where did everybody go?

                    FELIX
Just giving us a little privacy.

He takes both her hands, pulls her closer to him.
They are in the same position as they were when he
first asked to kiss her at the Valentine's Ball.

                    FELIX (CONT'D)
Becky, there's a question I asked you eleven years
ago that you never answered. So I ask again—may I
kiss you?

                    BECKY
But what if . . . what if . . .

Felix lets go of one of her hands and touches her
cheek. He isn't posing or acting—his movements are
very simple, very human.

                    FELIX
Becky . . .

                    BECKY
Yes? I mean, *yes*. I mean, kiss me. Yes, please kiss
me.

Their kiss starts slowly, tentatively, interrupted
by giggles, then building into genuine passion,
then slowing again into the sweetest affection.
They stop and look at each other.

                    BECKY
Wow. That cleared things up.

                    FELIX
And how.

She nearly crumples, and his arms go to support
her.

                    BECKY
I'm a little wobbly.

                    FELIX
I've got you.

                    BECKY
We're too old. I don't have the energy for this
kind of wild love. If you kiss me like that again,
you'll put me in a coma.

                    FELIX
I imagine we'll get used to it after a while.

                    BECKY
Felix, are you sure? Are you really, really sure?
Are you sure you don't want to marry me because
you feel sorry for me? Or you think you love me

just because you're used to me after all these
years or—

He kisses her again. She almost crumples again. He
catches her.

                    BECKY (CONT'D)
                     (groggily)
Okay, okay, you don't have to be so snappish
about it.

He pulls a suspicious little square box out of his
pocket. He holds it between them.

                    FELIX
Would you like to open it?

                    BECKY
I think so. I think I do. Yes, I do. Hey, whatdo-
youknow, I really do.

She takes it, opens it very slowly, wincing. It is
an oval diamond in a simple ring setting, the
stone as clear as a drop of water.

                    BECKY
Yeesh, it's huge.

                    FELIX
Only a carat. I knew you wouldn't want anything
ostentatious. May I?

She nods. He slips it on her finger, and she
shivers.

                    BECKY
Holy cow. This is really going to happen, isn't it?

                    FELIX
Please say it is.

                    BECKY
It is.

FELIX

It is?

BECKY

It is. It really is. And I'm the craziest and maybe
even the happiest woman in the world.

He kisses her suddenly, rapturously, and she laughs
and throws herself into his arms. They spin.

BECKY (CONT'D)

This will work. And we won't have to be alone. And
Polly won't have to be sad. And Hyrum—oh, Hyrum
will be thrilled!

FELIX

And you?

BECKY

I'm thrilled. I really am. Is that strange? Is it
possible? I didn't think it was, but now I'm—

He looks at her with those eyes that used to melt
her from the movie screen, that hadn't for eleven
years, but now make her feel softened into a pool
of butter.

FELIX

. . . the most beautiful thing I've ever seen.

BECKY
(scoffs)

You need to get out more.

FELIX

You can't tease me right now. I'm too smitten. I
won't be baited.

BECKY

Oh, you're such a charmer.

FELIX

And you're my sexy snake.

                              BECKY
Please, I'm so not a sexy snake.

                              FELIX
You are.

                              BECKY
Am not. I'm more hedgehoggy.

                              FELIX
But a *very* sexy hedgehog.

The subway car turns, facing the screen, and the
screen image becomes an evening landscape. Becky
and Felix kiss as the subway seems to drive into
the sunset.

FADE OUT

It was a classic ending, a Hollywood ending, and she really could
imagine herself on-screen, opposite the leading man in the romantic
comedy. Not as she had in *Blind Love*, a supporting cast member leaning on Felix's prowess. No, she was starring. She was living a movie.
Maybe she had been all along, and it took her this long to see it.

But did it work as a story? She was so close to it she couldn't tell.

If I can sell the screenplay, she decided, that will be the real test.

So she went through the script again, changing the names, loca-
tions, and obvious details. The Mike part was the hardest. She'd glossed
over it in her first draft, and found herself sickened by the merest idea of
revisiting his death, even in fictionalized form. So she tweaked. The
fictional husband, Brian, didn't hold a candle to the real Mike. He was
a paper doll of a man, eventually leaving his long-suffering wife to pursue a golfing career in the Philippines.

Her new character, Jennifer Baker, wasn't a Mormon (seriously,
who would buy a Mormon housewife as a romantic comedy heroine?).
Instead she was just a conservative, poster-wielding Republican. The
new Felix, Isaac Black, was a hot-fired liberal, and he wasn't British (too
specific—a studio would want more freedom in casting). Jennifer was
from Idaho, and Isaac was a rock star instead of an actor. They first met
in Detroit, where Jennifer was selling a song she wrote to a music producer. And then, just because it was funny, at their first meeting—
instead of just insulting each other and then going to dinner—Becky

had Jennifer go into early labor and Isaac take her to the hospital. But in essentials it was still the story of Becky and Felix.

As she went through the last scene, Becky realized that it was more about the author trying to figure out if she could love again. In the final draft, she scrubbed the climax clean of the uncertainty and made Jennifer fall totally and beautifully in love with Isaac.

Becky sent it to Karen with a Post-it note: "Does this work?" The next weekend, Karen made an offer on the script.

For two days, Becky couldn't stop dancing. She danced while she washed dishes, danced while she cooked dinner, danced in the car while driving the boys hither and thither. The money would really come in handy just then—but that wasn't why she danced.

"Thank you, Mike," she said while getting ready for bed. "Thank you, honey." It was a miracle, it was an against-the-odds buzzer-scoring victory. She *could* keep loving. She was not doomed after all.

Yes, the lightness in her middle, the shifting of her heart—all the signs indicated she was about to fall in love again. Wouldn't that be wonderful? Like in a movie. It wouldn't be like Mike; it never could, no matter who it was. But she felt so different, as if she'd been in a dark room and someone just turned on the light. The palsied part of her diminished, her old confidence began to thicken in her, and she no longer questioned every decision she made as a mother. She knew when to talk to Polly, what to say to Hyrum, how to comfort Sam. And it was all due, she thought, to knowing she could have another partner, a temporary partner, someone who would be a proxy father to her children, hold her hand and walk with her through the rest of this life. It was a beautiful idea, as beautiful as a ballad. And like a ballad, there was a touch of sadness curling the final notes.

The thought that it would be Felix made her thrill and sing—but also made her want to hide and shiver. Surely her reluctance was her worry that if loving him was possible now, then it had been possible then too. That she'd betrayed Mike all along. Taking in that thought was like swallowing a handful of quarters.

But the coincidences, the perfect path—it all points to Felix, she thought. And me. It was designed by a hand greater than mine. It has to be true.

Shame and guilt tarnished the joy somewhat, but it was not ruined. The story worked. Mike had given her the okay. Becky began to believe.

In which everything is decided at a high altitude

Becky was a wimp. There was no other explanation. She didn't call Larry, didn't jump on an airplane to surprise Felix on a Los Angeles film set or wherever he was. She'd painted herself into a corner—how could she write a fictional finale but set it in motion in reality? You can't force your own story into a Hollywood ending.

But then again, she didn't even call Felix. Or send him an e-mail. Or text him. Or anything. Wimp.

And what if . . . *duh, duh, DUH!* What if he was with someone else already? No, it couldn't be. The plan was perfect, complex and gorgeous, from Felix entering Annette's office to now—she was sure it was a divinely woven tapestry that wouldn't unravel randomly, not here at the end. But still she didn't know what to do. She prayed, she talked about it with Fiona as frankly as she'd ever dared speak mother to daughter. It was an astonishing thing, admitting to a child her own fears and vulnerability, to take advice instead of give. Astonishing and lovely too.

"Don't be so hard on yourself," Fiona said. "If you don't have a really definite idea of what to do, if your, you know, prayers and stuff aren't being answered clearly, then maybe the answer is, wait."

"My smartest girl," Becky said.

So she waited. She was not good at waiting.

A week after Karen made an offer on *The Rock Star and the Housewife*, Becky returned from the grocery store to find her street unusually populated—people loitering on lawns, walking around, looking at something. A pain of panic ripped through Becky and she prayed, Please let there not be a fire. Please let it not be my house. All four kids are at home.

There was no fire. Instead, when she pulled the minivan into the driveway, she spotted a helicopter in the park across the street.

Felix was standing beside it.

She jumped out of her car and almost ran to him, but stopped. She didn't know where the story was going to go from here. Her heart was still stinging, and failed hope would make the pain worse.

She started toward him at a casual pace, channeling her nervousness into nonchalance. "Don't you need a special permit to fly one of these around a neighborhood?"

"Indeed," Felix said. "Perhaps you haven't heard, but I'm wealthy and consequential."

"Uh-huh."

She tried to keep her tone light, to feel her way through a conversation with Felix as if they were as they'd always been, but there was a space between them now, drafty and chilled. He had not come for her, and the way they had parted in New York meant that he wouldn't be coming for her again. That spot on her heart was icy.

"It's good of you to remember Sam," she said after an awkward pause. "He'd been asking about the helicopter."

"To be honest, I'd forgotten until Fiona phoned."

"She did?"

"She said he was pining. I can't bear to hear of Sam pining. His face wasn't made for it."

Becky blinked. He was right. Sam had a round, happy face (like his father), and she'd always thought that his sad expressions looked out-of-place. It was the kind of thing she and Mike would have talked about, and she couldn't recall ever making that observation to Felix. To know he noticed Sam made her feel teary.

Sam hopped out of the helicopter, startling her out of tears.

"Mom! Did you see me? Did you see me up there?"

"Oh, you already went flying?"

"Yeah, it was great. It was noisy. I didn't know it'd be so noisy. We had to wear headphones and talk on microphones like astronauts. We were going so high I thought I would puke. But I didn't. Felix said we couldn't go into anti-grav because a helicopter can't carry its own weight up high where the air is thinner, so you'd need a strong force to break through the atmosphere, and I said that if he gave me a bowl of chili, I could maybe make a powerful blast." Sam laughed.

"Oh that's pretty language." Becky shook her head.

"He did say that," Felix confirmed. "Right on the microphone, right into my ear. The pilot laughed."

"So did you, Jeeves," Sam said, using the nickname Hyrum had given Felix. "A bowl of chili, Mom. Ha! I'm going to go call Jeff and tell him. He'll pee his pants—"

"Samuel Michael . . ." Becky said with a warning in her voice.

"Okay, okay, I'll watch my mouth." He scampered off to the house, leaving Becky and Felix in an odd kind of privacy—alone with half the neighborhood looking on.

"So your debt's paid," Becky said.

"Yes." His hands were in his pockets. He looked forlorn, his eyes on his shoes, glancing up briefly to take in the sight of neighbors shambling around the block. "I guess I'd better go before the police come after me."

"You said you had a permit!"

He smiled through eyes half-lidded. She swatted him on the shoulder.

"You better." Becky cleared her throat. "Do you want to come in for a minute at least? Have some dinner?"

"No, I'd better get going. I have somewhere to be."

"Oh." And that was it. He'd never come back again. She should say that she'd been wrong, that she'd had a dream about Mike, and Fiona had said it was okay, and that things made more sense now, and it worked in the screenplay so it might work for real. She should say all of that, and quickly before she changed her mind.

He turned away, climbing into the helicopter, and she knew she couldn't say it. She couldn't risk the blank look on his face, or a response like, "Don't embarrass yourself, Becky, let's just go our separate ways." Or his stone face. Definitely not his stone face. She couldn't be sure how he felt. She couldn't even be sure that she wouldn't change her mind, shy away and hurt him again. No, it was too dangerous. She was continually shocked to realize how much of her strength had been Mike.

"Okay," she said. "Good-bye then."

"Yes, good-bye." He sat in the helicopter, then turned back to her. "That is, unless you'd like a ride as well?"

She raised an eyebrow. His expression was suspiciously innocent as he held out his hand. She looked back at the house. All four of her children were standing on the front porch. Sam was chatting on the cordless phone, but the older kids were looking at her.

"Go on, Mom," Polly called.

Fiona was grinning.

"Felix, is something suspicious going on?" Becky asked.

"Absolutely." He took her hand and pulled her up.

And they went up and up.

She couldn't help it—she squealed as they zoomed over houses and veered toward the mountains. Breathless, they rose above clouds, hovering between white and blue, her stomach floating. For a moment there was only sky and sunlight melting into brilliance, and Felix too, then they dipped down over mountain slopes, skimming the tops of pine trees.

She thought it was just a scenic tour until the pilot landed the helicopter on the rocky top of a mountain peak.

"We'll be back," Felix said, nodding to the pilot as he helped Becky down from the helicopter.

"We will?"

"I certainly hope so. Unless you fancy the wilderness life and possess previously unexhibited survival skills?"

He took her hand and led her down a slope. He was holding her left hand, and his fingers briefly touched her ring finger, as if feeling for her wedding band. It was gone. She'd taken it off three days before, wrapping it in a tissue as she used to do when her kids lost a baby tooth, and put it in her jewelry box. The touch there gave her a thrill—of panic or anticipation, she wasn't sure.

They entered a grove of pines, and Becky held her breath when she saw what was waiting for her: a plaid picnic blanket, a basket full of blueberry muffins and chocolate croissants, bouquets of sunflowers wrapped in ribbons and dangling from the trees, and even a sweater her size, which she promptly put on against the mountain breeze.

"I thought you were done wooing me," she said, cozying into the blue sweater, smelling the sweet dryness of lamb's wool.

"So did I. But apparently, Mrs. Jack, you're not easy to forget." He started up a CD player hidden behind a stone, and "A Kiss to Build a Dream On" hummed over the mountaintop.

"Wow, you must buy CD players in bulk."

He held out his hand, she took it, and they were dancing under the sky.

She'd danced with him many times, but now she wasn't comparing his light manner of leading with Mike's big warmness, or worrying they were too close and careless, or even feeling befuddled and giddy as she had at the Blue Note. Now she was just dancing with Felix on top of the world. She was aware of the heat of his hand holding hers, the heat between their bodies, the subtle warmth of his breath on her neck. The touch made her skin feel warm all over, as if she'd just relaxed into a bath.

Very slowly, he pulled her in closer. Their bodies touched. Their necks touched. She found herself closing her eyes. Oh, he was such a little Don Juan, he really was. She took in his smell, and her breath thickened.

"You're making it hard to breathe," she said.

"I think you just complimented me."

"It's probably just the thin mountain air."

"No, it's definitely me."

He was right.

"I don't know why . . ." she started.

"What is it?" he asked with such tenderness, the words softened the hard edges from the world, and she melted into a Monet painting.

She had to answer. There was no hiding from anything inside the trees, dancing on pine needles and almost touching clouds. "I don't know why you love me."

She expected an eye roll or a grimace, but he kept that calm sweetness.

"I love that you make me laugh. I love that you know me, even my grimy underside, and though you see the whole world through a strict moral lens, you still approve of me. I love that you turn words like *Rudolf* into verbs. I love that you love Mike and your kids more than anything. I love you as a mother, I love you as a friend. I love your stubbornness. Three times you've had a chance to have me and you walked away, and I think I'll chase you to the ends of the earth."

"Oh," she said. It was a feat that she'd been able to say that much. There was no air now.

They kept dancing. She was testing out a new idea, this possibility of feeling differently about him. To feel him not just with her head and part of her heart, but with her whole body, to want him, to long for him in that way, missing him even when he was near.

I'm not ready, she thought, and her heart and stomach collided in dizzying panic.

But she wanted to be ready. All the providential evidence seemed to be shooing her in that direction. If she kissed Felix, maybe it would be clearer. Maybe she could see that she really could love him in that new way, that till-death-do-us-part way. A kiss could be Dr. Frankenstein's lightning, Wendy's pixie dust. A kiss might initiate one of those astonishing but oh-so-right transformations, like how a girl could start life as Rebecca Louise Hyde and end up as Becky Jack.

Her thoughts were startled away by a warm, tickly sensation—he had kissed her finger. The tip of her index finger, then her middle finger, then her palm. It took her several moments to realize that they'd stopped dancing. One arm around her waist, he was holding her body close to his, the other hand now pressing the inside of her wrist to his lips.

With a rush and a thud, there she was in the moment that meant everything. If she kept her face turned away, if she let him go, took a step back, made an offhand comment about the view, perhaps the question of Becky and Felix would stay frozen there between the trees, unanswered until it frayed and blew away. But she turned her face to his, resting her forehead against his cheek, and inside, she felt her heart turn to him too.

This is real, she thought. This is it. Isn't it? We can do this. We won't have to be alone.

He raised his hand from her waist to the back of her neck, his fingers stretching into her hair. His forehead touched hers. His eyes were shut, but she kept hers open, seeing this man in a new way—not the face of the actor on the screen or the friend who swept in and out of her life. His face was unrecognizable so close. A new face, a wonderful face.

"Becky," he whispered, "Becky, may I kiss you?"

It was the same question she'd put in her screenplay, the same he'd asked over a decade ago on the patio of the state capitol. She had laughed then. She couldn't have laughed now for all the world. Her throat was too tight to speak, her heart was jackhammering against her chest, her whole body felt loose. All she could do was nod her head just a little. She closed her eyes because she felt too terrified to see. Maybe the mountain had fallen away beneath them, nothing but sky all around, and they were sealed in the moment before the plummet.

What if? she couldn't help wondering, not nearly as sure as fictional Jennifer in the screenplay. What if he . . . what if I . . . what if it all ends, what if—

He clutched her hand as if they were about to take a leap and he didn't want to lose her, but for several wild, breathless moments, that's all that happened.

She ceased to be terrified of the kiss to come and instead panicked that it wouldn't.

Kiss me, she thought. Please, kiss me.

The waiting, the not knowing, made her entire body ache and she didn't think she could survive another second. She moved against him, she tilted her head until she could feel his exhale on her lips.

Excitement rumbled inside her, the kind of romantic glee she got from a good movie times a hundred. She'd fallen for Felix when he was Calvin the sexy pet shop owner. Now he was real, in her arms, wanting her. She wanted to want him too and felt a surge of frustration not knowing if she was holding flesh or cardboard or lights on a screen.

He leaned a little lower. His warm lips touched hers, once, softly. After the waiting, the touch shocked her as if she'd kissed a doorknob after dragging her feet across carpet. She winced and pulled back. Her face burned, and she felt as awkward and stupid as she had kissing Trent Harker at a school dance in tenth grade.

"Sorry," she whispered.

They tried again. A slow kiss, a warm kiss. It was sweet, like a flake of chocolate that dissolves on the tongue, but it didn't change her. She still felt distant and harried, as if she were a kite high in a windstorm and Felix only held her string.

So she wrapped her arms around his neck and kissed him, kissed him, and kissed him.

I'M KISSING FELIX, her thoughts seemed to scream. FELIX. NOT MIKE. ACK.

Shut up, she told her thoughts.

Survival instincts flared up, and her mind locked down, pretending she was with Mike, kissing Mike, loving Mike.

No, no, no. Experience this, she ordered herself. Kiss *Felix*.

She tried to keep her heart open, to allow the feeling of this contact to dissolve her walls. She tried. She was floundering. But she was not giving up.

She grabbed his face, put a hand in his hair and pulled him even closer. He responded, a moan escaping his throat. The soft and sweet kiss was gone. They were kissing passionately and feverishly now, roughly and achingly, in as many ways as she could, remembering her long-ago list of how to kiss, sometimes surrendering to Felix's mouth on her neck, sometimes bringing him back to her lips, always completely in that moment, fully with Felix, feeling Felix, kissing Felix. (And he kissed her back.) Sometimes he kissed her in a way that she felt in her joints, in her bones. Sometimes her body turned to sand. She kept kissing. She kissed him harder, trying to feel the part, acting better than she ever did in their movie.

But . . . (don't think, keep kissing) . . . but this isn't right . . . (shh) . . . I don't feel like I did when I kissed Mike . . . (don't compare, just kiss) . . . Felix is my friend, not my partner, not my lover . . . (but you want him to be, so kiss him until he is) . . . No, this hasn't changed anything . . . (stop thinking, I'm asking a question here, I need to know) . . . I think the answer is pretty clear . . .

He still held her. Felix Callahan, her best friend, her champion, her deliverer from the pillar of salt, that handsome, wonderful, blessed beast. He still kissed her, she still kissed him, but her thoughts took her a few steps back.

He's not Mike. He won't be quiet like Mike, easy to be around all the time. He's an effort; he has so many needs. And we're so different, I'll have to hide parts of myself from him, we won't ever be equal partners, not really. I'll always be comparing him with Mike, everything he does. That's not fair to Felix. And how will I support his career, his lifestyle, his everything, and still be the kind of mom my kids know and need? How do I become the Becky who marries Felix? So recently I was barely half a person—how do I change yet again?

She'd hoped passion and affectionate love would blaze through her with his lips on hers and silence the doubts and tear away her old feelings, leaving her a new shiny Becky, a Becky ready to love again. But . . . though she kissed him, she felt nothing deeper than her skin. She loved Felix. But not like Mike. She wasn't that new and shiny Becky. She was still old Becky, still tattered and sore and a little bit salty. Still Mike's girl.

The kissing slowed. She didn't want it to stop. She was terrified of anything being decided and discarded. Besides, it had been a long time since she'd been loved physically and felt as if her body were a precious and desirable thing. For the moment inside Felix's arms, the ache of not being touched and loved subsided some. But it was sand clutched in her fist, slipping away, almost gone . . .

They stared at each other, both their mouths open, taking deep breaths. She felt a hollow place in her chest, a space opened by hope that hadn't been filled by the kiss. In Felix's eyes there was a touch of longing, a feverish glint that hinted the kiss hadn't been enough and he was hoping for more.

That's what finally did it—that expression, not on a screen but directed at her. She felt that familiar pressure in her throat, rising up from her lungs. She pressed her lips together.

"What?" he asked, blinking the fever out of his eyes.

She pressed her lips harder, her eyes widened with the effort of holding back.

"Becky Jack, you are not—"

She hiccuped a little laugh. He seemed about to scold her, then held his breath. He was turning slightly red. She pressed her lips harder, he winced, then at once, they both laughed.

They laughed so hard they had to sit down to keep from falling down. They laughed so hard tears fell from their eyes. They laughed because their kiss of passion had been a belly flop, and they laughed to ease the tension that kissing and wondering had strung inside them. And they laughed because that was what they did together. Becky threw herself over Felix's legs, he leaned over her back, and they shook together with deep-bellied laughs that radiated through their whole bodies. It felt wrong to laugh so crassly in that idyllic setting, and Becky worried that they'd scare off wildlife, but she couldn't stop.

Becky panted for breath. "I can't believe . . . I can't believe . . . we went through all that. If we ever . . . need an idea for . . . for a comedy . . . all we need . . . pitch our story . . ."

The laughing made Felix cough and he tried to say, "Comedic genius," the words barely audible.

Once she could breathe, Becky rolled over so she lay across his lap and looked up at his face. Postlaugh hiccups tickled her chest. He wiped his face of tears and smiled as though he'd never been so happy in his life.

She sighed wistfully. "We really did our best though, didn't we?"

"I'd envisaged kissing you many times, Becky Jack . . . and not just kissing, I might add . . ."

"No, please don't add."

"But our kiss wasn't supposed to set you off into a hysterical fit. It was supposed to be . . ."

"Like a movie?" she guessed.

He nodded. "You would think I could arrange that much."

"Don't beat yourself up, sweetie. It's my fault."

"Yes it is."

"Hey, no need to be so pointy about it."

"And why not? You are the most impossible woman on this earth."

"And you are more caricature than man, thirty percent gay, and way overrated."

"Bloody hell, I really thought we had it that time. I thought—I was so sure . . ."

"I know! I'd had myself pretty near convinced too. I'd pictured us married, honeymooning, waking up next to each other in bed, and actually . . . actually . . ." She shivered with the thought.

He smoothed her hair from her forehead. "I was going to buy a house in Salt Lake City. I was going to *live* in it."

"And I was going to spend all that time in L.A. and go to movie premieres and shop—yes, I would have made a stab at fashion for you. I'd actually thought that through."

She reached her hands to his face, placing them on his cheeks, feeling the wonderful, rough skin of his jaw.

"I'm sorry. I . . . I'd hoped that kissing you would change me, allow the rest of me to heal over, but . . ." She sighed. "I do love you an awful lot."

"You're just not *in* love with me."

"But you still want to be friends."

"Exactly."

"You can't possibly love me as much as I love you, because my love for you is as big as this mountain and bigger even." She felt a pricking of tears in the corners of her eyes. "See? I'm almost crying I love you so much."

"Becky, we've discussed this. That can never be a compliment since you also weep for animated scraps of felt."

They lay there for a time, reminiscing about their years. Felix fed Becky bits of blueberry muffin whenever she spoke, making her spray crumbs into the air and over her own face.

"When did you first think you were in love with me?" she asked.

"I suppose it was gradual, but the first serious spark was during the *Blind Love* shoot. You said in order to kiss me, you had to pretend I was Mike. Those words ripped out my heart—or my ego, I'm not sure—"

"In your case, heart and ego are interchangeable."

"Exactly, and you took them both and mashed them and stepped on them and—"

"Dang, if only I'd known at the time—"

"You would have played it up, yes, I am aware of that. It bothered me that you had to pretend I was someone else. But I was still with Celeste, of course, and after Celeste, I was confused. Then in Mexico, I began to think, why not?"

"Before you go dating some young starlet again, just you make sure she understands the complex relationship you already have with another woman."

"That's all fine. I already explained it to her."

Becky elbowed him.

"Ow, I'm kidding. There's no one but you, darling. Yet. I haven't been with anyone since . . . well, since before our trip to Mexico."

That put a stitch in her heart. "Really?"

"Mmhmm. Well, except that one time, and really, no one on earth could blame me. I mean she—"

"For the love of all that is holy, no details please."

"If you insist."

"Listen . . ." She sat up, holding his face in her hands again before dropping them. "You're really great with my kids—really great. You have this weird idea that you're not a father type, but if you meet someone who has a kid or wants to, don't nix her for that reason alone, okay?"

He nodded.

"You're nodding," she said.

He nodded again.

"You're nodding, not arguing. Are you okay?" She felt his forehead. "You're a little warm. I've got some aspirin in my bag . . ."

"I may be changing my mind about the father thing. I had to in order to pursue you, didn't I?"

"Yeah . . ." She grinned. "That's cool. I'm glad something cool came out of this fiasco."

She ate another muffin and as the sugar hit her bloodstream, she realized she'd been trying to fit her life into a romantic comedy—it had seemed the only way to escape from the horror movie plot, the family tragedy drama. But maybe she'd been in the wrong genre all along.

She wasn't in a Hollywood movie; she wasn't the heroine of a romantic comedy. She was Becky Jack—mother, wife, widow. Lately, she'd mostly been a hatful of heartache, but sometimes she laughed too. So what that her story wasn't a tidy comedy or tragedy or romance or drama, or any one thing, but a big stew pot of stuff? At least she *was*. Tomorrow would happen, and the next day, and the next. Three years ago, that thought would have made her weep with weariness—but now, it was a relief. She'd healed that much at least, to be glad to keep going on. It helped to feel so certain she'd have Felix with her till death do us part, in one form or another.

"It's a shame we couldn't make this happen, because I think our craziness made a pretty good story. I wrote it into a screenplay and Karen made an offer."

"Have you signed anything?"

"Not yet."

"And the script is good?"

"Yeah, but to tell the truth, my first script—*Arm Candy*? It was better."

"Excellent. Two projects. We'll coproduce."

"Get off, I don't know how to produce a movie."

"You're bossy, and that helps."

"I'm not bossy—I just happen to be more capable than most everyone else."

"The salary is very good. Do this as a favor. It will save my inventing a secret trust fund and pretending it came from a long forgotten great-uncle so you'd accept the cash. You're terrible at selling real estate."

"I'm deplorable at selling real estate."

"Then it's settled. Have another muffin."

"What'll we call our production company?" she asked before taking a bite.

"Liverwurst Productions."

"Goose Liver Pate."

"To Liver Die in L.A."

"The Spleen's the Thing."

"Kissing Cousins. No, Kissing Friends."

Becky shivered. "I can't believe I kissed you like that. My tongue touched yours, and it wasn't even on a dare."

"To think I was prepared to . . ." He pulled a little foil square out of his wallet and twisted it between his fingers. It took Becky a moment to comprehend.

"You brought a . . . a . . . I can't even say the word in front of you. I can't believe . . . you actually—"

"I thought you would approve of my responsible—"

She hit him several times in the shoulder, and when he began to giggle, clearly unimpressed by her pounding, she yanked the blanket out from under him, rolling him off it with her foot. He'd begun to laugh again and could only make intermittent gasps and wheezes. When the blanket was finally free, she smacked him with it.

"I can't believe you!" *Smack, smack, smack.* "You are so naughty, after all this time, you thought I would—" *Smack, smack, smack.*

Felix tried to crawl away from the onslaught.

"You actually thought that I might . . . Here? Now? Enough to bring a—"

"I already . . ." Felix gasped for air. "It's Ol' Trusty, I always—"

"Are you trying to say that you're the sort of person who always keeps a backup, just in case? That it wasn't for us, it's just your 'Ol' Trusty,' and that's supposed to make me feel any better about you?"

"Yes," Felix wheezed. "But just so you don't feel bad, know that if you *had* been willing . . ."

Becky folded the blanket into a clublike shape and renewed her attack.

"Ugh! I can't believe you! I can't—"

He threw his arms over his head, trying to protect himself, his gasps for breath sounding painful. "Kidding! I'm—"

"Kidding? About which part? About your premeditation to seduce me on this mountaintop or—"

Someone cleared his throat.

"Excuse me?" The helicopter pilot was standing with his hands in his pockets, looking at the ground, his body half hidden by a tree.

Becky froze, still holding the blanket over Felix's head.

"We should go before nightfall. I'd like to lift off in thirty minutes." He cleared his throat again.

Felix held up a hand to say "just a moment" as he tried to catch his breath. He stood, brushed off his clothes, and looked every inch the English gentlemen as he said, "Very well. We'll be there in thirty minutes."

Becky and Felix both stood very still, watching the pilot walk back up the incline.

Felix cleared his throat. In a very tight, pained voice, he managed to squeak out the words, "Should we—" before they both succumbed. It was a couple of minutes before either could speak again.

"Ow," she said, holding her stomach. "I wonder how many calories I just burned."

"A lot. You should probably have another muffin."

Becky sat on a stone and ate while Felix folded the blanket. Laughing had shaken her up inside, exercised parts of her heart that had been tight and knotted since Mike died. But that stubborn ache was still there, timing throbs with every beat of her heart.

She ripped her muffin in half and something small and heavy fell out. "Did the baker loose a lug nut?"

Felix reached for it. "I'd forgotten—"

But Becky picked it up first. "Is this . . . a ring?" It was so encrusted with muffin it was hard to tell.

"It's a surprise for you. Or, it was going to be when things were supposed to turn out differently." He reached for it again.

"Hang on," she said, shifting it farther from him. "That's a big blueberry . . ." She flicked the blueberry off and gasped. "I mean . . . diamond. Wow. It's gorgeous. I am so keeping this."

He laughed lightly, thinking she was joking, and held out his hand. She sucked it clean of muffin and stuck it deep in the pocket of her jeans.

"When you bake fine jewelry into pastries, you kiss it good-bye. This one is mine."

"Really?" His look was surprised but pleased.

"I just . . ." She felt shy admitting this part. "I'd like a memento of what almost was. I'll trade you the Christmas diamond earrings for this, or I could pay you back—"

"It's all yours, darling." He sat beside her and kissed the top of her head. The touch made her sigh.

"I'm confused. We weren't meant for each other after all, not as companions, not for marriage, but what about the serendipity and God making his miracles manifest in my life, like Fiona said, and all the events linking together and the story working. There just can't be that many coincidences, can there? So what was that all about?"

Felix squinted. "And then the little trolls ate the elderberries and the horses sprouted wings—"

"Okay, okay, I'll explain better." She told him about the screenplay, listing all the coincidences of their relationship. "I thought that it was God arranging things so that we could be together after Mike, so I wouldn't have to be alone . . ."

Felix shook his head.

"No, it has to be! All those pieces set out for us, and we chose the paths that led to each other—to here. But not to be together . . ."

It had made such sense when Fiona had explained it. And sure enough, Becky's heart had twisted around, faced outward again, made loving Felix possible. But for what?

Becky sat upright, a jolt of adrenaline coursing through her. "It *was* God. I knew it!"

Felix felt her forehead. "You mentioned that aspirin . . ."

"See, thinking I was meant to be with you forced me to start to heal. To see that I'm not lost."

She'd only allowed herself one possibility for healing—that she needed another husband, a new partner, to not be alone. But she already had Mike, and Felix too, in a different way. And her kids. And herself.

There on top of the world, blueberry muffin in hand, she realized that would be enough for now. What a shackle-falling idea, it seemed to her, what a winged-feet idea.

"This whole thing . . . it was just to show me that I could be okay alone. Because I believed I could love you after Mike—I mean, *you* of all people. And so now I know that I really am healed enough to go on. The whole process pulled me out of that funk so I wasn't drowning in grief. Wow. God really is more mysterious and clever than I'd ever realized. Think about that. You are God's gift to this woman, Felix."

"I'm astounded it took you so many years to realize."

"I've always believed there was a reason you were in my life. I thought it was so I could—don't laugh—so I could save you sometime when you needed me. I didn't consider that it might be the other way around."

In the way she believed that the earth was round, she believed that the serendipity was divinely touched, a chain of tiny, perfect moments leading to that mountaintop. The sensation of witnessing heavenly mercy glowed inside her. Never had she loved everything so much—herself, Mike, their children, that tree over there, the rock by her foot, the sky, the world, God, the universe. And Felix.

"You've got to admit, there is something more than human to all this," she said.

"Just so I understand, you believe God takes the time to arrange years of events in our lives but doesn't just—" Felix swished his hand, the gesture of a magician making something disappear. She understood the questions in the silence: If God would do this much, why didn't he simply cure cancer? If he cared enough about Becky to lead her to Felix, then why hadn't he healed Mike?

It was a question that had pierced her too, especially when the house was empty and she lay alone. Three years later, her conclusion was that God could have healed Mike but didn't because it was beside the point. He allowed stuff to happen, and then took her hand to help her through it. Or in this case, put Felix in position to take her hand.

"It's all part of the Big Plan," she said. "God's job isn't to make anyone's life painless and easy, but to create opportunities for us to learn and progress. He knew what would happen to Mike, so all those years before he led me to you."

Felix shrugged, unconvinced. His fingers rose to sweep a strand of hair off her forehead. "You really are cute when you believe God helps you sell screenplays."

"Stop that. You said yourself back then that it was impossible. So why couldn't it have been God creating a little miracle so that we could meet? Our entire relationship has been one outrageous coincidence after another. There's no way this was all chance. Look at the evidence, Jeeves!"

He disengaged a bouquet of sunflowers from a tree and placed it in her hands. "It was karma, it was kismet, it was magic. It doesn't matter how it happened, just that it did."

"That's all you can give me? The Felix in the story converted."

"Really?"

"No. I couldn't even make your fictional counterpart see the light."

"I'll give you this much—if God exists, I hope he's your kind of god, the kind that would orchestrate all those events to bring us here on this mountaintop. That is a deity I could really dig. But . . ." he hesitated, and she could see the genuine struggle in his expression.

"Spit it out, sweetie."

"These months haven't been terribly fun, for either of us."

She hugged him, pressing her head against his chest, her ear to his heartbeat.

He leaned his head against hers and rubbed her back. "I don't mean to argue you out of your comfort, but this seems like a lot of torture to go through just for—"

"You're right!" She let go, hopping back and forth on the balls of her feet. "Maybe this means even more. I never thought I could love anyone again after Mike—not like that. But for weeks I almost believed I loved you, and for at least a few moments, I was convinced that I was head-over-heels. So in an extreme way, I proved to myself that I *can* love again. You see? I'm not only okay and mostly healed because of you, but now there's that added hope that I might be able to love someone else again. Someday."

"Ah. There we go." He was gazing at her, nearly glowing with affection. "You really are adorable when you get all crazy-eyed."

She giggled. "Thanks. I feel so weirdly happy. You didn't spike the muffins with something?"

"Besides diamond rings? Now enough with your fairyland talk and on to blessed reality. I'm quite prepared to shoulder the responsibility in your serendipity charade—discovering your next true love. It's just a matter of finding someone not quite as perfect as I am, one of your *own kind*. This is my arena, darling. I am going to—"

"Stop. No. Not you as matchmaker, not ever, and certainly not now. Let me clarify what I mean by *maybe* and *someday* . . ."

"So you say, but just wait until I start sending some delightful middle-aged Mormons your way."

"You know a plethora of upstanding LDS Utahns who are in the market for a forty-five-year-old widow with four children?"

"I know Robert Redford and—"

"And you think the Sundance Kid would go for me? Now, there's a real actor, a true heartthrob. That's so sweet of you to set us up! I wonder what colors I should pick for my bridesmaids—"

"*Ahem*, I meant that Bob lives in Utah and may know some people. I'll provide a handsome dowry for you and entertain your suitors in the parlor over nonalcoholic brandy."

"Don't you dare."

He rubbed his hands together. "Oh, this is going to be so much fun!"

"See? See what you did there with the hand clapping and the squealing and the matchmaking glee? This is precisely when you're thirty percent gay."

"It was a hand *rubbing*, which was intended to evoke an evil-genius persona. And I have never squealed in my life. But I will concede the matchmaking glee, because, my inscrutable lady, you're going to be falling in love again."

He swept her up and began to waltz, singing "Falling in Love Again" with an astounding Marlene Dietrich accent, which, truthfully, impressed Becky to bits. So she gave up. She was dancing with Felix on a mountaintop, and they were best friends again, and she would always, always be utterly and platonically in love with him. He would never abandon her, never leave a gaping hole, and even if he died someday, he was preserved like a lab specimen from all that alcohol he imbibed, so he wouldn't look or act much different.

And maybe she *would* fall in love again and not have to pass into old age alone, and maybe it would be someone the kids could really love too, and place a shiny little patch over the hole in their hearts. Someone like Felix. That kind of thing was known to happen, after all, and just then, with the sun pouring pure molten gold through the trees, and a sky directly overhead so close she thought she could swipe it with her outstretched hand, and air chilled and clear so that it went down her throat like a gulp of ice water—just then, everything was possible.

And she and Felix danced.

As often happened in unsuspecting moments, a sudden pain split her chest, reminding her that Mike was gone. But the ache was easier to bear there on top of the world, spinning with Felix. She missed Mike with exquisite longing. But she wasn't afraid of the loneliness. She would keep growing, keep changing, and the pain in her heart might lessen, and her isolation soften, and she still had a whole world to stretch and move in. There was a touch of excitement too, as if she were about to embark on an adventure. She aimed to make the second half of her life spectacular. Not better than the first—different, interesting, and worth the journey.

As they spun, Felix pulled her in till they were one person, together in the center of everything, the world whirling around them—and he kissed her on the mouth, the sweetest, best, friendliest, lovingest kiss.

"Dang," she said, "I forgot to eat the croissants."

Felix carried the basket and held her hand as they walked up the hill, Becky munching on a chocolate croissant. She realized how much they'd been touching, holding hands, embracing, kissing, cuddling, as if on that mountaintop they had a brief reprieve from the world and could experience what it would be like to be more than what they were. Her steps slowed, reluctant to return to earth and let this go. It might be a long time before she would walk like this with a man again.

He slowed to match her pace. "Nothing to hurry back to?"

"I wouldn't take another step if the kids weren't waiting."

"I imagine all four are sitting on the front steps watching the sky. Even Hyrum. Polly will be let down not to see a ring on your finger. Shall we take them out to a show to ease the disappointment?"

"Yes, let's. But this time, you buy admission and I'll spring for the treats."

"Don't forget the licorice."

Her heart warmed. He really had imagined himself becoming their surrogate father—not just accepted it; he'd looked forward to it. She planned to keep her best friend Felix around, playing soccer with her kids and filling Christmas stockings for as long as she could. It would be good practice until he stumbled into his own family.

Celeste has a child, she thought. And wondered if time and grace and need might someday pull the former couple together again. Though she would hold her breath and die before suggesting that to Felix.

"What are you thinking about?" he asked.

Her thoughts fled from Celeste and to the next nearest thought. "You know that old rhyme about the bear who went over the mountain to see what he could see? And what he saw was—"

"The other side of the mountain."

"Yeah. Well, here we are. I'd imagined it would be a lot different."

"Yes, so did I."

"But it's nice, the other side of the mountain. Not much different, but nice."

"And what provoked this rumination?"

"How I keep trying to force our story into a fairy tale, but from the beginning, it's been more like a nursery rhyme."

"Bizarre and adorable?"

"Just like you."

"With rings in your pockets and bells on your toes."

"Ooh, I should really invest in some toe bells."

Their steps kept slowing, stopping altogether beside the helicopter. Felix took both her hands, his face full of sunset. She glanced back down the mountain, wondering if she felt at all like Eve as she took Adam's hand and left Eden forever. Felix touched Becky's face, drawing her back to him. His finger stroked her cheek, and while there was no sorrow in his eyes, no fever, no worry, still there was a hint of hope in his voice when he asked, "Becky, are you sure?"

She knew what he meant. And she loved him even more powerfully for it. "Yes, I'm sure, Felix. And thank you for making sure."

He nodded once, resigned.

He didn't let go of her hand as they climbed into the helicopter, as they lifted up into the velvet blue sky. The evening was lush and unreal above the mountains, the clouds pulsing with gold and orange, everything more perfect than the end of a movie.

She'd been fearing the next silence, when she'd have time to consider that the hope that had been Felix was gone. And as the helicopter blades whirred, churning the world into white noise, and Felix was quiet, staring out the window, she winced and prepared herself for pain.

But it didn't come. There was still that twinge in her heart that told her Mike was gone, the ache of her skin because Mike no longer touched her, the dark tang of loneliness in her throat. She figured those would never go away completely. But they did not spread throughout her body, they did not bury her with grief. She ached—but her stomach muscles were still sore from laughing, and a twitch in the corners of her mouth told her that it wouldn't be hard to laugh again.

The helicopter dove at the valley. Becky snuggled into Felix and watched home draw near.

"I love you, Felix Callahan," she said over the headset. "I do. I love you so much."

"I love you, Mrs. Jack. I thank God for you."

Becky said, "Amen."

And they kissed one last time.

Acknowledgments

ooooooooo

Thanks to Victoria Wells Arms, Caralyn Beuhner, A. E. Cannon, Nadia Cornier, Dean Hale, Katie Henderson, Stephenie Meyer, Laura Middleton, and Elizabeth Peters for priceless feedback. A shout-out to Rebecca Castleton, Jen Hoge, Rosi Hayes, John Hayes, Mark Richardson, and Michael Snyder for helpful brainstorming and topical info. Huge slobbery kisses to the fine booksellers at the King's English and the noble librarians of the Beehive State, my home turf. Rick Walton's delightful picture book *Pig Pigger Piggest* (Gibbs Smith) made a brief appearance.

For unintended inspiration, *muchas gracias*: Katie Janke (my resident mother of four who, for the record, is not Becky); Bonnie Bryner (mother of five, who actually is Becky . . . just kidding, she's my mom); Libba "Bonnie Tyler" Bray (the "you broke it you bought it" line); Dean Hale (who is neither Mike nor Felix, but supplied a couple of their lines); Bill Bracy and Schnoppes; also Janae Stephenson and the Garden Geeks, Toni Butler, Marianne Lloyd, Christine Hale, Laurie Birky, and anonymous mothers at church, at the mall, at the hospital, etc. Take care what you say and do around writers—we're watching, always watching . . .

Reading Group Guide

These discussion questions are designed to enhance your group's conversation about *The Actor and the Housewife*, Shannon Hale's hilarious tale of the unlikely friendship between a suburban housewife and her dreamy celebrity crush.

About this book

Seven months pregnant and far from home, Becky Jack walks into the office of a Hollywood producer to sell her first screenplay and, much to her shock, meets silver screen heartthrob (and the object of her celebrity affection) Felix Callahan. They spend an awkward and unexpected day together and, though his cursing and drinking contradict her strict Mormon values, Felix and Becky somehow form an unshakable friendship.

Through the next decade, Felix and Becky experience tests of their bond they could never have anticipated. The everyday challenges of raising four unique children and running her household are exacerbated when Becky's community expresses increasing curiosity and doubt about her handsome, dashing best friend. When her sweet, supportive husband, Mike, expresses discomfort with Felix's role in Becky's life, Becky protects her marriage and ends her friendship. But as the years go by, both Mike and Felix's gorgeous French wife, Celeste, realize that the strange love their spouses have for each other is utterly platonic. Felix and Becky see each other through the good times, like costarring in a romantic comedy written by Becky and walking the red carpet together, and the bad, when Celeste leaves Felix for another man and then, worst of all, when Mike loses his battle with cancer. After Mike's death, Becky finds herself restarting her life as a widow, and eventually wondering if, after everything, she can find a new way to love Felix, 'til death do they part.

For discussion

1. What do you think accounts for the immediate bond between Felix and Becky? Is it their similar sense of humor? Is it possible to have platonic love at first sight? How does their first encounter compare to Becky and Mike's first meeting?

2. Becky often reflects on the dowdiness of her own appearance: her clothes, hair, weight, jewelry, etc. How do you picture Becky? Do you think she sees herself the way other people see her?

3. When Becky meets Hollywood producer Annette, she tells Becky they can "just deal woman to woman." (p. 3) What do you make of the relationships between women in the novel? Do Becky and Celeste develop a real friendship? While filming *Blind Love*, Becky detects the "tiniest arctic breeze" (p. 181) from Celeste, but for the most part Celeste is very sweet to Becky. Is there genuine affection between them?

4. On her Web site, Shannon Hale confesses she thought of several actors as she formed Felix's character. Is there a celebrity you think he resembles?

5. Becky says that Mike is "big as life" (p. 22) and consistently describes him as her perfect mate. How do they keep their marriage so strong? What are some of the challenges they face, and how do they overcome them?

6. What role does religion play in Becky and Felix's relationship? Does Felix respect Becky's Mormonism? Does Becky ever stop hoping to convince Felix to believe in God?

7. Becky constantly checks in with herself about her feelings for Felix, making sure that his presence in her life does not jeopardize her marriage, but she does feel comfortable harboring harmless crushes on her favorite fictional characters, such as "Gilbert Blythe, Mr. Rochester, Harry Hamlin as Perseus." (p. 47) Who are the fictional characters you've fallen in love with? Do you believe having a crush on a fictional character or actor is always "harmless"?

8. Becky often describes her own emotions using food, like when she says that Mike's sweetness "made her feel all warm and gooey, as if her heart were hot brownies." (p. 25) What are some other examples of this, and what do you think it reveals about Becky?

9. What do you make of Becky's list on page 118? Do you think it's possible to draw one firm line between appropriate and inappropriate behavior? Where on this list would you draw the line?

10. Usually being in Felix's world as his dear friend makes Becky feel special, but on occasion (such as at the cast and crew party or at the New York City nightclub) being in his world makes her feel insecure, ashamed, or neglected. What happens on these occasions? Why does Becky still want Felix as a part of her life? Are there times when Felix feels insecure while in Becky's world? Why or why not?

11. After costarring in a movie and attending numerous press events together, Felix and Becky eventually find themselves the subject of a torrid gossip television program. Were you surprised when this happened? Did Becky succeed in "avoiding the very appearance of evil"? (p. 125) Did reading this part of the story change the way you feel about tabloids and the paparazzi?

12. Were you surprised by Celeste's betrayal of Felix? Why or why not? Do you think her desire all along was to have a child? Did this justify her behavior for Becky? What about for you?

13. Many characters throughout the novel express their disapproval of Felix and Becky's friendship, saying at various moments that men cannot be friends with women unless they are attracted to them or that adult men and women cannot maintain strictly platonic friendships. Which characters feel most strongly about these questions, and which do you agree with? Can men and women just be friends?

14. Being a mother is the most important part of Becky's identity. What kind of a mother is she? How does she relate to her children? How does she compare to the other kinds of mothers in this book? When Mike dies, why does Becky begin to question herself as a mother? What do you think eventually helps her regain her self-confidence?

15. If you were in Mike's or Celeste's position, would you be comfortable with your spouse having such a close friendship with a member of the opposite sex? Why or why not? Would it change things if that friend was famous, rich, attractive, etc.?

16. Becky admires romantic movies and considers them important experiences for married women so they can remember what it felt like to first fall in love. What do you think is so appealing to women about romances?

17. Becky believes there was so much coincidence in her relation-
    ship with Felix that it had to have been divinely inspired. What
    does Felix think? Have there been unusual coincidences in your
    own life? How do you explain them?

18. Becky claims that romantic comedy is her favorite genre, but the
    book didn't have a typical romantic comedy ending. Were you
    happy with the ending or left hoping for a different outcome?
    What do you think Becky and Felix's relationship will be like
    going forward?

Suggested Reading

The Guernsey Literary and Potato Peel Pie Society, by Mary Ann Shaffer
and Annie Barrows; *The Friday Night Knitting Club*, by Kate Jacobs; *The
19th Wife*, by David Ebershoff; *The Beach House*, by Jane Green; *What I
Did for Love*, by Susan Elizabeth Phillips; *The Jane Austen Book Club*, by
Karen Joy Fowler

Shannon Hale is the author of *Austenland*, the graphic novels *Rapun-
zel's Revenge* and *Calamity Jack*, and six young adult novels, including
the Newbery Honor winner and *New York Times* bestseller *Princess
Academy*. She is at work on a seventh young adult novel, and lives with
her husband and two children in Salt Lake City. For more information
on *The Actor and the Housewife* and Shannon Hale's other books, visit
her Web site at www.shannonhale.com.